GHOSTS OF GUTHRIE

The Wantland Files Book 3

LARA BERNHARDT

THE WANTLAND FILES

GHOSTS OF GUTHRIE

BY LARA BERNHARDT

ADMISSION PRESS

*People who lean on logic and philosophy and rational exposition
end by starving the best part of the mind.*

— WILLIAM BUTLER YEATS

FAITH HEARD something in the hall. "Shh! What was that?"

Her friends Dakota, Parminder, and Yumeko shook their heads, eyes wide.

Faith held up her hands for quiet and tiptoed across the room. She turned the knob and cracked the door just enough to peek out. Nothing. She breathed a sigh of relief, clicking the door shut. "It was nothing. I still don't think we should though. Mom would freak."

Dakota held a Ouija board across her lap. "She'll never know! Come on. It's fun. Seriously. I didn't believe it would work the first time I tried it, but it does!"

Faith eyed the forbidden Ouija board, a knot of fear developing in her stomach. "Nah. We better not. Anyone want more snacks? I think there's some pizza left."

"Pizza at midnight?" Parminder asked.

"How can you think about food when we could be talking to ghosts?" Dakota asked. "Let's vote! Who wants to try it?"

Yumeko shrugged. "It's Faith's birthday party. If she doesn't want to try the Ouija board, don't make her."

Dakota's face fell. "But it's fun. We're thirteen, you guys. We can handle it."

"I've never tried one," Yumeko said, eyeing the board.

Faith took a deep breath. Her friends all clearly wanted to play it. What should she do? Risk discovery by her mother or disappoint her friends? Either choice could hold dire consequences. Why did Dakota have to bring that thing anyway? Her heart hammered. "If my mom and dad—"

"We'll be quiet." Dakota lifted a plastic piece with three felt-tipped legs from the box. She set it beside the board. "Who wants to go first?"

Yumeko scooted closer to Dakota. "I want to try it. What do we do?"

"Sit like this." Dakota crossed her legs. She unfolded the board and rested it on their knees to make a little table between them. "Hold your legs still. And keep the board completely flat. We don't want the planchette to slide off."

"The what?"

Dakota picked up the plastic piece. "The planchette. The spirits will use it to answer our questions. It's so cool! I can't wait for you guys to see."

Parminder huddled closer, leaning over the board to watch.

Faith took a deep breath, checked the hallway again, then knelt beside the board. She'd never seen one in person and couldn't help noting details. The words YES and NO were printed in the upper corners, GOOD BYE along the lower edge. All the letters of the alphabet arched across the center of the board in two rows, with the numbers one through ten in a line below that.

Dakota placed the planchette gently on its felt feet. "Okay. Yumeko, rest just your fingertips on the edge of it. Like this. Not too much pressure or you'll push it."

Yumeko nodded, focused on the board in front of her.

Dakota closed her eyes. "Oh, spirits, come to us. Answer our questions."

Yumeko stared intently at the board. "Nothing is happening."

"We didn't ask anything. What do you guys want to know? We should start with something simple."

"It's moving!" Yumeko squealed.

"But we didn't ask— H-A-P-P-Y B-I-R-T-H-D- A-Y."

Faith's stomach fell.

"Someone is talking to us!" Dakota shrieked.

"Did you two move it?" Faith asked. She slept in this room and didn't like the idea of an unseen entity creeping around. "Tell the truth."

"I didn't!" Yumeko said. "I'm barely touching the thing. Look."

"Ask it something!" Parminder said.

"Whose birthday is it?" Dakota said.

F-A-I-T-H

Three sets of wide eyes turned to stare at her.

Faith leaned back. "You guys, it's not funny. Stop teasing."

"Let's ask it about something we don't know," Yumeko said. "Will we all get A's this semester?"

"Hey! I'm supposed to ask the questions!" Dakota said.

NO

"Ha!" Yumeko said. "It doesn't want you to ask anyway."

"You don't even understand. The board was saying no, we won't all get A's."

GOODBYE

Dakota scowled at Yumeko. "You're not doing it right so it's leaving."

Someone knocked on the door.

Faith scrambled to her feet, waving her hands at the board, and whispered through gritted teeth. "Hide it! Hide it!"

The girls shoved the box and the board under the bed as someone knocked again, louder this time.

She crept to the door, peering over her shoulder to verify the forbidden game was hidden. Her friends all lounged casually, guilt and terror on their faces. She wanted to tell them to relax, but a third knock, slower and deliberate, focused her attention back on the door.

The moment she turned the knob to crack the door, her older sister, Rebecca, burst into the room, face illuminated by a candle. "Boo!"

"Rebecca, shut up!" she whispered as her friends squealed. "You'll get me in trouble. Mom and Dad said we better not wake them up."

Rebecca rolled her eyes. "If I can hear you guys from down the hall, I guarantee Mom and Dad hear you downstairs. Their room is directly below yours and you four are making enough noise to wake the dead."

"We are not!"

"What are you guys doing anyway? This looks like a pretty boring party. No makeovers? Movies? Nothing?"

"Makeovers?" Faith scoffed. "We're thirteen. We're not babies playing with makeup."

Dakota dove under the bed and retrieved the Ouija board. "Yeah. We're—"

Rebecca's jaw dropped. "Oh my God, Faith. Mom will kill you if she sees that. Seriously, you guys are playing with a Ouija board?"

"Don't tell," Faith pleaded.

Rebecca crept forward and knelt beside the board, pushing her long sandy-brown hair away from her face. "Did you try it? Does it work?"

"It was working until Yumeko didn't do it right," Dakota said. "It even wished Faith a happy birthday!"

"Okay, but you guys know it's her birthday. You could push the thing to spell that."

"I didn't push it!" Yumeko insisted. "And I didn't mess it up, either."

"Okay, so let's test it," Rebecca said. Her eyes glowed as she stared at the board.

"Rebecca, I don't think we should use it anymore," Faith said.

Yumeko moved behind Rebecca and began braiding her hair.

Faith wished her sister would leave. Rebecca had promised not to crash her sleepover.

"Here's what we do," Rebecca went on as though Faith hadn't spoken. "One of you draw a symbol on a piece of paper, fold it up, and hide it. The two of us working the board won't know what you drew. It'll be very scientific."

"That's a great idea!" Dakota shifted to face Rebecca, squaring her knees and placing the board between them. "Parminder, draw something but don't tell us what!"

"Faith, get a piece of paper for her," Rebecca directed, watching Dakota situate the planchette.

Rebecca is so bossy. This is my party. She almost told Rebecca to get out of her room. But her friends all looked to her so eagerly she withdrew a piece of paper and a pencil from her desk drawer and passed them to Parminder.

Parminder tapped the pencil against her lips, face scrunched in deep thought. "What should I draw?"

Rebecca waved her hands to hurry her up. "Anything! Just don't let anyone else see."

Parminder nodded and scratched the pencil across the paper, then folded it and passed it to Yumeko.

"Everyone close your eyes a moment and breathe deeply," Dakota instructed. "Imagine all your energy pouring into the planchette."

The girls sat in silence.

Dakota's most serious voice asked, "Are any spirits here with us tonight?"

Faith opened her eyes, heart pounding, and stared at the planchette, praying it didn't respond.

Nothing happened. She released a breath she didn't realize she'd been holding.

Dakota scowled. "Maybe it's stuck. "

Rebecca wiggled the plastic device and shrugged. "Seems to move easily enough."

The planchette swooped to the upper left-hand corner of the board. YES.

The girls gasped.

"Did you move it?" Dakota asked.

"I'm barely touching it," Rebecca said.

Dakota tried again. "Is there a spirit here with us tonight?"

No response.

Rebecca cleared her throat. "Is there a spirit here?"

The planchette drifted toward the alphabet, then settled again on YES.

Dakota stared at Rebecca. "It wants to talk to you."

The planchette slid off and returned to the word YES.

"Rebecca, this isn't funny," Faith said. "Put it away. Please."

"It can't hurt us. It's only a game," Rebecca said, using the I'm-much-older-and-know-better voice Faith hated so much.

NO

"See? It says it can't hurt us."

"Or that could mean, no, you're wrong, it's not just a game. You don't know."

"Scared of the lonely ghost, Faith?"

Sometimes she hated her sister so much.

"Whatever. She must be moving it," Dakota insisted.

NO

"Stop it, Rebecca. That's not funny!"

"One way to prove I'm not controlling it," Rebecca said. "Spirit, what did Parminder draw on the paper?"

The planchette jiggled but didn't shift from the word NO.

"What did Parminder draw on the paper?"

The board sat still.

Faith sighed in relief. "It doesn't know. It doesn't work." She began to giggle. Parminder and Yumeko joined her.

Rebecca scowled. "Spirit—"

S-T-A-R

Parminder's hands flew to her mouth, eyes wide.

Faith looked to Yumeko, unfolding the paper. She stared at it a moment before turning the paper for the girls to see. "It's a star."

"How did you know?" Parminder whispered.

"Look at the board," Rebecca said, her voice quivering. Faith had never heard her sister sound so shaken.

S-T-A-R S-T-A-R S-T- A-R

"Who are you?" Rebecca asked.

"Rebecca, stop!" Faith pleaded, near tears.

G-E-O-R-G-E

"George?"

YES

"Why are you here, George?"

D-E-A-D

"How did you die?"

H-A-N-G-E-D

"Rebecca, stop!"

"But it's working!" Rebecca's eyes gleamed. "Why were you hanged?"

H-O-R-S-E-S

Dakota broke her own rule and blurted, "Why will you only talk to Rebecca?"

W-I-F-E

"Your wife's name was Rebecca?"

NO

"Then what—"

I W-A-N-T H-E-R

Rebecca yanked her hands from the planchette as if it burned her fingers. She'd gone pale.

Dakota jerked her hands away and shrieked, "Don't ever do that! You can't handle a planchette alone!"

Rebecca's voice shook again. "That's enough. This thing is creepy. Put it away and I'll make you girls some mocktails in the kitchen."

"You guys," Parminder whispered. "The board."

The planchette jiggled, though no one touched it. Slowly it

drifted across the board, picking up speed until barely more than a blur.

W-A-N-T W-A-N-T W-A- N-T

Faith's heart pounded and her stomach twisted into knots. It was real. This board was not a toy and they had somehow made contact with an actual spirit. Not a nice spirit. Not the kind of spirit they learned about in Sunday school, who floated around heaven singing God's praises. They had no control over it.

Her best friends stood whimpering as the bewitched planchette continued the maniacal course across the board.

She had to stop it. Somehow.

Racing to the board, she dropped to her knees and grasped the white plastic piece.

"Faith, no!" Dakota screamed.

As her hand grasped the planchette, the closet door blew open. The candle flickered as a gust of air blasted through the room. The lamp beside her bed flickered on and off.

"Faith, let go!" Dakota screamed.

"I can't!"

The planchette changed trajectory, spelling a new word over and over.

R-E-B-E-C-C-A R-E-B-E-C-C-A

Faith looked to her sister for guidance, but Rebecca pressed her fingers to her temples, shaking her head back and forth. "What does it want? What do you want?"

Exasperated voices carried from downstairs. Her parents.

She grabbed the horrid plastic thing in both hands, pulling as hard as she could as it continued to spell.

W-A-N-T R-E-B-E-C-C-A

Sweat dripped from her temples, though cold shards jabbed at her stomach. "Let go! Go away!"

The planchette suddenly released her and flew across the room, landing under her bed.

Her hand felt like fire. She looked down to find a bright red welt burned into her skin—in the shape of the planchette.

Heavy footsteps thumped up the stairs. All the girls looked to each other, fear in their eyes.

Rebecca took charge. "Hide that thing! Where's the white piece? Just hide the board and the box! All of you, stop crying! Come sit down in a circle again and pretend we've been telling ghost stories."

Faith watched her sister flop onto the floor, waving wildly to the others to sit back down with her.

"Oh my God, Faith! Your hand! Never mind, I'll bandage it later. Right now we're in trouble."

"We're in more trouble than you think," Dakota said, settling beside Rebecca. "I told you guys not to handle the planchette alone. That's how you release the spirit into the world."

CHAPTER ONE

KIMBERLY WANTLAND STARED out the window of *The Wantland Files* van, marveling at the lush forests blanketing the rolling hills. Until her crew investigated Crescent Hotel in Eureka Springs, she'd never been to the Ozarks and couldn't get over how green they were. Nothing like the stark, barren mountains surrounding her hometown of Albuquerque. Back home, hues of beige, tan, and gray dominated. Seeing new places was one of the best things about her paranormal investigations.

Her show director, Michael, sang along to the radio as he drove them away from Eureka Springs toward their next destination. She glanced back at Rosie, her personal assistant/stylist/best friend, and Elise, the show's lead researcher, in the middle seats. Rosie must surely be feeling each mile that took her farther from Lorenzo, the ghost tour guide she'd started dating at The Crescent Hotel. How long would her personal assistant last in a long-distance relationship? She hoped it would work out. Rosie deserved someone who treated her well, after years of disastrous relationships.

Stan and TJ, her camera operators, drove ahead of them in the unmarked equipment van.

She flicked her eyes to the side-view mirror outside her

window, chiding herself for the umpteenth time for her lack of control. Sterling's BMW i8 still trailed along behind them. And she still couldn't catch a glimpse of him through the heavily tinted windows. So why did she keep trying?

She should close her eyes and sleep while she could. A nap could go a long way to recharging her batteries after a draining investigation. But she felt restless and couldn't seem to relax.

Another glance at the side-view mirror brought the realization she had no control and vague irritation with herself. If Sterling had wanted her beside him in his car, he would've suggested it. But he didn't. And she darned sure wouldn't be the one to ask. "I'll ride in the van with Michael, I guess," was the most she'd been able to bring herself to say, hoping to prompt an offer of a ride in his new car. He could have, nay should have, been in the corporate vehicles like everyone else. But no, he'd missed the convoy when they headed out from Albuquerque for the season.

Why did this irritate her so much?

The van crossed a bridge, which spanned a breathtaking valley. She forced her attention away from the mirror and back to appreciating her surroundings. She would see Sterling soon enough but didn't know when or if she would have the opportunity to see this beautiful part of the country again.

Rosie, seated behind Michael, leaned forward and patted her shoulder. "We'll need to stop for gas and a restroom break within the hour, girl. Don't worry. I'll have the perfect excuse cooked up to get you in his car by then."

"I don't know what you mean," she murmured, heat flushing her cheeks. Rosie knew her too well. Nothing escaped her best friend's notice.

Michael glanced away from the road just long enough to give her his patented eye roll from hell. "Puh-leeze. You're not fooling anyone. Just ride with Sterling. Seriously. It'll be a good chance for you two to bond and learn more about each other."

She opened her mouth to explain she didn't want to leave them behind to endure Sterling's insufferable arrogance and self-assured attitude, even for the chance to sit in that sweet ride with the cool butterfly doors. Cars didn't impress her, so what did she care? She didn't.

Before she could get one word out, Elise, normally withdrawn, cried out, "I call shotgun!"

"You can have it," Rosie said. "I'll be in the backseat with binoculars texting her tips and making sure she doesn't do anything silly."

"Rosie! I do not need relationship tips! Especially not from—"

"Uh-uh," Rosie interrupted. "I'm the only one of us currently in a relationship, therefore I am the learned scholar as far as you're concerned."

She crossed her arms. "I am single by choice. I don't have time for any of the nonsense relationships inevitably bring."

The three of them laughed. If her cheeks weren't red before, they were definitely flaming now. They could at least pretend the statement carried some truth. So she hadn't found the right guy yet. She was a busy woman.

Michael's cell phone rang. He glanced at the screen and passed the phone to her. "Randmeier. Better take it for me. He knows we're en route and that I'm driving so it must be important."

She accepted his phone, stomach in knots. What could be so important that their producer Randall Hoffmeier was calling? Was he upset with her? Had she done something wrong? Her pre-teen self squirmed within her, as if she were being called downstairs in trouble. She could still hear Dad's deep baritone calling, "Kimberly Annabelle Wantland! Come downstairs."

She shook her head, knowing she'd done nothing wrong, and accepted the call. "Michael's phone."

"Kimberly! Randall calling. Michael beside you?"

"Yes, sir."

"Good. We need to call an audible. Emergency situation. I'm

sure you'll see the request once you're settled, but we have some frantic parents begging for help."

"The season is already slated—"

"That's what I said when the interns first brought this to me. But the parents keep calling, desperate. And the case sounds like a doozy. Where are you guys right now?"

"I'm not certain. Still in Arkansas I think." She shrugged and looked at Michael for confirmation.

He nodded. "What's up?"

"Tell Michael you guys need to divert to Guthrie in Oklahoma. You're probably only about four hours or so away."

"But—"

"Their child is sick, Kimberly. I know you can't resist cases revolving around children. You have to go help. Besides, if this is as hot as I think it is, we can substitute it for any cases that fizzle and aren't exciting enough. I'll text you the address."

"Okay, I'll—"

He ended the call.

She stared at the phone before passing it back to Michael.

He cocked an eyebrow. "What was that?"

"He said—" Her phone chimed her text tone—echoing footsteps. An address materialized on her phone in a text preview box. "He said we're going to Guthrie."

CHAPTER TWO

THE SMELL inside the house burned Kimberly's nasal passages and the back of her throat. She fought her gag reflex and struggled to maintain a passive countenance. Each breath slammed against her olfactory senses, laying siege to her determination. If the onslaught continued, she would need an excuse to step outside for fresh air.

Oddly, no matter how many sideways glances she cut to her coworkers, not one of them responded with an exaggerated gag or a quiet nod of understanding.

The Johnsons circled around their dining table—Daniel and Ruth and their daughters Rebecca and Faith. A cross hung on the wall above their buffet. A plaque beseeching *BLESS THIS HOUSE AND ALL SOULS IN IT* graced the opposite wall.

Stan and TJ, primary and junior camera operators, indicated they were ready. Michael counted her in.

"In five . . . four . . . three . . ." He held up two fingers, then one, then pointed at her.

Show time.

"Mr. and Mrs. Johnson, thank you for reaching out to us and allowing us the privilege of investigating your disturbance."

"Please," Mrs. Johnson interrupted, "call us Daniel and Ruth.

And we can't thank you enough for being here. Especially on such short notice. I know you must have changed your schedule to accommodate us."

Kimberly offered her most comforting smile, mentally noting they would definitely need to edit out that last bit. With thousands of requests pouring in every day, most of which were declined due to time constraints, announcing they'd worked in this case as an emergency would only outrage the many turned away. Everyone considered their own case an emergency.

"Can you tell us the nature of the disturbance?" she asked Ruth. For once she didn't have all the details prior to the interview.

The woman glanced at her husband, nodded, and took a deep breath. "It was little things at first. Nothing that you'd pay attention to as an isolated incident. But they kept happening."

"What kind of things? Can you give us examples?"

Ruth waved her hands and looked to her husband. "Oh, you know. Little things. Something isn't where you know you left it. Things rolling off the counter. Things moving. Some things disappeared and we still haven't found them. Just gone."

"Such as?"

"First it was Faith's stuffed bear she's had since she was born. It was on her bed but vanished. Umm, one of my rings. Not expensive but great sentimental value. Rebecca's prayer book. We turned the house upside down and they're nowhere to be found."

"The radio came on once when no one was near it," Daniel said.

"That's right! I'd forgotten that. Strange but not anything that really caused more than a pause. One morning, though, Daniel's keys disappeared. It was more than just odd."

"Made me late for work," he reminded Ruth.

"Yes. We searched for over thirty minutes. Checked his pants pockets from the day before. Looked in the windows of the locked car. Counters, the bathroom, his nightstand. They were nowhere to be found."

"I always leave them in the same place. There on that hook by the front door." He indicated a wooden coat rack mounted on the wall. A row of hooks sat below a small shelf, with the inscription *HOUSE OF THE LORD* above it. A ring of keys currently hung on one of the hooks.

"I knew I hadn't disturbed them," Ruth continued. "I'm ashamed to admit we blamed the girls."

"We kept telling them it wasn't funny," Daniel said. "But that wasn't fair. They actually were helping search and didn't behave as though they'd played a prank."

"We knew for sure when it was time to take the girls to school. Both of them became quite upset at the prospect of a tardy. Suddenly, Snickers started whining and scratching at a shoe partly lodged under the couch." At the mention of his name, Snickers, a medium-sized dog of indeterminate breed, jumped to his feet, ears perked. "We couldn't get him to stop. We always leave our shoes by the door to reduce dirt and debris getting tracked in. I almost fussed at the girls again. Then I realized it was one of mine. I knew I'd left my shoes by the door, so I was really confused. I pulled the shoe from under the couch and it jangled."

"My keys were in the shoe," Daniel said. "And the shoe somehow got shoved under the couch."

"And the dog found it?" Sterling clarified.

"Yes. He's very smart," Ruth said, beaming at the dog. "And always tuned in to our emotions. If we're upset, he knows it and tries to help."

"He seems very sweet. What kind of dog is he?" Kimberly asked.

"We don't know. We rescued him from a shelter. He took right to us. We like to say he picked us."

Sterling smiled. "And he knew you were looking for keys?"

"He must have. He knows lots of words and tricks. He's very

smart. Snickers, come." Ruth snapped and pointed beside her. The dog went to her side and sat exactly where she pointed. "Give me five." The dog raised one paw and patted it against Ruth's outstretched palm. "Good boy! See? He's very clever."

Kimberly glanced at Sterling and steered the conversation back on track. "At that point you started paying closer attention to odd occurrences?"

"That's right," Ruth said. "Turns out, we'd all been noticing things moving and disappearing. Like Faith's Ladies of Fashion."

She turned to face Faith. The girl jumped and her eyes shifted, hands clasped so tightly the knuckles nearly glowed white. Kimberly knew the girl's pale complexion and sunken eyes could be attributed to her reported lengthy illness. But she thought the girl seemed anxious about all the attention on her as well.

"Can you tell us about that, Faith?" she asked gently.

Faith stared at her, then shook her head.

Ruth took over again. "Faith really hasn't been feeling well lately, as you know. The Ladies of Fashion were a gift to her from my mom, right before she passed. Mom collected them for years. Little porcelain figures of women in clothing and hairstyles from different periods. Victorian, Renaissance, Gothic. That sort of thing."

Kimberly smiled at Faith. "If you're interested in clothes and hairstyles, I need to introduce you to my personal assistant, Rosie."

Faith looked up long enough to return the smile, but then resumed staring at the table.

She's so skittish. Something seems off. Maybe she could read the girl's spectrum and gain some insight that way. Her experience with children of any age amounted to almost nothing, but anyone could see something scared this girl.

"The miniatures are stored in a display case," Ruth continued. "Two round, wooden levels covered in felt with a glass dome cover. They started moving."

Kimberly's eyebrows shot up. No one had told her this bit. "Moving how?"

"Faith is a little OCD about the dolls. She adores them, which is why my mom gave them to her. She keeps them arranged in perfect circles on their stands. But they started moving. Shifting. She'd come home from school and find them all clustered to one side or scattered about haphazardly. A few times she found the ladies had swapped positions. They were out of the order she keeps them in. She likes them chronological." Ruth stroked her daughter's hair. Faith looked like she was about to cry.

Sterling leaned forward on the table. "Well that sounds like . . . magic!" With a flourish, he reached behind her ear and produced a wrapped square of chocolate.

She suspected he could see the girl's distress and wanted to cheer her up. But this wasn't really the time for his tricks. She raised an eyebrow at him and glanced at Michael. He shrugged.

Faith wouldn't take the chocolate. Daniel and Ruth looked confused.

Sterling cleared his throat and left the chocolate on the table. "Tough crowd. In all seriousness, though, I can think of numerous reasons the dolls could be jostled."

Daniel nodded. "So did we. And yet we couldn't replicate the movement."

Sterling tipped his head and frowned. "What do you mean?"

"Faith keeps the case on her dresser. I tried bumping the dresser, shaking it, sliding the display case from one end to the other. We called Snickers into the room and had him raise up on the dresser. Nothing. The dolls didn't budge."

"They sit on felt," Ruth reminded them. "They don't slide around easily. It looked like someone moved them deliberately. But it always happens when the girls are at school and Dan is at work. I don't go in the room. I certainly wouldn't disturb the figurines."

"Very interesting. We will be sure to watch the dolls during our investigation," she said. Sterling cocked an eyebrow and smirked again. He would get his chance later. The interview was for the family. "But then things got worse, didn't they?"

Ruth's brow furrowed. "Yes. Things moving and disappearing is one thing. We wouldn't have called you for that. But Faith . . ." She reached for Daniel who took her hand and squeezed. "Strange things have been happening to Faith."

"Strange how?" Sterling asked.

"She has a burn on her hand from her curling iron. But it happened months ago at her birthday party. It still hasn't healed properly. She's woken up with strange scratches on her arms and legs. Once she . . . her arm looked like she'd been bitten. I know that sounds crazy, but her arm had what looked like a bite mark on it. Then the rash—" Ruth pressed her hand to her forehead.

"Rash?"

"A rash on her arm. Almost looks like poison ivy gone crazy and it won't heal."

Daniel rubbed his wife's back. "This has really taken a toll on all of us. Faith has missed a lot of school. Her teachers have been accommodating, sending lecture notes and her homework home. But the school has a policy about maximum absences."

Ruth sniffed and swiped a tear from her cheek. "The pediatrician can't diagnose what's wrong. He ran every test he could think of. They've drawn more blood than you'd think one little girl could safely give. He even ran X-rays and a CT scan. Rare blood tests. Allergy panels. I can't remember all the tests he ran. All negative. Even the rash won't respond to treatment. Cortisone shots do nothing. Oral steroids. We've been through gallons of calamine lotion."

"We've been to specialists now too. No help at all," Daniel added. "They're all confounded."

"She hasn't been herself lately. I don't know how else to describe it," Ruth said. "Withdrawn, down. She even raised her voice to me a few times."

"We don't allow behavior like that," Daniel said. "Disrespect.

But Faith looked shocked after snapping at her mother. And cried so hard afterward."

"She's not herself," Ruth repeated. "And then . . ."

Kimberly sat quietly, allowing the woman time to gather her nerve.

Daniel draped an arm around her shoulders. "It's okay. Go ahead."

Ruth took a deep breath. "I sometimes feel . . . a hand on me. At night. Touching me. It wakes me up. And it's not Daniel. Every time this happened, he was turned away from me, on the other side of the bed. I know what people will think, but it's not him and I'm not crazy."

This is more than just Faith's illness. I didn't get the full story. What had she walked into? This was a far more alarming disturbance that she'd expected. "I assume you're being touched inappropriately."

Ruth nodded. "I've felt a hand run down my arm. Once it slithered around my hip. And once it groped me . . . on my thigh." She shuddered. "I'm not crazy. I didn't imagine any of this, but I don't know what to do. I'm at the end of my rope."

Kimberly reached across the table and squeezed Ruth's hand. The woman's red chakra resonated, spinning brightly, indicating fear and survival dominated Ruth's emotions. "I can only imagine how violated you feel. We don't think you're crazy, and I promise—"

"Me too." The older daughter spoke for the first time since the crew had arrived for the interview.

Kimberly turned to the sisters. She'd never seen such somber children. Both of them stared into their laps. She sensed fear from the girls, much like their mother, but also something else. Something she couldn't quite identify. Guilt? Were they ashamed to have a camera crew recording their family's intimate secrets? "You've also experienced groping?"

Rebecca nodded.

Daniel jumped to his feet, brow furrowed and eyes full of concern. "You didn't tell us!"

"I didn't think you'd believe me," Rebecca whispered. "I thought maybe I dreamed it or imagined it. But if the same thing happened to Mom, maybe it was real."

The younger daughter raised her eyes. "I thought I felt someone touching me too."

Kimberly sat straighter, hoping she'd misunderstood the girl. "Are you talking about the scratches on your arms and legs?"

Faith flicked her eyes to her. The shame rolling off the girl broke Kimberly's heart. "Sometimes it scratches. Sometimes it rubs my back or pats my cheek."

Daniel pressed a hand to his forehead. "All three of you?" He paced away from the table, seemed unsure where to go, then returned, hands on his hips. "Do you know how helpless I feel right now? My wife and daughters all harassed and I can't stop it. Faith sick and no one can figure out why. I want to fix it. To do something."

Stan homed in on Daniel. TJ held back, capturing wide shots. She crossed to Daniel and rested a hand on his shoulder. "You did do something. You called us. We're going to help you figure this out."

Daniel's forehead wrinkled. "But I'm afraid . . . I'm afraid we're being tested. Maybe we shouldn't have called you."

"Tested?" she asked. "What do you mean?"

"Our faith in the Lord. Sometimes the devil challenges Christians. Tests their faith. What if this is a test? Everyone at our church is praying for us. And we believe we can overcome anything with God's help. But maybe we were weak. Impatient."

"Or maybe God brought Kimberly here in answer to your prayers," Sterling said.

Her jaw dropped. She spun to face Sterling, stunned by his sober, sincere attitude. Gone was the glib showman, constantly searching for attention and cracking jokes. He genuinely appeared to mean what he said. A man of science claiming God had sent her to help? She remembered him once mentioning being raised Catholic. Perhaps his religious upbringing remained firmly entrenched. They'd never discussed it.

"But if this is a demon sent to test us," Ruth said, "can she help?"

Sterling stood, resting his hands on his hips. "Are you kidding? Do you watch this show? Kimberly Wantland never fails. She will do anything to ensure your family is safe."

Daniel raised his eyebrows. "We saw some episodes of *Spook-Busters*. We know you don't believe in spirits. Why would you say that?"

"Look at it this way. You get the best of both worlds. I'll be here to investigate scientific explanations for the disturbances you're experiencing. If I find something, we fix it. Kimberly will search for alternate solutions to your problem. Either way, we don't leave until the issues are resolved."

"What do you mean scientific explanations?" Daniel asked. "Like what?"

"Well," Sterling began, "I noticed on the way in—"

"Let's not get ahead of ourselves," Kimberly interrupted. "Save those brilliant ideas for the investigation, Sterling." She beamed at him, hoping he could see in her eyes the gratitude for his praise. She couldn't wait to hear his initial impressions off camera and away from the family. She doubted she'd agree with him. But he was intelligent and might bring something valuable to the table.

She shifted to face Stan, speaking directly into his camera. "The Johnsons are plagued by a force growing bolder and more menacing by the day, powerful enough to move objects, sicken their younger daughter, and physically harass all the females in the house. Who is this spirit and what prompted him to lash out now?"

Sterling joined her, pressing shoulder to shoulder. "Or is something other than a spirit causing the issues disturbing this family?"

He looked to her, his piercing gaze searching hers. For . . . permission? Approval?

She smiled, nodded once, and continued. "Stay with us as Sterling and I search for the truth behind the haunting, tonight on *The Wantland Files*."

CHAPTER THREE

THE WANTLAND FILES van parked at the curb had attracted a few curious onlookers, Kimberly noticed as she gulped fresh air into her lungs, eager to clear the stinging stench of the house from her nose and throat. She needed Michael to tell them where to go. Her trailer wasn't here yet, and she wanted to get settled into her hotel room. She felt out of sorts.

Rosie walked with her. "I'm glad we came here. That girl looked so distraught. What are your initial thoughts?"

"I'm with you. The family needs help and fast. I didn't get anything specific, but what did you think about the smell in the house?"

"What smell? Rosie asked. "Freshly baked cookies?"

The growing group of people assembling nearby whispered and pointed but kept a respectful distance. Until one crossed the street—a woman carrying a paper plate of cookies covered in plastic wrap.

"Hello," she greeted them as she walked up the driveway. "I'm Dakota's mom."

This meant nothing to Kimberly. "Dakota?"

"Oh, sorry! Faith and Dakota are best friends. They've grown up together. I'm so glad you're here. These are for you." The woman beamed and held out the plate of cookies.

"We were just talking about cookies!" Rosie swooped between them and nabbed the paper plate. "I'll take those."

Kimberly knew her crew would devour them. "This is very kind. Thank you."

"They are the sweetest, kindest family. They don't deserve this."

"Any ideas what might have prompted the problems? How long have they lived here?"

The neighbor scrunched her face in thought. "They've been here since we moved in. And that's been . . . goodness, ten years. I still think of us as the new neighbors, but Dakota was three when we moved here."

She nodded, not really expecting useful information from a neighbor. "It's a gorgeous little town. Lots of history. I can feel it."

"But we're not far from one of the largest cities in the state."

"Well, thank you for these," she said, gesturing to the plate of cookies. "Let me know if you think of anything that might help us."

Sterling joined them. "Sweet! Cookies!" He helped himself to one and took a huge bite. "Those girls were not impressed by my magic. The older one told me she knows I had it in my hand the entire time. Yikes. So where will we be staying?"

"I haven't heard yet. Let's see if Michael knows."

Stan and TJ worked on unloading cameras, voice recorders, and other equipment from the van. Other crew members loitered about, awaiting instructions.

Elise's pencil scratched across her spiral notebook. "I'm so far behind. No preparatory research whatsoever. I'll be playing catch-up for days."

"It's okay. You'll get there," she reassured the frazzled young woman. "Cookie?"

Her lead researcher shook her head and glanced at her watch.

"I'll go see what time the library closes. It's only four thirty. I might be able to get a few hours in before we walk through the house. Did you get anything during the interview that might help?"

"Nothing helpful yet. We should look into previous owners, of course. History of the property. The usual." Kimberly marveled at the old wood-frame dwelling. "It's in impeccable shape. What would you guess? Victorian era?"

Elise adjusted her glasses and peered at the home. "No, built too late for that. I suspect Craftsman, but I will verify that. And definitely remodeled at some point. The kitchen is completely modern. And the exterior is well maintained. Some of the houses in this part of town are looking a little sad."

"This neighborhood is in pretty good shape," Rosie said, taking in the nearby houses.

Kimberly looked at the other homes as well, noting Elise was correct. The Johnsons' house stood out among the others, however.

A man stood in the street, staring at her. He smiled when she made eye contact, but no warmth lit his eyes. She shuddered.

Sterling took another cookie, ignoring Rosie as she batted him away. "This neighborhood maybe. But I saw at least one condemned place driving in. And I cringed when we drove over that one bridge. Wasn't sure it could handle the weight of the van. I worried this was about to turn into *The Wakefield Files*."

Kimberly gave him a hard stare. "Is that why you didn't invite me to ride with you? Hoping for the chance to take over the show?"

Sterling did a double take, shuffling his feet. "No. I would've loved company. But don't you always ride in the van? I know you don't like changing things, especially for me. I assumed you'd say no."

She sucked in a breath. He *did* want her to ride with him. Her heartbeat stumbled a few beats. "Not always. Riding in a van emblazoned with me on the side is a bit weird, honestly."

"If you don't like the van, why not get something new?"

"Corporate decision. I have no say."

"Well, I would've asked you to join me if I'd known. You should have asked."

"I couldn't invite myself. That's rude."

He laughed. "I keep forgetting. You don't see yourself the way others see you."

She scrunched up her face. "What does that mean?"

He rested his fingers below her chin, lifting her face to his. She forgot all about deciphering what he'd said. "Consider this a standing invitation. You are always welcome by my side."

"Got that, girl?" Rosie said. "You're always welcome to ride him. I mean, ride *with* him."

"Rosie!" Her entire crew watched, grins plastered on their faces. "Sorry about that, Sterling."

He shrugged. "Rosie is remarkably perceptive."

The warmth in his eyes sent an electric shiver through every nerve in her body. How did he always do this to her?

Before she could think of a response, Michael cleared his throat. "Sorry to interrupt but the clock is ticking. Turns out the Johnsons own the empty lot next door and don't mind us parking your trailer on it. I've called and told the crew to bring it in. And just the one since no one used the second trailer last week. I trust that's okay?"

"I. . ." Everyone watched her, silent, listening intently for her reply. She hated being the center of attention. Every move, every expression, every word scrutinized.

Sterling apparently misinterpreted her hesitation. "If I need—"

"No. We only need the one. I don't mind sharing." More silly grins from the crew left her feeling like she stood on an elementary school playground. They were all adults. Why did she feel so awkward around Sterling?

The smile that broke across his face sent her stomach

turning back flips. Then he curled an arm around her waist and squeezed. A warm, fuzzy rush buzzed through her body.

Michael clapped to get the crew's attention. "We're staying at the Stone Lion Inn. It's an historic home not far from here that's been remodeled into a bed and breakfast. The only downside is the limited room. Which means we all have to double up."

"Why not just find a motel like we usually do?" she asked.

"Randmeier booked the place. It's purportedly haunted and he's hoping for bonus material."

"Another haunted hotel? We just did that."

"I know. But he's the boss. I only follow instructions."

"Right. Seems like we have less and less input lately."

"Things have changed, sweetie. It's worth it though."

"I know. I'm not really complaining. Just minor venting."

"Besides, now you have me," Sterling said, elbowing her side.

"That's one change that *was* my idea," she reminded him.

"Not at first. Thank goodness my irresistible charm won you over."

"Okay, you two. Let's go find our rooms and grab some food so we can get back here and prep for walk through."

A man approached her as she reached for the van door. A wide smile broke across his face. The man from the street. The one who'd been watching her.

"You're the star, huh?" He gestured to her image on the van. "Ms. Wantland."

"That's me. Nice to meet you." She offered a hand.

He jerked his head toward the house. "Think this place is haunted? Gonna work your magic?"

She laughed. "Work my magic? I suppose that's one way to look at it. We won't be able to determine presence of activity or not until we run some tests and investigate. Don't worry, though. This home poses no threat to your neighborhood."

He nodded slowly, an odd look in his eyes. "You'll be staying at the Stone Lion Inn?"

Great. He overheard Michael. The guy kind of gave her the

creeps, though this was probably simply an awkward attempt at conversation. She preferred not to broadcast where she'd be sleeping. "Nice to meet you," she repeated, forced smile in place.

Sterling rounded the van. "What's the hold up, Kimberly?" He spotted the man. "Oh. Hey."

"I look forward to seeing more of you this week, Ms. Wantland." The man bowed slightly before heading down the street.

Sterling opened the door for her. "Who was that?"

"One of the neighbors, I presume."

"Guess you attract attention like that a lot. Especially from guys."

"It depends. Sometimes. And sometimes not so much. This one gave me the creeps. He heard Michael say where we're staying. That's unfortunate."

"Did he say something inappropriate?"

"No. Just something about him. I can't say what exactly. But I got a negative vibe."

Sterling frowned. "I'll keep an eye out for him."

She'd expected him to scoff at her concerns based on nothing more than a bad vibe. She tipped her head sideways and leaned against his shoulder. "Thanks."

He helped her into the front passenger seat. "See you at the inn. Michael said we'd all be doubling up. Think we'll room together?" He raised an eyebrow and smirked at her.

The look on his face was so ridiculous she couldn't help laughing. "Get out of here, you nut!"

He backed away, gaze penetrating until he turned and half-skipped to his car.

Michael threw the van in gear and backed out of the driveway. "You know, I intended to maneuver to be sure you had a room to yourself. But maybe I should come at it the other way and make sure you share with Sterling."

"Do it!" Rosie yelled from the back.

"Don't you dare," she told Michael as a warm flush crept up her neck and blossomed over her cheeks. Her racing heart told her loud and clear what she wanted to deny—the idea didn't sound so bad anymore. Some part of her rather liked the thought of rooming with him.

As the van cruised out of the neighborhood, she spotted the man who had approached her, still standing on the sidewalk. His eyes narrowed and his gaze locked with hers.

A shiver ran down her spine.

CHAPTER FOUR

KIMBERLY SIPPED tea in her trailer makeup chair as she waited for Rosie to finish applying a bit of powder to Sterling. Rosie had already mussed and gelled his hair. The addition of a second chair allowed her to sit beside him, which meant Rosie could easily shift back and forth between the two of them. But Sterling had insisted she be camera-ready before allowing Rosie to work on him.

They had moved into their rooms at the Stone Lion Inn, Sterling intervening to carry her bag for her. Her pulse continued to pound while the crew checked in, waiting to hear if she would be required to room with Sterling. A pang of disappointment settled in her stomach when she learned the two rooms on the first level, with the smaller single beds, had been given to the two of them. The other four rooms were upstairs and the crew would squeeze into them to fit the space.

After settling in, they'd walked a few blocks to the historic downtown area of Guthrie for dinner. Elise had gobbled a quick bite of food before dashing off to the library.

"Tomorrow we should take some time to explore the historical markers downtown," she suggested as Rosie brushed powder over Sterling's cheeks. "Nearly every other building had a marker in front of it."

"Great idea," Sterling said. "Rosie, you in?"

"Hecks, yeah. I love that they've retained so many of the original buildings here. I love the house we're investigating, too. How old do you think it is?"

"I'm sure Elise will know by tonight," Kimberly said. "Definitely an older house. Wonder what in the world caused that awful smell."

Sterling and Rosie both frowned at her in the mirror.

"What smell?" Rosie asked.

"The horrible smell in the house. It was so bad I could barely breathe."

Sterling shook his head. "The house didn't stink. Smelled like laundry detergent and cinnamon maybe. Didn't even have that musty odor some older homes develop."

"Neither one of you smelled anything bad?"

"Nope," Rosie answered.

"Must've been a greeting from the ghostly inhabitant. Or a warning."

"A warning?" Sterling asked.

"That my interference is unwelcome. Wouldn't be the first time. Rosie, if this spirit is already exhibiting hostility, we may need to gear up for a fight."

"I'm on it, girl."

"Maybe we should rule out simpler explanations first," Sterling said. "Make sure we can't easily determine causation before you gear up for Armageddon."

She turned her chair to face him, noticing how his eyes lit up when they danced with amusement. They practically glowed with delight. He enjoyed chasing mysteries as much as she did, even if they took different approaches. "What are you thinking might explain all the phenomena they described?"

"Let's see." Sterling threaded his fingers behind his head and leaned back. "The keys? Simplest explanation is that they fell from the hook into the shoe. The dog dragged it into the living room and under the couch and probably returned to play with it again when the family thought he 'found' it."

Rosie, standing behind him, cocked her head, clearly waiting for her reaction.

She sipped her tea, mulling over his suggestion. "Okay. I'll give you that one."

Sterling's eyebrows shot up. "Really?"

"It's a plausible explanation. What about the moving dolls?"

"The girl wants attention."

"I'm not convinced of that. Did you watch her during the interview? She was obviously uncomfortable. She barely spoke. Not the actions of someone eager for attention."

"She's probably scared now. She carried it too far and is about to be busted. Mom and Dad will be ticked when we debunk this sham."

"You think she scratched herself? Bit herself? Gave herself a rash?"

"All possible. Maybe she rubbed poison ivy on herself, is particularly sensitive to it, and now it won't heal."

"I disagree. Though I will admit I sensed some fear from her. Both girls, actually."

"You'd be scared too if something you couldn't see scratched you and made you sick," Rosie said.

"True. No doubt that's part of it. But there was an element of . . . I don't know, guilt, maybe? Something seemed off."

Sterling nodded. "Maybe the sister is in on it. They're guilty because they know they're about to be in trouble for tricking their parents."

She tried to see that as the reason behind the girls' emotional turmoil and couldn't make it fit. "The parents seem concerned and involved. Why would the daughters be forced to act out like that for attention?"

"I don't know. Yet. Maybe the dad is abusive. There are lots of possibilities that don't involve anything paranormal. Maybe it's a plea for help."

"What? Come on. I didn't get that impression at all. Besides all three girls are plagued with creepy hands at night."

He lifted his arms in a shrug. "Again, maybe the dad—"

"Ew, Sterling, stop!" Rosie said. "Please. I can't stand to hear an accusation like that tossed around."

"I agree with Rosie," she said. "Besides, Ruth said she was sure it wasn't Daniel. If it was, she wouldn't have been bothered by it."

Sterling held his hands up in surrender. "Only pointing out the existence of numerous possibilities. If you can prove this is a ghost, I'll believe it."

"That's always the goal," she said. "I'm not sure you'd admit it even if I could show you one though. The Johnsons seem to think it's a demon testing their faith."

He lifted an eyebrow. "You sound skeptical. I know you believe in demons."

"I do. And I suppose the fact I was assaulted by a terrible smell when we first arrived could support that. It just doesn't feel like one to me."

"I will note your loose interpretation of the word 'fact' once again. No one else smelled anything foul. That might suggest a medical condition on your part rather than a ghost."

"Except of course you know I can sense things others don't. How do you feel about demons? You mentioned before that you're Catholic. Catholics believe in angels and demons. Isn't that another way of categorizing spirits?"

He shifted in his seat. "No, not your definition of spirits. I believe we all have a spirit and we go to an afterlife when we pass away. But I don't believe in rogue spirits breaking free from their bodies and wreaking havoc in the lives of people."

She noticed how tense he remained as he spoke. He stared at his cuticles as if suddenly fascinated with them. This was a tough thing for him, she realized, balancing his religious convictions with his deep-seated belief in the structure and order of science. How odd that he could firmly believe in spirits moving on to heaven or hell but not believe they sometimes didn't make the transition. "Rogue spirits breaking free? They're not criminals. They're simply lost souls. I help them find their way to the after-life. And now you have the opportunity to help with the process."

"No. That's not how it works. When we die, we're gone. That's it."

"Everything is black and white with you, isn't it? Interesting. I wonder if the Johnsons will feel the same. I'm inclined to think not. They seemed more receptive. For that matter, they called us in, so they must believe this is something out of the ordinary."

"They're clearly deeply devout," Sterling said. "What about you? What religion do you ascribe to?"

"I consider myself spiritual, not religious. I have nothing at all against religion. I know many people find great comfort and support in their church families. And churches tend to give back to their communities. As long as they encourage people to be nice and do good things, I think religions are great."

"But you don't go to a church?" he asked.

"I spend my life helping people. If there is a higher power, I think I'm doing what I was meant to do. You did suggest that perhaps God sent me here to help. Ever consider that the God you believe in gave me this ability precisely so I could help the souls that don't transition successfully?"

He stared at her, forehead crinkled, and she could see he struggled with the notion. "I hadn't thought about it that way. That's . . ."

"Don't break Sterling's brain," Rosie said. "Aren't you two supposed to be starting this investigation, not discussing the philosophical nature of the universe?"

He stood, clad as always in black. "Good point. Let's get this under way."

"Hold on," Rosie said, dashing to the clothing rack. "One last touch for you, Sterling." She carried over a black leather jacket and held it out as he shrugged into it. "Fits like a glove! I saw it and had to get it for you."

He sized himself up in the mirror. "What do you think, Kimberly? How do I look?"

How did he look? The new jacket hung open enough to reveal the ribbed shirt hugging his narrow waist, hinting at the rippled abs beneath. She knew Rosie wanted to cast him as the bad boy, mussing his hair and adding the leather jacket to his black ensemble. But the desire for her approval in his dark eyes reminded her his rough exterior was only for show. He supported her unconditionally—had even saved her life last week—and was generous and caring.

"Fantastic. Like always," she responded.

He laughed. "You sound annoyed. I'm not sure if that's a compliment or not."

"Not annoyed. A little jealous. Five minutes and you look like that? Not fair."

He beamed and rubbed the back of his neck. "As long as the boss approves."

Her turn to laugh. "I don't feel much like the boss anymore. But thanks."

He crooked an elbow. "Shall we?"

She looped an arm through his.

Rosie's cell phone buzzed. "It's Lorenzo! I'll be right inside. I just want to say hi. He has a ghost tour starting soon."

Sterling opened the door for her. The wood frame house stood out from the others on the block. Though nestled in a nice neighborhood, the Johnsons' house was clearly well kept over the years. The roof looked new, the paint seemed fresh. Nothing peeled or faded with age.

Crossing the empty lot to the gorgeous wrap-around porch, Kimberly noticed a familiar face in the small group of people gathered in the street. She tightened her grip on Sterling's arm.

"Something wrong?" he asked.

She nodded toward the onlookers.

"Just some neighbors," he assured her. "Mostly kids, looks like—Wait. Is that the guy from earlier?"

"That's what I was about to ask you. It's him, isn't it?"

The man stood completely still, gaze fixed on her. When he realized she had noticed him, a slow smile spread across his face.

Sterling patted her hand. "I'll keep an eye on him. He'll probably lose interest. Don't people get tired of standing in the street watching you walk inside a building?"

"Usually. Every once in a while a fanatic will show up every day. I assume they're hoping for a *Poltergeist* ending."

"A secret Native American burial ground disgorging skeletal remains before the house is sucked into a vortex and disappears? Well, you're in the right part of the country for that ending. Maybe this will be the episode. We can only hope. Ratings would be through the roof."

She laughed. "I hope not. I rather like this house. Even I know how to separate cinematic exaggeration from real life."

"And I'm here to separate fact from fiction. You ready?"

She paused at the foot of the steps leading to the porch. The house loomed above as if daring her to enter. "I hope so."

CHAPTER FIVE

T̲he screen door opened. Kimberly scurried up the steps to a frazzled Ruth.

"I'm sorry we haven't left yet. Faith is having another episode. Please come inside. I hope you can help."

"An episode?" She released Sterling's arm and hurried inside, joining her crew in the large, open entryway. No foul odor greeted her this time. In fact, she agreed with Sterling—she smelled only cleanser, laundry detergent, and freshly baked something.

Michael looped an arm around her waist. "We just walked in. I was about to send someone to hurry you up."

"What does she mean 'an episode'?" she asked Michael.

"We're not sure yet."

A clatter of clicks preceded Snickers as he rushed to welcome her, claws struggling against the hardwood floors in his haste to reach her. He placed his front paws on her leg and peered at her expectantly. The dog ran to the sweeping staircase and then turned back as if waiting for her to follow.

"Look at that," Ruth said. "He knows you're here to help us."

Rosie's low heels clacked across the porch as she hurried to join them. "Sorry, girl! Lorenzo—"

A guttural growl from upstairs carried to them below. Snickers laid his ears back and whimpered.

Rosie froze in place, eyes wide. "What the heck was that?"

"Was that . . . was that her?" she asked Ruth.

Ruth wrung her hands and nodded. "This is part of the reason she's missed school."

"You didn't mention this during the interview."

"It's not something we enjoy discussing. We took her to a counselor, but she was fine during her sessions. Nothing happened. She hasn't had an episode in a while. We thought maybe she was getting better, though the illness won't subside."

Kimberly signaled to Stan and TJ, who already had cameras out recording. "Her bedroom is upstairs?"

Ruth nodded.

She followed Snickers as he bounded up the wooden stairs, marveling again at the architecture. As she turned at the landing, another deep growl echoed through the house.

Snickers sat in a doorway, signaling her destination. From the hall, she saw Daniel seated on Faith's bed, clutching his daughter on his lap as she strained and struggled to escape his grip.

"Faith," he murmured, "it's okay. Relax. We're just spending the night at a hotel. It will be fun."

"I won't go!" The low, angry voice was barely recognizable as that of the shy girl she'd heard during the interview.

Sterling joined her at the door, allowing the camera operators to pass through into the room. "Good grief."

"Still think she's faking for attention?"

"If she is, it's working."

"You guys getting this?" she asked Stan, knowing they were.

"I'm on the girl. TJ, don't forget wider shots to include Kimberly and Sterling. We need reaction shots as well."

She stepped into the room.

The energy surrounding her changed the moment she crossed the threshold. Darkness pulled at her. A thrumming sound filled her ears, obscuring all sound. Gray fog . . . no, mist swirled through the room. Quicksand sucked at her feet, rooting her in place. She pulled and pulled but could move no further.

The room's edges faded to black and her circle of sight diminished, growing smaller in diameter until all she could see was the little girl's face. Smiling at her.

Her heartbeat pulsed in her ears. *Whump-WHUMP. Whump-WHUMP. Whump-WHUMP.*

A twisted, distorted voice, like a distant echo crossing an unfathomable stretch of time and place, slithered down her ear. *You can't have her back.*

Faith's smile widened, her eyes squinting nearly closed under her creased brow.

The girl's gaze broke away, staring at something presumably in the doorway, wrinkling her nose before slumping sideways against Daniel's chest.

A hand clamped on Kimberly's shoulder. "You okay?" Sterling asked.

She blinked and looked around the room, now completely normal. Resting her hand on Sterling's, she stared over her shoulder at him. "Did you see that?"

"Judging by the look on your face and the way you're gasping for air, I'm going to say I didn't see what you think you saw."

Michael and Rosie joined her, but she moved to the bed and knelt beside a very confused-looking Faith.

"Oh, no." The girl blinked and peered up at her father. "It happened again, didn't it?"

Daniel hesitated, nodded, and squeezed her in a hug so tight it looked painful.

"What exactly happened?" she asked, eyes shifting back and forth between Faith and Daniel.

"She had another episode," Daniel said, pressing his chin against her head.

Sterling bent low beside Faith. "Episode? Is she diabetic or epileptic? You didn't mention episodes during the interview. Only illness. What do you mean 'episode'?"

"We don't know what's happening. But she isn't diabetic or epileptic. We told you the doctor ran every possible test on her and determined nothing was wrong. CT scans, MRIs, blood work. They couldn't find any medical reason for any of her symptoms."

Sterling turned away from the bed. His shoulders shook, and he appeared to be experiencing some sort of distress.

Kimberly rested a hand on his shoulder. "Are you okay?"

He faced her. Something flat and silver clogged one nostril. She gasped.

"I think there's something in my nose." He breathed in short gasps until he exploded in a sneeze. And blew a nail out of his nose. He held it up, grinning. "Well, that can't be good."

"Sterling! What the heck? You really scared me!" She punched his shoulder.

Faith recoiled from the sight, hiding her face in Daniel's chest. "Ew. Gross."

Daniel scowled. "Why would you do that? That's highly disturbing."

Sterling rubbed his neck and appeared truly perplexed. "The room was getting tense. Just trying to lighten things up. That one usually kills."

"We don't need magic tricks," Daniel said.

"I prefer to call them illusions," Sterling said.

"If we can please stay focused on the issue here," Kimberly said, giving Sterling a look, silently suggesting he cool it with the attempts at humor. She turned her attention back to the girl. "What do you experience when this happens, Faith?"

Snuffling from the doorway drew her attention to Ruth blotting her eyes with a tissue. "She doesn't know. Why is this happening to us?"

"Let Faith answer the question," she said, giving the girl a warm smile. "What happens during these episodes? What can you remember?"

The girl looked to her mother.

"It's okay, Faith," Kimberly assured her. "Tell me what happened. You're not in trouble. We only want to help. But we need to know what's happening before we can help."

Faith shuddered and took a deep breath. She glanced at each member of her family and a look of profound relief settled over her. "Well, we—"

"Faith, don't!" Rebecca yelled from the door.

Faith stiffened. The momentary relief passed as a weight seemed to settle over the girl again. "I came upstairs to finish packing. Mom and Dad said we could swim in the hotel pool, so I was looking for my bathing suit. That's the last thing I remember."

"You never remember what happens during your episodes?"

The girl shook her head.

Kimberly stood and raised her eyebrows at Michael. Time loss was not a good sign. If nothing medical caused the girl's memory lapses, that meant they could be dealing with a spirit able to take control of living bodies. And they rarely took control for good reasons.

"What happened from your perspective?" Michael asked. "You obviously experienced something when you entered the room."

She nodded but didn't want to share her growing suspicions in front of the family. "Let's just say we're up against something extraordinary. And he let me know it."

"He?" Michael asked. "You're sure?"

"In all honesty, that's a presumption. Intuition, maybe. Still, I heard a voice and thought it sounded masculine."

"It's a man," Faith whispered. "I know he is."

The girl's belief helped seal her own. They were dealing with the spirit of a man. Who was he? Why was he here? And why did he target Faith?

CHAPTER SIX

Snickers whined and gave a short yelp as he watched his family parade out the front door clutching suitcases.

Kimberly knelt beside him and patted his head. "Don't worry, little guy. They'll be safer away from the house." The dog whimpered and licked her cheek.

"I just can't keep the guys off of you," Sterling said and laughed at his own joke.

Daniel closed the back of the family's minivan. Ruth, Rebecca, and Faith all called out goodbyes to Snickers and instructed him to be a good dog.

Ruth opened the passenger door but hesitated, one foot in the vehicle. "You're sure you don't mind keeping him? I'm worried he'll get in the way."

Kimberly stood. "The motel has a strict 'no pets' policy regardless, but really, we don't mind. Lots of people in the crew to keep him company and let him go outside."

Sterling rested a hand on the small of her back. "He's already putting the moves on Kimberly, so don't worry. He's fine."

"Ha ha." She gave Sterling a look, hyper-aware of the warmth of his hand and the shivers it sent racing up her spine. "Really, he's fine. Please try to relax and have a good night's sleep."

After the van drove away, she turned her attention back to the house, aware Stan's camera captured her every move. "Activity in the younger girl's room is high. We need a sta-cam on the porcelain dolls. I'd love to capture movement in a recording."

"On it!" TJ said.

"Elise, I know you're scrambling on the house history. Did you happen onto anything yet?"

"Not specific to this house. I did discover Guthrie has a fascinating history."

"How so?"

"The town formed overnight. Literally. There was little more here than a train stop until April 22, 1889 when huge tracts of what was Native American Territory was opened for settlement in the Land Run. April 23, 1889, the population of Guthrie was approximately ten thousand people."

"In one day?"

"That's right. The town sprang up as mostly tents at first. Settlers had to register their claims at an office in the new town of Guthrie. Fights broke out. The plots of land were one hundred and sixty acres, so in some cases more than one person believed to have claimed it, not realizing someone else claimed it too."

"But it was Native American Territory before that?"

"Correct. Basically, the land was taken back from Native Americans who had been forcibly settled here on reservations."

"After marching the Trail of Tears," Rosie said.

"That's right." Elise nodded enthusiastically. "Appalling. Tribes were uprooted from their homelands at rifle point and forced to walk during bitter winter conditions. Men, women, children. No allowances made for anyone. Do you know how many died?"

"Thousands," Rosie answered. "Though historians disagree, possibly as many as six thousand. Maybe more."

"You know your history," Kimberly said.

"Family stories passed down. My ancestors survived the Trail of Tears and settled in Indian Territory only to get shafted again. The government took the land back and opened it to white settlers. For free. All they had to do was stake a claim."

"Rosie. How did I not know this?"

"Generations in the past. No point bemoaning it now."

"And your family moved on to settle in New Mexico after that?"

"Eventually. At least that's how the story goes. Not many records made the lengthy treks with them, so it's difficult to track."

"I never would've guessed Native American ancestry for you," Sterling remarked.

Rosie shrugged. "At this point I'm only a small fraction Native American anyway."

"I'm not happy this happened to your family," Kimberly said. "But I am glad you wound up where our paths would cross."

"Me too, girl. Me too."

"Hmmm," Sterling said, stroking his chin as if deep in thought. "Restless Native American spirits? The *Poltergeist* ending is looking more possible. Shall we start taking bets?"

She elbowed him. "I guarantee this house will not disappear into a vortex even if we discover a disgruntled Native American spirit is behind the disturbance. I suppose that could be plausible. Though why now? The house has been here—"

"Since 1930," Elise said. "Craftsman era, as I suspected. But I'm a little unclear as to when Ruth and Daniel bought it. I found no recent sales history in the generally accessible data."

"That is odd. We can ask them tomorrow. For now, let's just do a general walk through. Maybe I can get a feel for who has been disturbed and what caused him to act out now."

"Sounds good," Michael said. "Where do you want to start?"

She looked around. "I know this is a relatively big house, but after the hotel it seems tiny. Let's just wander each room and see where I get hits."

TJ barreled down the curving staircase. "Sta-cam is in place,

Ms. Wantland. Focused on the dolls but wide enough we can see anything by the dresser if they move."

"Perfect."

"Everyone ready?" Michael asked. He counted her in.

She closed her eyes, curled one hand around the quartz crystal on her chakra-stone necklace, and heard only the quiet shuffling of her crew. Focusing on the area around her, she drew a deep breath. "Will the spirit in this house talk to me?"

When nothing answered, she let her guard down a bit.

"The Johnsons are uncomfortable with your presence and behavior in their home. Can you tell me what you want from them? Why are you here?"

Whump-WHUMP. Whump-WHUMP. Whump- WHUMP.

A rhythmic *lub-dub* filled her senses. Was it her heartbeat? She pressed two fingers against her throat and found the whoosh of her bloodstream. *Ba-dum-ba-dum-ba-dum.*

"You okay, girl?" Rosie asked.

"Feeling dizzy?" Sterling took a step toward her.

She shook her head. "I hear something. Sounds like a heartbeat."

"I don't hear anything," Sterling said.

Rosie shushed him. "She's listening to a frequency most of us can't tune in to."

Imagining herself weightless, her feet free to wander, she allowed herself to be drawn, guided by the pull of the beating thrum.

Whump-WHUMP. Whump-WHUMP. Whump- WHUMP.

It called to her. Pulled at her. She crossed the entryway and stood at the foot of the stairs. The deep bass thumping grew to fill her ears. The sound emanated from upstairs.

She gripped the bannister and rested a foot on the first stair, almost sure she saw the upstairs walls reverberating in time with the pounding bass.

The dog barked, sharp and clear, filling the home with his terse rebuttal. The heartbeat ceased.

"Ms. Wantland!" TJ called. "In the kitchen."

She shook her head to clear the residual echoes of the beating thumps and hurried to the kitchen.

"Did you figure out what you heard?" Michael asked.

"No, but it came from upstairs. Maybe I'll hear it again later, when we move up there."

In the kitchen, TJ faced the pantry door, which stood slightly ajar. Snickers hovered at his feet, staring intently into the pantry. The dog waved his tail at the sight of Kimberly and *woofed* softly.

"Ms. Wantland! The pantry door just opened by itself! The dog barked, and when I turned around, he was standing here at the pantry. Nothing seemed weird, but I came over anyway. I was right here when it opened so I recorded it!"

"But it could have simply swung open," Sterling said. "It's open like half an inch."

"I heard it click," TJ said. "It was closed all the way, I'm sure of it. I heard the handle click and then it squeaked when it opened."

Snickers growled slightly, one edge of his lip curling to reveal his teeth.

"Is something in there, boy?" TJ asked.

"What's that?" Sterling asked. "Timmy fell down the well?"

"Sterling," she admonished, "dogs are known to have a sixth sense. They can be very useful during an investigation."

"Or maybe there's simply a mouse in the pantry. Anyone consider that? It's the simplest and most logical explanation."

Something struck her in the back. "What—?" She spun around. A roll of paper towels fell to the floor.

No one stood near the counter behind her.

"Did anyone see that? Get it on camera?"

"See . . . paper towels fall?" Sterling asked.

"They didn't just fall. The roll hit me in the back. It was propelled across the space. And no one was near it."

"Sorry, Ms. Wantland. I was still on the pantry."

"Stan?" Michael asked. "Did you happen to be recording Kimmy?"

"I had my camera on her. Don't know if the counter was in the shot though. I'll run it back." Stan stared at his camera viewscreen. "Sorry. Can't see the roll of paper towels."

"Not surprising. The creepy thing is never caught on the recording." Sterling crooked a finger at TJ. "I want to be sure we get this on camera. Mouse . . . nothing . . . whatever is in here I want to record it. Don't take your camera off this door while she opens it."

The dog continued to point to the pantry, one paw raised, ears laid back, eyes intent. His tail stuck straight out behind him.

A rustling sound inside the pantry, soft but distinct, stopped everyone. Snickers whipped his head sideways and whined at Kimberly, pawing at the floor.

She bent low, placing a hand on his back. "We hear it."

Sterling held a hand out, head cocked at the door, brow furrowed.

She couldn't help but smile. "Are you protecting me from the big, bad nothing in there, Sterling?"

He rubbed his hand along his neck. "You'll thank me when a mouse comes scurrying out the door."

She almost mentioned the pet mouse she'd kept as a child but opted not to share on camera. Grasping the handle, she verified the cameras were all on her and the pantry and opened the door. The hinges squeaked. She scanned the floor first, on the chance Sterling was correct. No mouse scampered from the cupboard or dashed to hide. No movement greeted her at all.

But every item in the pantry pressed against the right wall.

Cans stacked on top of one another formed pyramids and squares. Cereal boxes, spices, bags of rice and beans—everything sat squished to one side of the shelves.

Kimberly turned to Michael. "Reading on the KII?"

"It's a little elevated. Not too much. But maybe this

happened in a burst of activity before we arrived. EMF would have fallen to normal levels."

"Did anyone look inside the pantry before now?" Sterling asked. No one answered. "No one? Then I feel I should point out that the Johnsons could store their food this way. We have no reason to believe this was done by a ghost."

Silence. Then the crew burst into laughter.

She patted him on the back. "Good one. Thanks for keeping the atmosphere light."

He lifted one eyebrow. "I'm not joking. I mean it."

"I know. You poor goofball."

"What's that supposed to mean?"

"You'll believe anything, no matter how foolish, rather than acknowledge the potential existence of spiritual entities. Including that a family would store their food this way."

"You immediately assume ghost rather than looking for a realistic explanation."

She rested a palm against his cheek. "I'm not criticizing you. It used to bother me, but I've accepted it. You simply cannot allow yourself to believe in ghosts. But I do think it's kind of funny."

Sterling placed a hand over hers. His eyes burned with intensity and she knew ghosts were the furthest thing from his mind. She retrieved her hand. This was not the time. The little frisson of excitement that thrilled through her was not helpful to the investigation.

"Michael," she said, "let's be sure to ask the Johnsons how they normally stock their pantry."

Another wave of laughter rolled through her crew.

Sterling scowled. "Okay. Let's look at this from your approach. Why would your spiritual entity do this? What does shoving all the food to one side accomplish?"

"It got our attention. And proved he can. Moving physical items takes a lot of power and establishes him as an upper level disturbance."

"A 6.0 on the Wantland scale?" he asked, smirk curling across his face.

He remembered Kerry and Suzie from Crescent Hotel and their suggestion she establish her own classification to measure hauntings? She'd nearly forgotten all about it. But the analogy worked. "Sure. Around a six. He seems ready to rumble."

A flash of lightning flickered through the house. A low rumble of thunder shuddered the air moments later.

She glanced outside.

A noose hung from a tree limb in the backyard.

Her stomach dropped and she raced to the back door to peer out the window. The overcast sky allowed no moonlight. She waited for another flash of lightning but grew impatient.

She twisted the knob and yanked the door open, hurrying to the majestic oak whose leafy limbs held sentry over the property, an umbrella of protection.

No noose.

"Kimmy!" Michael chased her down. "What happened? Did you see something?"

She shook her head. Surely, she'd imagined it. But when she closed her eyes, she saw it so vividly—the coils of rope, the loop swinging lazily from the limb. This was so much more than a thirteen-year-old girl with a non-healing rash.

This would undoubtedly be a fantastic episode. But she wondered what exactly they were up against. And what would happen to Faith if they couldn't resolve the haunting.

CHAPTER SEVEN

KIMBERLY EYED the thick clouds threatening rain. Gusts of wind shook the van as Michael pulled into the driveway of the Stone Lion Inn. The huge white building with its wrap-around porch sat dark in the overcast gloom.

Michael parked and pressed the heels of his hands against his eyes. "Good work, everyone. Let's get some sleep. You okay, Kimmy?"

The swinging noose arced another elliptical across her memories. "Yeah. A little worried about this investigation. But I'm okay."

The sky flickered and rumbled. Fat drops of rain pelted the windshield. She watched TJ, Stan, and Elise make a mad dash with equipment cases.

Her passenger door opened. Sterling stood in the gap, an umbrella over his head. He held out a hand. "Hey, there, little lady. Won't you let this cowpoke escort you inside?"

She laughed. "Was that John Wayne?"

He tipped an imaginary hat. "When in Rome, little lady."

She accepted his hand and allowed him to assist her out of the van. She noticed he was careful to center the umbrella over her as he looped an arm around her waist and tucked her close.

Another jolt of lightning ripped across the sky, illuminating the Stone Lion in bursts of flashes. A peal of thunder followed immediately, rattling her bones. The swollen clouds released a deluge, the downpour beating against the ground, the trees, the umbrella Sterling shielded her with.

"I would be drenched right now if not for your chivalry," she noted, raising her voice to be heard above the storm's blustering rage. "This was very thoughtful. Thank you."

He guided her up the steps and to the door, safe under the shelter of the porch, and shook the rain from his umbrella. "My pleasure." The boyish grin that twisted his lips and crinkled the corners of his eyes sent an electric thrill buzzing through her. A warm flush crept up her face. No denying it. This man attracted her. A lot. When he looked at her the way he was now, she entertained thoughts that further pinked her cheeks. But what should she do with that?

Impulse control ensured she ate well and made smart choices that kept her out of the messes Rosie so often found herself in. What would happen if she tossed that aside, grabbed Sterling, and crushed him in a kiss so fierce it took his breath away? What if that opened the door to more? What if they became involved but then it didn't work out? They would be stuck together awkwardly working on the show. That's what would happen. And she couldn't believe the show wouldn't suffer from that shift. No matter how professional they tried to remain, the dynamic would be different and the audience would know.

Sterling cocked his head and lifted an eyebrow. "You're quiet. What are you thinking about?"

Crushing you in a fierce kiss before yanking your shirt off. She'd seen those rippled abs of his but never run her hands over them. She flushed again. "Nothing. Just tired," she lied.

"Well, let's get you to bed." One side of his mouth curled into a grin.

He opened the front door. Stan and TJ held cameras, debating placement.

Michael and Rosie clattered up the steps and under the porch roof, soaked to the bone.

"Nice, Sterling," Rosie said. "Way to share the love."

"Hi, Ms. Wantland!" TJ greeted her. "We're setting up to see if we can catch any activity while we're here."

"Good. Gotta keep Randmeier happy."

Michael wrung his shirt. "Hello? How about keeping me happy too? I feel like the four of us could have fit under that umbrella."

"A little water won't melt you. That's only witches."

"Sweetie, don't push it or the witch might emerge. This silk Brooks Brothers is dry clean only and might melt."

"Do we need to be worried about tornadoes?" TJ asked as another blast of thunder shook the house. A gust of wind rattled the windows, pelting rain against the glass panes.

"Not this time of year," Elise answered. "Tornado season is in the spring. I checked."

"I hope you're right," Michael said, heading for the stairs. He stopped to take in the vivid green wallpaper. "And I thought my shirt was loud. Good night, all. See you in the morning for footage review."

Kimberly giggled. "Maybe he doesn't melt, but the rain seems to have sent him into diva mode."

Rosie squinted at her as she rubbed smudged mascara from under her eyes. "Easy to say when you're completely dry. I am off to clean up and sleep. Have a nice night."

She didn't miss the subtle glance at Sterling and lift of the eyebrow from Rosie as her stylist headed upstairs. And she knew exactly what was on Rosie's mind.

She turned down the hall and headed for her room, fully aware Sterling would be on the other side of the wall as she slept. He fell into step beside her. She felt his presence before she saw him out of the corner of her eye. Pausing at her door, she turned to face him. She swore heat radiated from him. She shivered and ran her hands up and down her arms.

He stepped closer, concerned gaze searching her face. "You okay?"

"Just chilled."

He took her hand between his. "Good grief. You're like ice. It's not that cold in here. Sure you're okay?"

"A hot shower will help. And some sleep." Images of him curled around her in bed, that body heat against her skin, chasing the chill away, filled her mind. Her pulse quickened. "Well, goodnight."

"I'll be next door if you need anything. I mean it. Anything. Just let me know."

Unable to look away, she nodded, barely able to breathe. "I will."

"Goodnight."

She watched him walk to his room, noting how well his black jeans fit and how his broad shoulders swayed with each step. He unlocked his door and waved to her with a smile.

Her hand shook as she unlocked her door. Inside her own room, she took a deep breath. The bright colors, wild floral patterns, and jumbled collection of mismatched furnishings did nothing to calm her chakras or soothe her frazzled psyche.

What could she do with this chaotic mix of emotions Sterling stirred up in her? It wasn't getting better. If anything, it was getting worse. Spending time with him, she should become familiar and comfortable with his presence. So why did she find herself increasingly distracted? The pleasing slope of his shoulders hadn't caught her attention during the first investigation he'd worked with her.

Ugh. She needed Rosie. Although she knew exactly how Rosie would react and what advice she'd give.

She turned on the shower, spinning the hot water tap fully open. Steam began to fill the space as she dropped her clothes on the floor. Standing under the shower, she finally began to relax, the hot water soothing her aching muscles.

The noose she'd seen swaying from the tree in the Johnsons'

backyard boded poorly for the investigation. If the property had a murder in its history, the family seemed unaware. Hopefully, Elise would find something. Though she didn't want to be the one to break the news to the family.

She toweled off, tucked the towel snuggly under her arms, and went to dig through her suitcase for pajamas.

Another flash of lightning lit up the dim room as thunder rumbled. She jumped at the intrusion and glanced at the mirror over the dresser.

The silhouette of a person standing in the window reflected back at her.

She gasped and spun around, heart racing. The dark shape remained. This was not her imagination. Someone appeared to be standing right outside her window.

In the pouring rain? It made no sense. She closed her eyes. But when she opened them, the figure remained framed in the window.

She shook her head and tried again. No one could know where she was staying. Surely this was in her mind. Yet, the longer she stared, willing the figure to resolve into nothing, the less sure she became. Something was at her window.

Clutching the towel close with one hand, she lifted her cell phone from the nightstand with the other, selected Sterling from her contacts, and opened a message box.

You still awake?

She pressed the arrow to send the message and glanced again at the window.

The silhouette had shifted slightly to one side.

Not a tree. What was out there? *Okay, just go to the window and open it if you have to. Figure out what that is.*

But she couldn't do it.

Her phone lit up. Sterling.

I'm awake. What's up?

She quickly typed a response.

Can you come to my room? Please?

Three rapid texts popped up on her screen.

An emoji, one eyebrow cocked.

Be right there.

I'll grab pants.

Immediately she pictured him without pants. Did he wear boxers or briefs? Or boxer briefs? He would look incredible in boxer briefs, snug around his thighs and— She shook her head.

Pants. Right. Clothes. Meeting Sterling at the door in nothing but a towel would send the wrong message.

Three quiet knocks rapped on her door before she'd managed to wiggle into her nightgown. A glance at the window confirmed the dark shape remained.

Sterling's face displayed a mixture of confusion and anticipation when she opened the door. "I didn't dare hope this was anything other than business, but that nightie says otherwise. Is that new? Don't think I've seen that one before."

He'd put on pants as promised, but above the elastic waistband, his bare body distracted her. The sun-toasted skin, sleek lines, and belly button divot in his narrowed waist drew her attention, leaving her unable to speak and longing to touch.

His face morphed from amused to concerned. "You okay? You seem a little shaken up."

Unsure if her shaking hands were due to the shadow or her proximity to half-naked Sterling, she shook her head to clear it and forced herself to focus. "I saw . . . Someone is standing outside my window I think."

Sterling scowled and marched across the room.

But the silhouette was gone.

She joined him at the window. "No. It was . . . it's gone now but I promise I saw something. A dark silhouette. A person, I think."

He raised his eyebrows and crossed his arms, one corner of his mouth curling into a smirk. "Did you text me about a ghost?"

"No. No! It wasn't a ghost."

He moved closer. "You didn't need to invent a reason to invite me to your room."

"I didn't—"

"I would have come. All you had to do was ask." He leaned close, his woodsy scent further exciting her already fired up lower chakras.

Breathing so hard it nearly qualified as panting, she stepped back. "I didn't make it up, and it wasn't a ghost. Ghosts don't scare me. People do. Especially creepers who lurk outside bedroom windows staring in. What if you leave and he comes back?"

"Hey, hey." He pulled her into a hug. "You're really scared. It's okay. I'm here."

Pressed against his bare chest, she realized how terribly thin the material of her nightgown was. He realized too, she knew, feeling his orange chakra grow and resonate. But she didn't move. His strong arms wrapped around her felt too good, too reassuring. "Maybe he's gone."

"Want me to call the police?"

"They would probably be less likely to believe me than you are. He seems to be gone."

He leaned back and looked at her. "He? You sound sure."

She shrugged. "I've never been stalked by a woman."

Sterling glared at the window, released her, and jerked the flimsy translucent curtains together. "That doesn't help much but at least no one should be able to see you clearly. If you see the shadow again, call me. I'll leave my ringer on."

She grabbed his arm, a stab of panic at the thought of him leaving her alone consuming her. "Stalkers are the worst."

"I'll go walk the porch and see if I can spot anyone. Okay?"

"It's pouring rain. Are you sure?"

"The porch is covered. Can I bring you anything? Need me to wake Rosie for some sleepy-time tea?"

"No. Thank you. You guys need to sleep. I feel bad for keeping you up as it is."

He squeezed her hand. "I'm glad you reached out to me. Be right back."

After he left, she dropped her face into her hands. What was wrong with her? She forced her feet to carry her to the window. Her hand shook violently as she pushed one curtain to the side, just enough to peek out.

Another jagged charge of lightning shot fingers across the sky, illuminating the grounds around the inn.

Nothing.

No figures. No nooses.

Had she imagined it? Was she losing touch after all these years of reaching into the other realm?

A quiet tap preceded Sterling. "I didn't see anyone," he reassured her. He pulled her blankets back and patted the bed. "Come on. You need to rest. We all need you in top shape."

She crawled into the bed, and he tucked her in. If someone had told her six months ago that Sterling Wakefield would someday tuck her into bed, she never would have believed it. And the suggestion probably would have made her mad.

He patted her shoulder. "Better?"

"A little. Thank you."

He made no move to leave and she didn't want him to. She felt safer with him next to her. He wouldn't let anyone close enough to harm her. She could feel it in her bones. Protection and concern emanated from him.

"Should I stay?" The intensity in his eyes told her he was asking more than the surface question. "I could sleep on the floor."

"That sounds dreadful. You'll sleep better in your bed."

He tucked a lock of her hair behind her ear. "A bed is better than the floor. But anything for you."

A bed could include her bed. Her heart thumped as she envisioned scooting over and inviting him to join her. Imagined him sliding under the blankets beside her, shirtless, warm, his woodsy musk enveloping her.

She wasn't ready for that. As much as she responded to him physically, she had to remain in control. Allowing herself to dive into a relationship without carefully considering all the potential ramifications wasn't smart.

"I'll call if I see anything," she promised.

Disappointment flashed across his eyes, but he nodded. "If you call, I'll come running."

The door clicked behind him. A big part of her regretted the decision. But how would things change tomorrow if they changed so dramatically tonight?

Things had definitely already changed. Before Sterling, she would have called Michael or Rosie in a situation like this. She hadn't even thought of either of them tonight. She didn't think the proximity of Sterling's room had anything to do with that.

He'd gotten under her skin. And she had no idea what to do about it.

CHAPTER EIGHT

Kimberly woke to brilliant sunshine slanting across her pillow. She peeled her eyelids open and blinked, groping for her cell phone. 8:03 a.m.

Her head throbbed as she pushed aside the blankets and forced herself into a sitting position. The golden rays streaming through the sheer white curtains indicated the storm had passed.

Coffee. She needed coffee. Badly.

She listened for any sounds from the other side of the wall that might suggest Sterling was up and around but heard nothing. Maybe he still slept. He could have been waking up in her bed right now. How close had she come to spending the night with him?

A quick shower revived her. While she dressed, she tried not to listen for his gentle knocking on her door. And she tried to pretend she wasn't disappointed when no one knocked.

She joined her crew for breakfast in the dining room. No Sterling.

TJ stopped shoveling food into his mouth to bring a camera to her. "Ms. Wantland! Look!"

Michael stood. "TJ, let her have some coffee before you descend on her."

Her junior camera operator's crestfallen face melted her heart. He was clearly excited to show her something, and she loved his enthusiasm. "It's okay. What is it? Go ahead and show me." She grabbed a mug and quickly poured coffee, relieved to see a tiny pitcher of milk or cream and not the typical powdered creamer offered at most establishments. She would drink it black before adding corn syrup solids to her coffee.

TJ waited, nearly quivering with excitement, until she sipped from the mug. "Okay, watch the corner of the room." He angled the camera so that she could see clearly and pressed PLAY. "Riii-ight . . . there! See that? In the corner? Did you see the shadow?"

"I did. Just for a moment, but I saw it."

"That was in my room! Well, mine and Stan's. We had a ghost in our room!"

He replayed the recording. The diffuse shadow reminded her of the silhouette in her window. "Did you experience any distur-bances? Hear any noises or notice anything had moved this morning?"

Stan, seated at the table, shook his head. "Slept right through it. Apparently slept right through quite the storm too. I went for a walk this morning. Leaves and twigs everywhere. Even saw a tree knocked down." He crunched a bite of toast.

"Storms can bring out ghosts," she said. "All that energy powers them." The silhouette in her window had seemed so real. Had she been mistaken?

Michael whistled. "You're going to be a huge help when that new baby comes along. You'll sleep right through those night-time feedings. I'm sure Melanie will appreciate that."

"I'll adapt. Always do."

"How is Melanie?" Kimberly asked. "Everything okay?"

"She's doing fine. I think she's starting to worry about handling this without me though." He cleared his throat. "We're on the road a lot. And work nights."

The gravity of his words settled on her. Could Stan be thinking about leaving? She hadn't given any thought to the impact his wife's pregnancy might mean for the show. But this would be an enormous change for them. And she couldn't fault him for wanting to be with his wife and eventually the new baby. Melanie would need his help. Perhaps before the baby arrived. She couldn't blame either of them. But still. The show. The silence in the room told her the rest of her crew was arriving at the same conclusion. She glanced at Michael. His furrowed brow indicated this was news to him.

TJ fiddled with the camera. "Well, I'll leave the camera recording again tonight and see what else we get."

"That's fine," an unfamiliar voice commented. "Just don't run off any ghosts, okay?"

An older blonde woman entered the dining room, smiling and looking like she'd slept a full night. Kimberly envied the lack of dark circles under her eyes.

Michael jumped from his seat a second time. "Kimmy, this is Gloria, the current owner of Stone Lion. The woman Randmeier sent scrambling to accommodate us all."

Gloria waved away his comments and held out a hand. "It was my pleasure to welcome you. Nice to meet you, Ms. Wantland. Love your show. Glad to have you all stay and enjoy my inn. Feel free to record all you want but please don't scare the ghosts away."

Kimberly shook her hand. "It's a deal. I think the main investigation will require all my focus and energy. Have you experienced disturbances yourself?"

"I encounter spirits all the time. I have since shortly after I moved in. But they don't disturb me. Mostly they just go about their business and want to be left alone."

Rosie swallowed a last bite of blueberry muffin and reached for her glass of orange juice. "You sound so sure."

"Oh, yes." Gloria nodded vigorously. "I've seen the little girl. Pretty sure she climbed in bed with me once, though it may have been a different ghost."

"What little girl?" Elise asked, pushing aside her empty plate.

She peered at Gloria through her swooping cat-eye shaped glasses, pen ready.

"Augusta Houghton. Mr. Houghton had this home built in 1907 for his wife and their twelve children."

"Twelve?" Michael choked on his coffee. "No wonder the place is so big."

"Different time," Gloria said. "Large families were normal back then. Particularly among farming families. They needed the extra hands to help in the fields."

Kimberly watched Elise hunker over her ever-present spiral notebook, scribbling furiously. *Why take notes on large farming families?* she wondered as she savored another strawberry. That in no way helped with the Johnsons' troubles. "But back to the little girl?"

"Yes! Augusta developed whooping cough. Unfortunately, someone administered the wrong medication and the little girl passed away as a result of the mistake."

"That's so sad. The mother must have been distraught," Kimberly said. "And you feel you've seen the girl?"

"Definitely. I—"

Sterling walked into the dining room and scanned the faces gathered at the table. His brow crinkled as if in confusion. "Morning."

Kimberly's heart skipped a beat at the sight of him.

Apparently so did Gloria's. The woman straightened her blouse and smoothed her hair. "Oh, my. He's even better looking in person, isn't he?"

Rosie helped herself to another muffin. "Most people think so."

The grin on Rosie's face and teasing twinkle in her eyes irritated her.

"Maybe it's just that he's standing right here. Goodness, he must work out. Look at those arms."

Kimberly wasn't sure which annoyed her more—the woman's blatant panting and comments that Sterling surely overheard, or the fact that she felt exactly the same way about him. Why did she care if the woman noticed Sterling was attractive? Every woman on the planet seemed to find Sterling irresistibly hot. Nothing new. Yet, she felt something unfamiliar welling in her chest. Something painfully ugly and unpleasant that suggested she might consider scratching out Gloria's eyes so the woman could no longer stare at Sterling like she wanted to eat him with a spoon.

Was she . . . jealous?

"If I was a decade or two younger," Gloria sighed. "You're a lucky woman, Kimberly."

She shook the crazed nonsense out of her head. The tightness constricting her chest relaxed, and she smiled. "Thank you."

"Who just knocked on my door?" Sterling asked.

The crew looked around the table.

"Kimmy was last to join us," Michael said.

"Gloria came after me," Kimberly pointed out. Had this horny old woman been knocking on his door?

"How long ago, Sterling?" Michael asked.

"Just now."

"We've all been here at breakfast for some time. Did anyone go by Sterling's room? Maybe knock on it?"

All heads shook.

"I don't think I imagined it." Sterling rubbed the back of his neck. "But maybe."

"More likely it was Augusta," Gloria said. "She does that."

"Someone else in the house?" Sterling asked. "Housekeeping or—"

"No. The ghost of an eight-year-old girl."

Sterling reached for coffee. "Ah."

"I know, I know. You're not a believer. I was just telling everyone about her. She's one of our resident ghosts."

"Hold on. I need some coffee. It's too early to launch into ghosts without coffee." He poured a mug and heaped a plate with scrambled eggs, ham, and blueberry muffins, then took the empty seat beside her. He eyed her plate and frowned. "Nothing but berries? That's not enough food."

She thought she heard all the females in the room give a collective sigh. He worried about her. Cared about her well-being. She had to admit it was rather nice. "I'll have oatmeal in the trailer." The oatmeal he'd given her last week along with other supplies he'd outfitted her trailer with.

He beamed. "That's okay, then. I'm glad you like the snacks I got you. Add some walnuts too."

She couldn't handle the intensity in his eyes or the butterflies it sparked in her stomach. How could she eat anything with that fluttering thrill bordering on queasiness causing her stomach to turn flips? Glancing away, she sipped her coffee.

Sterling looked at Gloria. "You in charge here?"

"I'm the owner, yes."

"Do you have skim milk?"

"Cream."

He rested a hand on Kimberly's shoulder. "She prefers skim. If I get some, can I keep it in a refrigerator somewhere?"

"Of course."

"That's not necessary, Sterling," she said. "I don't need any special accommodations. Look I used the cream. You don't need to do that."

"It's no trouble. And I want you to be happy, not just content."

"But, really—"

"I want to do it. Arguing will get you nowhere."

Rosie raised an eyebrow and shot an I-told-you-so look of triumph across the table. Kimberly attempted to kick her but couldn't span the distance. The old table was too big.

Gloria sighed. "Kimberling is a thing. Adorable. Are they always like this?" she asked Rosie.

"Pretty much. They're a thing. They're just not ready to admit it yet."

She narrowed her eyes at Rosie but for once wasn't really

frustrated with her stylist. "You were telling us about the little girl who died here, Gloria."

"Right! Eight years old. Whooping cough. Wrong medicine. Now, I didn't know about that before I bought the place."

"You renovated it into a bed and breakfast, right?" Elsie asked, bent over her notebook.

"That's right. And I must've stirred up the spirits with the building modifications. I've learned that's not uncommon."

Sterling swallowed a bite of muffin. "And you believe a ghost knocked on my door? As opposed to one of the many living people present?"

"We were all here, dude," TJ assured him. "Honest. I wouldn't let anyone mess with you like that."

"Thanks. I appreciate it." Sterling returned his attention to Gloria.

"You can cock that skeptical eyebrow at me all you want," Gloria said. "I used to be just like you. Didn't believe in anything paranormal. And then I bought this place and moved in. I know what I've seen and heard."

Sterling, his plate of food devoured, crossed his arms and leaned back. "What exactly have you seen and heard?"

"I hear her footsteps. She runs up and down the halls. Scampers up to the attic where my son's old toys are boxed up. She used to get him in trouble scattering his things around his room after I'd told him to clean up. He'd swear he did and yet the toys were everywhere. What mom believes their child who swears he cleaned the room but someone else made it messy again? But eventually I saw it for myself. His room was clean when we left the house, but a jumbled mess when we returned. No one else in the house. These days I go upstairs and find the boxes upended, toys scattered. She knocks on doors. I've even had some guests report waking up to a little girl standing at the foot of their bed."

Kimberly rested her arms on the table. "Is the little girl the only presence you've detected? Any other manifestations?"

"I've had guests tell me about an older man in a top hat smoking a pipe. Maybe Mr. Houghton? That's my guess."

TJ moved to the seat beside Gloria and held out his camera. "Who do you think this could be?"

Gloria took the camera and watched TJ's recording. "Interesting. Did you see it in person? Hat? Pipe?"

"No, I was asleep."

"Without further distinction, I can't really say. But this could be Elmer McCurdy, the train robber."

"Train robber?" TJ's eyes widened.

Gloria laughed. "Don't worry. He wasn't much of an outlaw compared to others who roamed the area back then. He hijacked the wrong train. All he managed to do was steal a couple jugs of whiskey and forty-six dollars from the passengers. He escaped and hid in a barn, but a posse hunted him down with bloodhounds. He'd been drinking for days by then, using alcohol to dull the pain from pneumonia, tuberculosis, and trichinosis. He died in the shootout."

"What an awful way to go," Sterling said. "How old was he?"

"Only thirty-one."

"And he died here at the inn?" Kimberly asked. "Or near here? Was the train passing through Guthrie?"

"No, he was hiding outside of Pawhuska. Place called Okasa, near Bartlesville."

"Is that nearby?"

"Oh, no. Closer to Tulsa, really. His body was taken to the Johnson Funeral Home in Pawhuska."

"I'm confused," Kimberly said. "Why would he be haunting this inn? If he died nowhere near here his spirit shouldn't reside here."

Sterling leaned forward and propped one fist under his chin. He looked amused.

"The undertaker at the funeral home mummified him and—"

"Why would he do that?" Kimberly asked.

"No one claimed the body. He didn't want to bury him until

he was paid. But no one ever did. He wound up putting him on display in a corner of the funeral home and charging a nickel to see him."

"How macabre," Michael said.

No one in the crew moved. They'd all stopped eating, seemingly entranced by the grisly story.

"Gruesome," Kimberly agreed. "But that doesn't explain why he would now haunt this location."

Gloria continued. Her voice had dropped, her tone somber, as though they all sat around a campfire telling ghost stories. "Elmer's mummified remains were sold repeatedly, traveling around the country as a curiosity in various sideshows until people no longer realized it was a real body. The remains were presumed to be a prop. By the 1970s, Elmer's body hung in a haunted house in an amusement park in California. While filming an episode of *The Six Million Dollar Man*, the crew moved Elmer and his arm broke off, revealing human bone and muscle. The remains were identified, and a descendant of the family brought him back here to Guthrie for a proper burial so his soul could rest in peace. The cemetery is just down the road."

Kimberly's brow furrowed. She squinted at Gloria. "And you think his spirit left the cemetery and wandered over here?"

Gloria, apparently accustomed to a more excited reaction to her story, frowned. "I thought Sterling was the skeptic."

Sterling leaned back and crossed his arms, satisfied smile curled across his face. "I'm rubbing off on her."

"No, it just doesn't work that way. When a spirit is shocked from its physical body due to trauma or if a spirit is confused and not ready to leave this life, then it will remain where the body died. If Elmer is anywhere, he should be haunting the barn he died in."

Sterling cocked one eyebrow. "Now wait a minute. Last week you decided a spirit traveled around with a piano."

"Right. That spirit attached to the piano rather than the place of death. That is another relatively regular phenomenon."

"So maybe Elmer's spirit attached to the mummified corpse and traveled around with it. You can't change the rules every week."

"I'm not changing the rules. They're the same rules. If we accept that the spirit did in fact attach to and travel with the mummified body, then the closest it would be is the cemetery. Not here at the inn."

Gloria looked entirely too smug. "Some people think I disturbed the spirit. Some have accused me of black magic and dark rituals." She paused and made eye contact with each person at the table. "Which is nonsense. But my dinner theatre does end at Elmer's grave in the cemetery. Perhaps we intrigued him, and he followed us back one night. And decided he liked it here. Anything is possible."

Sterling held his arms wide. "That's right. Anything is possible. Anything at all."

She gritted her teeth. "No. That's not right. I—"

Michael stood and clapped. "We have footage to review for the actual investigation. Let's go see what the cameras caught last night."

Kimberly wasn't ready to give up, but Michael was correct. She couldn't waste time arguing something trivial when the Johnsons needed her help.

CHAPTER NINE

KIMBERLY GRIPPED HER QUARTZ CRYSTAL, breathing deeply in and out, willing herself to calm down and focus on footage review. *Anything is possible.* The woman knew nothing about the spirit realm and yet spouted nonsense as though she considered herself a learned professional. People like that made others in the paranormal field look bad. Her heart rate sped up again, frustration churning her emotions no matter how much she tried to forget about it.

Rosie joined the crew in the Johnsons' dining room, maneuvering around those transfixed by computer monitors, headphones clamped over their ears. Except Stan. The lead camera operator circled the space, recording anything that could prove interesting for the show. Her stylist pressed a steaming cup into her hands. "Chamomile. Drink. You need to calm down."

"Thanks, Rosie." She blew on the liquid and sipped.

"I can tell you're bothered by Gloria but try not to let it get to you. So she misidentified a ghost. She doesn't know any better, and it seems to make her feel good. At least she's excited about ghosts, right?"

Sterling chimed in. "I don't know why it makes any difference at all. Who cares what ghost she thinks she has in her house?"

"It's the principle of it. Her belief defies all logic. She hosts a dinner theatre and suddenly decides she's a paranormal expert."

Sterling laughed. "Do ghosts follow logic? Some people do follow your show for the entertainment value. Not to discourage you, but is the show that different from dinner theatre?"

"Of course it is. We have equipment and record interactions and I actually connect and communicate with spirits, whether people choose to believe it or not."

Sterling rested a hand on her arm. "I don't think Gloria takes it as seriously as you think she does. Don't waste energy getting worked up over her. It's not worth it."

"Look at it this way," she said. "Your PhD is in physics. How would you feel if someone was bent on believing something that completely defied one or more of the laws of physics and everything you know to be true?"

His face softened into a lopsided grin, and he stroked his chin thoughtfully. "I see your point. I'd probably be really annoyed at first and dead set on proving her wrong. I might even make it my mission to convince her of the truth. But then I think I'd come to realize her beliefs weren't hurting anyone, in some cases even helped people feel better, and let her do her thing."

"But her beliefs—" She saw something in his eyes—amusement or anticipation—and realized he no longer referred to Gloria. "Hey! You're talking about me, aren't you?"

Rosie giggled. "It's just part of her show, girl. She's not trying to fool anyone. She wants her guests to enjoy the dinner mystery. It's all for fun. And I'm sure they know that."

She relaxed. "That's true. I shouldn't let it bother me. Sterling, did you figure out who knocked on your door this morning?"

"I was hoping it was you. But no one was there when I opened the door."

She would never admit how close she came to knocking on his door. Or how eager she'd been to see him. "I didn't knock and run, if that's what you're thinking. We were all in the dining room together. And there was no one else in the house. How does physics explain that?"

"Maybe I only imagined I heard it. Wishful thinking that Kimberly Wantland was on the other side of my door, ready to walk to breakfast with me. I can think of lots of explanations."

She blushed, aware of Stan's lens capturing Sterling's comments about wishing she'd been at his door. "One of which is that a ghost knocked on it."

He shook his head but smiled. "No. That's not a logical explanation."

"If you knew which frequency to listen to—"

Michael rubbed his temples. "You two will never agree on it, Kimmy, so let it go."

"But I might be able to help—"

"Come watch footage review. We're working on the hand-helds. TJ went to get the sta-cams."

"We know we didn't see anything," Sterling said. "The most excitement all night was Kimberly racing out back."

Michael cocked his head. "That's right. What did you see out there that set you off?"

She heard Stan's camera whir as it adjusted, presumably to focus on her. She wasn't ready to share what she'd seen. Not until she knew more. "I'm . . . not sure. Let's see if the camera we left out back captured anything interesting. And I'll keep an eye out tonight."

Elise opened the back door. Snickers bounded in ahead of her. "Anyone know where the family keeps the dog treats? He was a very good boy."

Snickers yipped, wagged, ran in a circle, and dashed to the pantry. He snuffled the floor, then scratched at the door.

"I guess he knows the word 'treats.' Ruth did say he's very smart." Elise opened the pantry. Her eyes widened. "Guys? Did someone move things around in the pantry?"

"No," Michael said. "We left it to show the family."

"But it's—"

"We know," Kimberly said. "Everything is shoved to the right. We caught it on camera last night."

Elise shook her head. "No. I remember what we saw last night. But today it's normal. Look."

Kimberly joined her at the pantry door. All the items that had been mashed to one side now spread evenly across the shelves. Snickers pressed his head against her hand and whined. One paw nudged the bag filled with treats he clearly believed he deserved.

Sterling joined her. "Huh. I haven't been guarding the pantry by any means, but we all left together last night and arrived together this morning. Moving this many containers of food around would have not only taken time but also made a lot of noise."

Kimberly turned slowly to face him. "What exactly are you saying?"

"I'm stating the facts and attempting to draw a logical conclusion."

Michael nodded. "Astute observation. And you saw that the crew scrambled to set up computers when we arrived today so we could get right to work."

"I did." Sterling's brow furrowed. "This is odd."

"Are you actually admitting something unexplainable happened here?" she asked. "Something supernatural?"

He held his hands up. "I can't explain it *yet*. Supernatural is just a word for something we haven't figured out how to explain." He rested his arm on a shelf and raked all the contents to the right. Cans toppled and a box fell on its side. "Interesting. That made a loud, jumbled mess. But no one could have stood here long enough to quietly move each individual item without one of us noticing."

A thrill buzzed through her. He wasn't being his usual snarky self. He was listening and considering options. "So maybe you think this could have been . . . a ghost? Are you finally opening your mind to the possibility?"

He raised one eyebrow. "I'm saying I'm not sure how this was accomplished. It's a statement of fact. I've always maintained that if you could show me evidence of a ghost, I'd believe it. But not understanding what happened doesn't mean I think it was a ghost. Give me some time. Or some concrete evidence."

TJ raced downstairs and barreled into the dining room, skidding to a halt. "They moved!"

She waited but he said nothing more.

Sterling patted his back. "Slow down and breathe easy. We don't want an asthma attack. What moved?"

"The dolls! The little glass dolls in the girl's room. They've shifted around. I know they were in neat circles last night cuz I set up the camera right before we left."

"We had a camera on them all night?" Michael asked.

"Yes!" TJ held up the sta-cam. "And they moved. That means we should have a recording."

"Let's see it!" Stan said, focusing the camera on his junior operator.

TJ pressed buttons and stared at the screen. No one spoke.

This day was almost more than she could handle. Sterling seemed close to conceding potential paranormal activity in the pantry. TJ had managed to record activity. Perhaps this investigation was going to be easier than she thought.

TJ scowled. "What the—?"

"What is it?" Stan asked.

"Hang on. I'll connect to a monitor so everyone can see at once."

His tone had changed, she noted, watching him plug the camera in and bring the recording up on a monitor. He clicked the mouse, fast forwarded through images, scowled, and checked connections.

"TJ? What is it?"

He clicked again, repeating the same few minutes over and

over. "About three this morning the image gets grainy. Look. The images jump around like the camera is being bumped or shaken. Then the screen goes black."

"Batteries died?" Stan asked, recording their interactions.

"I made sure the camera had new batteries when I set it up. That was around two, I think. Brand new batteries only lasted an hour or so?"

"Does the camera turn on now?" Sterling asked.

"Well, yeah, but only cuz I put new batteries in. It was dead when I went up there. They should have lasted through the night."

"So what you're saying is you didn't capture the dolls moving, correct? We see them in perfect circles, the camera dies, then this morning they've shifted. But we have no proof someone didn't tamper with them."

TJ said nothing, mouth pursed into a tight line as he continued to rewind and replay as if hoping additional images would appear.

She watched the gray footage and saw the dolls in place before the screen shuddered as if someone shook the camera. The screen filled with static, the bedroom distorted into elongated shapes, and then the screen went black. Disappointment consumed her. Just once she wished they could manage to capture something so decisive, no one, not even Sterling, could dispute what she knew to be true.

But she couldn't let the others know how much this bothered her. "It's okay, TJ. This happens."

Sterling nodded. "Seems to happen every time. The camera always cuts out at the critical moment, just when you're about to record evidence. Convenient. This way you can make up whatever you want."

"It isn't convenient," she disagreed. "It's frustrating to all of us. However, this actually does offer evidence."

Sterling's eyebrows scrunched. "Evidence of . . . someone

tampering with the dolls and hiding it? That's how I would interpret it."

"Not at all. The sudden draining of the batteries supports the presence of a ghost. It consumed the energy from the batteries to manifest, thus the batteries were drained, and the camera died."

Sterling smirked and shook his head. "Right. Ghosts eat batteries. I forgot. Which means the lack of evidence becomes your evidence. Brilliant. You can never be wrong when you twist everything to support your beliefs."

She wilted as she watched him walk away. What just happened? Moments ago, he seemed ready to admit the possibility of ghost activity in the house and they thought they'd finally captured irrefutable proof of paranormal activity. In less than five minutes, both things were snatched away. No recording of the porcelain dolls moving without human assistance plus Sterling was back to disagreeing with her.

That moment when he'd seemed ready to concede, when his attempts to find alternate explanations seemed to support her view, had filled her with excitement. Working with a partner took on an entirely new, and appealing, aspect. For as long as she could remember, people had ridiculed, criticized, and disdained her ability to detect and connect with spirits. How refreshing to have someone by her side who could understand and connect with her.

That must be close to how the spirits she connected with felt. They wandered alone, displaced, confused, and ignored—or despised. No wonder they often latched onto her when they discovered she could see and communicate with them. That momentary rush of relief and excitement she experienced from Sterling would pale in comparison to the spirits' when they realized someone could finally listen. And help.

She needed to stop expecting anything different from Sterling. He was going to do whatever he was going to do. He had proven that. She couldn't let it bother her. "Come on, TJ. Let's go look at the dolls. I want to see them myself and see if I can detect any residual energy from them."

Michael snapped. "Stan?"

Stan lifted his camera. "On it."

Snickers, curled in a ball near Kimberly, jumped to his feet and ran from the room, barking.

Michael lifted his eyebrows. "Did he sense something?"

"I'll find out." The porcelain dolls would have to wait.

She heard the front door open. *What in the world?* Something must have gone wrong for the family. Why would they have returned?

—————

CHAPTER TEN

KIMBERLY FOLLOWED Snickers to the front door and watched most of the Johnsons trudge inside, bleary-eyed, yawning, and generally grumpy. The older daughter, Rebecca, was not with them. Snickers whined and jumped on each family member, licking their hands and wiggling with delight.

"Morning," she greeted them with her widest smile. "No one looks terribly rested. How was the hotel?"

Ruth patted Snickers. "We didn't get much sleep. Faith had a rough night. We took Rebecca to school, but Faith needs another sick day. Her rash flared up bright red and painful. I worry about her getting even further behind in her classes."

Faith stared at the ground despite her mother's comforting pat to the back.

Kimberly frowned. Moving the family away from the haunting should have reduced symptoms, not worsened them. "May I see?" She knelt beside Faith, who held out her arm. The area that had previously been pink and scaly was angry red and appeared blistered. She ran her fingertips over the tiny white bumps, closing her eyes and reaching out for answers.

The girl's chakras stirred, unaligned and spinning out of control. Anger and frustration dominated her emotional state.

79

And fear. The fear came from the girl, who wasn't the source of the other negative emotions. She pressed further, attempting to discern what presence overlaid its emotional baggage on the girl. Breathing deeply, she tried to siphon away some of the hostility while pushing positive energy toward the girl to replace it.

Faith shivered and pulled her arm away. "He doesn't like that."

Startled by the girl's response, she dropped her hand. "Who doesn't like that?"

Faith shook her head and climbed the stairs, plodding upwards as though compelled but unwilling. The girl turned toward her room on the second floor.

Kimberly looked to the parents.

"You see? She's not herself." Ruth's eyes filled with tears. "She's never behaved like this."

"We don't know what to do," Daniel said. "Did you find something last night that will help?"

"We're reviewing footage right now," Kimberly told him, staring after Faith. "But most investigations require more than one night, and this is no exception. We actually were headed up to Faith's room to see the porcelain dolls. I didn't expect you back."

"We didn't intend to return. I know you need access to the space," Ruth said. "Faith kept insisting she had to come home. We couldn't stand it any longer. I'm sorry. We will do our best to stay out of the way."

The family would impede progress no matter how much they tried to stay out of the way. She knew from experience that they wouldn't be able to resist eavesdropping and trailing after them, interrupting to ask distracting questions. And they would manage to be exactly where the crew needed quiet and concentration. It never failed. That was why the show put the inhabitants in a hotel. But it was their house and if they insisted on returning, she had to agree.

The daughter, though, seemed drawn back home. Something

seemed to want the girl here. Why would the spirit fixate on her? Interesting. What could be the connection? Maybe she could take advantage of the family's presence and speak with the girl—without the parents hovering nearby.

"Would you mind if I continue as planned? Could I observe the porcelain dolls in Faith's room? As long as she doesn't mind?"

"Of course," Ruth said. "Whatever you need. Shall I come with you?"

"Actually, how much do you know about the property history? We wondered if you might be able to answer a few questions for us."

"Probably most anything you want to know. It's been in my family for generations. Why?"

"Generations?" This was the best possible outcome she could have hoped for. "Elise!"

Her researcher trotted to her side. "Yes?"

"Ruth ought to be able to answer any questions we have about the property. She says it's been in her family for generations."

Elise flipped pages in her spiral until she came to a blank one. "Wonderful! Do you mind if I take notes? Can we sit somewhere? Tell me everything."

Ruth led Elise toward the living room. "My great-great-grandfather acquired the property in the Land Run of 1889. Someone tried to jump his claim before he had it registered . . ."

Haggard and unshaven, Daniel looked completely deflated, his drooping eyes conveying more than exhaustion. "Do you mind if I take a few moments to pray and collect my thoughts alone in my room? I'll close the door and stay out of your way."

That worked perfectly. If she could make some progress, she would be that much closer to helping the family get past this disturbance. "Of course. Rest and take care of yourself."

He started toward his room but then turned back to her. "Have you ever been unable to solve one of your investigations?"

"Never," she reassured him. "A few times I've determined

there was nothing paranormal in a location. But I can tell that isn't the case here. I will connect eventually and resolve this for you."

"And if it's a demon? Have you fought a demon before?"

She hesitated, choosing her words carefully. In her heart, she believed her childhood home housed a demon, which had tormented her as a child—an evil presence so powerful it had killed her mother. Her father had refused to accept her psychic gifts and barred her from the home, leaving it to her aunt when he passed, with strict instructions she never be allowed in it. She had recently purchased the house from her aunt, who insisted she honor her father's dying request not to "turn the family home into a television circus." Sterling had convinced her aunt to lift the restrictions, however, allowing her to investigate the house for the first time. Who knew what she would find there when she took her crew for this season's finale. "I believe I have encountered a demon, though I did not battle it. I was too young to know what was happening."

"What if this is a demon? Will you be able to handle it?"

"Let's not borrow worry. We can decide how to handle a demon if that's what we're dealing with. For now, I will approach this as any other haunting. You rest. Let me handle this for you."

After he clicked his bedroom door closed, she climbed the stairs to Faith's room. The door stood ajar, so she peeked inside. Faith lay on her bed, staring at the ceiling.

"Faith?"

The girl turned her head toward her but said nothing.

"May I come in? My camera operator tells me your dolls moved. I'd love to see them. Maybe I can get an idea of what's bothering your family if I can get close to them."

Faith sat up and swung her legs off the side of the bed. "He moved them. He was angry last night because I left."

She wanted to ask about "him" but held her tongue. The girl shut down every time she tried to question her directly. Perhaps she should simply listen. "Will you show me the Ladies of Fashion? They aren't really dolls, are they? They're figurines."

Faith slid off the bed and joined her at the desk. "Yes. Grandma loved them so much. I used to sit on her lap, and we looked at them together. We read all the stories about them and the history of the time. They're so fragile and delicate but so pretty. Grandma loved Clementine, the Edwardian lady best. She used to say that's when ladies still looked sophisticated and feminine. She said girls just dress like boys today."

Startled by the willingness to share, she hoped to keep the conversation going. The girl's voice had changed, too. She sounded much happier, more like a typical teen. "Which do you like best?"

"I always had trouble choosing a favorite. But I think Charlotte, the Gainsborough Lady. Her dress and hat are fancy but not too fancy. I wouldn't want to wear that every day though. It's too heavy and too much trouble."

"I agree. I don't mind wearing a skirt or dress sometimes, but our clothes these days are much more practical."

"Grandma said farmers never dressed like that anyway. She used to tell me stories about Guthrie from when she was a little girl and all of this land was farm country. Well, most of it. Her granddad was a lawman. He got this land in the Run and built this house smack in the heart of town. He lifted his family up from farming. Grandma Alta said her grandma Helen was a fine lady and wore gowns and dresses to show her status in the town. But Grandma Alta grew up on a farm. Grandma had to work in the fields, and she said fancy dresses would be impractical. She wore homespun and that was all. Girls didn't wear pants back then. Even girls who worked on farms. But on Sundays when she came to town to visit, her grandma Helen was splendid in yards and yards of fabric. Grandma wore her only dress every Sunday to visit and they ate fried chicken and homemade pie. When the Dust Bowl swept through this part of the country, Grandma's dad stayed on his farm to hold onto his land. She said those were some hard times. And her dad had to make up with his dad. They relied on his parents to get them through some lean years. Great-grandpa Henry said he wouldn't let his pride stand in the way any longer. It wasn't worth watching his children starve."

Kimberly's head spun from all the information the girl shared with her. Unexpected. But good. The quaint language the girl surely retained from her grandmother's stories. "So, you're living in the house your . . . great-great-great-grandfather built? This place has been in your family that long?"

Faith nodded. "Grandma was the sole remaining heir and it passed to her. And she left it to Mom. Our ancestors have always lived in the house, ever since the Land Run, when great-great-great-grandpa James staked his claim."

"That's fascinating." Asking the girl if she knew of any deaths on the property seemed in poor taste. "You had quite a connection to your grandmother, didn't you?"

The girl nodded. "She lived with us until the end. I kept her company when I wasn't at school."

"Have you lived here all your life?"

"No. We moved in when Grandma couldn't live by herself anymore and needed our help. That was about five years ago. Mom and Dad sold their house and we moved in. Mom knew Grandma wanted to leave the house to us anyway. Mom is an only child."

"I'm sure it was difficult when your grandmother passed away. Sounds like you were close." Could the grandmother be the one shifting the porcelain dolls? If Faith and her grandmother bonded over them, her grandmother's spirit could be trying to communicate with her granddaughter via the dolls. Yet the girl seemed so convinced the presence plaguing her was a male. And the grandmother would not hurt the girl.

"I liked coming home from school and telling Grandma about my day. She was going to teach me her dinner roll recipe that her mom taught her. But the arthritis got so bad she couldn't knead dough anymore. Now no one can make rolls like she did. Mom buys frozen rolls. They don't taste like Grandma's."

Hmmm. Unfinished business? Perhaps the grandmother did want to communicate. "Do you ever think maybe your grandma is still here with you in spirit?"

Faith looked at her like she was crazy. "Grandma went to be with Jesus. I'll get to see her again in heaven."

She felt the girl's chakras light up. Her throat chakra hummed deep blue. Terrible sorrow and longing. "Of course."

"But I miss her. I wish I could see her. Grandma wasn't afraid of anything. She would know what to do about the—" The girl glanced up and stopped herself with a little gasp.

She waited, eager for the conversation to veer toward the current haunting. "What's scaring you, Faith? You can tell me."

The girl shook her head.

"What do you think your grandmother could help with? I think I can help you if you tell me."

"It's my fault," the girl whispered. "Grandma would be ashamed of me."

Her own anger flared. She'd seen this before. Victims who blamed themselves and felt guilty, truly believing they'd done something wrong and were being punished. "Faith, this isn't your fault. Spirits act out because of their own anger or unfinished business. Not because of the people around them."

The girl crossed her arms, grabbed her shoulders, and squeezed tightly as if hoping to hold herself together. "It's my fault."

"I'm absolutely certain there is nothing you could have done that would cause any of this."

Faith shook her head as a tear fell down her cheek. Kimberly's heart ached at the sight of the girl's torment. She needed to solve this haunting and help the spirit translocate, not only so the girl could physically heal but also to prove she didn't cause it. Carrying guilt like that could damage a person permanently.

She took one step toward the girl, reaching out a hand.

TJ appeared in the doorway, camera in hand. "Ms. Wantland? I thought I should record the dolls. Am I interrupting?" He eyed Faith.

Faith appeared to have shut down for now and seemed unlikely to share anything additional. TJ offered a good diversion away from the dead-end conversation. "Good idea, TJ. Let's see if I get anything from them."

She held her hands over the glass dome of the display, closed her eyes, and relaxed. Her palms tingled. Something had left an ectoplasmic residue. Allowing her senses to stretch, she invited further input. Though her eyes were closed, her vision blurred. She detected a shift. Something from the spirit plane tugged at her psyche. What prompted it? Curiosity? A desire to connect? An aching for release through translocation?

A heartbeat pounded against her eardrums in the otherwise silent realm she tapped into. The beating grew louder and louder. Frantic.

She tried to pull back, but the unidentified entity held a firm grip on her. An invisible hand clutched her blouse.

Her breath hitched in her throat. She could feel her own heartbeat, distinct from the thrumming pounding in her ears. Images of vast fields as far as she could see filled her mind. She thought someone stood beside her but every time she turned, hoping for a glimpse, no one was there.

She followed the unseen presence, pressing through golden stalks heavy with ripe wheat, nodding in the breeze. Green rows of corn stalks rose above her, obscuring the sun's radiant beams. The silky tassels shuddered in a gust of wind, rustling in the summer afternoon swelter.

When she heard footsteps following behind her, she whirled but saw nothing. No one.

Who are you? What do you want?

Her lungs rattled with each breath. She coughed but could not clear them. Breathing, usually easy and without thought, became a chore. She gasped, pulling at the air around her but nothing displaced the fluid filling her lungs as if she'd sucked in a gulp of water.

Someone called to her from far away, the sound garbled by a great distance. Or perhaps water. Had she walked into a pond? Was she underwater? The world around her darkened until her vision faded, obscured. Where was she?

"Ms. Wantland?"

Who called her?

"Ms. Wantland!"

Sleep sounded good. She would lie down and sleep.

"Kimberly!"

Sterling's voice jolted her back. Her eyes flew open.

Everyone clustered in the bedroom doorway. TJ and Stan held cameras trained on her. Michael's hands pressed against his mouth, his brow furrowed. Elise stood silently, notebook clutched to her chest. Ruth and Daniel peered at her from behind the crew, fear in their eyes.

She blinked, trying to remember what she'd just seen. "What happened?"

Michael stepped closer. "We were going to ask *you*, sweetie. Faith said you were in trouble, that 'he' got you, and you needed help."

Sterling placed a hand on her back. "You didn't answer when we spoke to you. Your eyes were closed like you were asleep, but you didn't answer."

His eyes searched her face, worry creasing his forehead. Her palms tingled again. She jerked them from the figurine display. The figurines. She looked closer and sucked in a breath. "They moved again!"

Moments ago, she'd seen the porcelain ladies scattered haphazardly about the round display shelves, as TJ reported finding them this morning. Now, as if something had drawn them inward, they all clustered around the wooden rod in the center of the shelves.

Faith and TJ rushed to the dresser, each pressing against one side of her.

"They *are* different!" TJ said. "They moved again!"

She saw him adjust his camera, taking in the display case from all angles.

"Is the camera still recording?" Sterling asked. "I'd like to see what exactly happened to Kimberly."

"It is!" TJ said. "Maybe we caught them this time."

A small hand rested over hers. Faith peered not at the figurines but at her. "Are you okay? Did he hurt you?"

"Did who hurt me?"

"You said something, but I couldn't understand you," Faith said. "My mom and dad say I talk when he has control too. But I never remember."

She'd spoken? In a trance? This was unusual. Maybe she was dealing with something more dangerous than she'd suspected. "Please, Faith. Tell me what you know."

The girl stared at her feet, her voice barely a whisper. "He said his name is—"

Rosie spun her away from the display case—and Faith. *Where had she been? She wasn't here a moment ago.*

"Are you okay?" Her stylist/personal assistant/best friend held open palms over the air around her body. She knew Rosie read her psychic energy levels and chakra balance. "You're completely depleted, girl. Let's get you to the trailer. Footage review can go on without you."

She turned back to Faith. "But we were about to—"

"You need to be fully charged and ready for tonight. Save yourself for later. Come on."

Before she knew what was happening, Rosie dragged her from the room.

She caught Daniel's eye on the way out of the bedroom. "I learned one thing. This is no demon."

CHAPTER ELEVEN

KIMBERLY SUBMITTED to Rosie dragging her downstairs away from the crowd even though she really wanted to continue the conversation with Faith. The odd episode left her drained and woozy. She would speak to Faith later when she didn't feel like she was about to pass out.

Footsteps preceded Sterling as he thumped down the staircase. He caught up to them in the entryway and curled a hand around her forearm, tugging her to a stop. "What happened up there?"

"She overdid it, that's what," Rosie answered. "And we need to insist she rest and allow her energy and chakras to recharge for tonight."

"But . . . what *happened?* You were nonresponsive."

She struggled again to remember exactly what she'd seen.

"You connected with a spirit, didn't you?" Rosie asked. "I assumed you were communicating or trying to communicate."

"I was hoping to get something from the porcelain ladies. And I did see images. Felt things. But this was different. None of the visions had anything to do with the figurines. I wasn't in control at all. I'm not sure who communicated with me. And I had a lot of trouble breaking the connection." She turned to

Sterling. "You're a good anchor. Your voice brought me back. You always do."

Sterling beamed. "Glad I helped. Sounds like you need me around."

"Job security?"

"I like having a job, and this is a great job to have. But I think maybe you need an anchor on a personal level too." He placed a hand on her forehead. "You're not feverish. Don't look sick. I think Rosie's diagnosis of exhaustion is spot on. You should rest all day. We didn't sleep much last night, and I don't think you've had decent sleep in years. That's bound to catch up to you."

He meant well. His heart and throat chakras resonated with genuine concern. She let his slightly skewed interpretation of Rosie's diagnosis slide.

But Rosie didn't. "It's not lack of sleep. She's depleted psychically. Whatever took control drained her energy to share images. That's what spirits do to her. Usually to communicate and often to request help. Don't smirk at me, Sterling. I know what I'm talking about."

She rested a hand on Rosie's arm. "It's okay. Rest will help regardless. He can think it's lack of sleep."

"You must be exhausted. Or sick. You're going to let that go?" Rosie took a turn placing a hand on her forehead. "He's right. You're not feverish. You don't seem like yourself though. It's almost like you've been possessed."

She laughed. "I allow spirits to share and connect, but no spirit has ever taken possession of me—"

A male voice shouted outside. She jumped.

Sterling raised an eyebrow. "That sounded angry. Didn't it?"

Rosie crinkled her nose. "This neighborhood has been so quiet and welcoming. That's strange."

Another shout sent her to the window by the front door.

A man stood in the street at the end of the Johnsons' driveway. He clutched a sign in his hands, which he held above his head.

"What is he doing?" she wondered aloud.

Rosie and Sterling joined her as the crew appeared at the top of the stairs.

"What's that shouting?" Michael asked.

Across the street, a door opened and the homeowner peered out, apparently confused by the disturbance.

The sign-waving man continued to shout, the repeated yell morphing into what sounded like a chant.

She reached for the handle.

Sterling grabbed her hand. "What are you doing?"

"I can't hear what he's saying."

"Neither can I, but I can tell it isn't anything good. Don't go out there."

"But Rosie and I need to go to the trailer."

"Wait until the weirdo shouting in the street leaves."

"What if he stays all day?"

TJ thumped down the stairs. "I'll make sure you can get to your trailer, Ms. Wantland. Whatever it takes. Meanwhile, should I be recording?"

"And give the nut airtime? I don't know if I like that." Sterling scowled. Hands on his hips, he turned to Michael, who had also descended the stairs and joined them. "What do you normally do in situations like this?"

Michael stared out the window. "I'm not sure what exactly the situation is but we've never seen anything like it. What is that guy doing?"

Stan called from the dining room, "His sign says, 'Go away, witch.'"

"Witch?" She joined Stan at the larger window. "You just happen to have binoculars?"

Stan shrugged. "I always pack them. Bird watching is a habit of mine. I'm addicted."

"Huh. Never knew that. There are far worse addictions." She

watched the man as he shouted at the Johnsons' house, waving his sign to punctuate his words. "Witch? Really? I didn't even get called that in Salem. May I?"

Stan handed her the binoculars.

The lenses brought the older man directly in front of her. It was the same man she'd seen yesterday, watching her from the street, who had asked her if she thought the house was haunted. His thin, graying hair blew in the wind above a deeply lined face and intense eyes. This was no joke or prank. The man meant what he said. Her stomach churned.

Michael stared out the window. "They baked cookies for us yesterday and today this?"

Her hands shook as she lowered the binoculars. "I don't think he's one of the neighbors."

Sterling placed a hand on her shoulder, standing so near that the heat from his body enveloped her as she shivered. "Can I see this guy?"

He reached for the binoculars, which she gladly handed over. She'd seen enough. His hands adjusted the focus. "Wait. Is that the guy who was watching you yesterday?"

"I think so." She clutched her stomach and took deep breaths. She had to stay calm above all else. Her trailer sat parked in the lot next to the house, soothing teas and energizing oils waiting for her. Should she make a break for it? Would the man be content to yell from the street? Or would he get in her face? Or worse?

"What's happening?" Ruth asked.

She turned and found Ruth, Daniel, and Faith watching her. "I seem to have attracted some unwanted attention."

"Do you recognize him?" Sterling asked Daniel, offering the binoculars. "Is he a neighbor?"

Daniel took only a moment to respond. "Never seen him before."

"How did he know where to find you?" Rosie asked. "No one has posted about the detour investigation."

She shook her head. "No idea."

"I'm going to see what he wants," Sterling said, headed for the door. "And suggest he move along."

She turned to stop him, but he had the door open before she caught up to his long, determined steps.

The man's chants rang loud and clear as soon as the door opened. Sterling didn't hesitate as he crossed the porch and shuffled down the steps. He strode toward the man, who yelled even louder with an approaching audience.

"Witch, go home! Witch, go home!"

She took a deep breath and followed Sterling. Maybe they could reason with the man and convince him to leave them alone. Her stomach churned, her heart pounded, and a shiver ran through her. She hated confrontation.

"Hey, there," Sterling called to the man from about halfway down the driveway. "Can I help you with something?"

The man caught sight of her on the porch. He lowered his sign. His manic eyes blazed. "You can take that witch and get out of town." He pointed at her. "Daughter of Satan! Evil witch!"

"Hey, now, slow down," Sterling said. "Even if witches truly existed, which they don't, I can assure you Kimberly Wantland is no witch. She's a genuinely kind soul who wouldn't hurt anyone. She spends her days trying to help people."

"Witchcraft is the devil's work! It doesn't help anyone!"

"Okay, pal, that's enough," Sterling said. "This is utter nonsense you're spewing. Witches don't exist. Magic doesn't exist."

"She's cast her spell on you!" the man yelled.

"Not the type of spell you're talking about. Spells are nonsense. These supernatural beliefs were invented by humans to explain phenomena that confused them. These days science can account for what we once deemed magic."

For once, immense gratitude for Sterling's scientific explanations flooded through her.

"She admitted it to me! She admitted she's a witch!"

Hearing the blatant lie moved her to action. Indignation consumed her, burning away the fear, and her feet, formerly held in place by dread, carried her to Sterling's side. "I said no such thing. I never would because it isn't true."

The man's crazy eyes burned with delight. "Oh, yes, you did. I asked you yesterday if you thought this house was haunted and if you were here to work your magic on it. And you said you were."

She shook her head, frustrated. How could you argue with someone who refused to see reality? Or lived in their own version of it. "That's not what I meant at all. 'Work your magic' is a saying. I had no idea you meant actual magic. Believe me, if I had any power at all, I'd make you disappear right now."

The man's eyes bulged. He lifted a cell phone, stared into the camera, and yelled triumphantly, "She threatened me! She said she'll make me disappear. You heard it."

Sterling held an arm out. "Kimberly, go to your trailer."

She'd never heard his voice so grave. "But—"

"Now. Go. Do not say another word."

She backed away. Rosie met her halfway, just as the man began shouting after her. "Run, Kimberly Wantland! It will do you no good. God detests all who do evil in his sight. Justice will be carried out. Your day of reckoning is approaching."

Rosie followed her into the trailer and slammed the door closed.

Kimberly noted the lack of lock. She'd never needed one. Her trailer, sanctuary for years, wasn't meant to act as a fortress. She pushed aside a curtain and peeked out the window. Sterling appeared to be shouting at the man. Not good.

"How do we convince this guy I'm not a witch or a Satanist?" The words felt strange in her mouth. They didn't belong to her usual vocabulary.

"Girl, you don't. You can't argue with crazy."

"Sterling actually suggested to the Johnsons that God sent me to help them. And now this." She shook her head.

"Do you believe that?"

"It's easier to believe than his nonsense. I'm not evil."

"You don't need to convince me."

Sterling burst into the trailer, face red and fists balled. He breathed heavily as he paced. "Effing lunatic. Won't be budged. Laughed when I threatened to call the police. Said he's on public property and hasn't laid a finger on anyone. And that his religious views and freedom of speech are protected by the constitution. I sent you away to keep him from recording you. No telling what he will distort and edit that into." He looked like he might put a fist through the wall.

"He called me evil. Granted I don't attend a church anymore—"

"He's nuts. Don't listen to him," Sterling grumbled.

"I'll make us all tea." Rosie wrung her hands and seemed anxious for something to do.

"I donate to food pantries. School fundraisers. Children's hospitals."

"Don't forget those wishes you granted," Rosie added.

Sterling turned her to face him. "Don't let that man get in your head. You travel the country, sleepless and exhausted, sacrificing a personal life to help other people. People who have nowhere else to turn. Plus, apparently you give away a lot to charity. I know people who go to church and nothing more. That doesn't make them better. You're helping your way."

She worried her lip. "Is that enough? I don't know where my gift came from. What if the demon in my house—"

Rosie joined Sterling at her side. "Don't. We've talked about this. Your gift, your ability to connect, did not originate with that demon."

"Seriously," Sterling said. "Let's continue with that thought process. A demon bestows an incredible gift on a little girl. His long-term vision is that she grows up to help hundreds of people, rises to celebrity, donates to charities, generally makes people feel better about themselves, until one day . . ." He shrugged. "I'm at a loss. What's the evil master plan?"

She relaxed and slid into a chair, smiling in spite of herself. "You have a point. Just for the record, you said 'incredible gift,' correct?"

The electric kettle gurgled as it reached a boil. Rosie returned to the tea station, gripping Kimberly's shoulders in a quick hug on the way.

Sterling grinned. "If you truly can talk to spirits, if you genuinely assist lost souls in crossing to heaven, that is an incredible gift."

Warmth fluttered through her chest. "That sentence contained a lot of ifs, but I'll take it. Thank you."

His face clouded. "Speaking of for the record, that idiot out there recorded us. I'm certain he won't use it to make the show look good. And I'm afraid I lost my cool. Sorry."

Rosie pressed a steaming mug into his hands. "You got Kimberly out of harm's way for the moment. That's what mattered."

"Who is this guy?" she wondered, gratefully accepting her tea from Rosie. "How did he find us? Maybe Elise can track him down. If he has any online presence at all."

Sterling wrapped both hands around his mug. "I don't think he's going anywhere, unfortunately. We need a plan to cope with him." He seemed to see the cup Rosie had given him for the first time. "Tea? I don't like tea."

His phone lit up, pinging notifications again and again. Rosie's began to chime as well.

Sterling frowned. "Well, he just made research easier. He's blowing up Twitter, tagging all of us in his idiot rants." He turned his phone so she could see. "Meet Ezekiel Jackson. Zeke to his followers."

CHAPTER TWELVE

THE CREW GATHERED IN THE JOHNSONS' living room before the second night investigation as Elise shared what she'd learned about Ezekiel Jackson. Kimberly sat on the couch, Rosie on one side, Sterling on the other, everyone doing their best to ignore the periodic shouts from the street.

Normally, Kimberly attended every minute of footage review, but today she'd spent the afternoon in her trailer, afraid to cross back to the house. Rosie had administered a full body massage, applied numerous calming oils, and kept her tea mug full. Sterling stood guard at the window, keeping an eye on the protestor, and spent a lot of time on his phone.

Ruth had apparently baked cookies to distract herself. She cruised amongst the crew with a platter, offering baked goods and coffee to everyone. When she passed by Sterling, he pocketed his phone and held up his empty hands. He passed one hand over the other—and a daisy appeared. He held it out to Ruth.

"Thank you!" Ruth said, accepting the flower. "That was remarkable."

"How did you do that?" Kimberly asked.

"A magician never tells." Sterling helped himself to two

cookies from the platter. "And Kimberly likes her coffee strong with just a bit of milk added to it."

"Sterling! I don't need her to wait on me," Kimberly chided him.

"I'm happy to keep myself busy," Ruth said. "Anything to take my mind off everything going on is welcome."

Snickers had stationed himself at the window by the door, paws resting on the low sill. A deep growl rumbled in his throat anytime Ezekiel yelled. He rounded through the living room every few minutes, as if checking on his people. He sniffed hands, accepted pets, and looked generally concerned.

Ruth returned with coffee, which Kimberly gladly accepted. She'd attempted to nap but her heightened anxiety and Ezekiel's yelling had kept her from sleeping. The coffee would keep her awake for the investigation tonight.

Michael cleared his throat. "Elise, what did you find? Who the heck is this guy?"

Elise adjusted her glasses and focused on her notebook. "Sterling texted his name to me, but as soon as he started posting on Twitter, it didn't take much effort. Ezekiel Jackson established a church about twenty years ago—"

"A church?" Daniel asked, arms crossed.

"He calls it a church," Elise continued. "Church of True Salvation. He and his followers claim to base their beliefs on literal interpretation of the Bible. However, a quick Google search brings up a lot of posts disproving that. They're mostly seen as a hate group now. This is what they do—travel around the country protesting anything or anyone that they claim is evil or against God."

"That isn't a church," Ruth said. "True Christians continue the work Jesus began during his life."

"No one disagrees with you," Elise said. "Except maybe Ezekiel and his followers."

"What followers?" Sterling asked. "He's alone out there."

"They branch out to annoy as many people as possible at any

given time," Elise said. "He has people in numerous states today. But he does seem to be losing church members faster than he's attracting them lately."

"Maybe that's why he targeted Kimberly," Michael suggested. "Harassing a high-profile personality like her means more eyes on him. And more potential like-minded lunatics to add to his followers."

"We can handle him," Sterling said. "Let him try something. If he gets anywhere near Kimberly"—he formed a fist—"I'll be glad for the excuse."

She flushed. His presence during the afternoon had helped her nerves. But an altercation would not help anything. "I appreciate the sentiment, but we can't engage this guy."

"I have to respond some way," Sterling insisted, opening the Twitter app on his phone. "He took that recording of you and edited it to sound like a threat. He also recorded me getting in his face. Look at this. People commenting things like, 'I didn't realize Kimberly Wantland was so hateful.' That's garbage! He's the one spewing hate out there. He tagged the show, you, me, Michael, everyone who has a Twitter account."

"I don't think it will help," she said. "Like Rosie said, you can't argue with crazy."

Rosie shook her head. "I don't know, girl. You won't be able to change this guy's behavior, but I'm with Sterling. We need something to counter his lies. People will believe anything they see online."

"I hate this sort of thing," she said. "Michael?"

"Let's see if it blows over. Maybe tomorrow this will be yesterday's news, and no one will pay attention. I'll reach out to Randmeier as well and give him a heads-up that this could blow up even bigger on us."

"Okay," she agreed. "Let's hope for the best. What about footage review? Anything else helpful there? Did TJ manage to record the porcelain ladies while I was in Faith's room this morning?"

TJ squirmed in his seat. "I was focused on you. The display case wasn't in the frame when they moved. I'm sorry, Ms. Wantland."

Stan leaned forward, his camera logging the discussion. "The recording glitches and blips quite a bit though. I think that's when the presence moved them. And frankly we know Kimberly didn't move them. Too many witnesses. So, I think it's a good case for paranormal involvement."

"But if her hands aren't in the shot," Sterling said, "then she could have moved them. That won't fly as proof. Sorry. And I wasn't there to witness. We only have TJ's word for it, and he's biased. Plus, he admitted he wasn't watching her hands."

"But how could she lift off the glass dome without any of us seeing it?"

"No one was paying attention," he said.

"Faith was there, too," she reminded him.

"No offense, but she's the most likely person to be moving them. They're her dolls in her room. Without actually recording them moving, you have nothing."

TJ and Stan appeared to grind their teeth, but neither said anything more.

"Anything else from review?" she asked Michael.

"Not anything definitive or substantial. No voices. Nothing moving other than the items in the pantry."

"Also not caught on a recording," Sterling muttered.

"Okay, we know. You don't believe any of this," she said. Her head was beginning to pound, and she wished Sterling could focus more on being supportive and protective than disagreeable and contradictory.

"Just pointing out the obvious. It's my job," he reminded her.

She scowled and changed the subject. "What about the property? Anything helpful in the history?"

Elise and Ruth shared a glance. Elise flipped pages in her notebook. "The land was acquired during the Land Run of 1889 by Ruth's ancestors. Prior to that, most of Oklahoma Territory had been parceled out to Native American tribes, who were forced to move here when displaced from their homelands by white settlers greedy for land. Not a great part of our history, honestly."

Could angry Native Americans haunt the land? Had someone perhaps refused to leave his home again and died as a result?

"I can tell you lots of stories passed down through my family," Ruth said. "I had distant relatives who were true cowboys, for one thing. My great-grandfather used to say that a true cowboy had to do three things. He had to drive cattle from Texas to Kansas. He had to shoot a rattlesnake. And he had to hang a cattle rustler. Out on the trail, they didn't bother with dragging a rustler to the next town for trial. Anyone caught stealing was handled right there on the spot. It was a different time."

"A lawless time, it sounds like."

"Well, once the town established itself, they tried to be more civilized. My great-great-grandfather was sheriff of Guthrie when it was still young. Back then, outlaws hid in rural Oklahoma. Guthrie was capital of Oklahoma when we became a state, so he dealt with a lot of criminals."

Elise picked back up. "This site specifically, though, was claimed by her family. Someone tried to jump the claim before he registered it."

"Jump it?"

Ruth answered again. "That's right. One tent had been set up to register land claims. Men waited in line for days sometimes, trying to register their land. Another man tried to register the same parcel of land, though my great-great-grandfather had the deed in hand. The other man argued that he'd had the deed, but it was stolen from him while he slept in line. The man was discovered to be a criminal. Though he claimed he wanted to turn his life around and work an honest living, he clearly was up to his same tricks. Many did lose their claims though. My great-great-uncle also ran in that first run. He staked a claim for a farm. But then he got word that his wife had gone into labor. He returned home to be with her and by the time he got back, someone had jumped his claim."

"But here, on this land, no traumatic instances or problems?"

Ruth cocked her head. "What do you mean?"

"I can feel different history at each location we investigate. I can sense the history of the land itself, that of the dwelling, and the people currently living there. Sometimes it can be challenging to discern one from the others. If I know of any important events, that can help."

"I'll have to think about it," Ruth said. The woman's brow furrowed. "My grandfather was a pastor. Surely the home must be blessed with positive spiritual energy. We . . . we brought in our own pastor to say some prayers a few weeks ago. But the problems continued."

More shouting sent a growl rumbling through Snickers' chest.

"Now what?" Sterling asked. He got up and crossed to the window. "Great. That's the last thing we need."

"What is it?" She jumped up and joined him. A news van had parked across the street. A reporter and camera operator approached Ezekiel Jackson, who had increased his volume now that he had a new audience to perform for.

"We stand against witches and witchcraft," he yelled, waving his sign above his head as the camera operator focused on the reporter, who stood with Ezekiel and the house behind her, so Kimberly couldn't see the woman's face.

"That's News Channel Six," Ruth said. "And I think that's Cathy Rickman, one of their main reporters."

"Is this honestly such a slow news day that they have nothing more important to report on than kooks harassing people?" Sterling asked.

"He's making noise. Noise attracts attention," she said. "You know that better than anyone else in the room. Making noise is how you got on my show to begin with."

"I wasn't an ass," he muttered.

She would've disagreed at the time but didn't reply. No sense in digging up old annoyances.

Faith and Rebecca came downstairs, presumably from their rooms.

"What's happening now?" Rebecca asked. "This is so embarrassing. Everyone on the block can hear that guy shouting at our house."

"I'm afraid he may be on the news tonight," Ruth told her.

"Now everyone at school will know too!" Rebecca flopped onto the couch. Faith sat beside her sister, wringing her hands. Rebecca draped an arm around Faith's shoulders and leaned against her. "I'm sorry. It's not your fault."

Faith whispered so quietly no one else in the room seemed to notice. "It *is* my fault. You know it is."

"No. Not at all. Stop thinking that."

Kimberly drifted closer, hoping to glean more information. Why did Faith blame herself? What did Rebecca know? What name did Faith nearly disclose earlier? The girls went silent, and she didn't feel comfortable interrupting them.

Rebecca caught her watching them and pulled Faith's head onto her shoulder. Kimberly watched Rebecca comfort her younger sister and wondered how differently her life might have turned out if she'd had a sister. An older sister to look up to and watch out for her or perhaps a younger sister to care for. And if she had a sister, she wouldn't be all alone in the world. What would it be like to have someone always there for her, someone she could reach out to when she really needed to talk?

Ezekiel's shouting pulled her back from wistful thoughts to reality.

"The reporter and camera seem to have given him a second wind," Sterling commented. "He's not slowing down at all."

Ruth watched, then turned to Daniel. "What should we do? Call the police?"

"He *is* disturbing the peace. Not to mention upsetting the neighbors."

"Why don't we hold off on calling police?" Michael massaged his temples. "Let's send you guys back to the hotel. At least we can get you out of here, so you don't have to put up with this. I'm hoping to avoid confrontation. He could spin that to make the show look really bad."

"How much longer do you expect your investigation to take?" Daniel asked.

"I promise I'll do everything I can tonight," she said. "When we leave, I'm sure he will too."

A new thought struck her. What if he followed them? What if he continued harassing her at every investigation? She couldn't worry about that now. The Johnsons needed her.

"At least it's Friday," Rebecca mumbled, pushing herself off the couch. "No school for two days."

The family left to retrieve their bags for the night.

Kimberly pulled Elise to the side. "Did Ruth share anything with you about the property that could be useful to us?"

Elise shrugged. "She shared too much really. The area has so much history. Anything could be causing this. Maybe if you get something tonight it could help me know what to look at more closely. Our constant conundrum."

"It's a Catch-22, isn't it? I'm hoping you'll find something that can help me focus, but you need a hint for what to look at yourself. Let me know if anything grabs your attention."

Rebecca's voice carried down the stairs. "Faith, stop! You're not funny!"

Kimberly frowned at Michael, who raised an eyebrow and gestured they go upstairs. She nodded.

Ruth and Daniel already scrambled up the staircase and beat her to Rebecca's room. Faith stood in the doorway, completely still, staring blankly, one hand reaching toward her sister.

Ruth dropped to one knee and grabbed Faith by the shoulders. "Faith! Snap out of it! Come on. We need to leave for the hotel now."

Kimberly stood beside the family, overwhelmed by the psychic energy pouring off the girl. She grabbed her quartz and placed a hand on Faith's shoulder.

The girl cringed and whirled around. The deep, gravelly voice that came from her mouth startled them all. *"Get off me!"*

She retracted her hand. Something, someone, inhabited the girl. Had taken control of her. Spoke through her. She looked for a camera operator. Stan, of course, was on the scene, recording the odd behavior. She noticed Sterling, mouth open in shock.

Ruth stared on helplessly, wringing her hands. "Ms. Wantland?"

She placed both hands on the girl, focused all her energy, and 'shoved' against the entity, urging it away from Faith. It resisted, but she dislodged it. From the anger it left behind, she knew she'd taken it by surprise. The next time she challenged it, it wouldn't be so easily overcome.

Faith crumpled into her mother's arms, blinking and dazed. "What happened? Why am I in Rebecca's room?"

Ruth sobbed quietly. "Why? Why is this happening to us? Why my little girl?"

Tears streaked Rebecca's face.

"Come on. Let's get you out of here," she urged the family. "Quickly."

They grabbed their bags, and she ushered them down the stairs. She couldn't shake the feeling that the presence waited, recharging. She wanted the family gone before it could strike again.

The older house did not include an attached garage, which meant they would have to brave the protestor outside to get to their van.

"Just keep your heads down and keep moving," she instructed, suggesting the same approach she used when inundated with unwanted attention.

As soon as the door opened, Ezekiel shouted louder. "You house a witch! God hates a sinner! You will reap what you sow!"

Ruth glared at the man, arms around the girls as if attempting to shield her daughters from him. Daniel rushed to unlock and open the van doors. While the girls clambered in, Ruth broke away and walked down the driveway toward the street.

"Ruth?" she called.

Ezekiel's energy intensified as she approached. "God hates a sinner! You will reap what you sow!"

"How dare you claim to be a Christian?" she shouted back. "What are you sowing? Hate! A true Christian sows love and compassion. A true follower of Christ helps. He doesn't spend his time idly shouting at those trying to help."

"You house a witch! Yours is a house of evil!"

"Get away from my house!" Ruth yelled. "You're scaring my children and upsetting the neighbors."

"I'll scare the hell out of them! Scare them back to God!"

Daniel put his arm around Ruth's shoulders and turned her toward the van. "This is what he wants. He wants to make a scene and grab attention. Let's go."

"He's not a Christian," Ruth repeatedly emphatically, then yelled over her shoulder. "You are no Christian!"

She watched the family drive away to the safety of the hotel, then turned to Sterling, surprised to find him grinning. "What are you happy about?"

He held up his phone. "I recorded that entire exchange. Now your media specialist can fight back."

CHAPTER THIRTEEN

KIMBERLY PACED THE TRAILER, normally her refuge and sanctuary, feeling like a caged animal. A hard knot of fury stewed in her stomach. She wanted to be out exploring Guthrie, watching footage review with the rest of the crew, or driving back to the inn for a nap. Anything that would actually be productive and useful.

Most of all she was furious with the man in the street continuing to scream and accuse her of witchcraft, disturbing everyone in the neighborhood. She prided herself on discretion and professional behavior. The sideshow outside mortified her.

Rosie had gone back into the Johnsons' house for a private phone call. Sterling had left in his car hours before without telling her where he was going. Which left her alone to endure Ezekiel Jackson's continued harassment.

She was meant to be resting but the periodic yelling kept her on edge. She should ask Michael to take her back to the Stone Lion Inn. At least she could collect her thoughts and perhaps nap a bit there. Unless Ezekiel followed her. If his main intention was to harass her, he very well might trail after her no matter where she went.

Her phone rang. Glad for the diversion, she lifted it from her purse. The caller ID informed her it was Angela, the woman who lived in her house back in Albuquerque, a house sitter and caretaker while the show was on the road. Angela usually only called if she had a problem to report.

"Hey, Angela," she answered the call. "How are you?"

"I'm okay," Angela's voice assured her. "But something strange happened last night. I thought you'd want to know."

"Yes, of course. Did you hear a voice again?"

"No. This time all the family photos shifted suddenly."

"Shifted? What do you mean?"

"The photos on the wall moved so that they now hang crooked. Pictures sitting on shelves or dressers tipped over face down. All at once. Startled me, but nothing broke except the glass in one of the frames. It's an old school picture of you."

"Oh, wow. That's definitely significant. Someone or something is trying to get your attention."

"I thought so. But the way the glass shattered over your face scared me a little. Almost seems like a threat. Maybe they want your attention."

Angela normally didn't voice concerns about disturbances. Her house sitter usually seemed fascinated by the glimpses and hints of paranormal activity. Which made her the perfect woman for the job. "Maybe. Are you okay? Do you need a break from the house?"

"No. I don't. I'm okay. Do you want me to burn some sage or anything?"

Her heart skipped a beat at the idea. If her mother's spirit lingered in the house, she wanted the chance to connect with her. Anything that purged spirits from a dwelling could send her mother away. She strongly suspected a demon lurked in the house too, but as it wasn't hurting Angela, she couldn't risk such measures. "Please don't. I have permission to investigate the house. Finally. That will be this season's finale. If you can hold out a little longer, I'll handle whatever entity I find."

"That's so exciting! I'll be fine. Glad to help any way I can. Do you want me to keep calling with updates?"

"Yes. Anything out of the ordinary. We can keep a journal and try to get a handle on what we're dealing with. Thank you so much!"

"Talk to you later."

She hung up and dropped into a chair. Last week, Angela had called to report smelling floral perfume and hearing someone say Kimberly's name. This week the family photos were disturbed. Such markedly different disturbances seemed to indicate different presences in the house.

The door opened, startling her from concerns about her house. Sterling entered, balancing a pizza box on one hand.

She rushed to his side. "Where have you been?"

"Aw, shucks. You missed me."

She accepted the outstretched box and read the top. "Hideaway Pizza?"

"Yeah. Famous place here in Oklahoma. Highly recommended and reviewed on Yelp. I got one of the veggie options for you."

"It's here in Guthrie? Darn. I wish I could have seen it. I hate being stuck here. We all planned to wander around Guthrie and enjoy the history here. Now I'm trapped. Next time take me with you when you go on an all-afternoon outing."

"I thought you'd need to rest and relax."

"Impossible with that fringe lunatic out there."

"I'm afraid it's lunatics now. I noticed on my way in that he's acquired a friend."

"What?" She peered out the window.

"Hideaway isn't in Guthrie anyway. The original location is in Stillwater but now they've opened restaurants elsewhere in the area. I stopped by the one in Edmond, just down the street from the University of Central Oklahoma. I met an environmental professor. He agreed to test samples for me."

She opened the box, savored the mouth-watering aroma, and lifted a slice. "What samples?"

"Air. Water. Soil." He bit into a piece and groaned his approval. "We will rule out environmental contaminants that could cause hallucinations and rashes."

"You won't find anything." She inspected the dipping sauce. "Ranch? Ugh. Marinara is better for you."

He lifted an eyebrow. "How so?"

"Marinara is concentrated tomatoes so you have the benefit of antioxidants. Ranch is all fat."

Sterling cracked open the container and dunked his crust into it. "Mmmm. Delicious fat."

She shook her head but smirked regardless. "You are such a nut."

"Out of curiosity, what would you do if something tested positive for dangerous toxins?"

She swallowed before answering. "I would suggest the family get it cleaned up."

"Would you admit that's what caused the girl's illness?"

She selected a second slice. "If the house showed no signs of activity, sure. I'd absolutely consider that. But this location has a presence. How would you explain only one person in the house is affected by an environmental toxin?"

"Perhaps the younger girl is more sensitive. Perhaps children are more susceptible."

"Perhaps. But right now, that's speculation. Let's see what results you get from your samples. Even you looked shocked by the girl's behavior earlier."

"I'll agree she didn't look like she was pretending. That was odd behavior." He wiped his mouth with a napkin. "You don't mind?"

"Mind what?"

"Running tests to check for toxins?"

"Why would I?"

He shrugged. "I thought you'd balk. Feel threatened."

"Nope. I'm not anti-science. I'm . . . alternative inclusive."

He stared at her a moment before bursting into laughter. "Okay. I can work with that."

His gaze shifted to the look that always sent an electric quiver through her nerves. She squirmed. "What?"

"You're fascinating. Always a surprise. I like it."

The quiver burst into a full-blown case of butterflies in her stomach. She ducked her head and tucked a loose lock of hair behind her ear. "Well, I like having you around too."

"Oh, hey. The UCO stadium carries your name."

She did a double take. "What are you talking about?"

"I saw it when I was on campus. Wantland Stadium. It's not that common a name. Seemed unlikely to be a coincidence. Maybe you have some history here like Rosie?"

He was correct that a coincidence seemed like a stretch. She'd never met anyone else with her last name. Then again, assuming she shared common ancestry with every single person with the same last name struck her as equally far-fetched. "Not to my knowledge, but . . ."

But how much did she really know about her extended family? She knew her dad's sister, Aunt Dolly. Her grandparents had all passed on either before she was born or while she was too young to remember them. But she'd never even seen pictures of them growing up. Those family photos Angela reported toppling over or skewing on the walls were only of herself and her parents. Why no grandparents? Or anyone else? Why no photo albums of other branches of her family tree? Why no Bible diligently recording the names of those before her?

Why hadn't she ever asked her dad? Growing up, that was her only reality. And the relationship with her father had been strained at best after Mom's sudden death. She should have thought to ask, though, before it was too late.

"Hey. Where'd you go?" Sterling touched her knee.

"How far back can you trace your family history?"

He blew out a puff of air. "Oh, gosh . . . generations. I don't really know."

"So can the Johnsons. So can Rosie. I know nothing. How can that be?"

"No one told you anything?"

"Not that I can remember."

"Have you dug through all the stuff in your house since you bought it back? Maybe there are boxes of records somewhere? Maybe in the attic?"

"It didn't even occur to me to look. I haven't stayed there much. I'm always so busy with the show." She met his gaze and allowed herself a moment to relish the concern there.

"We'll find out. Honestly, I think you should pursue this from a medical history standpoint if for no other reason. Your aunt is your dad's sister, but your mom died young. You need to know if she suffered from a genetic anomaly you could have inherited."

"I hadn't thought about that. Good point. Wantland is my dad's name of course, but that could at least help me—"

Sterling's phone lit up, pinging repeatedly in rapid succession.

"What is it?" She jumped up and peered over his shoulder.

Sterling turned his phone toward her. "The five o'clock news story broke. We're taking hits left and right."

"I thought you were going to post that video of Ruth."

"I did. It helped drown out Jackson for a bit. Your fans supported you, as always. Left lots of negative comments about this guy. But now his supporters are fighting back. And the local news is reaching people nearby." He jerked a thumb toward the window. "And people nearby can come join him."

She watched his thumbs flying over his phone, fighting for her and her show. Their show.

"I'm posting again. You should retweet and encourage your fans to do the same. See if we can shut this down."

She flushed, unwilling to admit the truth. "I don't know how."

His thumbs stopped moving. He raised his gaze to meet hers, dark eyes below furrowed brows. "Don't know how to what?"

"Use Twitter. Usually Rosie posts for me. If anyone does."

"A smart, independent woman like you? I would've thought that would make you crazy."

She shrugged. "I didn't want an account, but my contract mandated it. So, I created one. But I don't like to share anything."

His adorable smirk quirked the corners of his mouth. "Now that makes sense. I've noticed your rebellious streak."

"I—"

He held up a hand. "Don't defend yourself. It wasn't a criticism. Rebellious hellions are sexy."

"Hellion? I—" She closed her mouth so quickly her teeth clicked. Sexy? Her? Had anyone ever called her sexy? Well, other than the creepy pervs who stalked her online and probably referred to anything with two X-chromosomes as sexy. "I'm not . . . any of those things. I'm just normal and ordinary."

One eyebrow cocked, that teasing look danced in his eyes. "By definition, a psychic is *para*normal and *extra*ordinary. And I love your fiery temperament when you get worked up. As I said, not a criticism. My life has only improved since you entered it. Way more exciting and satisfying."

Her mouth worked to produce words but had apparently become disconnected from her brain, which no longer issued command over anything. Her heart galloped out of control. Her stomach turned upside down. Her hands shook and sweated. Coherent thought escaped her. "But you . . . I thought . . . we don't . . . " She took a deep breath. "Thank you. I like having you on the show. You . . . you make things better. I appreciate it."

He threw his head back and laughed. "Progress. Slow, but progress. I'll take it. I wish you were as fiery and passionate about everything in your life. Come here."

Before she knew what was happening, he grabbed her waist, turned her around, and pulled her close, resting his chin on her shoulder. She could barely breathe. "What are you—"

He took her hands in his, raised her phone, and opened Twitter. "Instead of relying on Rosie or me to handle this for you, why don't I teach you how to Twitter? Then you can be in control."

His chest vibrated against her back as he spoke. His cheek brushed against hers. Hyperaware of the nearness of his lips, she gulped. "Okay."

"Super simple," he instructed. "See my tweet here? This button with the arrows is to retweet. And actually, you can set your account to automatically retweet anything I tweet, plus anything we tweet from the show's account. Let's do that. You won't be able to add your own message to the post, but I'm rather skeptical you will anyway."

At the moment, with Sterling pressed against her, she was skeptical she would remember anything he was saying. She nodded anyway, aware she would probably agree with anything he said right now.

"There," he said. "I have the video of Ruth ready to retweet with a comment. Go ahead and type in something to your fans. Tell them this guy is harassing you and ask them to retweet the video of Ruth. Something like that."

The door opened and Rosie hurried into the trailer, accompanied by continuous shouts from the protestors. Her eyebrows shot up. "Oh. Sorry."

"Sterling is just teaching me to tweet," she said, face flushed.

"Is that what we're calling it these days?" Rosie's mouth curled into a smile. "I truly hate to interrupt but we have company out there."

"Yes, I saw," Sterling said. "He has a friend."

"He has more than one," Rosie corrected him.

Kimberly extracted herself from Sterling's arms and peered out the window again.

A car had parked at the curb. Several people clambered from the doors, cameras and phones in hand. They all wore matching red shirts and ball caps.

"What is happening?" she asked, opening the trailer door for a better look.

The newcomers joined Ezekiel, increasing his presence to seven people. A neighbor jogging by watched the small cluster of people. One of the new arrivals shoved a camera in the man's face.

The jogger slowed his pace. "What are you doing? Why are you recording me?"

"We're allowed to be here," the man with the camera yelled. "This is a free country. We have a right to be on public property!"

The jogger swatted at the camera. "This is my neighborhood. Get that out of my face."

"You can't silence us!" the man yelled. His fellow red-capped compatriots joined in.

Kimberly heard bits and pieces of the uproar, all of them concerning freedom of speech and the right to be on public property.

"These new guys don't seem to care about Kimberly at all," Rosie noted. "They're just harassing the neighbors and yelling 'First Amendment' over and over."

"Great," Kimberly said. "That will endear us to the neighborhood. We're the ones who attracted them."

"Oh, no," Sterling said, typing on his phone. "We're being targeted by these guys."

"What does that mean?" Kimberly leaned against him to view his phone screen.

"Your own phone would be blowing up if you turned on notifications. That will be the next lesson. This new group is targeting the show, claiming we're trying to silence Ezekiel Jackson and keep him from voicing his religious opinions, therefore violating his freedom of speech, as guaranteed by the Constitution. They've sent out a call to arms to all members of their group."

"What does that mean?" she asked again, still confused.

"It means things are about to get really nasty around here."

CHAPTER FOURTEEN

UNSURE where to begin tonight's session, Kimberly stood in the kitchen, waiting for something to tug at her psyche. Sterling had gone outside to collect soil samples. The rest of the crew fanned out to conduct EVP sessions and monitor cameras.

The protestors had disbanded at nightfall, thank goodness. "They must need food and sleep like the rest of us," Sterling had commented as they drove away. "Guess they're not demons after all."

She disagreed with that assessment but breathed a sigh of relief, grateful for the break. Until TJ wondered aloud if a second team would show up for the night shift and put her back on edge. So far, no.

She grasped her quartz crystal and breathed deeply, grateful for a few quiet moments alone. So often people pulled at her from so many directions—the investigation, her fans, the promotional demands of the show—she felt like a drained battery in desperate need of recharge.

A few minutes alone was more decadent to her than a slice of lava cake. And healthier.

She withdrew inward, shifting focus away from all the distractions of the world, and focused her energy on her crown chakra, a lighthouse beacon she cast into the spirit world, inviting connection.

The darkened house faded away. The diffuse moonlight blurred and dimmed. Her skin prickled, goose bumps rising on her arms and legs.

A hand rested on her shoulder and pushed her forward.

She gasped and turned, eyes flying open. No one stood behind her, yet someone shared the space. She could feel the presence.

Closing her eyes again, she invited connection, determined not to break it this time.

She took several steps in the direction the hand had propelled her.

A soft heartbeat beckoned her. Concentrating on the sound, she moved forward, eyes closed, hands out.

She heard something fall directly behind her but fought the urge to look.

Expecting to collide with a wall or trip over furniture at any moment, she nonetheless allowed the heartbeat to guide her steps. The house around her became muffled, muted, as the heartbeat grew stronger. Vaguely aware of approaching foot-steps, she cocked her head at a sudden intake of breath.

"Ms. Wantland?" TJ discovered her just as another object clattered to the ground.

He would record, she was sure in the quiet recesses of her mind not occupied with the beating heart drawing her nearer. She lifted a foot and placed it perfectly on the first step of the staircase.

Dimly aware of garbled, echoing voices, she continued ascending the staircase. She knew when the steps ended, turned left and pressed forward, one foot after another, until the air around her clung to her skin and throat, thick as gelatin.

She peeled her eyes open. Faith's room. The pounding heart battered against her ears. The walls pulsed, reverberating with each bass beat. Beads of sweat collected at her temples and streaked down her face. She was pushed forward through the thick air. No, something pulled her. Both?

She dropped to her knees beside the bed, the beating so loud her head throbbed. Gritting her teeth against the pain, she thrust a hand beneath the bed. The space radiated heat like an oven, roasting her hand and arm. She groped the floor regardless, knowing the burning heat manifested on a psychic level and would not leave her physically harmed. Difficult to believe while her skin baked.

Her hand brushed past a blazing object. She clutched it, searing her hand as though she'd grabbed a hot skillet, the rhythmic beat throbbing against her palm. Fairly certain she screamed, she pulled the pulsating, living thing from under the bed.

She turned around. Her crew stood in the doorway. She wanted to reassure them everything would be okay. But her hand burned, and she couldn't breathe or speak.

She noticed something out of the corner of her eye and spun to get a better look. Letters scrawled across the wall sent her pulse pounding. Regardless of the heat radiating from her skin, the writing sent a cold shiver rattling down her spine. Bright red as though carved into flesh, the warning scared her more than anything they'd seen in this location yet.

The walls will run with their blood.

KIMBERLY SAT ON THE JOHNSONS' couch breathing deeply as her hands shook. Rosie plied her with soothing tea and rubbed her temples. No one on the crew had seen the threat bleeding from the wall. She'd seen it. Felt the malice oozing from each letter.

Michael sat beside her and rested a hand on her back. "You okay?"

"Yes. Shaken, but okay. And worried for the safety of the

family. This spirit is threatening them. He's out for blood. Faith is only the beginning."

Rosie lifted the poultice from her right hand. "I've never seen a spiritually charged object actually burn you."

Sterling sat beside her and gingerly rested her hand in his palm. He stroked the angry red skin with his fingertips. His touch sent a warm tingle through her body. But also stung the burn. She winced and pulled away.

His brow furrowed. "Your skin is hot to the touch. I don't see how you could fake that."

"I didn't fake it. Nor inflict it on myself intentionally. I'm not into self-harm."

TJ approached her, the planchette in his hand. He held the plastic device beside her burn. "Look. The burn matches the shape of this exactly. You can't heat plastic hot enough to burn."

"*Au contraire, mon frère*," Sterling replied, his furrowed brow showing his deep concern. "You can. The plastic would melt eventually. But skin burns at a lower temperature than plastic melts."

"But it was under the girl's bed," TJ reminded him. "What would have heated it up? It's not like she reached into a hot oven and grabbed it."

"Didn't say I had the answer." Sterling rubbed the back of his neck. "Just stating the facts."

Snickers whimpered and nudged past TJ, pushing through the people until he stood in front of her. He nuzzled her hand, sniffed carefully, then licked the afflicted palm.

"Hey, gross! Stop that!" Sterling said. He waved his hands at the dog. "Shoo! Go on! Shoo!"

Snickers jumped back a step, looking startled and confused.

"Sterling, it's okay," she said. "He can tell I'm hurt and is trying to help. Dogs lick wounds to help them heal."

Sterling scowled. "Dogs lick a lot of things, most of them covered in germs. Which he will transfer to your hand, which is currently injured and thus at increased risk for infection."

"It won't get infected. I think he's sweet." She patted her lap and smiled at Snickers. "It's okay. Come here."

The dog rested his head on her lap and licked her hand again. She stroked his furry head.

"Really?" Sterling said. "There's no way that's good for a burn."

Rosie scooted between her and Snickers. "I need to redress that anyway."

She watched her personal assistant spread a homemade concoction over the palm. Other than a base of aloe vera, she had no idea what was in it. The gel-based goo felt cool and soothing, however, so she didn't care. "Didn't Ruth say Faith's problems began with a burn that wouldn't heal? A curling iron burn from her slumber party?"

Rosie wound a handkerchief around the slathered hand. "Sure did. But I didn't believe that bit about the curling iron for a moment. The girl's burn looks nothing like the barrel of a hot iron."

"Why didn't you say something?"

"I'm not a rat. No way would I call out Faith in front of her parents and on television. Must be some reason she told them she hurt herself on a curling iron."

"You could've told me."

"Eh. I figured if it was important, you'd figure it out."

"Now she'll definitely be outed on television," TJ said. "We'll have to confront her."

Kimberly frowned. "I don't like that harsh approach. I think Faith nearly confided in me this morning. Let's give her another day. If she doesn't come to me on her own, I'll compare the planchette to her burn off camera before tomorrow night and see how she reacts."

"I'd prefer info sooner to later," Michael said, "but I can see how outing publicly is a bad idea. No one say a word. We will wait for Faith to come to us."

Rosie finished bandaging her hand and held her palms over

the wound, eyes closed. "Let me know if this is too much."

Sterling looked back and forth between them. "She's not touching you. What would be too much?"

"Reiki," she murmured as her hand around the burn warmed gently. "She's using healing energy. It stimulates the immune system and encourages blood flow."

"Ah. I'll go make an ice pack. I think you'll find that far more effective than dog saliva and 'energy.'"

"Get out of here, you non-believer," Rosie said, fighting a smile. "You'll break my concentration."

"That's perfect, by the way," she told Rosie. "I can tell you're drawing the heat away."

"Good. When he gets back with the ice pack, you let him put it on your hand."

"I will." She frowned a bit, miffed Rosie felt the urge to comment.

Rosie cocked an eyebrow. "I mean it. He's helping the best way he knows how."

"I know. I will."

"Good. He's very protective of you."

"Hello? I can read his spectrum. I know how he feels better than anyone."

"He's good for you. Don't hold him at arm's length. Or push him away. You never know how long you have with someone so make every moment count."

A wave of sorrow rolled off Rosie. What was that about? Had Lorenzo dumped her? No, no, no. Her stylist was so happy with him. He couldn't have dumped her. "Rosie, what's wrong? What haven't you told me?"

Sterling returned with a plastic bag full of ice, which he was wrapping a kitchen towel around. "Here you go. Let's get some ice on that burn."

Rosie rocked back on her heels. "Excellent timing. I just finished."

She needed to know what was upsetting Rosie. "But—"

"Later." Rosie glanced at Sterling. "Please."

Sterling situated himself beside her and rested the ice on her hand as if she were made of glass. "How's that?"

Even if she hated him—and she didn't—she wouldn't have been able to resist the concern on his face, his tender touch, or the warmth she felt beating in his heart chakra. Her own heart skipped a beat before softening a little.

But Rosie knew her well. Her protective barrier clamped down hard on her softening heart. She fought against it. "Much better. Thank you."

He beamed, and she thrilled at his crinkled eyes.

"Keep an eye on this," he said. "Whatever caused the burn, if it doesn't improve soon, I'm going to insist you see a doctor."

She wanted to remind him that Faith's parents had taken her to the doctor too, and nothing came of it. Only resolving the haunting, cleaning the house of the malicious entity bent on harming the family, would allow the wounds to heal. Explaining that to him would be a waste of time. He would never believe it. "Agreed. But I'm sure it will clear up."

Snickers padded across the room, sat at her feet, and whined.

"What is it, little guy?" she asked.

The dog laid back his ears and stared down the hall.

"I think he wants to show me something," she said.

"I think he just wants your attention."

Snickers curled his upper lip at Sterling, then whined at her again.

"Can you show me?" she asked.

The dog yipped and scrambled backward several steps, toenails clacking on the hardwood floor.

"What's that, Lassie?" Sterling cupped a hand around his ear. "You say Timmy fell down the well? Again?"

She swore Snickers gave him the stink eye. "He knows you're teasing him, Sterling. Stop."

Sterling threw his hands in the air and rolled his eyes.

She stood to follow Snickers, who scampered down the hall

and up the stairs, stopping every few feet to ensure she followed. He led her to a closed door. He stared at it intently, one paw lifted from the ground, nose quivering.

"What is this, boy? A closet?"

The dog whimpered, touched the door with his nose, then backed up a few steps.

She grasped her crystal and placed her bandaged hand against the door, hoping for an indication of what drew the dog.

"Do you feel anything?" TJ asked, recording the entire scene.

She appreciated the boy's intuitive instinct and suspected he was a sensitive as well. He always managed to be where she needed him. "Nothing overwhelming."

Snickers scratched at the door.

Sterling crossed his arms. "Maybe that's the closet where they keep the dog treats? Tossing out the most simple and obvious possibility."

"Dogs are very attuned to spirit activity, Sterling."

Sterling sighed, grasped the knob, and cracked the door.

"Wait! You don't know what's behind that!"

He peeked through the crack. "Oh, my gosh."

Her heart hammered. "What? What is it?"

He pushed the door open. "Absolutely nothing. Stairs. And, no, they're not dripping in ectoplasm. Or glowing. Or covered in vines. Or anything else weird. Just stairs."

"Where do they lead?" she asked, tentatively peering into the small enclosure. It wasn't large enough to really be called a closet. The space housed only a ladder built directly onto the wall.

Sterling tipped his head back. "Up. They lead up."

She glowered at him. "You're so helpful." She pushed past him and settled her foot on the first rung. As she reached to grasp a step above her with her uninjured hand, ready to climb, he gripped her waist.

"Uh, no. I'm not letting you climb up there first."

"Sterling! Let go!"

He lifted her off the ladder entirely too easily, despite her attempts to hold on. "Nope. You can follow me up."

"You can't do that!" she huffed as he deposited her feet back on the hallway floor.

"Sorry, but I can. One of the perils of weighing all of a hundred pounds. Eat a burger and put on some weight."

"You don't even believe the dog has a reason for leading us here." She smoothed her shirt and attempted to push past him a second time.

His arm shot out to block her. "True. But that doesn't mean their attic is a paradigm of safety. I'll check it first, and you can follow."

Caught off guard by his nearness, she opened and closed her mouth a few times, struggling to think of a witty retort and failing miserably. Retorts weren't her thing. She worked alone. Or at least she used to. She watched him climb the ladder until her gaze lingered on how nicely his jeans curved around his butt. She shook her head, averted her eyes, and scrambled after him, convinced Snickers would prove more helpful during the investigation than Sterling.

CHAPTER FIFTEEN

AT THE TOP of the ladder, Kimberly accepted Sterling's outstretched hand. He tugged and she landed on the floor. "Whoa."

"Yeah, seriously. Gain a little weight. You're so light you'd be easy to grab off the street and shove into a car."

She shook her head and blinked. "I'm sorry. What?"

"You worry so much about stalkers, but you weigh nothing. Put on some weight so you'll be harder to kidnap."

"I suspect Patty Hearst might not agree with that tactic." Brow furrowed, she started to explain all the ways that was wrong. Then she noticed the glint in his eye and the corner of his mouth slightly upturned. She squinted and gave him a shove. "You goof! I never know when you're teasing."

"Good. Though you seem to be catching on. And honestly a couple pounds wouldn't kill you." He poked her in the side.

She jumped. "Stop that!"

"Oh, you're ticklish. I will file that away for later." He rubbed his hands together.

She pointed at him. "Don't even think about it!"

A thump ended their conversation.

She whirled. "What was that? Did you see something, TJ?"

TJ sounded sheepish. "I had the camera on you two, recording you flirting."

After she'd just been thinking how he always managed to catch the right moment on camera. She bit her tongue to keep from saying anything discouraging though. "We weren't flirting. Either of you see a light switch?" The light from the opening below illuminated only the area around them, and she didn't relish the idea of running her hands along unknown surfaces.

"Here," Sterling said. With a click, he stood in a pool of light from a bare bulb hanging from the ceiling. He let go of the light pull and brushed his hands together. "Cobwebs. My favorite."

She turned, taking in the dimly lit attic. The sloping ceiling followed the roofline, narrowing at the edges. Dust accumulated in furry film on the tops of stacked boxes. A few pieces of old, worn-out furniture sagged in the dark, low corners, napping in their shadowy resting places.

What could Snickers have detected? Why did he lead her here? She clasped her quartz stone, breathed deeply, and opened her senses to any disturbances. Her burned hand throbbed painfully. She did her best to ignore it and focus on the attic. "Anyone see anything amiss? Something out of place? Anything to explain a thump?"

"Maybe a tree branch banged against the side of the house," Sterling suggested.

She went to the window and peered out. "Good suggestion. But no tree branches within striking distance."

"I appreciate you considered the explanation," Sterling said, exuding delight from his heart chakra.

"Would have made things easier."

Trees reminded her of the noose she'd seen swinging from the tree in the backyard. She shivered and rubbed her hands up and down her arms.

"You cold?" Sterling asked.

She realized she was. The attic could store sides of meat. Her teeth chattered as she answered. "It's chilly up here."

TJ and Sterling shared a glance, brows furrowed.

"It's actually the opposite of chilly," Sterling said. "It's warm and stuffy."

She looked to TJ for confirmation, but he shook his head, eyes concerned behind his thick-rimmed black glasses. "I'm roasting. But let me switch to the FLIR."

While TJ shuffled cameras, she reached out with her sixth sense. A burning odor irritated her nose, like ozone after a lightning strike. The air crackled with residue, raising her hair on end. Her skin prickled.

She looked down. A small jumble of objects lay on the floor. Squatting, she took a closer look before picking up a teddy bear. Something metallic fell to the floor and rolled away. She grabbed it before it rolled out of sight.

"What did you find?" Sterling asked.

TJ moved closer, cameras in hand. "Look, Ms. Wantland! I'm using both cameras at the same time! I've never even seen Stan do this!"

"Good job, TJ. Sterling, it was a ring," she said, peering up at him. "I noticed this cluster of things, picked up the stuffed animal, and the ring rolled away."

Sterling bent down and poked through the items, lifting a small book, a necklace, and an ink pen. "What is all this mess? They just tossed this stuff up into the attic? The rest of the space is pretty well organized and well kept. Why this pile of junk?"

"I don't think this is junk. Look at the ring. It looks vintage and potentially valuable."

Sterling put his hand out to accept the jewelry. When she brushed against him, he grabbed her hand. "Your hands are like ice!"

"I told you I'm cold. It's freezing up here."

"And I told you it's stuffy and hot. Not cold at all. I'm sweating."

"I guess you have a higher metabolism."

"Not that high. More likely you're going into shock from that burn on your hand. I think you need medical attention."

"You're both wrong," TJ said. "She has a cold spot directly around her."

"What?" Sterling asked.

"Come see. It's quite clear. Vivid and distinct blue aura around her signature body heat."

"Come see? I'm standing right next to her. I don't feel a cold spot."

"You're not close enough. It's specifically affecting only her. Never seen this before. I think it might be an attack."

"That makes absolutely no sense."

TJ shrugged. "But I can see it quite clearly. Look."

She sifted through the other objects in the little pile as TJ and Sterling squabbled over the FLIR images. Pack rats collected "treasures" into little piles like this, but they hid them in their nests. She didn't see signs of rodent activity. Besides, this was out in the open, not tucked away in a nest.

She picked up the small notebook, turning it over in her hands. *My Daily Prayers* the cover read above a picture of a cross, a dove, and water. Not a notebook. A prayer book. She looked again at the items. Ruth had mentioned in the family interview that things had disappeared from the house. Were these the missing belongings?

She reached for the teddy bear, but the terrible odor she'd smelled when they first arrived at the Johnsons' house filled the attic. She could barely breathe, the acrid stench burning her throat and lungs. Foul air choked her until she coughed. Her head began to pound. Pressure built as though two massive hands rested on either side of her head, squeezing like a vise grip.

Waves of nausea struck. She leaned forward on her hands as the room around her lurched, the floor tilting askew. Afraid she would slide along the slanted floorboards, she tried in vain to grab onto something. Dizzy, she couldn't move. She heard TJ and

Sterling call out to her, but she couldn't answer. Hands grasped her hunched form, pulling her, until strong arms scooped her off the floor.

She rested her head against Sterling's chest as he cradled her in his arms, comforted by his scent, which overpowered the rotten odor surrounding her. His heavy footsteps clunked against the attic floor, extracting her from the foul environment. As they drew closer to the door and fresh air, the pain in her head subsided a little. His lips brushed her ear. "Can you get down the stairs?"

She nodded, anxious to leave the horrid space. Who was this entity attacking her for intruding? He lowered her feet to the floor but kept her tucked close, one arm curled around her, steadying her against his warm body. She longed to press her frigid hands against him.

"Let me go down first. You can even sit on my shoulder if you need to. TJ?"

"Yeah?"

"You getting all this?"

"Yes, sir!"

"I want someone to see this and try to argue there's nothing in this house making people sick. I'll go back up and collect samples, maybe use a carbon monoxide tester."

"And hopefully we can catch the spirit on the FLIR. Nasty little beast, isn't he? Went right for Ms. Wantland. Full-blown attack."

Sterling shook his head and reached to steady her as he descended the steps out of the attic. Fighting nausea, she managed to turn herself around and place her hands on the floor. She felt about with a foot until it connected with the first step. Wobbly, she didn't trust herself not to tumble to the floor below. Sterling somehow managed to situate himself just below her. "Here. Sit on my shoulder. Or at least lean on me for support."

Too weak and disoriented to argue or attempt the stairs independently, she did as instructed. Somehow, they inched their way back to the floor below.

As soon as he neared the ground, Sterling yelled over his shoulder. "Rosie! Kimberly's sick! Come quick!"

Shaking, she slid from his shoulder, gripped the handrail, stepped off the final stair, and lowered herself to the floor, leaning against the wall. Sterling crouched beside her. He rested a hand against her forehead, patted her cheek, and peered at her anxiously until Rosie flew up the staircase and took over.

Snickers whined nearby. She turned to assure the dog she was okay, that she would be fine. But he wasn't looking at her at all. He peered up the stairs, his gaze intent as though watching something.

She motioned to TJ, who bent low to hear her. "Let Stan get this for the show. You take the FLIR and see what the dog is watching. Maybe you can capture something helpful. Have Elise record Snicker's behavior. Something dreadful is up there. I need to know what we're dealing with."

"Yes, Ms. Wantland." The junior camera operator rushed to carry out her instructions.

Rosie rubbed lemon oil on her temples. Sterling snatched up the bottle and caressed her hands with the invigorating oil. The fog began to lift from her mind. Her sour stomach lingered, and for one horrible moment she feared she would vomit right there in the hallway, on camera, in front of Sterling.

"You look extremely pale," Sterling noticed. "White as a ghost, if you'll pardon the pun."

She clutched her abdomen as another wave of nausea overwhelmed her.

"Come on, the joke wasn't that bad," Sterling said. Though he kept his voice light, she saw concern in his eyes.

"What is it, girl?" Rosie asked.

"I feel like I'm going to puke. That horrible smell filled the attic while we were up there."

She saw Rosie look to Sterling, who shook his head, his brow deeply furrowed.

"What else?" Rosie asked.

"My head felt like it was going to explode. It still hurts, though not as badly."

"And she complained of cold," Sterling added. "She was shivering, and her hands felt like ice. I suspect she's going into shock."

Rosie pawed through her satchel, much like a traditional doctor's black bag but filled with the herbs, crystals, oils, and teas she used to support Kimberly's psychic health. "She's not in shock from that little psychic burn. She's been attacked by a spirit that wants her gone. But he doesn't know who he's dealing with. Kimberly never quits. And I'm here to keep her going."

Sterling sighed and shook his head a bit. "How can I help?"

Rosie withdrew dropper bottles full of tinctures then placed her hands in front of Kimberly and closed her eyes. "Your spectrum is out of whack. You're scared."

She lifted one eyebrow and smiled. "I could have told you that."

Rosie peered at the bottles, presumably weighing her treatment options.

Snickers whined. Kimberly turned to see why and heard a scuffling from the attic. TJ worked his way down the ladder, something tucked under one arm.

"I think I found what caused the thump upstairs, Ms. Wantland." He carried a simple file box. "I found it on its side."

She eyed the plastic container, hinged lid clasped in place. No lock. No label. She retracted her hand from Sterling—still massaging—and reached for it.

The box nearly jumped from TJ's hands and into hers. Startled, she dropped it in front of her. The dull thud it caused sounded identical to the thump they'd heard upstairs. Then again, did thuds and thumps really differ all that much?

Snickers spun around, teeth bared, and crept closer, nose quivering, snuffling so hard he snorted like a pig.

Sterling scowled and held out a hand. "Stop that! Go on! Shoo! Is this dog bipolar? What the heck?"

Crouching low, the dog wormed his way past Sterling until he reached the box.

Sterling threw an arm in front of her. "I won't have that mutt bite her. She's endured enough injuries."

Kimberly watched closely. "I think he's disturbed by the box." Though she defended Snickers, she didn't push Sterling's arm away. She wasn't sure enough to risk a bite.

Sterling scooped it up. "What the hell is in it?" He popped the clasp and rocked the lid back. "Oh, my gosh."

She heard a collective gasp from the gathered crew. Scarcely able to breathe, she managed to whisper, "What is it?"

He spun the box as she leaned closer.

"Paperwork," he announced, inspecting a page. "Boring, filed paperwork. Property documents, looks like to me."

"Property documents? May I?" She reached for the box, but before she could grab it, one page from the very back of the box slid to the floor beside her.

Sterling shook his head. "What the—" He peered into the box, shook it slightly, and tapped the side. No other paperwork slid out.

"I have a camera on Kimberly. Caught the phenomenon," Stan assured them.

Burning hand throbbing, arm hair standing on end, she reached for the official-looking page. The thin, yellowed paper crackled between her fingers then sizzled with charged energy. Her eyes scanned the faded letters, typed so long ago. It was a claim deed issued by the Homestead Office to James Loveless on April 24, 1889.

Why did the spirit bring this to her attention? The family's ancestors had no reason to cause problems or inflict harm. Who did? Whatever presence had infiltrated the house and targeted

Faith seemed willing to do anything to get what he wanted. But what did he want? Powerful and fired up, he must have a strong motivation feeding his manifestations.

Michael squatted beside her. "What are you getting from it? Images? Visions? Connection?"

"It's charged, but I'm not getting anything else. No helpful information."

Sterling continued to fiddle with the box. "What caused that to—"

The hallway lights flickered. The closet door leading to the attic slammed shut.

"I think it's time for another family meeting," she said. "Tomorrow morning as soon as we can gather them together."

<h1 style="text-align:center">CHAPTER SIXTEEN</h1>

KIMBERLY DUG at her eyes as Sterling pulled his i8 into the Stone Lion Inn driveway. She ached from head to toe, muscles screaming for rest, head pounding, eyes watering and gritty. Her burned palm throbbed, reminding her of this spirit's potential to inflict damage.

Sterling parked, ran around the car, and extended his hand to help her out. "I'm exhausted. I don't know if I can keep up with you."

She'd predicted he'd soon tire of her demanding schedule but was too tired to enjoy even a moment of being right. When she stumbled over her own feet, he caught her. Eh, who cared about being right anyway? She leaned against him and murmured, "I'm glad you're here."

They discovered Stan and TJ checking cameras in strategic locations.

"Batteries are good," Stan shared. "We'll see what we catch tonight."

She nodded, not terribly concerned about this location. The main investigation occupied her thoughts, the girl's health her paramount concern.

Sterling hesitated when they reached her door. "I'll leave my phone on again, but I can't promise it will wake me. I suspect I'm going to sleep like a coma patient." His mouth stretched into a yawn as if to verify his concern.

"I understand," she assured him. "I expect to be sound asleep myself." This was why intimate relationships were impossible for her. Work took all her extended waking hours and then some. How could she add an additional demand to the schedule she juggled? It wouldn't be fair to the other person. She was fortunate Rosie turned out to be such a wonderful friend. Otherwise, what support would she have?

Rosie. She forgot to ask her personal assistant why she looked and sounded so down. Something had happened. She needed to find out what.

"Hey." Sterling shook her slightly. "Are you falling asleep on your feet?"

She shook her head. "Sorry. Mind wandering. I'm completely out of it. Better say goodnight before I collapse."

"Goodnight." He pulled her close, enveloping her in a hug. As he leaned back, his lips grazed her cheek.

The not-quite-kiss sent a jolt coursing through her veins. She sucked in a breath before stammering a reply. "Goodnight."

"Sweet dreams." He squeezed her hand.

"Sweet dreams." *Where did that come from?* She didn't say things like "Sweet dreams." She opened her door and bolted into the room before she did something stupid like follow him into his. After closing the door behind her, she leaned against it. Her gaze crept to the window, sheer curtains still drawn from last night. No dark silhouette hovered there. Thank goodness.

Her heart hammered in her chest. That didn't qualify as a kiss. Not even a peck on the cheek. He'd barely touched her, yet he sent her heart racing. Must be the fatigue. She needed sleep.

She skipped the shower, wiping her face with a makeup-removing cloth and sliding into pajamas. She fell into the bed.

But couldn't sleep. Her thoughts galloped out of control, causing her stomach to churn. She still didn't know what entity harassed the Johnsons or why. She'd experienced some visions, but they didn't seem to add up to anything. The pieces weren't clicking together.

What was wrong with Rosie? What was she going to do about Sterling? How did he spark such an overwhelming response in her with so little effort?

She rolled over and pulled the blankets over her head, wondering if she would be this restless and out of sorts if Sterling was in the bed beside her, snuggling close. *Ugh*. She needed to solve this haunting and move on. But her brain wasn't going to make any progress in its current addled state. She tried to go to a comforting, relaxing happy place. And could think only of Sterling spooned around her, nuzzling her neck, his presence reassuring. She didn't worry about strange noises in the night or menacing shadows at her window when he was close.

Why was that? And what did she want to do about it?

KIMBERLY SAT at the huge wooden table the next morning nibbling toast. She'd finally drifted into a few hours of fitful sleep. And felt completely unrested, like she'd been hit by a truck. She sipped the very dark coffee she'd filled a mug with. She would need a lot of coffee to keep going.

Her crew looked just as exhausted. No one chattered. Rosie stared at her phone morosely, picking at a muffin. TJ had cleared his plate and appeared to be reviewing recordings. Even Michael, who normally attempted to energize morale, sat quietly and seemed to be brooding over something. This did not bode well for the day. Negative energy never helped.

Sterling stomped into the room, haggard, his eyes sunken. He looked like he hadn't slept either. And he looked pissed. His eyebrows crunched together into an angry point above his stormy eyes. He poured coffee and slouched into a chair across the table from her. He didn't take food and he didn't address anyone. Out of character for him.

Was he upset that she had responded to his first gentle attempt at a kiss by fleeing into her room? It hadn't been intentional exactly. She hadn't thought about it. He'd surprised her, that was all. Still, she could see how that could have been interpreted as a rejection. She wasn't close enough to be able to read his spectrum. She couldn't be sure.

She opened her mouth to attempt light conversation and see how he responded. But before she got one word out, Gloria bustled into the dining room. "Good morning!"

The crew let out a collective groan in reply.

"Is breakfast okay? Ms. Wantland, I made sure we had some skim milk this morning."

"Oh, thank you. Yes, breakfast is wonderful. We're all a little beaten down by the investigation, I'm afraid. This one is kicking our butts."

TJ piped up. "Check this out though. We got some super-cool footage here at the inn last night! One of the cameras caught the attic door slamming. And another camera was in the hall on the other side. Which means we can see no one was on either side of the door at the moment it slammed! The footage is time stamped."

Gloria beamed. "I love it! What did I tell you? This place brims with activity."

Kimberly drained her mug and stood to peer over TJ's shoulder, withholding exuberance until she'd seen it for herself. She paused. She was starting to sound like Sterling. Michael and Stan moved so they could see. Sterling leaned over to watch as well. She tried to read his spectrum, but her own energy was such a jumbled mess, she couldn't focus.

"Okay," TJ started. "This camera we left in the attic. I was hoping to catch, like, the boxes of toys topple over, like Gloria said she sometimes finds them. I haven't seen anything like that yet, but around one thirty this morning, the door closes. Watch."

Her junior camera operator hit PLAY. They all leaned in closer to the small screen, mesmerized by the black and white images of the attic. Sure enough, as they watched, the door swung closed. It slammed. Hard. Which meant there was force behind it. This was not simply a door drifting closed due to an air current or an incline that allowed gravity to finally gain the upper hand.

"See?" TJ turned bright eyes to Kimberly's face, as if gauging her reaction. "Now watch this." He picked up the other camera. "Watch the timer. They're the same. At one thirty . . . there! Nobody in the hall and the door closes by itself."

All faces turned toward Sterling. While Gloria clapped her hands with delight, Kimberly waited for Sterling to offer an explanation—a thin thread, not visible on the recording, attached to the door handle, used to pull the door even though no one is in the hallway when it happens. Or something.

Sterling pressed his fingers to his mouth, apparently deep in thought. He gestured at TJ. "Can you put a camera in the hall outside my door tonight?"

TJ did a double take. "Yeah. Sure, man. Of course."

She glanced at Michael and Rosie who both returned her dumbfounded expression. "Did something . . . Are you hoping to record something in particular?"

Sterling worked his jaw, mouth pursed, before he answered. "I want to find out who's knocking on my door at night."

"It happened again this morning?" Kimberly asked.

He shook his head. "It happened all night. Every time I fell asleep, someone banged on my door. But every time I opened it, the hall was empty."

Gloria clapped again. "It's her! It's Augusta. This is what she does! Knocks on doors and climbs in bed with people. I think she's lonely and wants someone to play with her."

Kimberly scowled at her. "You know he doesn't believe in ghosts. Plus, he's sleep deprived. He clearly doesn't share your delight. Please be considerate."

"At first I was afraid your nighttime creeper was back," Sterling said. "I thought you needed me. But time after time, no one was there. Whoever it was is darned quick. I'm going to be impressed. I mean, I got pretty irritated and just waited by the door the last couple of times. Opened it immediately. No one."

"Did you get any sleep at all?" Kimberly asked.

"Not really. I feel awful. Never been so tired in my life." He ran a hand down his face.

Michael went back to his seat and threw back the rest of his orange juice. "Listen, we can get through footage review without you. You can join us later."

"I mean, I think I slept from six to eight. Once the sun started coming up, it stopped."

"Go back to your room and sleep a few more hours. It'll do you a world of good."

"You sure you wouldn't mind?" Sterling asked.

"Not at all. It happens."

"Did y'all see what a stir you're causing?" Gloria asked.

"Stir? You mean Jackson and his First Amendment cronies?"

Gloria flipped on a television and switched to a news station. The cameras recorded a big crowd outside the Johnsons' house. Kimberly watched, horrified, as the camera operator panned down the sidewalk, focusing on angry faces and signs demanding she "Get out of Guthrie or else!"

She regretted the toast she'd eaten as her stomach churned anew. "How has he managed to draw together so many people? And so quickly?"

Michael shook his head. "It is rather impressive. In a terrible way."

"And so early in the morning," Rosie added. "Don't they have jobs?"

"It's Saturday, darlin'," Michael reminded her.

Rosie sighed. "So they jumped out of bed early to be here? They ought to have better things to do with their time. Like sleeping in."

"I can't cope with that," Kimberly whispered.

"Asshats," Sterling murmured. He pushed away from the table and headed for the hallway that led to their rooms.

Her heart fell as she watched him walk away, but she knew some sleep would be good for him and wanted him to feel better. She called after him, "I hope you get some good, uninterrupted sleep this time." She turned to Michael. "Maybe we can conduct footage review here. I don't think I can handle all that yelling and negativity."

Gloria seemed eager to help. "I'll let you use whatever space you need. You say the word and it's yours."

Kimberly smiled her gratitude. The woman may have been a bit overeager for her taste most of the time, but she clearly wanted to help. "Thank you for that. Can we, Michael?"

"Sweetie, the equipment is all set up at the house. The computers, the cameras. We can't. Besides, you said you want to meet with the family this morning."

"The family." She looked at Michael, then the others in the room, concern creeping across all their faces. "What will they do? Should we suggest they don't return home at all? They'd be much better off staying at the hotel."

Michael pulled his cell phone from a pocket. "I'll call and make sure they're aware of what's happening."

Sterling rounded the corner from the hallway, shrugging into his leather jacket. "I'll take her, Michael. No sense having her step out of the van with her face on it. No way we can sneak her past them if we announce her presence that way. You ready, Kimberly?"

"I thought you were going to sleep?" she said, jumping to her feet. Even though she knew he really needed to rest, she couldn't lie to herself about wanting him by her side. This gesture meant the world to her.

"And leave you to that pack of wolves? I don't think so." He pulled his keys from his pocket and nodded to the rest of the crew. "You guys be careful when you arrive. No way to be surreptitious in the company vehicle."

Stan stood and wrapped one hand around a fist. "I'll get the crew inside."

Sterling visibly shuddered. "I believe you will."

CHAPTER SEVENTEEN

Staring out of the windshield, Kimberly blinked several times but still couldn't believe her eyes. Who were all these people? Somehow, they were even more terrifying in person than they'd been on the television screen.

A news van sat parked across the street from the Johnsons' house, apparently hoping to catch a confrontation between her crew and the protestors, who no longer simply congregated on the sidewalk—their numbers had increased to the point that they spilled into the street as well, impeding cars attempting to creep past. Still, though they clogged the sidewalk and choked the street, not so much as one toe crossed over onto personal property.

Sterling pulled his car to the curb several houses down from the Johnsons'. "Someone needs to call the police to clear these guys out of the street. Someone not connected to the show." He adjusted his sunglasses and blew out a breath. After a quick glance over his shoulder, he shifted into reverse, rested his arm on her seat, and drove backwards. He maneuvered through the neighborhood until they were several blocks away then pulled into the empty driveway of an abandoned ramshackle ruins of a house.

A blast of negative energy radiated from the decaying remnants of a home. She raised a palm as if to shield herself and grabbed her quartz.

"You okay?" Sterling asked.

"Someone died here. Long ago. A woman. Violently. Gruesomely. Blood splattered . . . all over the room."

"Great. Of all the houses in all the neighborhood, I pulled into the driveway of murder house. Well, it looks the part." He threw the car into reverse and tried another driveway. "Better?"

She breathed a sigh of relief as the onslaught of negative psychic energy ceased. "Yes, much. Thank you for not questioning or doubting."

"I have a plan. It will only work once if it works at all. Get in the back and lie down." As she followed his instructions and clambered awkwardly into the cramped back seat, he wriggled out of his jacket and passed it to her. "Good thing you're so tiny or you wouldn't fit back there. Put this over yourself. Hide under it the best you can. The tinted windows will help."

She complied, realizing what he intended. Head on the leather seat, his leather jacket over her, she was surrounded by and very aware of the rugged scent enveloping her, partly Sterling's own particular fragrance. Before she could reign in her thoughts, she envisioned Sterling draped over her instead of the jacket. *So not the time.*

She stayed still, unable to see a thing, dreading what would happen when they reached the house. Why target her? Why? She wasn't hurting a soul. What did they hope to accomplish other than causing her and the Johnsons distress? She marveled that Sterling managed to stay so calm and levelheaded. Thank goodness he was here. Even sleepless and painfully tired, he insisted on making sure she got safely to the investigation. What would she do without him? She propped up on one elbow and peeped out from under the jacket.

"Won't they recognize you?" If he decided her show was

more trouble than it was worth, would he leave? She didn't want to go back to running things solo.

"Get back down!" He batted at her with one hand. "I don't know. Maybe. They might. Ezekiel posted that video of me arguing with him. Still, I'm not the target. Okay, here we go. Stay covered."

She heard the rowdy crowd as they approached the Johnsons' house and hated crouching down and hiding. The car slowed, and she heard Sterling murmur, "Come on, move. You're not allowed to impede traffic flow."

Curiosity pushed her to sit up and see what was happening. But she wasn't ready to provoke the inevitable confrontation just yet.

"Listen," Sterling said, his voice hard. "As soon as I turn into the driveway, all that attention will turn on us. I'll pull as close to the house as I can. You run for the door, okay?"

"They have to stay in the street, don't they?"

"In theory." Sterling's low timbre and hard tone scared her more than the periodic shouts from the crowd punctuating the mid-morning quiet of the neighborhood. "I'm at the driveway."

The car lurched and spun to the right, tossing her in the back seat as Sterling gunned the engine and whipped into the drive-way. She fought to hold herself steady as the car jerked to a sudden stop.

The butterfly door whooshed as it rose. Sterling popped out of the car and tipped his seat forward. "Go!"

She scrambled to straighten while remaining under the jacket and threw herself out the door. Terrified of tripping and sprawling face-first to the ground, she watched her feet, head ducked, heartbeat pounding in her ears.

The crowd went momentarily silent, presumably as they caught sight of her and collectively worked through the event unfolding in front of them. When one of the protestors yelled, "It's her!" the chanting and derogatory noises and comments erupted in earnest.

Tempted to sneak a glance, she fought the urge and scurried up the steps to the family home. To her surprise, the door opened as she approached, and Ruth pulled her inside. After waving a trotting Sterling through, the woman slammed the door, uttering something about God truly getting the last word.

Kimberly lowered Sterling's jacket and stated the obvious. "You're here."

Ruth nodded. "Michael called to warn me of the crowd and suggest perhaps we stay at the hotel, but we were already here by then. We came home early. Faith is not in good shape. She's staring into space. Won't answer us. Won't eat. Daniel and I have prayed so hard. I refuse to let myself believe that God isn't listening, but it's getting more difficult. We're good Christians, we go to church, we help others and strive not to sin. Faith is on the prayer chain at our church as well as other prayer chains at other churches. With so many praying for her, how can this be happening? How can God allow this to happen?"

Though she hadn't couched it in religious terms, Kimberly knew exactly how Ruth felt. She'd just been thinking virtually the same thing. Not normally a hugger—the influx of energy often flooded her when she experienced unbridled physical touch—she nonetheless grabbed the woman in a hug.

Ruth relaxed against her. Apparently hungry for comfort, the woman siphoned energy rather than dumping her own. Kimberly pushed positive energy toward her.

Ruth looked calmer when she lifted her head and wiped her eyes. "Do you pray, Kimberly? Will you pray with me?"

She hesitated and almost declined but realized prayer would further comfort Ruth. "Sure. Let's pray."

Ruth extended one hand to Sterling. "Won't you join our prayer circle?"

"Of course." If Sterling found this ridiculous, he hid it well, grasping their hands solemnly and bowing his head.

"Lord, we thank you for this day," Ruth began. "We thank you for Kimberly Wantland, her assistant Sterling, and the rest of her crew, who have adjusted their schedules to come to our aid. We thank you for the gifts you blessed Kimberly with, allowing her to help your children in need. We ask for your loving presence today. Guide Kimberly as she works to solve our problem. Guide Sterling as he works alongside her. Guide the entire crew as they seek to help us. Lord, we beseech you to protect us from evil forces that seek to harm your children. In this and in all things, we pray. Amen."

Not surprising, Sterling, raised Catholic, joined Ruth's final closing. "Amen."

Shocking, at least to Kimberly, she echoed, "Amen."

Sterling glanced at her as Ruth squeezed and released their hands. Why shouldn't she affirm Ruth's prayer? Maybe she would categorize herself spiritual rather than religious, but she wasn't anti-theistic. She sensed warmth and peace flowing from Ruth as she intoned the prayer. If it brought her and Daniel comfort, great. The more happiness and positive energy flowing through the planet, the better the spiritual atmosphere for everyone.

Snickers, who had been lying at Ruth's feet with his nose resting on crossed paws, stood. "Ahf-ahf."

Ruth graced the dog with a smile and a pat on the head, prompting his tail to wag. "We didn't train him to do that. But doesn't it sound like he's trying to say amen?"

Kimberly kept her smile firmly in place as she saw Sterling struggle not to laugh. "He's a very good dog. I can tell. He's been helping with the investigation, too."

"I'm glad to hear he hasn't been any trouble," Ruth said. "I'm going to start a big pot of coffee and will keep brewing all day. I doubt any of you got more sleep than we did, and we feel dreadful."

"I'll need it," Sterling said. "Thanks. Doubt we will venture out to the trailer much."

Kimberly's stomach sank. "I'll have to at least once. For makeup."

Sterling nodded. "We'll manage. They're just yelling. It can't hurt you."

If only he realized how that sort of negative energy affected her. If he felt it too, he would realize his statement wasn't entirely accurate. But she knew he meant physical injury, not spiritual distress. Though she felt the stress and anxiety in her body.

Ruth, on her way to the kitchen, stopped and turned back. "Don't you feel that, though? Something ominous in the air? Like a bad omen. It feels heavy and makes me anxious."

"I do," Kimberly said, surprised someone other than her picked up on the shift. "I think the toxic energy from the crowd is feeding the presence. Strengthening it."

"That sounds like a demon to me." Ruth frowned. "But you said it's not one."

"No, I believe this is a spirit with a personal vendetta. Someone once human, who lived and died with unfinished business and is seeking resolution. In fact, I think we're dealing with a very powerful—"

The crowd outside erupted once again. Snickers raised his hackles and scampered to the door, low growl rumbling in his throat.

She moved to the window and pushed the curtain aside only enough to peek out. From the side of the company van, her face peered back at her thoughtfully next to *The Wantland Files* logo. Protestors shook signs with extra vigor and shouted with more fervor as the doors opened. Stan jumped out first. He planted his feet, crossed his arms, and squared off against the crowd as if daring them to try anything. Michael, Rosie, and the others unloaded.

Her pulse kicked up a notch watching the agitated crowd.

"See?" Sterling said, resting a hand on her lower back. "Just noise. It can't hurt you."

"Maybe not physically, but it throws me off balance and drains my energy. Which won't help the investigation."

Ruth threw open the front door and ushered the crew inside, casting some serious stink eye on the noisy gathering in the street.

Rosie rushed to her side. "You okay, girl?"

"Yes. Sterling got me inside no problem."

Michael directed everyone to ignore the distractions as best they could and get started on footage review. "You okay, Kimmy?"

She pulled her gaze away from the angry mob and nodded. "As okay as I can be, considering."

"Come join us when you're ready. And then we can speak with the family when they're ready."

Ruth's forehead crinkled. "Speak with us again? We intended to stay out of the way."

"Kimmy has a few more questions for you. Hoping you can clarify some things, maybe offer a few more details."

"I think we've told you everything. But I'll let Daniel know. He wanted to be alone to pray. I think he's in our bedroom."

"Why don't I help with coffee and tea?" Rosie offered.

Michael clapped his hands together. "Let's get started on review, folks."

Everyone dispersed, leaving her alone again with Sterling. He stood with arms crossed, head cocked, and seemed to be evaluating her, lips curled in a bemused half smile.

"What's that look for?" she asked.

"I was surprised you agreed to pray with Ruth."

"Why?"

"Thought you don't approve of prayer and religion."

"I don't disapprove. Praying is Ruth's way of sharing positive energy. Everything she said was kind and supportive. Of course I welcome that. I need all the positive energy I can get to combat that negativity out in the street."

He shook his head slightly. "Every time I think I have you figured out, you surprise me. And for some reason, I like that."

"You like that I surprise you?"

"I like that you're complicated and interesting. You keep me guessing. You make me want to know more."

The intense look in his eyes seemed to search out her innermost thoughts, as if he hoped to catch a glimpse of her soul. She squirmed, not sure she was ready to share as much of herself as he appeared to be seeking. Laying bare her easily crushed heart didn't appeal to her. Even if this man was starting to convince her he would handle it with utmost care. Even if he did demonstrate genuine concern for her wellbeing, her wants, her needs. He protected her. Shielded her. Seemed ready to fight for her.

Maybe that was the problem. Men she'd dated typically focused on what she could do for them. Not initially, of course, but eventually the relationships settled into the same pattern again and again, draining her until she had to call it off. But Sterling didn't take. He offered. He gave. And, she realized, that made her suspicious. What did he want? He must want something in return. No guy had ever treated her this way and certainly never given her anything without wanting something in return—even if that something was only control. If she allowed her feelings for him to control her behavior, eventually the relationship would sour. And she didn't want that. She'd grown accustomed to his presence.

Something behind her caught his attention. His eyes cut away, the burning intensity gone.

"Ms. Wantland?"

She turned to see a hesitant Rebecca slinking into the living room, dragging a reluctant-looking Faith. "Hi, girls. How are you today?"

Rebecca crept closer, eyes darting toward the kitchen. "I . . . we—" The girl glanced at her sister. "Faith and I . . . did something. It's my fault. I made her."

"It wasn't your fault. It was mine," Faith insisted, tears in her eyes. "It was my birthday party. I'm the one that did it."

Rebecca hugged her sister. "No. I'm the one who made you. I was excited. I should have known better."

Kimberly looked at Sterling. He shrugged.

"Girls? What is it? What do you think you did?"

Faith lifted her head from Rebecca's shoulder. "I had a slumber party for my birthday. One of my friends brought a"— she dropped her voice to a whisper—"Ouija board."

Kimberly lifted a hand to her mouth. As she suspected, the planchette that burned her hand was involved.

"A Ouija board?" Sterling lifted his eyebrows in amusement.

Ruth entered the room with two mugs of coffee. "What about a Ouija board?"

The girls jumped and went silent, staring at the floor.

Ruth looked back and forth, eyebrows furrowed. "What is happening?"

Kimberly sighed and reached for her coffee. "I think it's time for the family meeting."

CHAPTER EIGHTEEN

THE FAMILY SAT in the dining room again, the two girls snuffling while their parents looked confused. Kimberly brought the planchette to the table. "I found this last night under Faith's bed. It burned me." She turned her hand over to reveal her angry red palm.

Ruth jumped to her feet. "Are you okay? How did that thing cause a burn—" She turned to look at the girls. "That looks like Faith's burn. Rebecca! You told us it was from a curling iron."

Rebecca buried her face in her hands.

Daniel gave the planchette a hard stare. "What exactly is that?"

Kimberly took a deep breath. "This is a planchette. It's used in conjunction with a Ouija board."

Ruth gaped. "You girls used a Ouija board?"

Still weepy and sniffling, the sisters nodded.

"You had one of those in our house?" Daniel asked, his voice low.

When the girls didn't reply beyond frightened sobs, Kimberly spoke. "Apparently a friend brought it to Faith's birthday party."

"You girls know better than that," Ruth said, her voice rising, eyes wild. "I just can't believe—"

"I didn't know she had it!" Faith cried. "It was in her bag! I didn't know until she—"

Daniel interrupted. "And everything we've ever taught you about standing strong in the face of temptation went out the window?"

Rebecca spoke up. "Faith tried to say no. She knew it was a bad idea. She told everyone not to play. It was my fault. I pushed her. I was curious and thought it would be fun."

Daniel's dark countenance grew sterner, his eyes stormy with anger. "You actually played with this thing?"

The girls sobbed and nodded.

Sterling shifted in his seat. "If I could say something."

Kimberly's heart broke for the stricken girls, and she didn't know how to help them. She nodded encouragement at Sterling and gestured for him to continue.

"We're talking about cardboard and plastic. I don't understand why everyone is so grim. This is like finding the spinner from the Game of Life under her bed or a hotel from Monopoly."

"Sorry, no," Daniel said. "A Ouija board is designed to channel spirits. Dabbling in the occult is dangerous. And you girls know better. We will discuss your punishment later."

The girls seemed unable to form any response other than more tears.

Sterling shook his head. "Seriously? It's a game. You're going to punish them for playing a board game?"

"They will be punished for breaking the rules. This is a God-fearing house, and we don't allow anything related to the occult in it."

Sterling seemed unable to let it go. "Come on. Surely you can't—"

Kimberly could see his approach would get them nowhere.

"Thank you, Sterling. Let's pause here and ask the girls to explain what happened that night."

Rebecca and Faith stared at their folded hands, contrite and silent.

She used her most reassuring smile and tried again. "Girls, can you tell us what happened that night?"

Faith shook her head and gulped a breath. Rebecca shook her head.

She looked to Sterling.

He shrugged. "They're terrified. They've been told they broke rules and sinned by playing a game."

Daniel shifted his gaze. "Please don't question how I run my household."

Sterling tightened his lips, as if struggling not to say something. But then seemed to lose the battle. "You strike me as a smart man. I can't see how—"

"I'm also a God-fearing man. I don't expect an atheist like you to understand."

"Atheist? I'm Catholic!"

Daniel raised an eyebrow. "A Christian who doesn't believe in spirits and demons?"

"I don't believe in paranormal activity or the occult. And I don't believe something from beyond the grave is making your daughter sick."

"No offense, but I don't see how you're any help to us then."

"Are you kidding me? I'm your best chance of help because I'm looking for real causes of illness rather than nonsense."

"Religion isn't nonsense," Daniel insisted.

"I'm not saying it is! I'm saying I don't think a ghost is making her sick."

Negative energy levels bubbled higher, raising the psychic temperature in the room until Kimberly sweated as though fully clothed in a sauna. She raised her hands to calm them, flooding the space with soothing energy, but Michael shook his head slightly. He spun his hand at TJ and Stan to indicate they keep rolling. Only she realized the impact the arguing was making on the space around them. Exciting footage or not, she had to do something.

She continued to send positive energy into the room hoping to stem this heightened emotion and cool their tempers before it resulted in a meltdown. "Everyone, please calm down. The hostile presence feeds on this type of—"

Daniel jumped to his feet. "I'm sorry. I guess I missed the part about you being a medical doctor, Sterling. Where did you get your degree?"

A cabinet door slammed, but no one took notice. She spun toward the kitchen. No one was there. She caught TJ's eye and motioned for him to shift to the other room.

"I received my doctorate in physics," Sterling said. "From Stanford. What about you?"

"Physics? You do magic tricks." Contempt dripped from Daniel's words.

"You're the one hoping for a miracle. You said you had your minister come over to pray. Do you truly believe his magic words will help your daughter?"

"Magic words? You're the only one who uses magic words, magician."

"No, I perform illusions that trick the mind. And that's because I understand how things work. How people can be distracted and fooled into believing what someone wants them to believe."

Kimberly sweltered in the oppressive heat generated by the anger the two men felt toward one another. She grasped her quartz and opened her sixth sense wide, releasing as much calming influence as she could generate.

The crowd outside grew louder, presumably agitated by something. The yelling took on a hostile edge.

She raised her voice. "Please, could we allow the girls to continue?"

Ruth joined her. "Yes, Daniel, please let Ms. Wantland talk

with the girls. Rebecca, Faith, go ahead. We're not going to punish you. We need to know what happened."

Rebecca glanced at her father. Daniel scowled and took his seat.

"Dakota brought it," Faith began.

"Big surprise." Daniel rolled his eyes. "Do her parents even go to church?"

"Shush!" Ruth scowled at him. "Go on, Faith."

"Parminder and Yumeko wanted to play too. I was scared but they all thought it was just a silly game."

"Which it is," Sterling said.

"Shush," Kimberly admonished. If he wasn't careful, he would work up Daniel again.

Rebecca finally spoke. "I mean, like Mr. Wakefield says, it's just a game. The girls were, like, telling me it told Faith happy birthday, but, like, they all knew it was her birthday. I assumed they were pushing it."

Sterling nodded. "Correct. That is how they work. The people playing subconsciously shift the pointer where they want it to go and answer the questions themselves."

Rebecca shook her head frantically. "No. No, that's not what happened. I thought so too, but it told us things no one in the room knew."

Sterling gave her a gentle smile. "I know it feels real. But it's a proven phenomenon. Known as the 'ideomotor effect.' People using a Ouija board truly don't know they're moving it. That's why they think it's caused by a spirit."

"You don't understand," Rebecca told him. "I had one of Faith's friends draw something on a piece of paper and hide it. No one else in the room knew what she drew. And the board spelled out star. Over and over again."

Faith shuddered. "It's true. The board would only talk to Rebecca and after it told us Parminder drew a star, it kept spelling Rebecca's name. And then said he . . . wanted her."

Daniel formed a fist and brought it down on the table. "I've heard enough of this."

"He didn't finish spelling that. We don't know what he was going to spell." Rebecca's rebuttal sounded like she didn't believe it herself.

"Dakota got upset when Rebecca let go of the planchette. She said operating the board by yourself releases the spirit into our world again."

"Think about that, though," Sterling said. "If you believe a spirit was moving it, wouldn't the spirit have to be in our world to operate the board?"

"No," Daniel answered. "You don't know what you're talking about. It was reaching across from the spirit realm, unable to do anything on its own without the assistance of a host inviting it to communicate. But if a spirit is released, if it crosses over to this world again, then it can act on its own. As we have witnessed. And this one has been molesting my wife and daughters."

"That is the most ridiculous—"

She hastened to intervene. "Then what happened, Faith?"

The girl took a deep breath. "We all freaked out when it spelled out 'star' and didn't want to play it anymore. But it started moving without anyone touching it. He spelled Rebecca's name again and again and wouldn't stop. Kept saying he wanted her. No one was touching it! I yelled at it to stop but it kept going. I didn't know what to do so I grabbed the planchette to make it stop. But it kept going and my hands were stuck to it. I couldn't let go." She buried her face in her hands.

"What happened next?" Kimberly prompted. "It must have stopped."

"It did finally," Faith said. "The planchette sort of jumped out of my hands when I yelled at him to go away. I didn't know where it went. And my hand hurt so badly we kinda forgot about it."

"You keep saying *he* spoke to you. Why do you think the spirit was male?"

"He told us his name," Rebecca whispered.

"Can you tell me?" Kimberly asked. "If we can figure out who he is, I might have a better chance of connecting with him and figuring out what he wants."

"Don't speak his name!" Daniel said. "Isn't it clear what he wants? He told them. He wants my daughter. Not only Faith, the one he's hurting, but also Rebecca, whom he seems to have perverse designs on."

"But I need to know. It can help my investigation. If I can help resolve his unfinished business, I might be able to assist him in crossing over."

"He doesn't want to cross over, does he? He made a point of coming back."

"Sometimes spirits are confused following their death. He may not realize he's dead. Or he may know but have no idea what to do about it. Please. This is important."

"Come on," Sterling said. "What difference does it make if they say his name? Who cares?"

Daniel crossed his arms. "Speaking the name can give him power."

"No, speaking his name will give Kimberly power over him. At least, that's what she says and why not believe her theory?"

"Fine." Daniel waved his hands in defeat. "Tell her, girls."

Rebecca gulped. "He said his name is George."

Ruth clutched her chest. "George? No. Oh, no. He's real."

CHAPTER NINETEEN

THIS WAS UNUSUAL. Kimberly knew she was missing a key part of the story. But Ruth's response to the spirit's name startled her. And changed everything. If Ruth knew who the ghost had been, perhaps the woman also knew what he wanted and why he was upset. Normally, determining the identity of the spirit was the most difficult part of an investigation. The identity was vital to learning what it wanted, how to resolve its unfinished business, and finally helping the lost soul transition to whatever came next. Though she had assisted with many translocations, Kimberly had no idea what exactly the next plane of existence entailed. She hoped it was something like the traditional idea of heaven, where the spirits she helped could finally find peace. But her surprise was nothing compared to Daniel's response.

"You knew about this?" he demanded of his wife. "All this time? And you didn't say anything?"

"No. Well, yes. A little. Not really. I didn't think any of it was real."

"Didn't think what was real?" Kimberly asked.

"I always thought it was my imagination," Ruth murmured. "It can't be real. Why would God allow this to happen?"

"Allow what?" Kimberly pressed. "What did you think was your imagination?"

"Before we moved to this house, years ago when Rebecca was a baby, I could have sworn I heard a voice whispering her name when we'd come visit my mom. And I noticed little things when Mom was still alive—things moved or out of place, the stove left on, a dirty skillet in the refrigerator. I attributed it all to her worsening dementia. Oh, God. We left her in the house alone with him!"

"Alone with whom? Who is he?" Kimberly struggled to keep her cool and not snap at the woman, though her impatience grew to the point she felt ready to pop.

Ruth stared at her hands clenched on the table. "George. George McIntosh. At least I assume that's the George we're dealing with. He must have held a grudge all this time."

"And now he's been released by the Ouija board and is out to get my family," Daniel said. He put an arm around Ruth. "Don't worry. We'll fight him together."

Sterling chuckled. "Guys? It's a common name. George. Spinning wild stories of revenge based on a supposed revelation from a cardboard game is . . . I don't even have the words for it. It's just so ludicrous."

"Why would this George have a score to settle with you and your family, Ruth?"

"George McIntosh was the man who tried to jump our claim in the Land Run. My great-great-grandpa's claim. George was Native American. He refused to leave the area, even after the federal government opened the land for settlement. At least that's how the story was passed down."

"He refused to leave his home after the government stole the land from the indigenous people," Rosie muttered.

Ruth glanced at her. "Well, I wasn't there. I didn't steal anyone's land. I just live in a house that's been in my family for generations."

"Then you can understand how the tribes felt when they were uprooted from their homelands," Rosie said.

Daniel scowled. "But we didn't take anything. We're not to blame. It's in the past now."

"Not completely in the past if George is still here," Kimberly said. "Why don't you tell us the rest?"

Ruth nodded. "George apparently refused to move. He had already marched here in the Trail of Tears and wouldn't go any farther. When the government seized his land, he found himself homeless and resorted to crime. After the Land Run, he tried to jump the claim that he insisted was his land. But he didn't prevail. He made threats against my great-great-grandpa James and his wife Rebecca. Later he was accused of stealing horses and was hanged."

A shiver ran down Kimberly's spine, an electric jolt that suffused all her limbs. *Hanged.* The noose she'd seen the first night, swinging from the tree out back.

Elise paused in her frantic scribbling and flipped through several pages of her notebook. "Didn't you tell us James was instated as Guthrie's first sheriff?"

"That's right." Ruth's voice held a measure of pride.

"James acted as sheriff, judge, and jury?"

Ruth bristled. "The town convicted George of stealing horses. That was a big deal back then. People's livelihoods depended on their horses, which were an expensive investment."

Daniel frowned. "Look, I don't like this implication that my wife is to blame. You're talking about things that happened well over a hundred years ago. What's she supposed to do? Leave the house to this ghost?"

Sterling snorted. "That would be really stupid. Especially since ghosts don't exist."

Daniel jumped to his feet. "Oh, shut it, magician! I've heard enough out of you for one day."

"Illusionist! And what's the problem? You can't handle hearing the truth?"

"What truth? You're a belligerent, close-minded, arrogant—"

"The truth is Ouija boards are a game, not a way to contact spirits. Michael Faraday disproved them ages ago. Before your Land Run even. But the spiritualist movement just won't die. There is no George. No ghost at all."

"You're calling all of us liars?"

"Not liars per se. Just confused."

"I'm confused why Kimberly Wantland added you to her show. Other than that, I'm well aware of what's happening."

Kimberly felt the toxicity in the room skyrocketing. Worse than before. Sweat beads collected at her temples and her heart pounded from the anxiety all the negative energy produced. She had to intervene. "Okay, let's all just—"

Ruth stood beside Daniel. "You don't know. You haven't been here, coping with this day in and day out. How do you explain that both my daughters and I have all experienced the same hands groping us in the night? How do you explain Faith's ongoing illness that no doctor has been able to diagnose?"

Kimberly had not seen the soft-spoken woman so fierce. Sterling appeared startled by the woman's outburst too.

"I don't have the answers yet, but that doesn't mean—"

"You think we're all crazy?" Ruth demanded.

"No one said 'crazy' and no one will," Kimberly insisted. She had to take control of this spiraling situation. "Now if everyone can please take a deep breath and calm down."

But the psychic heat in the room continued to climb. Her attempts to add cooling, positive energy were no match for the massive amounts of negative energy. The crowd outside grew louder again. The sour energy pressed against her from all sides. She could hear voices but could no longer make out the words. Her crew began to take sides, adding to the cacophony. She thought Michael attempted to calm everyone but couldn't be sure. His voice at least seemed more stable than the others.

The mob shouted louder and louder. Sterling raised his voice. Daniel raised his to match. Ruth and Rosie seemed to be squabbling about something. Elise recited facts from her notebook pages. Stan skulked around the perimeter of the room, attempting to catch it all and yelling for TJ to "get over here now!" TJ yelled something back from the kitchen. What was happening? They all looked ready to throttle each other.

Kimberly closed her eyes and grasped her quartz, sending all her psychic energy to her indigo chakra, allowing it to grow and resonate and seek out spiritual entities in the space. She walked through the fields again, her hand brushing the tops of ripening wheat, golden in the shimmering sun. She meandered through corn stalks, drooping tassels nodding in a gust of wind. Hawk cries pierced the air above her as she found herself in an endless open field, a massive herd of bison painting brown Rorschach blotches across the grassy plains as it morphed with shifting movements.

The images shifted, and she stood in the dusty dirt road of a new town. Skeletal wood frames and tents dotted the noisy chaos. Lines snaked from some of the tents. She could barely make out the hand-drawn signs UNITED STATES POST OFFICE and CLAIMS OFFICE. Wagons and horses kicked up dust clouds as they flew past her. Everyone seemed late for an appointment as they zipped about the newborn town.

Which seemed to strain at the seams from the influx of people suddenly burgeoning the cramped space. She smelled sewage, saw piles of garbage. Smoke filled the air from innumerable fires.

A fight broke out in the line at the claims office tent.

Kimberly heard slamming. Lots of slamming. She opened her eyes. Her crew and the Johnsons still bickered. The lights flickered. From the living room, she heard the television blaring. A radio in the house switched on and boomed music. Something smashed against the front of the house, startling everyone into silence.

She blinked and reoriented herself to her surroundings, still recovering from her visions. Her crew likewise blinked and shook their heads as if trying to remember where they were. Daniel ran to the front door.

Sterling stared at the light fixture. "Electrical problems? Is the wiring old?"

Ruth wrung her hands. "This has never happened before."

Daniel ran back to join them. "Some of the people in that mob outside are throwing garbage at the house. I'm calling the police!"

She followed him to the kitchen but nearly bumped into his back when he stopped abruptly.

"What . . . what is this?"

She peered past him. All the cabinets and drawers in the kitchen opened and closed, the erratic movements frantic. The pantry door flew open and slammed shut.

Sterling appeared mesmerized as he stepped into the kitchen and turned in a slow circle, watching the bizarre antics. His gaze landed on her. "How are you doing this?"

She shook her head. "I'm not."

TJ whirled with his camera, aiming it at one shifting drawer and cabinet door after another. "This is insane! This is incredible! I can't believe this!"

"This is evil," Daniel said. "The work of the Devil."

Sterling stepped closer to a drawer and caught it in his hands when it popped open like a Jack-in-the-Box. He pulled the drawer from its tracks and turned it, running his hands all over it before bending down to inspect the empty space around the tracks. "No strings. No magnets. I don't see anything. Kimberly, how are you guys doing this? I need to know. This isn't funny."

"No, it's not funny," she agreed. "But we're not doing it."

Ruth screamed from the dining room. "Ms. Wantland! Come quickly! Something is wrong with Faith!"

Kimberly dragged her attention away from the kitchen cabinetry and raced back to the dining room with Elise, Daniel, and Sterling close behind. Michael and Rosie stood over the girl who thrashed on the floor, illuminated by the flickering light bulbs above. "What happened?"

"She just fell down and started convulsing," Rosie said.

"What's wrong with her? What's happening?" Ruth cried.

Kimberly knelt beside the girl. She placed her hands gently on her shoulders. The girl growled and gnashed her teeth. "Rosie, we need sage."

"What's happening?" Daniel asked.

"Call an ambulance," Sterling whispered.

"I forgot to call the police!" Daniel said.

"Call both." Sterling squatted beside her.

She'd never felt so helpless. This presence was powerful, and it was angry. "Well, Sterling, you may get your crazy ending after all. I believe we are dealing with a poltergeist."

CHAPTER TWENTY

KIMBERLY DESCENDED THE STAIRCASE, drained and discouraged. The EMTs had found nothing physically wrong with Faith. The girl had stopped convulsing and appeared exhausted but normal by the time the ambulance pulled into the driveway—temperature and blood pressure were normal, and Faith reported she felt fine and had no memory of the instance. With nothing to treat, the EMTs left. Ruth tucked Faith into bed, then stood over the girl wringing her hands and looking at Kimberly to fix it. And she didn't know how.

Kimberly crossed into the entryway, seeking the comfort Sterling would offer. Before she located him, she discovered Daniel speaking with a police officer.

"I'm sorry, sir," the officer said as she drew closer. "Everyone in the group denies throwing anything. They all claim everything in your yard was here when they arrived this morning."

"They're lying!" Daniel said. "Look at that. Why would we do that to our own yard? We wouldn't."

The officer glanced over his shoulder at *The Wantland Files* van and then leaned sideways for a look at Kimberly. "Maybe some of the neighbors are disgruntled about the general hubbub disrupting the neighborhood?"

"No way. We're good friends with everyone on this block. You can interview them all. Maybe they saw someone throwing things."

"Well, I did knock on a few doors. People either weren't home or didn't happen to see anything."

"But you can't possibly believe we would throw trash in our own yard! That's nonsense."

"I understand your frustration, sir, but without photos or something to corroborate your complaint, I'm afraid it's your word against theirs. And they have more 'witnesses' on their side."

"But—"

"I know. I don't like it either. I'm afraid my hands are tied, though. I'm sorry. If they act up again, try to record them doing it, get some irrefutable proof they can't deny. Then we can run them out of here. Meanwhile try not to provoke them." He continued to eye Kimberly, whether from sheer curiosity or in distaste, she couldn't tell.

Daniel thanked him and shook hands, then closed the door.

"I'm so sorry," she told him. The dejected look on his face was more than she could bear.

"Why should you be sorry? You're here at our invitation trying to help us. The people outside should be apologizing. And cleaning up the mess they made. 'Try not to provoke them.'" He shook his head and sighed. "And I should be apologizing. To you and to Sterling. I can't understand it. I never raise my voice or insult another. That . . . wasn't like me."

She rested a hand on his shoulder. "I know. It wasn't your fault. The stress is getting to you. And the negative energy of the crowd feeds the poltergeist, who then provokes the people around him, raising the negative energy more. It's a vicious cycle that powers the spirit."

Daniel shook his head. "And no amount of praying seems to help. I'm going to check on my girls. If you'll excuse me."

"Of course. Please do. Let me know if you need anything."

She heard Sterling's voice and followed it to the living room. He stood near the big front picture window, apparently recording a Confidential Corner. Even from across the room she could tell his heart wasn't in it. The kitchen incident had shaken everyone. She couldn't blame them.

"Something strange happened today," Sterling said. "I'm a little rattled. I also got the results back from the toxicity screenings. All negative. No signs of environmental toxins in any of my samples. I won't lie. I'm disappointed. But facts are facts, and I'd be a huge hypocrite if I attempt to refute or ignore them. I don't have an alternative theory right now, particularly in light of what I witnessed today. But I'll keep working on it."

She hadn't heard anything about the test results. As much as Sterling had been banking on environmental influences making the girl sick, he must be very disappointed.

Sterling caught sight of her and nodded slightly, his lips twisted in a slight frown. Stan lowered the camera, but Sterling gestured for him to keep rolling. He opened the curtains wide, the protestors framed in the window.

"You're backlit," Stan muttered.

Sterling shifted to one side, waited for Stan's approval, then jabbed a thumb over his shoulder and continued. "This is unacceptable. Make no mistake. I don't support or condone this in any way. If you think this behavior is tantamount to disproving psychics and other paranormal activity, you're wrong. This is harassment and bullying, plain and simple. These guys claim to support religion and free speech. But apparently only their own. They want to silence Kimberly and anyone else they don't agree with. I support the truth, and that mob out there isn't preaching it."

He indicated Stan should cut before crossing to the couch and flopping down. He dropped his head into his hands.

Kimberly hesitated, not sure if he needed company or needed to be alone. Stan caught her eye and tipped his head at Sterling, eyes giving her the signal to go to him.

She crossed the room and sat beside him. He leaned against her.

"I am so sorry," he said. "I don't know what happened back there. It's so unlike me to lose my temper. I don't know how Daniel got under my skin like that. There's no excuse."

"He feels the same. But it wasn't your fault. It's all the toxic energy from the crowd feeding the poltergeist."

"The crowd has turned nasty for sure. I'll give you that. How's the little girl? I can't believe the EMTs didn't find anything wrong with her."

"She's in bed. She's awake but won't respond to anyone. And the EMTs didn't find anything *physically* wrong with her. I know exactly why she's ill."

"I guess you heard the toxin screenings came back negative. I was so sure . . ."

"I heard. I'm not surprised, but I know you're disappointed and I'm sorry." She rested a hand on his back and rubbed. His storm of emotions crashed against her so hard she gasped.

"What's wrong?"

"Worried about you. You're all shaken up inside. Your emotional prism is refracted every which way."

"My rainbow is a mess? Is that what you're saying?" He cocked an eyebrow and chuckled softly.

Remembering the night she explained chakras to him and how their spinning, colorful energy rendered everyone a walking rainbow, she flushed. He'd taken her hand in his that night, looked at her for the first time with the burning intensity that rattled her to her core. Much the way he looked at her right now.

"I am shaken. You're right about that," he said.

"Take a deep breath." As his lungs expanded, she pushed positive, soothing energy through her palm.

He shivered and sucked in a breath. "I love the results, but I'd still love to know how you do that."

"I'm sharing my energy with you." He wouldn't believe her.

But he claimed to value the truth so why not give it a go? "I'm holding back negative and sending over pure positive energy. You need a boost."

"Mmmm the force is strong with this one," he croaked in what she assumed was his best Yoda impersonation.

She giggled. "Not going to tell me how silly that is?"

"After everything that happened in the kitchen earlier? That's the least bizarre thing I've heard today." He raised an eyebrow and seemed to think carefully before speaking. "You know, electric eels have the ability to conduct bursts of electricity and shock nearby animals. I don't know how they do it. I can't do it myself. But I'd be a moron to deny they can. Maybe you have some unidentified ability that allows you to manipulate currents."

Her jaw dropped. She almost felt the ground vibrate with the massive shift in his attitude. "Wow. I never expected to hear that. Not from you."

"Yeah, well, I never expected to witness something like I saw today. Or feel . . . I don't know. Warmth? Happiness? I feel something radiating from you. I know I'm not imagining it. It's almost like a little jolt but not unpleasant like a shock. All this stuff about ghosts and demons, though . . ." He tossed his arms in the air and let them fall.

"I know. It goes against everything you believe. You didn't grow up with this like I did. But I still think you may have some latent sensitive abilities. We should leave that for another day. Baby steps." She gave him another dose of energy.

He sat up straight and gasped. "Seriously. That's causing euphoria. A high almost. You're like a drug. You'll turn me into an addict."

"Oops. Too much at once. Sorry."

His hooded eyes burned, searching hers. What did he hope to see? "I can't help but wonder what you'd be like in—"

"In?"

He shook his head and broke the penetrating gaze. "Nope.

We're having a nice moment. I'm not gonna ruin it by being a dude." He took her hand. "I need you to tell me everything in the kitchen was all an illusion. Please. Otherwise I don't know how to deal with this. None of this makes sense."

"It's not entirely making sense to me either," she admitted. "Poltergeists normally aren't out for revenge. They're mischievous troublemakers for sure, and never easy to deal with. But this one has a mean streak. And I can't figure out why. What am I missing?"

One side of his mouth curled into a wry grin. "We're both talking in English but we're not speaking each other's language at all."

She squeezed his hand. "I know it's scary. I remember how I felt when I first realized I sensed things in this world no one else could. You're finally witnessing it for yourself. It was difficult enough on me as a child. This goes against one of your core beliefs. Believe me when I tell you it's going to be okay. I won't let anything hurt you."

His smile spread across his face. "My own personal ghost bodyguard? Tiny little thing like you? Somehow, I believe it. And I like that you want to protect me."

She stood, overwhelmed by the situation. "I'm restless. I can't just sit here. And I don't think I can sit through footage review."

Ruth walked past them, a box of trash bags in hand. "Faith seems to have fallen asleep. Daniel is going to stay by her. I need to do something with my hands. Something useful. I feel so helpless."

"You're going outside?" Kimberly's heart skipped a beat at the idea of facing the angry mob on the other side of the door.

"I'm going to clean up the garbage those horrible people threw in my yard."

"But they're still out there. And wound up."

Sterling joined in. "And probably empowered since the police didn't do a thing."

"This isn't the first time Christians have been persecuted." Ruth squared her shoulders. "And it won't be the last."

How ironic Ruth believed she was being targeted for her faith when this all started with people using misguided religious beliefs to accuse Kimberly of witchcraft.

"Wait," she said as Ruth reached for the doorknob. "I'll go with you."

"What? No, you won't!" Sterling insisted.

"You should stay inside where you're safe," Ruth agreed.

"No way. This is all my fault. I'm supposed to be helping and instead I've made it worse. I haven't figured out how to clear the poltergeist, Faith is still sick, and I've attracted zealots. The least I can do is help clean up the mess."

Sterling sighed. "Then I'm going too."

___

CHAPTER TWENTY-ONE

___

EZEKIEL'S FOLLOWERS and the First Amendment nut jobs went crazy as soon as Kimberly stepped onto the porch. Fear rose with each step toward the lawn. She felt like she was back in middle school, terrified of the older kids, ostracized and ridiculed, small and helpless. Unlike those days when she truly was isolated, however, today Sterling and Ruth stood beside her, shoulder to shoulder.

Papers, soda cans, empty snack wrappers, and other detritus littered the manicured and edged yard, emerald grass blades crushed under garbage. Her stomach churned.

"'Where two or three are gathered in my name, there am I,'" Ruth said. She shook open a trash bag, bent and picked up a wrapper. "Shame on you!" she scolded the crowd, which quieted to watch the drama unfold. "Didn't your mothers teach you any manners? Trash from trashy people."

The group booed her admonishment.

Kimberly spotted a fluorescent-orange chip bag and picked it up. "You actually eat this junk?" she yelled. "Do you know what it does to your bodies?"

The crowd went silent, then burst into laughter, jeering her. "Yeah? What do you eat, witch? Bat wings and toad stools?"

Sterling patted her back. "Valiant effort. But I think it missed the intended mark. Maybe you should leave the insults to someone else."

"Their daughter is sick! They're suffering enough. How can you be so heartless? Leave them alone."

Ezekiel yelled. "We cannot stand silent in the face of evil!"

"What evil?" she answered. "These people haven't done a thing to hurt anyone!"

"You've brought sickness to the house, witch. We're here to end it!"

"I didn't make their daughter sick! I came to help her."

Someone hacked and spat—and actually hit her. She'd been spat on. Revulsion and rage filled her. She clenched her fists and stormed toward the street. "How dare you? Which one of you disgusting—"

Sterling looped an arm around her waist and scooped her up. "No way. That's exactly what they want. An enraged target lashing out at them, closer and easier to reach."

She couldn't see straight. Anger hazed her vision as she shook. "So we just let them do whatever they want?"

"No." He stood her near the porch and pulled his phone from a pocket. "I'll have TJ come record. If they do it again, we've got them."

Encouraged, numerous protestors snorted and hacked. Yellow glob after yellow, slimy glob flew through the air and fell on the lawn. They couldn't reach her at this distance, but she gagged at each wet thwack that hit the ground.

She had brought this on the Johnsons.

Ruth began to sing a psalm about being lifted up and protected from foes as she continued to pick up trash.

TJ emerged from the house, camera held high. "Hey, douchebags! Who wants to be recorded harassing these nice people?"

Though the crowd buzzed like a hornet's nest poked with a

stick, the spitting stopped, allowing them to clean in peace. No one dared fling additional garbage.

Rosie and Elise came looking for Kimberly and joined them cleaning up the debris. Soon, neighbors pressed past the protestors and helped too, scowling at the unwelcome intrusion. Kimberly recognized the woman who had brought over cookies and had referred to herself as Dakota's mom. The woman hugged Ruth and grabbed a trash bag, ready to pitch in. A girl about Faith's age—Dakota presumably—stood near her mother and stared at Kimberly with wide eyes.

"Hey, Kimberly," Sterling called. "Look at this."

She didn't immediately spot him, but a quick search led her to the backyard.

The hanging tree.

He was hung for stealing horses.

She shook off the ghosts of the past and the cold shiver that wracked her body, focusing on Sterling. "What is it? What did you find?"

He squatted beside the tree. Decorative brick defined a flowerbed encircling the trunk, setting it off from the lawn. Fresh mulch covered the soil.

"Look at the plants. This area is clearly maintained. And yet the flowers are drooping and withering. The stalks are all yellowing. Some of them are flat out dead now. Nowhere else in the yard. Only here."

"That is strange. Maybe you should've sent samples from this area for testing. This does seem to indicate the ground has been poisoned in some way."

"I did. Noticed it the first day. One of the first samples I collected."

"And that came back negative too?"

"Completely. And yet it's progressing. Look." He showed her pictures on his phone. "This was from the first day. Then yesterday. Now today."

She stared up at the tree. The ground below it was poisoned, but not from anything Sterling's tests would detect. Wedging one foot between dying plants, she placed both hands against the trunk and breathed deeply, allowing her sixth sense to connect with events of the past.

Talk to me. What happened here?

A breeze lifted the ends of her hair. She opened her eyes. The world around her had shifted. Empty fields stretched into the distance. Tents and wood frames defined a young town sprouting from the prairie. But directly in front of her stood a tree—a sturdy oak.

A noose hung from a thick branch, swinging lazily in the breeze. An angry mob screamed and jeered.

"Thief!"

"Hang him!"

Rough hands gripped her arms, propelling her forward. Terror pulsed through her body with each rasping breath, each stuttering heartbeat. Angry fingers shoved her onto a rickety platform and dropped the noose over her head.

"What did I do?" she called out helplessly, her voice that of a terrified and confused man. "I only tried to protect my land. I claimed it fair in the run."

"Jumping another man's claim isn't fair, you thief!" The man who answered sported a sheriff's star on his shirt. "And stealing horses! We won't stand for it!"

She scanned the faces in the crowd, hoping for compassion. Each man echoed the same sentiments.

"Thief!"

"Claim jumper!"

"Cattle rustler!"

The rope rubbed against her neck as she twisted it, panic setting in. She raised her bound hands, noting the darker skin tone, and pointed to the sheriff. "I never stole nothing! He stole the claim from me while I waited in line. I fell asleep. When I woke up, my claim was gone."

"You lie, redskin!" the sheriff insisted. "How dare you

accuse me?"

She looked again to the angry crowd, hoping for a sympathetic face, anyone who might take her side and save her—well, save the man whose history she currently relived. Finally, one pair of eyes gazed on her with sadness and fear. She cried out to the woman they belonged to, the only person who might help her. "Rebecca! Please! You know the truth!"

The fair-skinned woman wept. "George!"

The sheriff curled an arm around her waist and pulled her close. "Now, now, Rebecca. Don't let him disturb you. Go on back home."

The young woman hesitated. She was the only one in the new town who had ever shown George kindness and mercy, sneaking food to him and a warm blanket when the weather turned cold. He loved her. He'd made promises to her. She'd returned his affection. Until Sheriff James grew sweet on her and noticed the attention she spent on George and the time they spent together.

The thick rope tightened around her neck, scratching the delicate skin, restricting airflow.

"Please, Rebecca. Don't let them."

James shoved Rebecca. She sprawled to the dirt, kicking up a cloud of dust. "Go on, now! Git! You'll have the finest home in town right here in the nicest location. Don't ruin it for yourself by making me mad."

The sight of the gentle woman knocked to the dirt blurred her vision red. Her blood boiled and she struggled against the bindings.

"Look at that! We've made him mad!"

The crowd laughed and spat. "Hang him!" they cried over and over.

"You gonna come down from there and teach me a lesson, Red?" the sheriff taunted. "Gonna protect the lady?"

She struggled again, outraged by the injustice of everything —losing ancestral land, watching this arrogant, selfish buffoon help himself to anything he wanted, and the crowd so easily swayed by anything the sheriff told them.

"Git, Rebecca!" Sheriff James' voice took on a threatening tone. "You're distressing the prisoner."

Rough burlap descended over her eyes, drawn tight behind her head.

Shoved from behind, she swung forward. Her feet found no purchase, though she scrambled with all her might. She gasped in vain for air until darkness clouded all thoughts save one:

Innocent.

CHAPTER TWENTY-TWO

KIMBERLY SAT with Rosie and Sterling in the trailer. Her neck still throbbed and ached, though no red marks had appeared. She'd expected bright red welts and bruises, the history of the land had replayed so vividly across her psyche.

Despite downing three cups of calming tea, she could not relax or slow her adrenaline-fueled racing heart.

Sterling held one of her hands, caressing her with gentle fingertips. "Rosie? What else do we do?"

Distracted with her phone, Rosie took a moment to respond. "Sometimes it just needs to run its course."

He frowned at Kimberly. She shrugged. She didn't know what was up either.

"Hey, girl." She nudged Rosie. "You've been distant since yesterday. What's going on?"

Rosie waved a hand at her. "Don't worry about it. Focus on the case. This family needs your undivided attention."

Something *was* wrong. "But now I can't focus because I'm worried about you. Is . . . is it Lorenzo?"

That tore Rosie's attention from her phone screen. "Lorenzo? No, no, no. Nothing to do with him. We're fine."

Fleeting relief that she didn't have to worry about a meltdown and several weeks of post-dumping depression was replaced by fresh concern. "If not Lorenzo, what?"

"I don't want my personal problems interfering with work."

"We're not the typical nine-to-five here. We're family. Come on. I'm really worried now. I need you to tell me what's going on."

Rosie's shoulders slumped. "Apparently my dad had a mild heart attack yesterday."

She jumped to her feet. "And you didn't tell me? How is he?"

Rosie held up her phone. "I'm texting Mom. He's in the hospital, scheduled for a procedure tomorrow."

She grabbed Rosie and crushed her in a hug. "Sounds like you need to go be with him and your mom."

"All the way back home? We're here. Working a case. And it's a tough one."

"I'll get online and book the flight myself if you want to go."

She'd never seen Rosie cry. But her personal assistant's eyes watered and her voice quavered. "Thanks, girl. I don't know. Let me call them, okay?"

"Of course. Find a quiet room in the house for some privacy. Take all the time you need."

The noise from the crowd filled the trailer as Rosie left, dabbing her eyes. Kimberly, already weak from her encounter with the hanging tree, wilted under the high toxicity. She hung her head and rubbed her temples.

Sterling guided her back to a chair. "That really wears on you, doesn't it?"

She nodded, each yelled taunt piercing her temples like a metal spike, as shrapnel seemed to rattle about her skull. "I'll be useless tonight. Poltergeists thrive on caustic emotions and disbelief. I don't. They drain me. Leave me exhausted and powerless. How will I finish this investigation?"

Sterling ran a hand up and down her arms. "Relax. It'll be okay. Wish I could give that jolt of energy back to you."

"That's sweet. Thank you."

"Well, I did hear Ruth saying she was calling her church prayer hotline. She said the prayer request will reach hundreds of people."

Already low and depressed, she found mustering a positive response challenging. "She's contributing the way she knows how. This helps her feel active rather than passive."

Sterling scoffed. "I suppose. Let's hope her prayer line participants believe hard enough."

The harsh edge of his words sliced through her, revealing a new level of bitterness in him. "And yet you're the Christian and I'm the witch. What's going on with you?"

He dragged a hand down his face and mumbled, "Maybe the whack jobs out there are getting to me too."

"I sense this runs deeper than that. Not wanting to be duped by charlatans is one thing. Disparaging someone's beliefs is something else entirely."

Resting a hand on his back, she felt rage and fury. She longed to gather him into a hug and ask, "What happened? Who hurt you?" She stayed quiet and let him move at his own pace.

He pressed a fist to his mouth, his resolve appearing to waiver. "I worked at a hospital two summers in a row during high school. What they used to call Candy Striping, but they just called it the Junior Volunteer Program when I was in it." He stared into space, lost in the memory. He sought eye contact. "I've never told anyone this."

"It's okay," she soothed. "I'm here and I support you whether you share this or don't." While she tended to feel much , better after a heart-to-heart with Rosie—relieved and refreshed—she sensed that Sterling felt threatened and didn't want him to feel pushed. "You don't have to. Only if you want to."

"Juniors don't do much. But my assignment included some basic patient care. Grunt work, you know? Fill water pitchers or get cups of ice. Fetch blankets. Answer call lights and get the nurse."

"That sounds like excellent volunteer work," she said.

"The second summer, a little boy was admitted to the floor. His case seemed simple enough, but he kept getting sicker. I went home Friday and worried about him all weekend. He was still there Monday morning. The parents refused medication and testing. They refused the doctor's urgent plea to transfer him to another hospital with a specialist. Instead, they called their pastor to pray for the boy. He told them not to let the doctor speak negative words over the boy, not to refer to the boy as sick. The pastor convinced the parents that if their faith was strong enough, God would heal their boy. They called the prayer line. Got people all over town praying."

"Prayer can be comforting to people in stressful situations."

"Granted. Sure. Pray for health. Pray to guide the doctors' and nurses' decisions. No problem. But they denied all medical care and left it to God. I kept going by the room, offering to get water or whatever they might need. I was desperate to help. Hell, I was praying at that point. Praying for a miracle that the parents would come to their senses and let a doctor help. The boy died and I watched the mom wailing over him as he turned blue. Then the nurse noticed I was in the room and escorted me out."

"Oh, Sterling."

"He died! The pastor insisted their faith wasn't strong enough. BS! What if God sent that doctor to heal their boy? That might have been God's will. And then the pastor had the nerve to blame the parents, to tell them their faith wasn't strong enough." He dropped his face into his hands.

She curled her arms around him. He melted into her embrace, head on her shoulder. Without much energy, she couldn't do more than console him. "I'm so sorry."

"He blamed the parents when all they did was follow his advice. He murdered that boy."

Deeper understanding clicked into place. The tidbits he'd shared made sense—being duped as a little boy, witnessing faith abuse that resulted in a child's death. What other pain did he harbor in his aching soul?

He sat up, rubbing at the corners of his eyes. "Sorry."

"Nothing to apologize about. That's what friends are for. I'm glad you felt like you could share with me."

That brought a hesitant smile to his face.

The door opened and Rosie returned, slamming the door on the boisterous crowd. "Ugh! Can they go away?"

"Hey! How's your dad?"

"Mom says he's stable. He says he's great."

"You got to talk to him? How did he sound?"

"Pretty normal actually. Said he isn't too old to 'whup' me if I race home for no reason."

"This isn't no reason though."

"No, but he insists he's going to be fine. The cardiologist is going to put in a stent tomorrow and a nutritionist is going to work with Mom to develop a heart-healthy diet he can stick to."

Sterling gagged. "Healthy? Ick."

Kimberly leaned forward in her seat. "I can help with that!"

Rosie grabbed her hands and squeezed. "I know, girl, but let's be real. No way will he start eating oatmeal. Baby steps."

"But oatmeal is soooo good! Maybe he hasn't tried it the way I make it. I add—"

Michael burst through the door into the trailer, shaking his head. "That crowd is getting out of control."

"Getting?" she asked. "They didn't hack on you."

"Ew. They need to go. But I don't know how to get rid of them."

"Don't worry. Ruth called her prayer line." Sterling rolled his eyes.

Michael raised an eyebrow but continued when Sterling added nothing more. "I'm used to people praying for me. Let's hope this prayer group has more luck. But what I came to talk about was footage review. We've noted a few odd things but nothing as strong as the kitchen incident we all witnessed."

Sterling cleared his throat. "Which we still haven't explained."

She rested a hand on his shoulder. "We're trying to explain it, Sterling. Any voices on the recordings? Any clues as to what he wants?"

"Again, English and yet not the same language," Sterling said. "I mean what really caused the kitchen to erupt like that. I read that use of fracking to extract oil from the ground in this part of Oklahoma has been causing earthquakes. But that wouldn't be isolated to a single room. That would have shaken the entire house."

"An earthquake?" Rosie asked. "Come on. I love ya but you're reaching so hard right now."

"Can't you just admit you experienced a paranormal episode?" Kimberly said.

"Nope. But speaking of episode, Kimberly had another of hers. Out back by the tree. I can't figure out why, but all the plants around it are dying."

"I think the ground is poisoned," she said, shivering at the memory.

"What did you see?" Michael asked.

"That first night I thought I saw a noose hanging from it. That's what I saw in the backyard."

Rosie shuddered. "With a body hanging from it?"

"No, empty. But it scared me."

"And you didn't mention it why?" Michael asked.

"I blinked and it was gone so I wasn't sure. Even if I knew I saw it, that wouldn't necessarily mean it was related to this investigation. This land has soaked up a lot of history through the years. I can feel it. But now I think the hanging is part of the issue here."

Rosie snapped her fingers. "Didn't the girls say their Ouija board ghost told them he was hanged?"

"Yes. And I believe I just experienced it. What Sterling is

calling an episode. I connected to past events and witnessed the hanging. As George."

Michael gasped. "The theory is true? Our ghost is George, hanged for claim jumping and cattle rustling? He's angry and wants revenge on the family?"

"George was hanged, that's true. But something is off. To the moment he died, George maintained his innocence. He believed it. I felt his confusion and betrayal. He only wanted his land, and no one would listen or help him."

"Ruth said her great-great-grandfather James became sheriff. And that George jumped his claim. If he jumped it, the land wasn't really his. You only experienced George's opinion on the matter."

"Pretty sure I saw Sheriff James too. He didn't strike me as terribly altruistic. He seemed aggressive and even hostile toward Rebecca, a tiny, young thing who couldn't hurt a fly."

Michael propped his chin on a fist, brows knitted above his eyes. "Still, you may be seeing only his slanted view of what happened. Maybe he's become angry over the years. Wandering the shadow world between this existence and the next, not really part of either. We've seen that happen."

"Spirits in the veil do sometimes become confused and agitated. And that could be affecting his recollection of those past events. I need to connect with George, get a feel for his current state."

"It plays, doesn't it? He lost his land, couldn't get it back, was hanged, and now is taking revenge on Faith, the descendent of the man he believes wronged him."

"Maybe. That makes sense logically. Doesn't feel quite right though."

Sterling shook his head, a smirk curling his lips. "Logically."

Michael massaged his temples. "The clues so far seem to point in that direction. Until we have another lead to pursue, I think we need to move forward assuming we're dealing with

George and that he's making Faith sick. Maybe you can convince him to move on peacefully."

TJ burst into the trailer, gasping for air as he pulled an inhaler from his pocket. "Ms. Wantland."

Sterling stood and moved beside him. "Didn't I tell you to text instead of running around?"

"I . . . forgot." He sucked deeply on the inhaler. "It's Faith. She's . . . not right."

CHAPTER TWENTY-THREE

KIMBERLY WATCHED Faith thrash in her bed, teeth bared. Daniel attempted to restrain her as Ruth sobbed in the doorway, consoled by Rosie and Elise. Rebecca hovered in a corner, wringing her hands, tears glistening in her eyes. TJ and Stan shifted about the room, capturing the strange events as well as the family members' reactions to them.

Faith growled and shoved her father, throwing him across the room. Sterling's jaw hung slack.

Daniel stood and adjusted his shirt. "You're still going to claim this isn't a demon possessing my daughter?"

"I know this seems bad. And I'll admit this spirit is exceptionally powerful. But believe me, it could be far worse."

"Please, Ms. Wantland," Ruth pleaded. "Help her. I'm ready to make a deal with a demon if that's what it takes."

Kimberly whipped her head to face the anguished mother. "Don't say that. Never say such things."

"I'm sorry. I didn't mean it. I just want my daughter back."

"You don't want to invite a demon into your home. This ghost is challenging enough."

"How can you be so sure?" Daniel asked. "What's the difference between a demon and a spirit?"

She thought back to the afternoon her mother had died, remembering the cold emptiness that had sucked all the joy out of the house, the menacing fear that had gripped her, an anxiety she couldn't understand or explain. Terror and iciness accompanied demons. But she didn't know how to describe that to someone who had never experienced the raw soul-unnerving presence.

"A demon . . . is like the opposite of the feeling you get when you walk into church," she attempted to explain. "Instead of warmth and acceptance and love, you feel isolation and cold and fear. I don't know how else to tell you. This doesn't feel quite the same to me."

She took a deep breath and wrapped her unburned hand around the quartz crystal on her necklace. She sat on the girl's bed, reaching out with her indigo chakra to establish a connection. Though a connection could only be offered and never forced, she had a feeling this spirit would actively fight to avoid her. Why? Even confused and lost, most spirits wandering the veil were eventually open to her assistance. Once they resolved their lingering issues, she was able to help them cross over to the next existence where they could finally rest at peace.

What was different here? And why couldn't she figure it out? Something eluded her.

She placed her palms on the girl's shoulders. "Faith?"

Faith sniffed the air and turned her head sharply. The girl stared at her, a slow smile splitting her face. Her eyes rolled back in her head until only the whites remained visible. A deep voice, low and gravelly, filled the room. "Kimberly Wantland. Give up now. This family is mine."

Sterling pushed away from the wall he slumped against. "What the fu—"

"Language, Sterling," she cut him off.

Faith's head twisted to face him and mimicked, "Language, Sterling."

She'd never seen anything like it. Was she wrong? Was this in fact a demon possession instead of the spirit possession she assumed she was dealing with? How was the spirit able to take such complete control over the girl? It was powerful, in control. Terrifying. And it seemed to be growing stronger. "I still think the energy from the crowd outside is feeding this spirit. No one contribute. Nothing negative. Counter the hate outside with love. Flood this room with positive energy. Pray if that helps guide and control your thoughts."

Sterling's harsh tone jarred her. "Kimberly, if you tell us not to speak negative words over this girl, I'm out."

Startled, she took a moment to respond. "This isn't the same thing, Sterling. I need positive energy to help Faith. I'm not asking you to believe. I'm not asking you to save her."

He puffed out a breath and shook his head. "Sorry. I can't do this."

She watched him go, disappointment settling in her stomach, an indigestible knot of frustration. Though she wished he'd stayed, she had to move forward. She rested her palms on the girl's shoulders. "George? I want to talk to you."

Faith giggled, a horrible, menacing sound. That deep, incongruous voice gurgled up again. "You can't talk to George."

"Please? Let me talk to George. Let's talk about what happened at the tree."

Faith stiffened, grabbing the bed sheets in her fists. The girl thrashed from side to side. "No! No George!"

Kimberly pushed psychically, hoping to cast out the spirit controlling the girl. Whatever it was. "Let me talk to Faith then. Faith? Faith, sweetie? Come back to us."

Faith's legs worked the air as though pedaling a bike, head lashing back and forth. The girl went still suddenly. Her eyes rolled back in her head and one side of her mouth twisted into a grotesque smile. "This is not your fight, Kimberly Wantland. You should worry about your mother instead."

The unexpected turn in the conversation sent a jolt of surprise racing through her like an electric shock. She jerked backward and stumbled over her own feet as she retreated from the bed.

Michael and Rosie gasped.

Ruth stopped reciting the Lord's Prayer mid-sentence. "Your mother? What does she mean?"

Before Kimberly could gather her thoughts or slow her breathing, a creaking noise drew her attention. The closet door slowly swung open.

Clothes fell from their hangers. Shoes spilled from the space. Dolls dropped from a shelf and crawled toward her.

TJ shouted. "The porcelain ladies!"

Kimberly turned in a circle, watching the room around her come to life. Jaws hung open, eyes wide, as her crew and the Johnsons took in the spectacle. The Ladies of Fashion promenaded about their tiny circular display shelves. Music and voices blared through the house.

Ruth pressed her hands to her ears. "What is that?"

"Sounds like a radio or television switched on. Maybe both."

"What's happening?" Rebecca appeared in the doorway. As her gaze fell on the shoes and dolls clomping and lurching across the room, the teenager screamed. "What's happening?"

Michael yelled a warning. "Kimberly! Look out!"

She turned again to discover Faith's possessions from the closet encircled her. They kept a distance and moved no closer, marching round and round her.

From somewhere in the house, she heard Sterling call, "Hey, guys? I can't get the radio to turn off."

As if to prove a point, the Christian rock blared louder, reverberating through the walls, the bass shaking framed pictures and photos.

The dolls and shoes drew closer, the circle tighter.

Michael took a step toward her. She threw her hands out. "A poltergeist makes a lot of noise but can't hurt anyone. Stay back. Someone is finally trying to communicate with me."

Michael frowned and raised his voice to be heard over the

cacophony filling the house. "Are you completely certain this is truly a poltergeist?"

Was she? No. But she had a feeling and hoped she was correct. She grasped her crystal. "George? Are you there? Are you causing this? Come talk to me. Let me help you."

The dolls, books, and figurines stopped moving. The house went silent. A book fell from the nightstand by Faith's bed. Kimberly stepped over shoes lying in a heap near her feet and walked to the bedside table.

She picked it up, scouring the printed pages for clues. "I don't understand what this means. Deuteronomy? What are you trying to tell me?"

Faith turned to face her. When she spoke, her grave voice hinted at malice. "No one of illegitimate birth shall enter the assembly of the Lord."

CHAPTER TWENTY-FOUR

THE DARK HOUSE, now silent, seemed to seethe, resting for the next assault against her, Kimberly thought as she wandered alone through the rooms. The moon shown above the gnarled oak out back as she passed through the dining room and glanced out the window. A shiver hurried her meandering pace to the living room. She peered past a curtain and into the still street. The black pavement, empty since the protestors disbanded at nightfall, glistened under the pale moonlight, shimmering like a creek cutting through the neighborhood.

Faith had slept, virtually comatose, since the episode. Neither cold nor feverish, they found no reason to summon medical attention. But the family remained in the house rather than leave for a hotel. They couldn't move the girl in this state. Ruth had busied herself straightening the room, returning items to the closet, rearranging the Ladies of Fashion, and replacing the Bible on the nightstand. Kimberly, still shaken from the reference to her mother, didn't help with cleanup this time. She didn't watch the footage with the rest of the crew either. The entire experience had etched itself deeply into her mind. She fought to keep herself from running out the door and never coming back. Between Ezekiel's crowd of angry followers screaming at and threatening her and the personal turn this investigation had taken, all she wanted to do was run away and hide.

But then what would happen to Faith?

She turned from the window and flopped onto the couch, dropping her head into her hands. A young girl suffered and so far she'd done nothing to help. Snickers clicked his way into the room, approaching her quietly, head down, whining softly. When he reached her side, he sat and rested his head on her leg, large brown eyes gazing up at her.

"Hey, little guy," she whispered, petting his furry head. "Thanks for the encouragement."

Rosie tiptoed into the room, slid onto the couch beside her, and pressed a mug of tea into her hands. "Here. Drink."

"Thanks." Kimberly held the mug to her face and breathed deeply, allowing the steam to relax and soothe her before she sipped it. "I'm glad your dad is okay. I will never forget how supportive he was when you first joined the show. He may have been my first fan."

"Absolutely he was. I mean, he was super happy I finally had a job that might lead somewhere. But he liked you and was fascinated by the show. Did you reach Angela?"

Kimberly shook her head. She hadn't brought herself to attempt reaching out to her house sitter. "I didn't try yet. It's the middle of the night. I don't want to wake her."

"I get that. It was so creepy hearing that little girl mention your mom, though. How would she know?"

She swallowed hard. "Clearly the spirit possessing her."

"Yeah, but . . . how would he know?"

"I have no idea. This has never happened before."

"Sterling is really shaken. You might go talk to him."

"Where is he?"

"TJ showed him footage from Faith's room, and he went to sit in there. He's miffed he left and missed the excitement. But the radio blaring music and not responding to the power button spooked him."

"We're all a little rattled, I think."

"This one has been crazy for sure. You okay? I mean, I know you're not."

She leaned her head on Rosie's shoulder. "No. Not at all. I've attracted fringe lunatics. I'm powerless to fight back against them so they stand out there draining my energy, leaving me to investigate with lessened ability. I haven't figured out what the spirit wants. If I can't figure out the root problem, I can't solve it and resolve the haunting. And on top of everything else, all the talk about demons has dredged up memories of Mom and the day she died and how helpless I felt. I'm scared. I'm scared and I have no idea what to do next. Not for Mom. Not for Faith. I don't think I can do this."

Michael happened into the room for the last bit. "You can. You have to. Who else can?"

"I'm depleted, Michael. I'm next to worthless in my current state. The crowd and the poltergeist combined are too much. I can't fight them both."

"The situation isn't fair to you, I agree. We need to get rid of the protestors."

"Anything we do to run them off, they'll twist to their advantage. They turn me into the bad guy no matter what."

"We have a permanent camera out front now. So far nothing helpful, but one of them will trip up eventually."

"Unlikely. They know the camera is there. They are professional manipulators. I'm not a witch, we haven't suppressed anyone's rights, but try to convince their thousands of followers. Some people believe anything they read online."

Michael sighed. "You'll figure it out. You always do."

"And what happens to Faith if I don't?"

"You will."

She placed her mug on the coffee table and squeezed her temples. "Why can't someone else figure it out for once?"

A yell carried downstairs. She, Rosie, and Michael jumped to their feet and raced up the staircase.

The rest of her crew appeared to be en route to Faith's room, so she turned left and followed them inside.

The girl remained motionless on her back, eyes shut.

Sterling, however, stood in the center of the room, eyes wild as he twisted back and forth.

She went straight to him, placed a hand on each side of his face, and forced eye contact. "Hey. Hey. Shhh. What happened?"

"I was . . . the closet . . . the doll . . ." He shook his head. "I must've fallen asleep and had a nightmare."

"Can you tell me about it?"

His gaze traveled to TJ. "Not on camera."

"Okay. You guys can all go back to what you were doing."

"But this is where the action is," TJ said.

"TJ. Please." She shot him a look, eyebrows raised.

"Fine."

The crew filed out, leaving her alone with Sterling and an unresponsive Faith.

She rested a hand on Sterling's arm.

He dragged a hand down his face and blinked several times. "I was sitting in the chair in case Faith had an episode or something. I heard a click and the closet door started to creep open. It squeaks, so I heard it opening. I swear I—you'll think I'm crazy, but I swear there was a light shining inside. Not from the bulb. Just a glow. And then this doll came walking out. I guess it was a doll. An old creepy doll." He shuddered.

"Why would I think you're crazy? The same thing happened to me earlier."

"No. This wasn't real. It couldn't be. Something like that isn't possible."

She crossed to the closet and flipped the light on.

Sterling shuffled his feet. "What are you doing?"

She bent and picked up a threadbare cloth doll from the floor. The yarn hair frizzed out of its braids. One button eye had broken in half and barely hung on by a thread. She held it out to Sterling. "This?"

His startled jump answered her question even before he spoke. "That's not possible. How could I dream something I didn't know about?"

"You're either clairvoyant or you weren't dreaming."

"Clearly there is at least one more option because neither of those can be true."

"How would you explain it then? Logically?"

"I must be losing my mind."

"No. You're learning to use it in new ways." She took his hand. "Come on. Stay by me. The poltergeist has probably exhausted its energy for now, but it will torment you relentlessly given the opportunity."

"What about her?" He gestured to Faith.

"Let's let the family sleep while they can. We can check in on her while we patrol the house."

"You think she's okay?"

"I wouldn't leave her if I didn't. I want to try to connect with the spirit, but it expended energy teasing you with the doll. It will probably be quiet for a bit. And if not, the cameras will catch anything big that happens."

She spotted TJ in the hallway. "Be sure to check the cameras in Faith's room. Activity may have drained the batteries."

"Sure thing!"

"And stay quiet," she whispered. "I know we usually have the house to ourselves, but the family is here so be respectful."

"Yes, ma'am!"

She led Sterling to the living room and asked Rosie to make some tea for him. "He's been targeted by the poltergeist so something soothing and relaxing."

"I don't like tea," Sterling protested. He called after Rosie as she headed to the kitchen, "Don't waste your time. I don't want any."

Ruth turned the corner into the living room, tying a robe.

"Sterling, you woke her up yelling about tea."

"Didn't yell."

"He didn't wake me. I haven't slept a bit all night. I'm too worried."

"See?" Sterling said. "I didn't wake her. Didn't yell. And don't want tea."

"Why do you have that doll?" Ruth asked.

"I wanted to ask you the significance," Kimberly answered. "It looks quite old."

"Very," Ruth confirmed. "My great-great-grandmother made it for her daughter, my great-grandmother, and we've passed it down ever since. We don't handle it anymore for fear of damaging it."

"I'm so sorry. Sterling experienced an incident with it, and I was hoping to find out if it's relevant to the investigation or not."

"What happened?"

"Nothing," Sterling insisted. "I fell asleep and had a dream. Nothing happened."

"Sterling was startled by the closet opening and the doll . . . falling out of it." She opted not to share the part where he'd seen it walking. He clearly wasn't accepting the idea. "This is a family heirloom?"

"Yes." Ruth nodded emphatically. "Treasured. We've passed it down all these generations. But we didn't let the girls tote it around or love on it too much. We put it away once they were toddlers for fear it won't survive much cuddling."

This made no sense. The porcelain figurines and the doll, handmade with love and treasured by the family—these weren't the types of things a poltergeist should antagonize the family with. What was happening here?

Ruth held out a hand. "May I put it away again?"

"Yes, of course." As Ruth wrapped her hand gingerly around the fabric, the doll sizzled with psychic energy.

A yell from upstairs preceded TJ rushing downstairs.

Kimberly jumped to her feet as he entered the living room.

He held out his arm. "I think something bit me!"

Sterling shook his head. "No. Nope. Uh-uh. This is not okay. Elise, did you find anything on Indian burial grounds around here? Maybe moved when the houses went in? Kimberly, you promised no *Poltergeist* ending!"

Elise attempted to launch into a dissertation on the history of the land.

Sterling held up a hand. "Indian burial ground. Yes or no?"

"No record of one," Elise conceded.

More footsteps brought Daniel, with Rebecca close on his heels, rubbing her eyes.

Ruth stared at TJ's arm. "What happened? Was it Faith? Did she bite you? I'm so sorry."

"Bite him?" Daniel asked. "Will this hellish trial never end?"

"Everyone calm down," Michael soothed.

Why would Ruth think Faith bit him? Then again, TJ hadn't stipulated yet. "Has she bitten someone?"

Ruth's cheeks flushed, apparently in embarrassment. "She has snapped at us a few times."

Michael held his arms wide. "And you didn't mention this to us why?"

"Has she been tested for rabies?" Sterling asked. "Has she suddenly developed an aversion to bathing?"

Kimberly held up both hands. "Everyone, quiet. Let TJ speak."

Cradling his arm, TJ took a deep breath. "It wasn't the girl. She was sleeping when I got to her room. I checked the batteries and then kinda looked around to see if I could figure out what scared Sterling. I mean, like, figure out what animated the doll. Right?"

Sterling cleared his throat. "I must have dreamed it. As strange as that seems, it's the only explanation. The doll couldn't have been walking. Sleep deprivation can cause hallucinations and I'm beyond exhausted."

TJ shook his head. "No, dude. There's something in the attic.

I heard a noise while I was in the girl's room. Sounded like footsteps in the attic. I went down the hall to the attic door and noticed a light glowing. As soon as I opened the door something grabbed my wrist and bit me!"

Ruth's hands flew to her mouth. "Faith has shown us bite marks on her arms. We . . . we thought she was biting herself."

Daniel sighed heavily and shook his head.

Everyone in her crew looked to her.

"Okay, we already knew we were dealing with something vicious and powerful. Let's all take a few minutes to collect our thoughts and breathe." What good would that do? She had no idea, but they all seemed to expect her to say something.

"I'll . . . I'll get the first aid kit." Ruth's voice quavered. As she passed Kimberly, the woman rested a hand on her arm. "Don't give up on us. Please don't leave."

Kimberly took hold of Ruth's hand and squeezed. "I'm not going anywhere."

CHAPTER TWENTY-FIVE

SNICKERS LAY UNDER THE TABLE, head resting on Kimberly's feet as she sat, worrying over each bit of information they'd collected so far. Restless, she longed to pace, move about the space. But she couldn't bring herself to disturb the dog. His attention comforted her, and she sensed he intended it to.

Her crew had gathered around the table with her. She had the land claim, the doll, and the bible in front of her. How did it all tie together? She'd asked Rebecca to repeat the entire conversation with the Ouija board several times. But she knew something was missing.

"Anything on the recordings?" she asked Stan.

Her head camera operator glanced up from his computer screen. "They're blurry. Disjointed. Lots of static. But TJ did catch the light under the attic door. I'm trying to isolate where he got bit, see if he caught any images. Maybe we can determine what we're up against. But to anyone else, the images will look like faked click bait. Not much to go on."

Rosie rubbed Kimberly's temples. "You're getting too worked up, girl. You need to relax."

"I'm trying. But it's so frustrating. The puzzle pieces won't come together. Heck, I feel like I have a jumbled assortment of pieces from different puzzles."

"You're not getting anything at all?" Michael asked.

"Like the recordings, it's jumbled and non-coherent. I know there's a presence here. I know it's male. I know he's miserable and wants to make everyone in this house miserable. What I don't know is how to convince him to connect with me and let me help him."

Silence descended on the group.

After a moment, Ruth whispered, "You know, my mother talked about George quite a few times. I assumed she was remembering someone from her past. And everything I read about Alzheimer's advised not to question or argue. So I just let her talk."

Kimberly sat up, leaning across the table toward Ruth. The woman hadn't mentioned this before. Perhaps she could glean some clues from the elderly woman's conversations. "What did she say about George?"

"Oh, I don't know. At the time I didn't pay all that much attention. Honestly, I worried she was remembering some old boyfriend from when she was younger, and I didn't really want to hear about that. But she would say that George came to visit and check on her." Ruth stopped fiddling with her wedding band and looked up at her. "You know, I'd forgotten this, but she told me once that George was so happy when I chose the name Rebecca."

Kimberly frowned and grasped her quartz. This case was giving her a headache. "What you're saying doesn't make any sense."

Sterling finally contributed to the conversation. "Kimberly, the ramblings of an Alzheimer's patient don't typically make sense."

Ruth nodded. "I agree. Especially toward the end. Except when she talked about George, she seemed lucid. She was calm, more like herself before she got sick. And the less coherent in general, the more she told me about George."

The more her grandmother's mental faculties deteriorated, the more she'd talked about George? Did the loss of social norms and expectations open people to input from the spirit world? Interesting to contemplate. "I understand but that's not what I meant. Her mother's experiences sound positive and reassuring. Why would George hurt Faith and terrorize the family when Ruth's mother reports such positive interactions that appear to indicate he's been here many years—maybe more than we realize —and had ample opportunity to cause problems before now?"

Ruth dropped her head in her hands. "What if he did hurt her? What if some of her skin lesions weren't expected wounds due to thinning skin and clumsiness? I should've been here. I should have done more. You just never see the end coming. You always assume you'll have another day."

Kimberly grasped the woman's hands. "I don't think George ever hurt your mother. I think he was here keeping her company when you were busy with your family. You were blessed to care for her into her later years, and I know you did everything you could."

Unlike me. I stood by while something attacked my mother. Didn't even call for help.

Enough. She couldn't dwell on the past. All she could do was solve the current haunting. And plan to investigate her childhood home the moment her schedule allowed it. Dwelling on the past would change nothing.

Overwhelmed with the urge to shield and protect this family, she motioned for everyone to gather around. "Come on. We can figure this out. Everyone think. The property claim was disputed. James insisted George stole it and vice versa. James hung George for crimes that George insisted he didn't commit. If that's all true, George would be here looking for revenge against the descendants of the man who wronged him."

Nods and murmurs of agreement circled the table.

"That makes sense until we factor in the evidence"—she glanced at Sterling but he didn't roll his eyes—"that George has possibly been here on the contested property for generations. Conceivably since the hanging. But the family never experienced anything malicious until Faith's birthday party. What set him off?"

Sterling looked around the table, sighed, and leaned forward. "No one else, huh? Really? You're going to make me do it?"

Caught off guard, Kimberly asked, "Do you have a theory, Sterling?"

"Remember Occam's Razor? 'The simplest explanation is usually the correct one.' If we were talking about people, I'd say you're describing two different people. You accept spirits exist around us. If I also believed in them, I would say you're describing the behavior of two different spirits. Judging by the 'evidence' you just laid out."

She nearly slapped her forehead. "Of course! That would explain it. You're a genius! The girls must have released a second spirit with the Ouija board."

Sterling's head rolled back, and he looked at the ceiling. "Great. I'm a genius figuring out ghost logic. Terrific. Exactly what I never wanted."

"No, this is great!" she enthused. "Just the break in the case I needed! Now I can approach this with fresh eyes and maybe make some progress. It's not George we need to connect with. It's someone else! The question is, who and what do they want?"

"You know," Sterling said, "my very first episode, you decided you had a second ghost in the house. Seems like someone else could have arrived at this conclusion."

"But we needed you to see it for us this time." She grabbed his hand and squeezed. "Sometimes we need fresh eyes."

His features softened. "A fresh perspective never hurts, that's true. I guess I'm okay with it. Seriously, though. What else could be happening here? Thoughts anyone?"

Snickers lifted his head from her feet. He stood and ran to the stairs, whimpering.

She exchanged confused looks with her crew, then followed the dog.

Faith padded silently down the staircase in her nightgown and bare feet. The girl's eyes, though open, seemed unfocused.

Ruth moved to intercept her daughter, but Kimberly grabbed her arm.

"Is she normally a sleepwalker?"

"No, not to my knowledge."

"Don't disturb her."

Faith hesitated when she reached the first floor, swaying in place. The girl changed trajectory, walked to the radio, and switched it on.

Ruth tried again to go to Faith, but Kimberly held an arm out, blocking her. "Let her. Please. We need information."

Faith twisted the dial until the music faded, melting into crackling static.

The girl turned her empty, glazed gaze on Kimberly and whispered, "George wants to talk to you, but James won't let him."

Michael gasped. "Two ghosts confirmed. Well done, Sterling."

She didn't know if Sterling responded. She didn't dare take her eyes off Faith. "James? What does he want? What could possibly be upsetting him? He had everything he wanted."

The radio popped and hissed. A hesitant voice, thin and shaky, burst from the speakers, the vowels stretched between tentative consonants. "Hello?"

This time she heard Sterling respond.

"What the hell?"

Her co-host crossed to the radio, lifted and shook it.

"Can you hear me?" The hazy voice increased in volume and intensity, then tapered off.

Sterling dropped the radio. "It must be picking up a local transistor or CB frequency nearby."

"We hear you, George," she assured him. "What do you need to tell us?"

"Can't . . . project . . . long . . ."

"He's weakened. Too weak to effectively communicate this way. I need the Ouija board!"

"Then why did he have Faith turn on the radio in the first place?"

"He's trying to get our attention," she said. "Someone go get the planchette from Faith's room! Where did you guys hide the board?"

Faith remained silent, vacant stare in her eyes.

Rebecca looked horrified. "We didn't—"

"Is that demon board still in my house somewhere, young lady?" Daniel's booming voice seemed to shake the walls.

Ruth laid her hands on his arms. "Daniel, please calm—"

"It's not here!" Rebecca cried. "Dakota took it back home!"

"Go get it!" She pointed to the front door. Her crew remained motionless. "Someone get the planchette from upstairs! TJ? Go get the board. Rebecca can show you which house."

TJ glanced at Michael.

Sterling had picked up the radio and turned it over and over in his shaking hands. Brow furrowed, he mumbled to himself. Everyone eyed her warily, as if she'd lost her mind.

What was wrong with them? This was it. They'd been hoping for a break and here it was. One of the ghosts wanted to communicate with her. George had used the Ouija board before and probably felt most comfortable with that medium.

"Kimmy." Her director cleared his throat. "It's nearly eleven o'clock at night. We can't go pounding on neighbors' doors. You know that."

"But . . . he's trying to tell us something! This could be the break I need."

She heard a distant *lub-dub* from somewhere in the house. The planchette called to her, pulsing with a message.

"Kimmy, we're not—"

"Then get the planchette and some paper!"

"What kind of—"

"Any blank paper! Hurry! We don't have much time."

She saw Michael gesture to TJ, who turned and ran upstairs. She grabbed her quartz and breathed deeply, taking control of her emotional state, forcing focus and calm. She must not lose control while operating the Ouija board.

Ruth left and returned with a sheet of copy paper.

Kimberly sat at the dining table and rotated the paper to a landscape position. "I need a pencil or pen."

Elise held out a pen.

"Thank you." She started in the top corners, scribbling the words YES and NO before transcribing the alphabet, the numbers one through nine plus a zero, and then the word GOODBYE below that. Familiar enough with Ouija boards to create her own, the facsimile was not bad at all. The spacing was a little off but it would do.

In fact, it was good enough to offend Daniel.

"I don't want that in my house," he insisted.

"It's a piece of paper with writing on it," Sterling said. "What could you possibly object to?"

"The writing is the important part. Just like the Bible is sacred and precious with the word of God, this paper is now contaminated with evil. It's used in occult practices. Good intentions or no, I must insist."

He reached for the paper. Kimberly crossed her arms and leaned forward protectively, shielding the paper.

"This piece of paper can't hurt you," Sterling insisted. "Let her do her bit."

"Daniel." Ruth's voice held a steely edge that Kimberly hadn't heard from the woman before. "Faith needs us to be strong right now. Whatever it takes. We invited Ms. Wantland into our home to help us. I believe she can. We can't stand in her way. If she needs to do this, we need to trust God will protect us and step back."

"Where has trusting God gotten us so far?" Daniel asked, his voice shaking. "Where is He while my daughter fights a demon?"

"That's why He sent us Kimberly. Because He knew we couldn't fight this alone." Ruth rested a hand on Kimberly's shoulder. "Lord, guide Ms. Wantland as she seeks to help our daughter, Faith. Give her strength to use the gift you saw fit to grant her and to drive out the evil that has taken hold in our home. In your name, amen."

As murmured amens echoed the prayer closing, warm energy flowed through her.

She could do this.

TJ placed the planchette in the center of her homemade board.

She looked around the room at all the eyes on her. Grasping her quartz, she closed her eyes and breathed deeply, clearing her thoughts and emotions. Only an empty vessel could effectively channel a spirit while remaining in control.

"Who will operate the board with me?" No one answered. She looked around the room. "No one?"

"My family and I will not participate." Daniel's tone told her arguing would be pointless. "I'll allow you to use it, but we will not involve ourselves."

"Fair enough. Guys?" She looked to her crew. "Don't all volunteer at once. Really? Sterling? This is your chance to not only witness but experience paranormal phenomenon firsthand."

"After all, it's only a piece of paper. Right?" Daniel said.

Sterling glanced at Daniel before answering. "What do I do?"

She took the paper in one hand, the planchette in the other, and settled in the living room floor, legs crossed. "Sit here. Close. Mirror me."

He lowered himself but remained about a foot away.

"Close. Our knees need to touch to support the letter board. Actually, this paper is so flimsy we need—"

Elise thrust a clipboard at her. "This should do it."

"Thanks, Elise." She wiggled forward a bit more and held her fingers above the planchette. "Okay, Sterling, we will rest our fingers along the edge like this. Don't apply pressure and don't push it. Don't say anything. Try not to think negative thoughts. You don't need to believe. Just be blank."

"Be careful," Rebecca said. "Please."

"It's just a piece of paper," Sterling muttered.

She closed her eyes and took a deep breath to center herself. "George? We're here. We're listening."

Nothing happened. The planchette remained still.

"George, Faith says you want to tell us something."

She glanced at the girl, rooted in place, vacant eyes staring at nothing. The girl seemed to be fighting back, her head turned toward them. Perhaps she had felt the spirit's hold on her weaken.

Refocusing on the makeshift Ouija board, she tried again. "George, we're trying to figure out what happened here. We want to help. I saw that you were hanged."

She felt an electric charge from the planchette buzz through her fingers. The plastic piece shimmied, then drifted in an arc across the paper, stopping on the word YES.

Sterling's eyes lifted to meet her gaze. "I'm barely touching this thing."

"I know. Don't freak out on me."

"I never freak out."

She hoped that was true. "George, is James in the house with us?"

The planchette slid away from and then back to YES.

"Did the Ouija board release his spirit?"

YES

"Why is James here, George?"

R-E-B-E-C-C-A

She heard Rebecca gasp. "Why? Why me?"

"But he's making Faith sick," she said. "Why is he hurting the family?"

R-E-B-E-C-C-A

"But I didn't do anything!" Rebecca insisted.

"What did Rebecca do, George?"

M-I-N-E

"What?" Rebecca said. "What does that mean? I didn't do anything."

"Did you move the doll, George?"

YES

"Why did you move it?"

M-I-N-E

"Who is yours, George?"

R-E-B-E-C-C-A

"What did you do, Rebecca?" Daniel demanded.

"Nothing! I—I played the Ouija board with Dakota! But I didn't think anything would happen!"

F-A-I-T-H

R-U-T-H

Daniel moved closer. "That's enough! He's threatening my family. He's clearly the one who's been molesting my wife and daughters at night."

NO

"Kimmy?" Michael's voice broke through the chatter. "You got this? What's happening?"

"Are you saying all the women are yours, George?"

YES

This wasn't going at all as she expected. She'd been so sure she had it mostly figured out, that James was the one causing harm. But as the girls had reported, George seemed fixated on them.

"George, we don't understand."

"I think we understand plenty," Daniel said.

W-A-N-T R-E-B-E-C-C-A

"That's enough!" Daniel yelled. "I want this disgusting thing out of my house!"

S-A-F-E

"Wait!" Kimberly yelled. "We're missing something!"

"He wants me safe?" Rebecca asked. "I didn't . . . we didn't . . . let him finish, I guess. I thought he meant . . ."

"You want Rebecca safe?"

YES

Footsteps thumped above them.

"What is that?" Michael asked.

She turned her attention from the board and listened. "Sounds like footsteps."

"From upstairs?" Michael asked. "No one is up there."

She quickly confirmed his assessment, taking a headcount. All the family and all her crew remained in the living room.

"Is that coming from the attic?" TJ asked. "That's where something bit me."

"It's probably a squirrel," Sterling suggested.

"Dude! That does not sound like a squirrel," TJ said.

"We're all here," Ruth repeated. "What could it be?"

She watched everyone duck and flinch as the thumping increased in volume and intensity.

"No one is up there!" Sterling said.

Movement from the planchette drew her attention back to the Ouija board.

W-A-N-T T-H-E-M S-A- F-E

S-A-F-E

H-E I-S C-O-M-I-N-G

"Mommy!" Faith cried out suddenly. "He's coming! He's back!"

Ruth raced to her daughter's side. "What is it, baby?"

Kimberly watched the girl quake in fear.

Ruth looked to her helplessly, as she held the girl close. "She hasn't called me 'Mommy' in years."

"He's coming!" the girl repeated.

H-E I-S C-O-M-I-N-G

The radio blared static as lights blinked on and off.

The footsteps thumped closer, sounding as if someone ran down the hall of the second floor.

K-E-E-P T-H-E-M S-A-F-E

She watched the board spell, and something clicked. She knew what she needed to do, knew what George asked of her. "Sterling, let go!"

As the footsteps thumped down the stairs, she threw the board to the side and jumped to her feet.

She saw him. A bright manifestation of James from her vision of the past. Though gauzy and translucent, she recognized him. The same cruel smile cut across his face. His eyes homed on Faith, who seemed rooted to the spot, terror in her eyes.

"Leave her alone!" She crossed the room and jumped in front of Faith, shielding the girl from the spirit, opening all of her senses to envelop him.

She seized under the impact, muscles paralyzed by the sudden incursion. James' memories played vividly across her mind. She saw him hang George and felt him delight in the triumph of the moment. She experienced blood-curdling fury and watched him beat Rebecca mercilessly, felt the jarring impact of each blow. He took her for his bride, longing for the town's approval while still furious with her. He drank to excess. He frequented the town's brothel, abusing the women there too. All quietly, hiding his dark side from the town, so they wouldn't know their sheriff was not the man of God he pretended to be on Sundays. She watched Rebecca scream in agony during childbirth, saw the newborn. Drank deeply from a whiskey bottle. Rage and images of George filled her mind.

She understood. She knew. And she'd seen all she could stomach. She attempted to sever the connection with James, but he fought back. He showed her more and more, apparently aware how much it disturbed her—and delighting in it. He enjoyed inflicting pain. He refused to release her. Psychically, she wrestled with him, pushing him away. When she felt his hold weaken slightly, she gave one huge push, forcing him out, closing the connection.

She fell to the ground, panting and nauseous.

Rosie and Michael knelt beside her.

As she fought to catch her breath, she looked up at Ruth. "Have you ever had a DNA test?"

CHAPTER TWENTY-SIX

Sitting on the couch, Kimberly rubbed her temples, struggling with how to share what she'd learned with the family. This wasn't how her investigations normally played out. She liked bringing closure and peace to spirits and the living alike. What she'd just seen didn't indicate a happy ending was forthcoming for anyone.

The one good change was that Faith had woken from her trance-like state. Presumably James had exhausted all his energy fighting Kimberly. But she knew he would return as soon as he could. She would have to be ready to prevent him gaining hold of Faith again. The two sisters sat on the couch, Faith tucked beside Rebecca, who held her younger sister fiercely.

Once again, Kimberly noticed a stab of jealousy. The girls clearly shared a bond she couldn't begin to imagine.

"Why did you ask about a DNA test?" Ruth asked, wringing her hands. "We have our family records all the way back to the Land Run in 1889."

"And nothing before that?" Elise asked.

"Well, no."

"I couldn't find anything on James Loveless prior to the land claim from the Land Run. Seems a little odd for someone so intent on establishing himself in Guthrie."

Ruth shrugged. "How many of you can trace your roots back that far? People didn't keep good records back then. It's not that unusual."

Elise shuffled through a folder and extracted a sheet of paper. "True. But that also made it easier to falsify records. Look. Here's an example of a family tree missing a name. One wife of one of eight brothers is left off, though all the children are included."

Ruth's eyebrows crinkled. "Maybe the mother died?"

"No," Elise said. "In that scenario, the name would be struck through. But still recorded and left there even after the man remarried. I discovered that it was common practice back then not to record the names of Native American brides who married into white families. And in rural areas like Guthrie, additional records either didn't exist or were lost through the years."

Kimberly could see Elise's roundabout approach was only further confusing Ruth. "We don't have a missing name though, Elise."

"Right. Not in this case. I only meant to illustrate how far people would go back then to hide Native American blood."

Rosie tsk'ed loudly.

"It was a different time," she comforted Rosie.

Rosie crossed her arms. "In some ways, maybe. And in some ways, things haven't changed much at all."

Kimberly couldn't refute that. She'd witnessed people harassing Rosie numerous times—and been called a few hateful terms herself when she'd defended her friend. For that matter she had the equivalent of an angry mob after her. She remembered the hanging—lynching—she'd experienced psychically and shuddered.

Ruth glanced at each face. "Hide Native American blood? I don't—"

She shifted to sit next to the woman. "I experienced visions when I intercepted James' spirit. Sweet, gentle Rebecca was meant to stand next to him in public and make him look good—a strong, upstanding citizen—and provide him with heirs. But Rebecca was already involved with George when she caught his attention. He invented charges against George and had him hanged to get to her, but what he didn't know is that she carried George's child."

"But he was the sheriff. Everything passed down through the family records indicate he was a good man." Ruth's eyes filled with tears. "You must be wrong."

Faith lifted her head from her sister's shoulder. "He isn't good, Mom. He never forgave great-great-great-grandma Rebecca."

"He never forgave *her?*" Rosie interrupted. "I'm sorry but that's garbage. He coveted another man's woman and killed to get her. He lied about cattle rustling and claim jumping to do it. And he got away with it because of the color of George's skin."

"Faith is giving us James' point of view, Rosie. No one here feels that way or supports his behavior."

"But . . . we don't look Native American," Ruth said. "Sure, we have dark hair and we're maybe not as pale as say someone from Scandinavia, but—"

"I don't either," Rosie said. "My skin tone is darker than yours, but that's because my more recent ancestry is Hispanic. And you do have high cheek bones."

"Do you happen to have any photos from back then?" Elise asked. "Maybe a few generations ago, the influence would have been more evident."

"No, nothing that old," Ruth said. "I just can't believe this. And you think George has remained on the property all this time?"

Kimberly nodded. "I think so. The sudden and bewildering lynching displaced his spirit. I think he wanted to remain close to Rebecca, even after death. I suspect he's been watching over the family ever since."

"Hold up," Daniel said. "My wife and daughters have felt hands on them in the night. Wouldn't that mean the ghost has been molesting his own descendants?"

"No, not at all. I believe only James has been harassing you. And if George was really the father of Rebecca's child, James is not related by blood. Did Rebecca and James have any children together?"

Ruth shook her head as Elise dove for her folder and extracted a family tree. She pushed her glasses up her nose and peered at the paper. "Only the one daughter."

"The beatings Rebecca took from James could explain that. I wouldn't be surprised."

"And James' spirit just suddenly appeared?" Daniel asked. "How do you explain that?"

Kimberly glanced at Sterling, fully expecting a snarky response about making up whatever they wanted to. But he stood at a window, staring silently into the dark night, apparently disengaged from the conversation. She almost went to him, wondering if he was okay, but the conversation continued.

Rebecca's voice shook as she spoke. "Did we release him with the Ouija board?"

She hesitated. Every eye but Sterling's turned to her. Daniel looked ready to declare he'd told them about the evils of the occult. The girls appeared overcome with guilt, trembling as they clutched each other. Ruth looked like she couldn't take another blow after learning the hidden scandal from her past. Though she couldn't explain what had kept the spirit relatively dormant over the generations, the Ouija board most likely presented the open invitation James' spirit had been waiting for. But she didn't want to add to the family's stress.

"It can be difficult to know exactly what provokes a spirit to action," she said, carefully choosing her words.

Her crew reeled at her reply. Stan briefly lowered his camera, eyeing her with crinkled brow. Even Sterling turned from the window.

"But don't you think—" Michael began.

"I think we should focus on how to help this family now that we know what's plaguing them and why."

Ruth hugged herself and burst into tears. "So Great-great-grandpa James wasn't my ancestor at all? He was a criminal who murdered my true ancestor? My entire life has been a lie."

Daniel grabbed her and held her close. "Your life is not a lie. You are a good woman. You're my wife, and these are our girls, and we're good Christian people. Nothing that happened all those years ago changes any of that." He looked at his huddling daughters and opened an arm. "Come here, girls."

Rebecca and Faith dove into their parents' embrace.

Still clinging to her family, Ruth asked, "Why Faith? Why is he singling her out?"

"I . . . I held the planchette alone."

Rosie nodded. "That would do it."

Sterling shook his head and seemed finally prompted to join the conversation. "Come on. You honestly think she's the first kid to ever play with one of these boards alone? Surely no one truly believes a piece of plastic is the cause of her illness."

"I'm sure she isn't the first," Kimberly said. "But in this instance the board was spiritually charged and highly active at the time. It's the caustic energy of the spirit causing her illness. And I think James would have found a way regardless. If he were strong enough, I believe he'd be making all of you ill."

Daniel hugged Faith tighter. "She's better now. That's the important thing."

Kimberly took a deep breath but didn't speak, unsure how to share the other bit of information she'd learned.

"Right?" Daniel asked. "You fought him off. Faith is better. The spirit is gone now, isn't he?"

Once again, she felt the weight and responsibility of all eyes on her, everyone looking to her for answers and solutions. She finally had an answer, but it wasn't a good one. And she wasn't sure the solution was a good one either.

"Unfortunately, no," she began. "Normally once I connect with a spirit, I know what it wants, know its unfinished business tethering it to this world. Once I know that, I help the spirit resolve its business, find peace, and transition over to the next realm."

Daniel cocked his head. "Normally? You mean you can't do that this time?"

"No. James wants blood. In his mind, George won."

"James lynched him!" Rosie said. "How the heck is that winning?"

"James didn't find out about the baby until after he'd coerced Rebecca into marrying him. Then he had no offspring of his own. George's true descendants live on the land he believes rightfully his that he claimed in the Land Run. George stayed close, watching them generation through generation. James' spirit is consumed with fury and indignation. His plan failed."

"But what's done is done," Rosie said. "He can't have children now."

"And who cares?" Michael asked. "I'll never have kids. You may choose not to have children. It's not the end of the world."

Before Kimberly could answer, Elise responded. "It was everything back then. Large families worked fields, cared for parents in their old age, and proved a man's virility."

"She's absolutely right. James played it off as not needing children since he was sheriff and not a farmer. But he grew resentful of the presumption that a weak man can't produce children. Or that perhaps he wasn't able to have sex. Eventually he blamed Rebecca to deflect any criticism of himself."

"Of course," Rosie said. "It's always the woman's fault. She doesn't do enough, isn't exciting anymore, won't loan him enough money, doesn't jump and run to placate his every whim, doesn't give him enough kids."

Kimberly cleared her throat. "Rosie. Not every guy turns out to be a jerk." She glanced at the girls. "After all, you have Lorenzo now. He's been great."

"Yeah, yeah. We'll see if that lasts. Doubt I'll be that lucky."

"Back to our problem," Daniel said. "I still haven't heard how this case is so different."

"James posed as a law man, a good citizen. But all for show in public. That wasn't his true self. He brutalized his wife and the prisoners in his jail. He bullied people to get what he wanted. And he liked it. His spirit behaves the same way, if not worse. Our spirit is our true essence, with no inhibitions, no threat of punishment."

"But surely his soul will be punished in hell," Ruth said.

She grabbed her quartz crystal. "He didn't cross over when he died. Perhaps he feared being called to account for his behavior. I don't know. I can't even confirm the existence of heaven and hell. I've caught glimpses of something on the other side of the veil. And I know James doesn't want to cross it."

"Whoa," Michael said. "How sure are you?"

She locked eyes with him, hoping to impress how serious this problem could be. "Completely. He will not cross willingly."

"You don't have a spell or something?" Daniel asked.

The question startled her. "A spell? No. As I keep saying, I'm not a witch."

"And spells don't exist," Sterling muttered.

"Oh, yeah?" Daniel asked. He pointed at the handmade Ouija board. "Still believe *that* is just a piece of paper with writing on it?"

"I don't know what to think," Sterling admitted. "But if Kimberly says spells don't exist, I believe her."

Daniel glanced at her, his jaw tight, then nodded. "Fair enough."

"What about prayers?" Ruth asked. "Maybe there are prayers we can say? You know, like an exorcism?"

"Didn't you say you tried that?" Elise asked.

"Well, our minister came to the house and prayed with us," Ruth said. "We didn't actually pursue a Catholic exorcism."

Daniel nodded. "I looked online and Faith does show many

of the symptoms of demonic possession. We thought about reaching out to see if we have a qualified exorcist nearby. But the process can take six months just to get approved. We needed help faster than that."

"So we called you," Ruth said.

No pressure.

"The Catholic Church is very careful with that process," Kimberly said. "They've taken a lot of flak over the years, as I'm sure you can understand given the angry mob we've amassed in just a few days."

"But can't you—"

"No. I cannot perform an exorcism. Only carefully trained priests are qualified for that. However, it's moot anyway, since we've determined this is not a demonic possession. We're dealing with a strong spiritual entity, but not a demon. We did manage to overcome his control over Faith for now."

"But what's to stop him from taking control again?"

"Nothing. In fact I fully expect him to as soon as he's regained the power required."

"You're saying we're helpless? There's nothing you can do?"

She looked to Michael, asking a silent question, wondering how he'd respond. Would he approve the method she was about to propose?

He lifted an eyebrow and shrugged, his hands open to her. He was leaving the decision up to her. And she knew she didn't have a choice.

"Maybe not." She looked around the room at all the expectant faces watching her, trusting her to lead them, waiting to hear the solution. "I can attempt a forced translocation."

Someone in her crew gasped.

Rosie looked resigned, as if she had expected this. "Oh, girl."

Ruth and Daniel watched the reactions, faces twisted in confusion.

"What is that?" Daniel asked.

"If successful, I would force James' spirit to cross over into the next realm."

"Then he couldn't hurt Faith anymore?" Ruth asked.

"He would truly be gone, yes. His spirit would no longer remain in this world among us."

"Let's do that then!" Daniel said.

"You have to understand, I've never attempted this before," she cautioned. "Never."

"And it's highly dangerous," Michael said. "It's one thing to assist in a peaceful crossing. Quite another to force a spirit who doesn't want to go."

"What other options do we have at this point?" Daniel asked.

Kimberly looked to Michael, then Rosie, then Elise. Each of them shook their heads. She would have to do this, whatever the cost, whatever it took. She couldn't leave this house without ridding them of James forever. She faced the family and took a deep breath. "No other options. I'll have to dislocate him. We don't have a choice."

CHAPTER TWENTY-SEVEN

THE STONE LION INN welcomed them, the glow of the windows drawing them up the steps. The old dwelling sighed a warm breath of air around them as they escaped the cool night outside.

"Oklahoma's weather is all over the place," Sterling said, rubbing his hands together and blowing on them. "Wicked thunderstorm one day, hot and humid the next, now tonight it's downright chilly."

"It's doing terrible things to my hair," Rosie said as she stared into the hallway mirror. "What a nightmare."

Kimberly threw an arm around Rosie's shoulders. "I think the greater concern is the asshole ghost we're up against, but sure, your hair."

Michael clapped his hands to quiet them all. "Everyone take five and then meet back here in the dining room to discuss our agenda tomorrow."

Kimberly caught Elise's eye. "And research forced translocations."

Elise lifted her cell phone before returning her attention to the screen. "Already on it."

"Thanks! Do I smell coffee? Or am I having a stroke?"

Rosie lifted the pot from the buffet. "The coffeepot is full!

And there's a notecard in front of it. 'Thanks for all you do. Gloria.'"

"Guess she knew we'd have a late night. Lights on. Coffee waiting. Very thoughtful of her. Or maybe she's hoping to win Sterling's affections." She laughed entirely too hard, casting a glance to see how Sterling responded.

"She's just being a good hostess. It's her job," he said.

"Besides," Rosie chimed in, "she already knows someone else has captured his attention. And she's too old for him anyway."

"Hello?" Michael said. "We can't finish until we start, and I for one would like some sleep tonight. If you don't want to take five, can we get started and discuss Gloria's motivation behind the coffee later? Off the clock?"

"Yikes," she said. "Someone gets salty when he's sleepy."

Michael gave her a withering look. "Honey, you haven't seen salty and you know it."

Stifling a laugh, she kissed his cheek. "I know it well. Let me run to my room. Be right back."

"Be quick about it! You've already wasted more than the five minutes I gave you!"

Sterling fell into step beside her. "I think a bathroom break is in order. I get the feeling it's going to be a long night. Why footage review now instead of in the morning?"

"In truth, we don't really need footage review at this point. We will be looking for anything that might give us an advantage over James tomorrow and trying to develop a plan of attack. Elise and I try to figure out how to force him to cross over."

"You need some positron colliders." He looked at her sideways, clearly hoping she'd get it.

"I've always prided myself on my organic approach. But today I actually wish that was real." She stopped, cocking her head in thought. "Wait a minute. You're a physicist. What do you think?"

He stopped and lifted an eyebrow, half a smile crooking his face. "What do I think about what?"

"Designing some equipment for me."

"You want me to create imaginary equipment from a fictional story for you to use in real life?"

"Well, it doesn't sound like a good idea when you say it in that tone of voice. But you could build real equipment. Something that could try to disrupt the energy field or inhibit a harmful ghost from manifesting. Or maybe we could even trap one like this, that refuses to cross over and is wreaking havoc in people's lives. We have EMFs and the SEEPS and other equipment. Why not take that technology and adapt it?"

He blinked a few times and started laughing. "I appreciate your confidence in my abilities. But even if I thought something like that was possible, it isn't my area of expertise."

She extracted her key and unlocked her door. "Maybe just keep it in mind. That could be really useful to the show."

Sterling remained beside her, lingering in front of her open door. Did he want to be invited in? Was he contemplating her suggestion rather than laughing it off?

She searched his eyes, but his gaze was drawn to something behind her. Whatever held his attention caused his brow to furrow. He grabbed her arm and pulled her into the hallway, wedging himself between her and the bedroom.

She knew him well enough to know he didn't startle easily or overreact. Her pulse kicked up several notches. "What is it?"

"I saw someone at your window. Shadow of a person. I'm sure of it."

"Like I saw before!" She peered over his shoulder. "I don't see anything."

"Whoever it is, they walked away."

A shadow passed across the window.

She jumped, heart hammering. "That's not a ghost. I'm not getting any psychic energy from it."

"You don't have to convince me. I see it and I don't see ghosts."

"What do they want? What do we do?"

Sterling took out his phone. "Go ahead and use the restroom or whatever you need to do. Pretend like everything is normal."

"I can't go in there. Not with that creeper at the window."

He dialed and waited.

Michael walked down the hall. "What's going on? I thought I made myself clear—"

She held up a hand. "Quiet!"

Sterling spoke into his phone. "Yes, ma'am. This is Sterling Wakefield from *The Wantland Files*. We're staying at the Stone Lion Inn and we have a Peeping Tom outside Ms. Wantland's window. Please send an officer immediately. This is the second time he's been here, and I want this guy caught."

"What?" Michael asked as Sterling hung up.

"They're sending someone."

"Peeping Tom?" Michael craned his neck to see into her room.

The shadow crossed the window again.

Michael jumped. "Oh my God. Nope! I don't do stalkers." He turned and headed back to the dining room. "I'll be hiding away from windows."

"Thanks a lot, Michael. Appreciate the concern," she called after him.

"You have Sterling. He can earn his keep."

"Hey! I earn my keep! I—" Michael had turned the corner. "He really is salty when he's sleepy."

She peered at the window again. "Now what?"

"Act like we haven't noticed him. I need to let Gloria know what's happening on her property. The police may need to speak with her."

"Let's go together. I don't think we should separate."

He cocked an eyebrow. "Okay."

In truth, she hated the idea of him showing up at Gloria's bedroom door alone in the middle of the night. But she'd never admit it to him. Besides, she genuinely felt safer with him near. She didn't want to admit that either, but deep down, she knew it was true. Some strong, independent woman she turned out to be.

They were saved the awkwardness of waking the owner, however. Gloria rounded the corner, frown firmly in place. "I hear we have a disturbance?"

"I've called the police," Sterling said. "Not sure if we're dealing with an overly enthusiastic fan or one of Zeke's freaks, or simply someone unhinged who gets his rocks off peeping in random windows. But I'm not taking any chances with Kimberly. Have you had trouble like this before?"

Gloria shook her head. "Not to my knowledge." The inn owner hazarded a glance and gasped. "I see him. That's so creepy."

They stood in the hallway, watching the shadow cross back and forth.

"Should we be doing something?" Gloria whispered.

Sterling shrugged. "We should really act normally. Other than calling the police, there's not much we can do."

"How long do you think this will take?" she asked.

TJ's voice startled her. "Michael said there's a stalker!"

She jumped before realizing who had crept up on her. "Let's go back to the dining room."

"Agreed," Sterling said. "Worst thing we can do is tip them off before the police arrive."

They waited, pacing and drumming fingers, until a knock on the door jolted them to attention.

Gloria opened the front door, the entire *Wantland* crew crowded behind her, to a police officer with Zeke in handcuffs.

Zeke's fury blasted Kimberly, red chakra radiating his supernova hate, eyes boring into her. "You will not prevail. I will take you down."

She shuddered, stricken by the intense power of hatred. "Please, I just want you to leave me alone."

"Never. Not until I'm sure you're done forever." Zeke struggled to move closer, but the police officer's grip held firm. "'Beware of false prophets, who come to you in sheep's clothing, but inwardly are ravenous wolves!'"

"Are you saying I'm a false prophet? Because I'm not the one spewing crazy nonsense to a church I invented. All I do is help people. Not trying to convince anyone of anything."

"You turn people away from the true God with your practice of witchcraft!"

"No, I don't. The Johnsons are Christians. Their faith is strong. I'm not attempting to challenge their religious beliefs in any way."

"You are a menace to believers everywhere and I will see you and your show ended."

Sterling stepped in front of her. "Officer, you heard him. He's threatening her."

The policeman turned to Gloria. "Ma'am, does this man have permission to be on your property?"

"No."

"I'm taking you in on trespassing as well as voyeurism. We don't tolerate Peeping Toms."

"I wasn't peeping! I have no interest in this woman that way. I was patrolling."

"You're harassing," Sterling said. "You can believe whatever you want to, but you have no right to harass and threaten."

"Are you pressing charges?" the officer asked.

Michael hesitated a moment. "It won't reflect well on the show, but I think we have to. We'll all rest better if we know he can't return tonight."

"I'll take him in, but no guarantees how long we can hold him. Some slick lawyer typically bails out nut jobs like him pretty quickly."

"We're close to wrapping up the investigation," Michael said. "We should only need another day."

"I'll press charges," Gloria offered. "He can be mad at me instead of Kimberly or the show. He's trespassing on my property after all."

The officer tipped his hat. "Will do. You folks have a nice evening." He pulled Zeke along with him, reciting his rights as he went.

Zeke yelled over his shoulder, "You can lock me up, but you can't stop us!"

Kimberly blinked at Gloria, dumbfounded. "Why would you do that?"

"He'll move on once you do. I can take the heat for a day. And we women on the fringe have to stick together, don't we? The witches and psychics, the outspoken and opinionated. Other people want us to fall in line and be 'normal' whatever that means. But we know better. The world needs us just the way we are."

Shame twisted her insides. To think she'd been jealous, almost hostile, toward this woman who was risking her own peace and safety to support her. "I . . . thank you."

"Of course, dear. Besides, I knew your mother. I'm sure that's the true reason you decided to stay here. I've been waiting for you to approach me. You could've simply asked."

The shame dissipated, searing shock and excitement rushing in to replace it so fast it gave her emotional whiplash.

The crew turned as one, mouths agape. Rosie rushed to her side and lifted her jaw to close it before holding a bottle under her nose.

"Breathe," her personal assistant instructed. "Deeply."

She took a deep breath of the eucalyptus oil Rosie held.

Gloria watched the reactions with a furrowed brow. "You didn't know? None of you?"

"That you knew my mother? Not at all. I didn't even know she lived in this area. We've been searching for any information—"

Elise stepped forward. "I've researched extensively. We didn't find a thing. Are you sure?"

Gloria laughed. "Very sure. We weren't best friends or

anything, but I knew her. Knew of your dad too. You searched using her married name? Wantland?"

Elise's face melted from confusion to withering disbelief. She glanced at Kimberly as if to ask, Can you believe this? "Of course. Vanessa Wantland."

"Vanessa? No. Her name was Veronica. Veronica LeBlanc when I knew her in high school."

Elise scowled. "That can't be right. Why would she change her name?"

"To hide, I presume. She and your dad skedaddled out of town overnight without a word to anyone. I never saw her or heard from her again. I missed her but couldn't even write to her. Didn't know where they'd gone until it was too late."

Sterling squinted. "Then how do you know Kimberly is her daughter?"

"Her death made the news. Not national news, of course, but it was public, and we learned about it back here. Horrible. Then this brilliant daughter of hers turned herself into a celebrity. She shares pictures on her social media for Ronnie's birthday."

Kimberly gripped Gloria's arm, her heart thudding erratically. "What did you call her?"

"Ronnie. Everyone called her that. Gosh, I could probably dig up an old yearbook if I looked hard enough."

She stared off to the side, vision blurring, her friends' images distorted through the haze of tears welling in her eyes. "Dad used to call her Ronnie, and I never knew why. They never told me a thing. Why didn't they tell me? What were they hiding?"

"Weren't you just a little girl, sweetheart?" Gloria asked. "They must have been dealing with something extremely serious. Why would they tell a young child?"

"But later, Dad could have told me. Something. Anything." Remembering how her father had withdrawn from her, a tear escaped her eye and dripped down her cheek. He had blamed her for her mother's death, she knew that. But oh, how she wished they had leaned on each other for support in that dark time, rather than growing more distant. Dad was all she had after that terrible tragedy. "I was only ten. I didn't know CPR. I don't know what he expected me to do—"

Gloria grabbed her in a hug. "I'll find my old yearbooks. I'll search for anything I can about her, okay? You stop blaming yourself. I know whatever happened, it wasn't your fault. You just focus on your investigation."

CHAPTER TWENTY-EIGHT

THE RESEARCH into forced translocation yielded little information beyond the scope of what Kimberly already knew. She and Elise had read anything and everything they could find online, including a few blogs with the opinion no one could force a ghost to transition. She closed that tab and puffed out a long breath, rubbing her temples.

"I'll need everyone's support of course," she told her crew, gathered around the Stone Lion Inn dining table.

"We'll be there," Michael said.

The others nodded in agreement.

Rosie clasped her hand. "I'll be there, girl."

"Me too," Elise said. "Giving you all my positive energy."

She glanced at Sterling, unclear of his current emotional state.

"I'll be right by your side," he assured her. "Surely you know that by now."

She smiled and nodded, hoping he could bring positive energy to the equation. Otherwise his presence would be less than helpful. This was one time he needed to check his skepticism and just be supportive.

"I'm really worried about the protestors, though," she said.

"All that negative energy will feed the poltergeist all day, amping him up. He will be difficult to overpower fully charged like that."

Sterling held up his phone. "Not to be a Debbie Downer, but have you seen the latest on Twitter?"

Dread spread through her, cold and discouraging. "You know I haven't. How bad is it?"

"Zeke's videos are going viral. Quite a few more people claim they're on the way here to join the protest. The crowd could be monstrous tomorrow."

She dropped her head and rubbed her temples again. This headache wasn't going anywhere. "Great. Just great. This is the absolute worst-case scenario for a forced translocation."

What else could go wrong?

"Zeke is encouraging his followers to bring mirrors tomorrow," Sterling said. "He says they can reflect sunlight into homes to cause disruption in the neighborhood and increase public outcry without breaking the law."

There was her answer. "Terrific. Well, I had intended to avoid them altogether by sleeping in and going to the house late in the day. We know what we need to do. No need for footage review. Technically we don't need to head to the Johnsons' house until we're ready to perform the translocation."

"And leave the Johnsons to deal with this?" Michael asked.

She felt tears and fought them. *Don't let them see you cry. They will follow your lead. Be strong.* "Leave the family to deal with the mess we brought to their door? You know I can't do that. What time is it?"

"It's . . . a little after one a.m.," TJ said. "I'll go check the sta-cams and set one up in front of Sterling's door for the night."

Sterling, slouched in his chair, lifted his eyes. "Thanks, man. Appreciate it."

Michael yawned and stretched. "Let's all head to bed. Sleep as late as you can. Kimmy, you especially. Your health and well-being are critical. We can deal with the jerks. You sleep and rest up for tonight."

Tomorrow night, she almost corrected him. But he was right. She dug the heels of her hands into her dry, weary eyes. "Deal."

Chairs scraped the wood floor as her crew stood and gathered their belongings, all exhausted and ready for sleep.

Rosie grabbed her arm. "What's up? I can tell something is wrong."

She shook her head. "Nah. Just tired. And worried. See you tomorrow."

"Okay, girl. I'll be snapping Lorenzo for a while, so text me if you need anything."

She had no idea what snapping someone meant but was too eager for bed to prolong the conversation by asking. "Thanks. I will."

Rosie turned to go upstairs, pausing to take a selfie of herself in front of the bright green, floral wallpaper.

TJ, ever energetic with the thrill of youth, nearly bumped into her as she headed down the hallway to her room. "His camera is all set, Ms. Wantland! I'm gonna check the others! Goodnight!"

"'Night, TJ."

"He adores you," Sterling commented from behind her.

She watched TJ virtually skip down the hallway. "He adores the job. He loves what he does."

Sterling yawned widely. "Do I understand we have permission to sleep in?"

"Correct. No hurry to get to the house."

"Good. I'm a zombie." He took her hand and fiddled with it, seemingly in no hurry to go to his room, despite his professed exhaustion.

"I am too. We should probably go to bed." She didn't withdraw her hand and he didn't release it. He turned her arm over, massaging the palm with his thumb. Exhausted though she was, her heart hammered, sleep the furthest thing from her mind.

"Thank you," he said.

"What for?" Her breath caught in her throat as his hand worked up her arm, kneading the muscles gently.

"You've been very kind. Haven't made fun of me once when I see strange things."

"I see strange things all the time."

"But I don't. And you've been nice about it. Never once said, 'I told you so.' I appreciate it."

She sensed his internal struggle. He'd seen things that didn't correspond to his firmly held beliefs. He couldn't reconcile the two and didn't know what to do about it. Adding fuel to the fire wasn't her way. She'd learned at an early age not to engage in arguments about the supernatural. They never ended well. No matter how sure she was about the existence of spirits, someone who didn't possess her gifts and couldn't see them would insist she was wrong. She walked away rather than waste the energy. Just admitting he had seen things that made him uncomfortable was a huge step for Sterling.

"When did saying that ever help any situation?" she asked.

He spotted the sta-cam and lifted his eyebrows. "This will record the person knocking on my door at night?"

"I don't think it will record a person, but, yes, assuming the culprit returns, the sta-cam should capture the interaction."

"You think it's a ghost?"

"I know no one on my crew would knock on a door in the night. We're all too exhausted and want all the sleep we can manage."

"I seem to be attracting the supposed ghosts on this investigation."

"Spirits can be like cats," she said. "They like to harass skeptics. At least the ornery ones."

He laughed. "The ornery skeptics?"

"I meant ornery ghosts, but . . ."

"What would that possibly accomplish?"

"Hey, they have to do something to fill the time, right? They're lost, confused, and possibly bored. For centuries. That's why most of them welcome the chance to move on and finally rest in peace."

He stared at her hands, then tipped his head toward his door. "You could come in and help me listen for it to come knocking."

"It might not even come back tonight," she said.

He turned the full intensity of his blue eyes on her. "I'd welcome your company either way."

She took a deep breath as the implication of his words hit. The butterflies in her stomach danced about, encouraging her to take a chance. But the little voice in her head struggled to maintain control. So many things could go wrong if it didn't work out. "I think maybe—"

"I give the best massages. Let me work all the knots out of your back and shoulders. You'll sleep like a baby."

Oh, wow. That sounded amazing. Did she truly believe it would stop at a massage? Did she want it to?

"Let me shower and change first, okay?"

His eyes lit up and his orange chakra spun, bright and vivid. "Sure! Five minutes?"

"Give me ten?"

He squeezed her hand. "Take all the time you need. Just don't change your mind."

He knew her too well. As soon as she undressed and stepped into the hot shower, she began rethinking her decision. This would be a huge change. What if she regretted it in the morning? Did she know him well enough to risk getting closer? But what if she held him at a distance and never allowed him to get closer? The thought caused an ache in her chest. That meant something, didn't it?

She heard Rosie's voice telling her to just go for it already. When was the last time she'd done something for herself just because she wanted to? Thrown caution to the wind and gone for it, no thought to the future, or what might happen, or potential ramifications to the show? She couldn't remember a single example.

Sterling demonstrated genuine concern time and again. And possessed a protective quality no one had ever shown toward her. He had nothing to gain from playing her. Already a celebrity, he had women lined up down the street trying to get close to him. But he was here with her, not interested in anyone else. He'd even managed to get rid of Zeke for her. Why should she push him away?

They were both mature adults, mutually attracted to each other, and capable of keeping it professional in front of the cameras. For that matter, the crew and fans seemed to be pulling for them and hoping they would hook up.

Rosie's voice once again barged through her thoughts. *Girl, go get him.*

Heart galloping, stomach churning, she turned off the shower and quickly toweled dry. Glancing at the time, she quickened her pace. Eighteen minutes had passed since she'd left Sterling's door. What if she'd taken too long? What if he'd fallen asleep waiting?

She wiggled into her satin nightgown, ran a brush through her hair, and slathered night cream on her face. Loaded with vitamins and peptides and age-defying ingredients, she never skipped an application. Beauty might be eighty percent what you eat compared to twenty percent skincare, but she needed every percent she could get.

No makeup, hair damp and stringy, she started for the door, then rushed back to brush her teeth. Just in case. One last glance confirmed how plain and ordinary she looked. But he'd seen her this way before and claimed to find her most attractive without all the effort. She glossed her lips anyway, a tiny shiver running through her abdomen as she thought about his mouth on hers. Her orange chakra resonated for Sterling as his glowed for her.

Taking a deep breath, she hurried to his door before she could talk herself out of it, raised a fist, and tapped softly in case he'd nodded off to sleep.

The door swung open to reveal a scowling Sterling.

Not the reaction she'd expected. She immediately regretted her decision.

But his features melted, his furrowed brow smoothing as he grinned. "Hi!"

"I'm so sorry! Did I wake you?"

"No! Not at all. I just didn't expect you."

"You expected someone else?"

He laughed. "At one thirty . . . make that one forty-five in the morning? No, I thought you were the mysterious knocker. I'd given up on you."

"I took too long. I should have—"

"Don't apologize. I'm glad you're here. I almost texted ten times but decided that would be way too thirsty."

"I've been over there worrying, talking myself into it, out of it—"

"Why are we torturing ourselves?" He opened the door wide. "I believe you were promised a massage."

The air sizzled as he closed the door. She swore sparks crackled as he took her hand to lead her to the bed. She sucked in a breath.

"You okay?" he asked.

"I'm nervous," she admitted.

"Because? I don't want you to feel pressured."

"I don't. I've just never felt this . . . electrified when I'm near a guy."

His eyes softened, to the point he almost seemed to tear up. "I feel the same way." He stepped closer. His spectrum burned like fireworks arcing across her psyche.

"And I can feel your orange chakra pulsing. Along with my own chakra glowing for you. It's almost more than I can bear." Her voice developed a breathy quality she'd always scoffed at in movies and books.

"You're glowing for me? That's hot." He looped an arm around her waist and drew her closer. "You feel me pulsing for you?"

Indeed she did. On more than one level. Her body responded, melting at his touch, quivering and eager to commune. "What happens if things fall apart?"

"They won't. But regardless, what happens off camera stays off camera. I won't share anything you don't want me to. On the show, things are different. The fans only see my skeptic persona, not the real me. Well, glimpses of the real me, I suppose." He brushed his hand over her cheek. "I would never do anything to hurt you or our show."

She believed him. He spoke the truth. All seven chakras along his spine resonated for her, naked and raw, his longing laid bare right alongside his genuine concern. His heart chakra swelled to outshine the orange chakra in his groin, the green light spinning even brighter than the orange ball of desire.

Her chest swelled in return, emotions threatening to spill into tears. Though this seemed impetuous on some level, on another, it felt completely right. Meant to be. "I feel the same way. I can't imagine the show without you. Or my life without you."

He enveloped her in both arms, resting his chin on her shoulder and cupping the back of her head in one hand. "I meant it when I offered a massage, but if we don't get to that immediately, I can't promise I won't skip it. I am, after all, a heterosexual male, you are insanely gorgeous, and I am absolutely crazy about you."

Insanely gorgeous? Without her makeup? If she'd been on the fence about this guy, that would have decided it. But she wasn't. She was crazy about him in return.

A knock on the door startled her. She nearly jumped away from him, guilt flooding through her. What would she say? How would they explain her presence in his room? And who the heck was knocking on his door at this time anyway?

"Hey, relax. Why so jumpy?" Sterling asked. "We're single adults. Nothing to hide or be ashamed of."

"Of course. You're right. Yes."

He sighed. "Want to hide in the bathroom?"

"Nope. No. They'll learn eventually so . . ." She gestured to the door, indicating he open it.

He cracked the door and peeked into the hall. "Son of a bitch. They got me again."

She went to his side, prepared for an empty hallway.

And was greeted by a little girl.

CHAPTER TWENTY-NINE

"Augusta?" Kimberly asked the girl.

The little girl's face lit up. She smiled broadly and curtsied.

"It *is* you. Why are you pestering Sterling? You have lots of other people you could be waking up in the night."

The girl shrugged and clamped her fingers over her mouth as if to hide her smile.

"Yes, I know he's cute. But you won't win him over this way."

Sterling's brow furrowed and he squinted. "What are you doing? Talking to imaginary friends? Whoever knocked and ditched is long gone, so maybe we could pick up where we left off?"

She knew nothing she said could dissuade him from his adamant belief. And suddenly, she found she very much wanted him to believe her, to know she wasn't a sham or a huckster or a crazy person. She'd said many times he wouldn't believe in ghosts even if he saw one with his own eyes. But would he? And could she help him to see? She decided it was worth trying.

Taking his hand, she wrapped it around the quartz crystal on her necklace and placed her other hand on his back, pushing psychic energy through him. She had no idea if this would work, if there was any way it could work. But he'd demonstrated some latent sensitive abilities so perhaps—

Sterling jumped, threw his arms out, and stumbled backward. "What the hell? What did you do to me? I thought I saw . . . I thought I saw . . ."

"Did you see the little girl?"

His head whipped around to look at her. "How did you know? How did you know that? What is happening?"

"It's okay. It's not—"

He clutched the sides of his head and slid down the wall. "This isn't possible. What did you do to me?"

Perhaps that had been too much. She crouched beside him where he hunkered on the floor. "I'm sorry. I thought you might possess some sensitive proclivities. You've mentioned seeing and hearing things, but you haven't embraced your abilities. I thought maybe if you saw with your own eyes . . ."

He glanced from the floor back to the girl. "Oh God. She's still there. I still see it. I'm going crazy!"

He began to rock. What had she done? Never in her wildest imaginings did she think he would become so completely unhinged.

She gathered him in her arms. He leaned against her chest. Stroking his head, she crooned, "It's okay. Nothing will hurt you."

The little girl's spirit looked distressed and stepped closer, as if she, too, wanted to comfort Sterling. That was the last thing he needed right now.

She waved a hand at the girl. "Go on. You're scaring him. Go up to the attic and dump a box of toys. TJ would love to play with you."

The girl's face brightened. She turned and skipped down the hallway toward the staircase.

"Look. She's gone. See?"

He lifted his head and stared at the empty hallway. "I'm going crazy. Or hallucinating."

"Come on." She pulled him to his feet. "Let's get you in bed. We've had enough excitement for one day."

He nodded and allowed her to lead him to his room. She clicked the door closed behind them, knowing the moment was ruined.

Still shaking, he slid under the sheet and blankets, allowing her to tuck him in.

She brushed unruly locks of hair off his forehead. "I promise you're okay. I'm really sorry. I didn't mean to freak you out. You were so upset by the knocking, I thought you'd feel better if you saw what caused it."

His silence unnerved her. Brash, swaggering, sure-of-himself Sterling she knew how to handle. That side of him she knew. And had come to appreciate when he stepped in on her behalf. Shaken, somber Sterling worried her. Normally he spouted whatever thought crossed his mind. Left to guess what he was thinking, she assumed he was upset with her. Maybe even contemplating leaving the show.

What would she do without him? Not that long ago, she would have been delighted to see him walk away. Now the idea wholly unnerved her.

Clearly, her presence was unwelcome. She stood to leave. "Well, goodnight."

His hand shot out and gripped her wrist. "Don't leave me. Please. Stay here."

He lifted the blankets, his bare chest and arms inviting her in.

Before she could stop to think, she crawled in beside him. He arranged the blankets over her before clicking the lamp off.

Only a bit of anemic moonlight reflected off the mirror illuminated the room. Burying his face in her hair, he breathed deeply, sighed, and relaxed.

Strong arms enveloping her, she snuggled against the contour of his body, luxuriating in the warmth radiating from his skin, his woodsy, earthen scent. He exuded masculinity from every pore.

She knew the moment he fell asleep. His entire body melted heavily against her as his muscles went slack.

In her last moments of consciousness, she listened to his deep, rhythmic breathing, felt his heart thumping in his chest—and had never felt more at home in her life.

Bliss.

***

KIMBERLY WOKE WITH A START, unaccustomed to another body in bed with her. The two of them must have slept like the dead, so to speak. Neither had moved a muscle. His arms remained curled around her, tucking her snug against his body, which radiated heat like a small oven.

Normally she woke shivering, irritated by the sun's rays rudely blasting her in the eyes and waking her from the precious little sleep she managed. This morning, the golden morning light seemed to be encouraging her to wake and enjoy the beginning of a new day, inviting her to savor the moment. Which she did. Remaining absolutely still, she basked in Sterling's warm cocoon, enjoying his soft breaths against her neck, the weight of his head against hers, the slope of his forehead and nose that seemed to nestle perfectly against her cheek. She didn't so much as turn her head to check the time.

All too soon, he jumped, snorted, and rose onto his elbow. He blinked a few times as if getting his bearings before his eyes cleared and his gaze landed on her. His features broke into the widest smile she'd ever seen.

"Good morning," he murmured. "You stayed. You stayed with me all night."

"Hope that's okay. No regrets?"

He glanced down at his waist. "I regret my pants are still on."

His unexpected response left her fighting to quell a giggle. "We both fell right to sleep."

"Damn. Biggest mistake of my life."

She lifted a hand to his cheek. "There's always next time."

He cocked an eyebrow. "I like the sound of that. Actually, even better—don't move."

He hopped out of the bed so fast he stumbled and nearly sprawled to the floor but managed to catch himself.

"Be careful! What are you doing?"

He stumbled into the bathroom, spun around, and held up one finger. "Don't move. Be right back."

She fell back on the pillow and nearly squealed. When she heard water splashing in the sink and the scritching of rapid tooth brushing, she sat back up. "Are you brushing your teeth? That's not fair!"

He leaned out of the bathroom, foaming at the mouth, and spoke around his brush. "What?"

"You can't be minty fresh if I have morning breath."

He spat and started back to bed. "I promise I won't notice."

The intense heat in his eyes combined with the burning desire radiating off him drove straight to her core. As he untied his pajama pants and strode across the room, her pulse raced and a gasp escaped her parted lips. All thoughts of her toothbrush in the other room were driven from her mind.

A knock on the door interrupted her thoughts. And the moment.

Her head whipped to the clock on the bedside table. "What time is it?"

He dragged a hand down his face. "Don't know. Thought we got to sleep in today."

"Nine o'clock. Not that late. But someone is looking for us." She met his gaze, disappointment and frustration evident. A cold shower wouldn't have killed the mood more completely. Someone always pulled at her and demanded her time. Could he accept that? Or would he be another guy who moved on, unable to handle the weight of responsibilities she carried? She wouldn't blame him. No one wanted to feel like they took a back seat to everything else. She would find a way to make time for him—for them—if he gave her a chance.

He scowled as he crossed to the door and cracked it just enough to peek out.

She heard TJ's voice ask, "Have you seen Ms. Wantland?"

She held her breath, half expecting Sterling to throw the door open and gesture to her in his bed. But he didn't. He remained firmly lodged in the open space.

"What difference does it make?" he asked TJ. "I thought we didn't need to hustle this morning."

"I came to grab the sta-cam. Michael told me to rouse you guys. Something's happened and he wants us to discuss. But Ms. Wantland doesn't answer and I'm worried."

"Relax, kid. She's probably in the shower."

"Oh, yeah! Didn't think of that. Well, can you listen for her and tell her to meet in the dining room as soon as possible? Michael says."

"Sure."

"Thanks! See you at breakfast!"

Sterling closed the door and trudged back to the bed. "Apparently we have been summoned."

She sighed. "Sorry. Welcome to my world. The universe isn't cooperating."

He ran a hand in little circles over her back. "Don't sweat it. Things happen. That's life. And frankly I don't much care if the universe cooperates or not. You're worth waiting for. Raincheck?"

Worth waiting for? She nearly swooned. All her life guys had told her how lucky she was to be with them. She didn't realize until that moment how much she longed to hear a man think he was lucky to be with her.

But she didn't tell him that. She couldn't. If she admitted how deeply his words touched her, the emotions would be too much, and she'd stand there blubbering like an idiot. She swallowed the swelling emotional storm and managed one word. "Definitely."

She stood, ready to go back to her room and prepare for the day.

He grabbed her wrist. "Can I ask you something?"

"Of course."

"Last night . . . what you did . . ."

She squirmed at the memory of him trembling in the floor.

"Have you done that before? With anyone else?"

With anyone else? What did he mean? "Done what exactly?"

"In the hallway. You rested your hand on my back, and I can't explain it, but it was like a blurry image came into sharp focus. I swear I saw . . . but that can't be."

"You saw a ghost." She entwined her fingers with his and squeezed. "The first time is always terrifying. I'm sorry. I truly thought if you could see what was knocking on your door, you'd be relieved. I didn't think it through."

"But how? You've done this before?"

"No, actually. Never." Funny. Why hadn't she? "It's never occurred to me to try. I guess since I suspected you have latent sensitive abilities, I thought . . . No, I didn't think about it at all. We have such a connection, something I've never felt before. I opened my energy and shared with you. Backfired though."

"I'm not convinced I wasn't hallucinating. Sleep deprivation apparently caused me to fall asleep with you in bed next to me. Clearly, I was not in my right mind. I like this idea of a shared connection though."

"Me too. It's very nice." She peered at him, feeling all at once vulnerable and exposed, while safe and protected. She couldn't decide if she liked it or not and struggled not to close down.

The look he gave her sent tingles through her body. But he broke the spell and led her to the door. "Okay, off you go before I can't control myself any longer and we both get in trouble for not attending the impromptu meeting this morning. Dash to your room before they come looking for us again and discover you in mine. I know you don't want anyone privy to your private life."

"Oh, they're about to know. That sta-cam TJ retrieved was aimed right at your door all night. They'll see me go in and then not re-emerge."

CHAPTER THIRTY

THEY WALKED down the hall together. Just before turning the corner into the dining room, Kimberly took a deep breath and grabbed Sterling's hand.

He smiled, then his brow furrowed. "You sure?"

"I have feelings for you. If I hide them it'll look like I'm embarrassed. And I'm not. Cautious, sure. But with you, this feels right. I want my best friends to know."

He squeezed her hand, eyes sparkling, and she felt his heart chakra spin and glow. "I want to shout it off the rooftops. Or blast it all over my socials. I want everyone to know."

She cringed. "Ugh. Rosie will never let this go. She'll be saying she told me so for . . . well, forever."

"I also want everyone to know you're off the market. Officially."

"In reality, I wasn't on the market. You on the other hand—"

"No worries. Don't waste energy on that. Public persona Sterling might attract attention—like you do—but only you see the real me. And you squeeze out all thoughts of anyone else."

He understood what life in the public eye was like. Rosie *was* right. He was a good match for her. And he even appeared to be mildly sensitive. She'd continue to gently encourage him to use his gift and to develop equipment for them to use. With a little training, he could be another paranormal investigator. The two of them would work together, crusading side by side, resolving disturbances.

"You ready?" he asked.

With a nod, she turned the corner to join her crew, ready to step out with Sterling.

But not one set of eyes registered their entwined hands—not even Rosie's. They were all captivated by the television or phone screens.

"There you are!" Michael said when he finally noticed them. "Where have you been? We need our media specialist. Get on this. You okay, sweetie?"

She nodded, brow furrowed. "Of course. I'm great. Just confused because I thought we were taking it easy this morning."

"Oh, sweetie. That was before. You haven't seen any of this?" Michael swept his arm to indicate the local morning show.

She lifted her gaze to the television and sucked in a sharp breath. She'd thought the Johnsons' street had been crowded before. Nothing prepared her for the angry mob clogging the neighborhood this morning. They yelled and shook fists and waved signs demanding JUSTICE FOR ZEKE! Some of them actually appeared to be foaming at the mouth.

Sterling looked up from his phone. "How did this happen? Zeke should have been in jail all night at least."

"Everyone gets a phone call," Michael said.

"This is bad," Sterling said. "Some of them are calling to forget peaceful protests—"

"They've been peaceful so far?" she asked.

"—and come armed today. They even have a couple hashtags for it. #can'tsilenceus and #nosilencers."

Stan's back stiffened. "Silencers? As in for guns?"

"That's one interpretation. Yet these are also vague enough

they can argue it isn't a threat. That they're referring to us and refusing to be silenced."

Michael's face twisted into a scowl. "Surely they're all talk. One shot fired and every one of them could go to jail."

"I don't care if they're bluffing. Or most of them are anyway. Talk like this encourages fringe nuts who take it seriously. And one shot is all it would take to hit Kimberly. No way." Sterling's voice held an edge she rarely heard from him.

"No way, what?" she asked.

"No way are you going back there today."

"I have to. Who else will help the Johnsons?"

"Look, this is not a simple Twitter storm. These are potentially real threats made by people a few blocks away. Social media cannot fight this."

"But no one else can fight James."

"I'm calling Ruth," Michael said, lifting his cell phone to his ear. "I'll see if it's as serious as the news makes it look."

She watched Michael step out of the room, then discovered Sterling biting his lower lip. "What's that face for?"

"You won't quit, will you?"

"Quit the case? I've never bailed on an investigation. I definitely won't bail on this one. If I leave, Faith could . . ." She couldn't bring herself to say it out loud.

"But this is different. Your life is in danger."

"So is Faith's."

"You can't save everyone."

"Probably true."

"Sometimes you need to take care of you first."

"That's your job now."

He clearly hadn't expected that response. He started to speak several times, his mouth opening and closing as he tried to formulate a response. He blew out a deep breath. "What if we confuse the crowd with a double? They won't know which one is you."

"Then they have multiple targets. I won't risk putting anyone else in danger. Including you. You don't have to come if you're worried—"

"Oh, hell no! If you go, I go." He pulled her to his chest and wrapped his arms around her.

This gesture did not escape Rosie's notice. "Ummm, have you changed your relationship status without alerting the important people in your life?"

Before she could respond, Michael stepped back into the room. "Ruth says it's okay. Her prayer group stayed up all night. Kimberly will be safe."

Sterling released her. "That's a joke, right?"

She felt the irritation roll off him, his red chakra flaring.

"She seemed pretty convinced. Also she said there's a police officer outside the house today."

"That's more encouraging."

Michael gave Sterling the look. "You really think I'm gonna walk our girl into a dangerous situation? We all took care of her before you were here."

"Still, should we consider putting her in a Kevlar vest?"

"Do you have one?" Michael asked. "Cuz we don't. Never needed one."

"Sterling, that seems extreme," she said.

"Extreme is necessary when we're dealing with extremists."

"Personally," Michael said, "I think we'd be better off getting to the house as early as possible. Before more zealots have a chance to amass."

"We need to do something to protect Kimberly," Sterling insisted.

This wasn't how she saw this morning going. She didn't realize the weight of stress that had been alleviated with Zeke's incarceration until she felt it settle firmly back in place, crushing her previous euphoria. Not only had they not taken care of him, he'd managed to make the situation worse. She appreciated Sterling's concerns but leaving the Johnsons to cope with this mess alone simply wasn't an option.

"I agree with Michael," she said. "But Sterling is correct that we will need to be especially cautious. Let's go."

"Kimberly rides with me," Sterling said, and she went warm and squishy at his protective insistence.

Gloria joined them from the swinging kitchen doors, clutching something in her arms. "I'm glad I caught you. I wanted to wish you luck today in your investigation. And I found an old yearbook up in the attic. Along with a dumped box of toys." The woman rolled her eyes and shook her head. "Precocious ghosts I have here."

"Yes," she agreed, eager to know what Gloria found and wanted to share with her. "Your yearbook?"

"From high school. Ages ago. But look. Here's your mom." She opened the pages to one she'd marked with a finger. "See? Veronica LeBlanc."

Her mother stared back, a wide smile for the camera, but hesitant shyness in her eyes. She wondered what secrets were held behind them. No question about it. Though her face was rounder, not yet lined with the stress of adult responsibilities, and her long hair was styled and sprayed in wings and huge bangs that curved over her forehead, this undoubtedly was her mother. Any mild skepticism she'd felt vanished. She brushed her fingers over the image, tears brimming her eyes. "It's her. She was so young."

Gloria laughed. "We all were back then, dear."

"What do you remember about her? Did you know my grandparents?" She envisioned Gloria having sleepovers with her mother, perhaps giggling long into the mornings, sharing secrets and deepest desires. "What did she like? What did she do? What did you guys talk about? Was she dating Dad back then?"

"Oh, goodness. I didn't know her that well, I'm afraid. I never met your grandparents. And I'm not sure how she met your dad. I don't think they started dating until we were at UCO. He was a legacy there, of course. His great-grandfather CW Wantland coached football back in the twenties. The Wantland Stadium is named for him and his wife chose the Broncos as their mascot." Gloria eyed both Kimberly, hanging on her every word, and Elise, pencil scratching feverishly across her spiral notebook. "You really didn't know any of this?"

Kimberly shook her head. "The more you talk, the more I realize I know nothing about my mother and my family history. Or my father for that matter. I had no idea he had roots in this part of the country. None."

"We share more history than we knew," Rosie said, "since both our families were here a few generations ago."

"That's . . . this is . . ." Her knees felt weak. This was wild. So much information coming at her so quickly.

Rosie hooked an arm, propping her up, and offered her a bottle of eucalyptus oil. "Breathe. It's okay. Just more proof that we were meant to cross each other's paths."

She breathed deeply, allowing the scent to suffuse her senses and bring a modicum of calm to a situation that had spiraled off in a direction she never saw coming.

"I'm so sorry," Gloria said. "I didn't intend to upset you. I truly thought you must have been aware of some of this at least. I felt certain that's why you came to Guthrie."

"No, though the current investigation has brought up my mother once already. I couldn't imagine how the spirit knew, but if Mom lived here . . . What else can you remember about her? Anything?"

Gloria's eyes squinted as she considered. "I remember when her family moved to Guthrie. We were in high school—always a tough time to relocate. I never heard why they moved but I want to say maybe they came here from New Orleans, though it's been quite some time and I can't swear to that with any certainty."

She looked at Michael, who nodded. They had an investigation on their schedule in New Orleans. The perfect opportunity if Gloria's memory turned out to be correct.

If Gloria noticed the shared look, she didn't register it. "We had a few classes together, and we ate lunch together. She was so sweet and easy-going you couldn't help but enjoy her company. She always seemed to hold back a bit though. In retrospect, we never discussed anything serious or personal. We lost touch when we went on to college. I want to say they married just after graduating from college, but again, I could be remembering that wrong. And then suddenly I heard they moved. Never heard from her again."

Elise pushed her glasses up her nose and peered through them at Gloria. "Veronica LeBlanc. Possibly from New Orleans. Went to UCO. Got married and moved. Anything else that might help us?"

"If I think of anything more, I'll let you know."

Elise turned her large almond-shaped eyes on Kimberly. "I got it all. Don't you worry. This opens all sorts of potential, new avenues we didn't have to search before. I'm sure we can make some progress now."

She managed a smile and a nod for Elise. Fortunately, Michael came to her rescue.

"No one will argue how great this is," he said. "But let's give Kimmy a chance to absorb this. Perhaps we should table the research until we finish this investigation. We were about to leave for the Johnsons' house."

Elise glanced up from her notebook, where she'd returned to scribbling notes and thoughts, and adjusted her thick frames again. "Of course. I just got excited. But yes, we should focus on resolving the Johnsons' disturbance."

Kimberly wrestled to bring her own thoughts back to the investigation. The conversation with Gloria may have lasted only a few minutes but had completely derailed her thoughts and attention. Not good for the investigation, but a big part of her wanted only to pursue these new leads now, to heck with every-thing else.

But the Johnsons were waiting for her to help their daughter. Zeke's protestors waited for her. Dislocating James would be the most dangerous interaction with a spirit she'd ever undertaken. Though she longed to use this new information and push aside all else, she couldn't grant herself that luxury. She had to set aside her personal issues and force herself to concentrate on work. "Yes. Michael is right. This is going to be one of the biggest challenges we've ever faced. Let's go."

Sterling looped an arm around her. "Okay, but you're riding with me."

CHAPTER THIRTY-ONE

THE SILENCE in the i8 allowed Kimberly to turn over and over the bits of information Gloria had shared with her, looking for something to help her feel better. Why had her parents hidden so much from her? All this time, she thought if she could just get back into the house to conduct a full investigation, she might find some answers. But the atomic bomb of information Gloria had just dumped on her indicated far more than simply a mysterious death. And emphasized, as if she needed a reminder, how very little she knew about her mother and her family history in general. She had long mourned the early loss of her mother. Now she was realizing how much she'd missed out on by losing her so early. And why had her dad never told her? What about Aunt Dolly? What did she know and had never shared?

Sterling took one hand off the wheel as they sat at a red light and rubbed her back. "You okay?"

"Not really. But I have to be."

"This is good. You were just saying how little you know about your family. Now maybe we can get some answers."

We. With that one word he reminded her that as scared and alone as she felt at the moment, she wasn't. She had people who cared and were there for her. She grabbed his hand and squeezed just as the light turned green and he resumed driving.

"What was my dad hiding? Why didn't he ever tell me anything? If they ran out of town overnight without a word to anyone, they must have been running from something. But what?"

"Gloria said she didn't really know them that well. Let's not get carried away. Maybe it felt to Gloria like they moved suddenly. But if she wasn't in contact with them, she wouldn't have known their plans. And if they weren't best friends and had lost touch, why would your mom have left a forwarding address? This may well have a simple explanation. Don't assume something mysterious is the cause."

She nodded. He was right. His level-headed practicality brought a calming element to the moment. And right now, whatever the information unearthed at some point in the future, that's what she needed. Though his paranormal skepticism had often rankled, his pragmatism soothed. "Thank you. I needed to hear that."

Sterling turned the i8 into the Johnsons' neighborhood—and immediately slowed. Cars and pedestrians jammed the street. He navigated as safely as possible toward the Johnsons' house, twisting and turning, until they could do no more than inch forward.

The protestors stood shoulder-to-shoulder thick. No longer content to merely fill the street and sidewalk directly in front of the Johnsons' home, they now spilled through the neighborhood in both directions, up and down the block.

Kimberly watched in horror as the crowd turned and recognized either the car or her—or both. The mob sent up an angry cry and descended upon Sterling's glorious i8. She buried her face in her hands, unable to watch. "Oh, Sterling. Your car. We should've ridden in the van."

"I thought we had a chance of sneaking you in this way. Ah, well."

"'Thou shalt not suffer a witch to live!'" As soon as one of them hurled this in her direction, others picked it up and soon the chant filled her ears.

Heart thudding at what without much mental acrobatics could be interpreted as a death threat, she shivered. "Okay, maybe I should have listened about the Kevlar vest."

"Gotta love people using the Bible to justify hate," he said. "And so much for Ruth's prayer group."

Though they inched forward excruciatingly slowly, the Johnsons' house came into view. "Maybe if you can manage to get into the driveway—"

A new noise caught her attention, and nearly drowned out the cacophony of the crowd. Composed of many voices, it sounded like singing. She craned her neck to see over the people encroaching on the car. "What is that?"

Sterling finally crept up to a point that her door was flush with the Johnsons' driveway. A line of women in white dresses blocked the entrance to the driveway. Was this some new method of harassment they'd developed?

"What in the world is this?" Sterling asked.

At the sight of her, the women smiled and stepped aside to reveal an empty driveway, lined by more women in white. The women dropped their arms, then lifted them in sync. Billowing yards of fabric swooped upward, creating a tunnel to guard her passage.

More women stood along the curb in front of the Johnsons' house. They sang the Lord's Prayer, their beautiful harmony nearly drowning out the crowd's ugly taunts and jeers.

"Is this Ruth's prayer group?" she asked Sterling.

"If so, I'm impressed."

Wings. They'd created wings, which they held aloft, obscuring her from view of the protestors.

She opened the car door and stepped out, completely shielded, and walked through the guarded walkway to the door, where Ruth stood beaming to welcome her inside.

From the wraparound porch she watched Sterling and the entire crew approach the house, unperturbed by the agitated crowd. All their faces appeared as equally perplexed but delighted.

She also caught sight of a police cruiser. The officer leaned against the vehicle, arms crossed, nonchalant but present, ready to intervene. His presence likely quelled potential violence, but the prayer group's protective wings and singing washed her in peace and positive energy—which she needed more than anything today. Though she rarely prayed in the traditional sense, she closed her eyes and sent a beacon of thanks and gratitude into the world.

Warriors. Warriors for good. That's what these women were. Profoundly grateful they'd come out to support her, she waved her thanks.

"This is your prayer group?" she asked Ruth.

"Yes! They stayed up all night sewing the wings." The woman's face reflected the pride she clearly felt.

"My kind of prayer group," Sterling said. "Seriously, this is brilliant."

"This is incredible. I can't believe they did this for me."

"Of course, we did. We believe in standing up to hate in every form. They'll stay all day, so you'll be able to move back and forth to your trailer."

Ridicule, ostracism, skepticism, scoffs, and threats. Those she knew with great familiarity. She'd grown up with it and developed a thick skin to protect against it. But this? Protection and support? Defiance of her critics? Outside the little circle of her crew, this was rare indeed. The overwhelming show of support moved her to tears.

She threw her arms around the woman. "Thank you."

Snickers reared onto the screen door, whimpering and clawing the frame.

"Bad dog! No scratch!" Ruth scolded. "He knows better than that. He's never allowed out front."

The dog ignored the scolding and stared intently at Kimberly. He rumbled low in his throat, ending with an insistent, "Woof!"

"Something is wrong," she told Ruth.

When Ruth opened the door, he didn't make a break for freedom. He turned and led them to the living room, peering over his shoulder twice to ensure they followed.

Faith knelt in front of a small table, fingers crooked over the edge, staring at an old radio, the dial set between stations. Static crackled from the speakers.

"A dial tuner? How old is this antique?" Sterling asked.

"Ancient," Ruth answered. "It belonged to my mother when she lived here. We never use it, but I couldn't get rid of it."

"I'm surprised it still works."

"So am I."

Kimberly stepped closer, watching Faith, who stared as though mesmerized at the radio. The hissing static morphed and took shape. Though the words weren't clear, Kimberly caught the cadence and pattern of sentences.

And then a whispered, *Kimberly*

She jumped and caught her breath, the threat in the voice palpable.

James knew she was coming for him and wanted her to know he didn't intend to leave.

"What's wrong?" Sterling asked.

She gestured him closer and raised her hand to his back. Before she made contact, she asked, "May I?"

He hesitated a moment before giving a brisk nod.

She guided his hand to the quartz hanging from her necklace and tried not to think about how near it hung to her breasts, then rested her hand on his back and channeled a tiny jolt of psychic energy to his chakras.

He gasped, his eyes wide. "You can hear that?"

She nodded. "Can you make out words?"

"What's happening right now?" Michael asked.

She noted everyone in the room staring at them, baffled, but shook her head. She didn't want any interruptions.

Sterling cocked his head as he strained to understand. "No distinct words, though it's clearly meant to be threatening. Or at least to frighten you."

He got it. He understood. She gazed at him with new appreciation, as he shared a moment with her in a way no one ever had. "Agreed."

"What is happening?" Michael asked.

"Kimberly?" Rosie asked. "You okay?"

Sterling stared at her as if she were the only person in the room. The fear was gone from his eyes, replaced with wonder. "How do you do this?"

"I don't know," she answered honestly. "I just do."

"Someone want to let the rest of us in on it?" Michael asked.

"Shared moments are nicer when everyone is included," Rosie said.

"Ummm, Ms. Wantland?" TJ's hesitant voice broke through to her. "The KII is off the charts. One hundred and fifty and climbing."

That value broke the spell. "One fifty? We've never seen a level that high."

Loud thumping sounded upstairs. Lights flickered. All the electronics in the house flipped on at the same moment—the television, more radios, the home Alexas—and all of them screeched static at full volume.

Still holding the KII, TJ spun in a circle, as if unsure where the threat emanated from.

The thumping upstairs continued, intensified.

Rebecca ran to her mother's arms, terror on her face. Daniel held them both.

Stan turned every direction, trying to record everything at once.

Elise clutched a handheld recorder, possibly attempting an EMF session.

All at once, everything stopped. In the silence, every person in the room looked to her, hoping for an explanation.

Faith, who hadn't budged during the commotion, turned slowly over her shoulder and addressed the room. "He's back."

CHAPTER THIRTY-TWO

KIMBERLY SAT at the head of the dining table, aware of the pall James' display had cast over the house and everyone in it. Downcast eyes, chins resting on fists, and anxious pacing surrounded her. Her crew attempted to carry on with footage review as normal. But at any unexpected noise, everyone froze in place, staring toward the ceiling and electronics, waiting for the next round.

Daniel sat up straight and addressed her across the table. "What did you learn about forced whatever-you-called-it?"

She knew her answer would disappoint him. "Not much. Most don't believe it's possible and those who do don't recommend it."

"Why not?"

"It's dangerous. I'll need to open a pathway to the other side, latch onto his spirit, drag him to the portal, then sever the connection and push him across at nearly the same moment."

Daniel rubbed his face. "You can't capture him somehow?"

"That's the plot of *Ghostbusters*," Sterling said.

"No mechanism currently exists to capture and contain spirits," she said, looking to Sterling. "I wish we had that capability. Would make my job a lot easier."

Sterling smirked and shook his head.

"Meanwhile we have the biggest angry mob yet, spewing hate and negative energy this way. Combined with our own dread and fear. James will feed on it all day."

Ruth leaned forward. "Can't the prayer group block that?"

"Sadly no. It doesn't work that way. However, their positive energy will boost me, which will help immensely. Poltergeists thrive on doubt and negativity. And target the most vulnerable." She looked pointedly at Faith, who sat alone, staring out a window.

What more could she do? Zeke and his nuts outside. A spirit determined to stay and torture the family. A girl terrorized and in danger of a spirit taking control of her. The enormity of the situation weighed her down. The stress and anxiety levels in the room threatened to sink her. She needed to do something.

Nothing was worse than feeling helpless. She had decided long ago that her abilities were meant to be used to help others, that this was not a random quirk that the universe gifted her. She was meant to use it. Days like today, though, when she couldn't figure out how to best overcome the challenges she faced brought back all the times she had failed, all the times she had done nothing, the years of torment and ridicule from others.

How she couldn't save her mother—and how her dad never forgave her.

Rosie, who knew her so well, must have recognized her distress. "Come on, girl. You're coping with a huge emotional shock. Let's isolate you in the trailer and spend the day relaxing and charging you up for tonight. I can control the environment to some extent in the trailer. We need to prepare you for this showdown."

What would she do without Rosie? Her personal assistant always knew what she needed.

TJ yanked off his headphones. "Ms. Wantland! You didn't tell us Sterling saw a ghost last night!"

Every eye in the room turned in her direction. Sterling squirmed in his seat.

"We're not really certain what we saw. I think—"

"No, this is legit! He says he sees a ghost and totally freaks out!" TJ slammed a fist into his palm. "And I compared footage from the sta-cam by his room to the one in the attic. You tell her to go dump toys and like five minutes later the box of toys falls over. This is wild."

Michael looked to her for confirmation, but she wouldn't respond. She lifted her eyebrows, trying to communicate they should not get into this right now. Apparently, he didn't get it. "Sterling, did you see a ghost?"

Sterling ran a hand over the back of his neck. "I can't confirm that. Kimberly and I . . . I don't know what we saw."

TJ gestured her over. "Come see! Come watch the footage. It's all right here. Sterling freaks out and the toys dump over a few minutes later."

"I believe you. I don't—"

"Can you stop saying I freaked out?" Sterling's tense voice matched his emotional state. His increasing agitation lapped at her senses from across the room. If this continued to escalate, he could grow into a tsunami of negativity he didn't know how to deal with.

TJ grinned. "I mean, I don't know how else you would describe this but—"

"Not right now, TJ." She knew her younger camera operator had grown accustomed to teasing and bantering with Sterling. But he didn't recognize that Sterling wasn't playing this time. She needed to curtail the conversation fast. "Let's discuss this later."

TJ's eyes glinted. "But we have Sterling on record saying—"

"TJ." She allowed a harsh edge to her tone that she normally worked hard to control. "Let's discuss it later. Just the two of us."

The young man's face fell. She understood that he couldn't fathom why she wasn't gleefully jumping all over this, eager to show the world that Sterling Wakefield saw a ghost. And to be honest, not that long ago, she would have. But things had changed. TJ would have to trust her. Or at least follow her direction.

She felt Sterling's emotional storm die down, but now TJ was upset and confused. She joined him at his computer. "Show me the box of toys?"

"Yeah, sure." He obliged, playing the recordings for her. "Here's where you tell her to leave, cuz she's scaring Sterling, and to go dump over some toys cuz I'd be happy to play with her." He clicked over to the other camera. "And here, if you see the time stamp, just about five minutes later, the box of toys falls over and spills everywhere."

She watched a few more minutes. "Anything else after that?"

"Not that I found."

"She's bored. Like any little girl would be, trapped forever in the same place, cooped up all day. And most people don't see or at least don't acknowledge her. That's sad."

Rosie rested a hand on her arm. "Girl, you're bringing the room down. Weren't we headed to your trailer?"

"I have a question," Daniel said. "I'm not about to claim to understand anything that's happening here, but if the spirit is going to sit and charge up all day, as you say he will, wouldn't it be better to fight him now, while he's weaker?"

"That would be ideal, yes," she confirmed. "But where is he? It's the paranormal Catch-22. The spirit needs to be strong enough to manifest and make its presence known before I can engage it. Not as simple as playing Hide and Seek, unfortunately."

"But," Michael said, "perhaps we could lure him out before he's fully amped. Maybe try provoking him and see what happens?"

"I'm game," she said. "As soon as Rosie has me completely charged and revitalized. This dislocation is going to take every-thing I have."

CHAPTER THIRTY-THREE

KIMBERLY THREW her hands in the air. "Nothing!" She pressed her fingers to her temples and stared at the items surrounding her on the floor—all the personal items they'd used in an effort to engage James. They'd attempted to lure him out all afternoon. Nothing. Not a sound or a movement or a blip. No EVP or temperature fluctuations. Mostly they'd loitered around the house feeling useless. "What am I missing? What am I doing wrong?"

"You're doing everything right," Rosie assured her. "But you're wearing yourself out. Let's give you a break and go to your trailer."

Kimberly looked to Michael for guidance. "I think she's right. I think James is deliberately hiding from me, recharging. And I'm wasting time and energy trying to goad him into interacting."

He nodded. "Go rest. We tried, but this isn't working."

Sterling pulled her off the floor. He held up his hands, fingers wide, eyebrows raised, then cupped his hands together as if holding something precious. He blew into them, then lifted the top hand to reveal a square of chocolate. "I think dark chocolate helps revive you."

She laughed despite her exhaustion and dull, persistent headache and accepted the square. "Did you learn that from Harry Potter?"

"No, I've learned what makes you happy." His eyes burned with intensity. She suspected he was as eager for their next night together as she was. A little shiver ran through her body. Maybe they could sneak off to her trailer alone—

Rosie looped an arm around hers. "Okay, lovebirds. That's enough. We have an investigation to finish here. We'll be in the trailer, Sterling, when you're ready for makeup."

Rosie led her down the staircase and outside, where they both ducked their heads while they dashed through the angels' protective tunnel.

In the trailer, she sank into her chair and rubbed her temples. She was ready to put this investigation behind her. Nothing about this was going as anticipated. She'd never dealt with this sort of situation before.

Rosie busied herself making tea. "What's up? Something is still bothering you. I can tell. More than just being worn out."

She sighed. "You always know, somehow. I don't know how to put it into words, but this doesn't feel right."

Rosie sat down beside her. "What doesn't? The investigation?"

"Not the investigation itself. I've helped a lot of spirits cross over. Usually they find resolution which results in a voluntary crossover. They're ready to go at that point. It's their decision and they feel good about it. And then I feel good because they experience relief. I've helped the spirit as well as the family dealing with the disturbance."

"Right."

"But James doesn't have anything to resolve. He isn't lost or confused, needing guidance. He knows exactly what he's doing and doesn't want to go."

"So you'll force a translocation."

"That's the plan, yes. It just feels wrong to force it. Honestly, it feels a bit like murder."

"Murder? That's a little extreme. He's a spirit. Already dead."

"But he exists here in our world. Not in the same way we do, of course. But he exists and wants to stay."

"To terrorize a family. Girl, you are overthinking it. No one else would consider this murder."

"Most people don't believe in spirits to begin with, so of course they wouldn't see it that way. But they're very real to me. I sense them, communicate with them, connect with them. They lived and breathed and retain memories of those lives."

"You've determined James was a total dick when he lived. You yourself said he has probably avoided crossing over because he fears facing ultimate justice. How can you worry about him? He should have crossed over when he died. If you could stop a wanted murderer, wouldn't you?"

"Yes. But I wouldn't want to carry out the death sentence."

Rosie pursed her lips. "I can see this is really bothering you. But let's explore other possibilities. If you don't force James to cross over, then what?"

She sighed. "He remains and continues terrorizing the Johnsons."

"Which really isn't an option."

"I know. I don't have a choice. But I don't like it."

"You need to find a way to let it go. You need to be completely invested when you face him."

"I will fight for the family, no matter what. The living take precedence over the dead. But I fear this will haunt me."

"Better the memory of James haunts you than his spirit makes Faith sick, right?"

She clenched her fists. "Yes. Of course."

"Okay, then. Let's get you charged up and ready for this showdown."

KIMBERLY SIPPED at her third cup of tea before setting it aside. "I'm going to float away, Rosie. No more tea."

Rosie stopped massaging her temples. "How are you feeling? Anything more we can do?"

"I don't think so. I'm as ready as I'm going to be."

The trailer door opened, and Sterling appeared. "Ladies, your presence is requested for a one-time only, sold-out event. Appearing on demand in Guthrie, Sterling Wakefield will defy physics and logic before your very eyes."

She exchanged a glance with Rosie, who shrugged. "What's happening?"

Sterling clapped and drew one hand in front of him in an arc. He used his on-stage voice. "Due to popular demand, I will perform one of my most famous illusions. An illusion which stunned and astounded audiences around the globe."

"You've performed around the globe?" Kimberly asked.

"Well, mostly in Vegas," he admitted. "Back in the day before I had a television show. I should keep my skills sharp in case I need to go back to that."

She didn't like the sound of that. It reminded her that eventually this show would end. "Popular demand, huh? The family has been remarkably unimpressed by your magic tricks thus far."

"Okay, fine. I want to perform it. You're right. Nothing has impressed them. This one has to. Besides, we need something to cheer everyone up. It's awful in there. The tension is unbearable. I've never seen teenagers so down and mopey."

"They're scared, Sterling. But lightening the mood before we launch an attack on James isn't a bad idea. You can potentially lift the positive energy level. Rosie?"

"Let's do it." Rosie rose and opened the door, allowing late-afternoon sunlight to stream into the trailer.

The moment the door opened, the prayer group "angels" unfurled their wings again, forming safe passage to the house. She made eye contact with each of the women as she passed, thanking every one of them. They'd gone sleepless last night and given up an entire day to support her in helping the Johnsons. They deserved so much more than thanks.

When she walked into the Johnsons' house, Snickers' claws skittered across the entry floor as he scampered to greet her. He stood on his hind legs, licked her fingers, and turned in circles.

Sterling shook his head. "I swear that dog has a crush on you."

"Why aren't you ever this happy to see me?"

His eyebrows shot up. "I thought licking you in public was off limits. My bad."

She squealed as he looped his arms around her and pretended to lick her cheek. Her laughter echoed through the house as he scooped her up and spun her in circles.

Michael rounded the corner from the living room. "Is that . . . Kimmy?"

"I've never heard Kimberly laugh so loud," Rosie said.

"I haven't either," Michael said. "And I've known her since college."

"Of course, I've never seen anyone sweep her off her feet like that either." The silly grin plastered on Rosie's face told her she was correct—her best friend would never let her hear the end of it.

One hand to his cheek, Michael shook his head. "Neither have I. Who knew?"

"Ms. Wantland?" TJ approached her, his brow furrowed, stealing glances at Sterling. "The recording last night . . ."

"Yes?" She wasn't ready to revisit Sterling seeing a ghost. She rather wished the sta-cam hadn't even been there. She squirmed until Sterling put her feet back on the ground.

"Well, I . . . I watched through to the end, and I . . ."

The shift in his chakras and the way he stared at Sterling clicked. She realized he wasn't talking about Augusta. He'd pieced together that she'd spent the night in Sterling's room.

Apparently, Sterling realized it too. He draped an arm around her shoulders and kissed her temple.

TJ gulped, blushed, and dashed out of the room.

Rosie scrunched up her face. "What was that?"

"His lingering crush crushed," Sterling said.

"Stop." She elbowed him in the ribs.

"Her reputation is tarnished in the eyes of her young admirer."

"It's not like that and you know it," she said, as Rosie's eyes bugged out of her head and the rest of the crew seemed to be trying to piece the clues together.

"I know it. He doesn't know it, and I'm not setting the record straight."

Rosie's head ping-ponged back and forth between them. "What? What isn't like what? Spill the tea, girl!"

Sterling wrapped his arms around her waist and propped his chin on her shoulder. "She spent the night in my room. TJ saw her go in with me on the sta-cam. Looks like it upset him. Junior just found out Mommy and Daddy sleep together."

Heat rushed to her cheeks. "Sterling!"

She hazarded a look at her crew, their faces in varying forms of delight and shock.

"I can't believe you spent the night with Sterling," Rosie said. "And didn't tell me!"

"We've been a bit distracted with—"

"All that time in the trailer and not one word?"

"Well, true, but we were—"

"Unacceptable! You know I'm supposed to know all the details before anyone else."

"The truth is I don't have any details to share. You're not missing out on anything. I swear."

Rosie raised an eyebrow. "Sterling? Does she speak the truth?"

"Alas, she does. No hot gossip. Yet. Give me another day or two."

Her face burned. "I am really uncomfortable with this conversation right now. Someone change it quick."

Michael's eyes danced with delight, his mouth twisted into a sly grin. "Nope. I'm with Rosie. Let's hear a little more about last night."

"Ugh." She rolled her eyes and extracted herself from Sterling's arms. "A little help here?"

Sterling clapped, then waved his open hands several times. "Ladies and gentlemen. If you'll all move to the living room, a remarkable and astounding feat awaits you."

Michael scowled. "This doesn't sound like hot gossip. What's happening?"

"Sterling's going to entertain everyone with a trick."

"Not a trick." Sterling covered his eyes with his hands and slowly drew them to the sides. "An illusion."

Faith giggled. Kimberly couldn't believe it. The girl actually looked happy for the first time since they'd arrived. And though she attempted to look bored, Rebecca was clearly intrigued by the idea. Sterling had the right idea.

"Yes! Everyone into the living room." Kimberly ushered everyone into the large room and took a seat on the couch.

Once they all settled, Sterling set his phone on the coffee table and pressed the screen. Dramatic music began to play. He turned his back on them, looked over his shoulder, and spun around.

He held a pack of cards in one hand. He made eye contact with them while the music surged. With a flourish, he shook the cards out of the box. He shuffled the deck and fanned the cards several times. He gestured to Faith and held out the cards, indicating she select one. Though timid, the girl did as he instructed.

"Show everyone in the room your card," Sterling directed. He covered his eyes with his empty hand. "Everyone except me."

Faith seemed to be enjoying herself. The girl's eyes glowed as she turned the card around. She'd chosen the four of hearts.

"Now put it back in the deck."

Faith followed his directions, and Sterling shuffled the cards over and over. As the music built in intensity, he began dealing the cards onto the table. They watched the cards revealed, one by one. The four of hearts never appeared.

"Did you see your card?" Sterling asked.

Eyes wide, Faith shook her head.

"What the heck?" Rebecca asked. "Where did it go?"

Sterling held up his hands, fingers wide. He flipped them back and forth several times. Smoke began to curl from his mouth. Everyone in the room gasped. He tipped his head, cocked an eyebrow, and held up one finger. He opened his mouth, revealing something inside. He extracted a card, held it up as he unfolded it—and revealed the four of hearts.

Kimberly drew in her breath and clapped. "How did you do that? That was incredible! I have goosebumps!"

Sterling glanced her way, clearly quite pleased with her delight. He held the card out to Faith. "Is this your card, ma'am?"

Faith nodded. "How did you do that?"

Sterling bowed. The room filled with cheering, clapping, and comments of disbelief.

The energy of the room shifted from dark and miserable to upbeat and cheerful. Sterling had done that. He made everyone feel better. Watching him return the cards to the package, her feelings for him intensified. She no longer worked alone. And she liked it.

She didn't have to work alone. In a flash, she considered all the paranormal interactions she'd experienced since beginning the investigation. *Of course. That was it.* She knew what she needed to do. It would be dangerous, but she'd have to risk it.

A thump sounded above them, a heavy crash that seemed to originate in the attic.

Faith gasped. The room went silent.

Everyone turned to her. But this time she had a plan.

"Sounds like James is ready for us. And now I'm ready for him," she said. "We've been going at this all wrong. Move the personal items to the attic, bring the homemade Ouija board, and fire up the SEEPS. We're going to wake all the ghosts in this house."

CHAPTER THIRTY-FOUR

KIMBERLY WATCHED one pair of legs after another disappear into the hole in the ceiling as her crew prepared the attic for the final showdown.

Rosie hovered at her side, bag of crystals, oils, herbs, and whatever else she kept at the ready clutched in both hands. "I feel completely unprepared."

Kimberly watched Stan and TJ foist the SEEPS up the narrow steps. "So do I. But we have to act now. After the brief respite Sterling provided, Faith is rapidly deteriorating. I think James has reestablished a connection without us realizing it. He's keeping his tendrils in her all day, ready to pounce the moment he's ready. I should've recognized what was happening sooner."

"I'm worried that—"

Michael's head appeared in the trap door to the attic. "I think that's everything except you two. Kimmy, want to come inspect the troops?"

She grabbed the steps and started up. Halfway, she heard a whimper and looked down to discover Snickers' front paws on the lower steps of the ladder. He stared at her mournfully. She knew he longed to follow and wanted to help.

"No, puppy. Not up here. This is no place for dogs."

He whimpered again, more forcefully this time.

"No. Your family needs you." She pointed down the hall. "Go to Faith's room. Protect Faith."

Snickers looked where she pointed, then, as if he understood, barked at her once before trotting down the hallway.

She took a deep breath and scurried up the steps, bracing herself for another olfactory assault. But that proved unnecessary. The attic smelled a bit musty, but nothing more. Stan and TJ checked camera angles and discussed the best way to include as much in the frames as possible. Elise meandered the space, speaking softly into a digital recorder, probably gearing up for an EVP session, if not already conducting one. The SEEPS sat quietly in one corner, waiting to be turned on. She rubbed her sweaty hands together and hoped this worked.

The large oak tree out back remained stoic and harmless. No visions of a noose plagued her. Perhaps now that she had shared the vision of the tree's gruesome history, the image would not return. She shuddered, wishing she could clear it from her memory.

Peering out the window that overlooked the front of the house, she saw Zeke's amassed followers remained—and more appeared to be climbing out of cars to join the gathered group. Was the police cruiser still out there? She couldn't tell. Not good.

Sterling joined her, bumping her with an elbow. "I distinctly remember you telling me that spirits are all around us all the time. So why are the investigations invariably at night?"

"Astute observation. The short answer is that we see the majority of spirits better at night. The theory is that rods, which are more active in dim light and only detect black and white images, better detect the gauzy, ethereal spirit apparitions than the cones, which provide vision during the day and see colors. Basically, we remove the competition at night and use the correct vision tools to see them."

The corners of Sterling's mouth twitched. "That's at least

based in science. However, the counter argument is that nothing is there at all. Our eyes aren't perfect and sometimes trick us. We think we see something out of the corner of our eye, but then it disappears when we try to focus directly on it. Which has led to the belief in ghosts, when in fact nothing was ever there."

"Except when it is. Believe me, I'm quite familiar with that theory. And I know some people are so desperate to see ghosts that they imagine what they want to see. I get that. But what you're describing supports the phenomenon. Rods are found at the edge of the retina and catch what's in our peripheral vision. Cones are centrally located. So as soon as we change our focus to look directly at whatever we saw out of the corner of our eye, the cones take over—and can't detect the ephemeral spirit."

Sterling laughed. "And yet again, we both say the same things, yet draw different conclusions. Somehow, it doesn't seem so silly anymore. Maybe there really is something to it."

She heard skepticism in his voice that belied his true feelings. But no way would she push too hard. This was progress. Best to keep it light and let him work it out for himself. "Oh, the ghosts are really here. But only an extraordinarily luminous spirit can be seen in daylight by the naked eye."

"Super powerful? Especially ferocious? Amped, as TJ likes to say?"

"Newly deceased."

He sucked in a breath. "Like when you thought you saw your mom."

She nodded and turned away, staring out the window again. "Look at this. More people pouring in to support Zeke. All of them look ready to go all night. What if we never get rid of them? What if they follow me around the country?"

Sterling took her cue to change the subject. "They must have lives to get back to. Jobs? Families? Seriously, how are they able to be here?"

The mob, perhaps incensed by the presence of the angels, increased in volume, calling for an end to witchcraft in general and *The Wantland Files* in particular. And her most of all. The hostility and ferocity of these shouted insults aimed at her landed with real force, each blow depleting her reserves.

As if he detected her waning energy, Sterling stepped closer, wrapped an arm around her waist, and pulled her backwards against him. He leaned down and pressed the side of his face against her head. "I'm here for you. We all are. Don't let them bring you down."

She relaxed against him, grateful for his soothing presence. Her spine tingled, and she realized it responded to his nearness. Though he was taller than her, and thus their chakras didn't perfectly align, hers prickled at the proximity of his as they resonated together. Perhaps this was the source of the electric tension she felt near him. Their chakras, their most intimate centers of self and existence, called to one another.

The prayer group angels began singing again, jolting her out of her reverie. *Focus,* she chided herself. She could explore and enjoy Sterling's chakras later. Right now, the Johnsons needed her full attention.

She squeezed Sterling before releasing him and turning away from the window to take in the attic, breathing in the space and situating herself in it. The Ouija board lay in the middle of the floor. Her plan hinged on it. She'd asked the Johnsons to trust her and allow her crew to bring Dakota's board back into their home. James had connected through this exact board the night of Faith's birthday sleepover. She wanted to recreate the conditions as closely as possible. Except of course, the Johnsons would be nowhere near the board.

It was time. No reason not to get started. Except her own fear, which she couldn't allow to stop her. "The family is in Faith's room?"

TJ's head popped up from behind a monitor. "I have a live feed from a sta-cam in the room. I see them all on the screen."

"Let them know we're about to begin."

Elise spoke into a walkie-talkie, listened for the response, then gave her a thumbs up.

"Ready, sweetie?" Michael asked.

She took a deep breath and shook out her hands to dispel some of the nervous energy. Once she'd situated herself near the Ouija board, she faced Stan's camera and nodded.

Michael held out a hand, all five fingers spread as if for a jazz ensemble, and counted down. "In five . . . four . . . three . . ."

She watched him fold back his middle finger, then point to her—the signal it was go time.

"We're in the Johnsons' attic for what I hope will be our final encounter with James. Earlier attempts to engage him today in Faith's bedroom proved fruitless, though her room was the origin of this haunting and she has endured the majority of James' hostilities." She gestured to the Ouija board. "Faith and her friends established contact via Ouija board, as we've already determined. What I hadn't considered is a protective presence from family ancestors, who I believe remain in Faith's room, perhaps her closet, doing their best to shield the family from this new and malevolent spirit, released into the house by the Ouija board."

She turned to Sterling and held out a hand. "Sterling and I will operate the Ouija board to establish a direct connection with James, who I believe slinks away and hides here in the attic to recharge. Once connected, I will attempt to force him to cross over."

Sterling took her hand and joined her. "I'm still not a fan of the plan, but I remain convinced this is merely a piece of cardboard and don't believe it can result in harm to anyone."

He locked eyes with her and for the first time since they'd met, she saw a glimmer of doubt. His convictions no longer carried the weight they once had. But he sat on one side of the board.

She lowered herself opposite him and situated the board on their knees, then addressed the camera again. "Make no mistake,

James is an evil and powerful spirit, fully capable of inflicting real injury on living tissue."

Meeting Sterling's eyes once more, she smiled encouragingly —and felt a deep pang of guilt that he didn't know the second half of the plan. None of them did. They would never agree to it if she told them. It would be the most dangerous thing she'd ever attempted.

CHAPTER THIRTY-FIVE

Kimberly and Sterling rested their fingertips on the edges of the planchette. Elise and Rosie lit candles throughout the attic. The dancing flames crackled and flickered, throwing obscure patterns across the walls and casting an orange glow over the space.

She met Sterling's eyes across the Ouija board. Harsh shadows from the candlelight played across his face, highlighting his cheekbones while casting dark pools below his eyes.

"Are you ready?" she asked.

"Whatever you need."

The property claim, dating all the way back to the Land Run, rested near her. She sometimes used personal items that held special meaning to a spirit when they were alive in order to remind them of their life and connect with them. Once reminded, she could help them cross over. James would unlikely respond in that way. He didn't need reminding—he remembered his life and was focused only on punishing the descendants his wife had born with another man. Never mind the fact James had known Rebecca was pregnant before taking her as his wife. Never mind that he'd killed George, the man Rebecca truly loved, and beaten Rebecca mercilessly. He couldn't see his own sins and believed himself justified to seek revenge.

What would prompt him to show himself? How could she convince him to let go of Faith and connect with her instead? Particularly since he had no interest in connecting and even less in crossing over.

"Are any spirits present with us?" she tried. *Lame*. What was she, a teenager playing with ghosts?

Sterling stared at the motionless planchette. He glanced up at her and whispered, "Want me to push it around a little?"

"Definitely not, though I appreciate the sentiment behind the offer. We want James to respond on his own."

"What if he doesn't?"

"That would be a problem." Her plan hinged on the spirit connecting with her. And she hadn't considered a Plan B. This had to work. She tried again, more forcefully this time. "James, we'd like to talk to you."

The candles continued to flicker and suffuse the space with soothing lavender scent. One of them popped in the silence that filled the attic. The dull roar of the protestors carried from the street to where she sat. For a moment, she actually wished she possessed the magical abilities the yokels outside accused her of. Then she could simply summon the spirit and force him to do as she bid.

She would have to be smarter. How could she, in effect, summon him? What was important to James in life? He may have been a complete jerk in his private life, but he somehow established himself as an upstanding citizen of Guthrie, a pillar of the community, rising to the rank of sheriff and overseeing justice in the burgeoning town. Or his own justice.

But Elise found no record of a James Loveless prior to the Land Run claim. Oklahoma had been a hideout for outlaws on the run for a reason—they could disappear into the wild land and elude capture. Who had James been before he showed up for the Land Run? In the wide-open plains and unsettled territory, generations before the Internet and social media, people reinvented themselves routinely, hiding past crimes, previous identities, and the ghosts in their personal histories.

She didn't have facts, but her intuition rarely misled her. No true upstanding citizen had reason to run from his past. "James, I know what you did before you moved to Guthrie. Before Guthrie even existed."

The candle flames went completely still. Coincidence? Or did she have his attention?

"I know what you did," she repeated. "You lied. You stole. And when you decided to start fresh in Oklahoma Territory, the Land Run was your perfect opportunity. But nothing changed. You still lied and stole."

"Ms. Wantland?" TJ said. "Something is happening in Faith's room. She . . . doesn't look good."

"What's happening?"

"She's thrashing around on the bed. Daniel is trying to hold her down, but she's too strong for him."

She had James' attention. "You may have fooled the other people who settled in town. But we see who you really were. You stole the land claim and you stole your wife. Nothing changed."

"Faith just threw Daniel and shoved past Ruth," TJ said.

"We all know who you really are, just like Rebecca knew. You're a liar and a cheat. And a murderer."

The flashlights in the room began to flicker as a low rumble trembled along the attic floor she sat on.

"Kimmy?" Michael's voice trembled. "What are you doing?"

She pushed harder, knowing she'd found the sore spot. "You were nothing but a criminal, on the run, avoiding capture. You still are. And I'm going to tell everyone."

She felt more than heard the angry roar that ripped through the house. Every flashlight in the room switched on and off in the darkening space. The overhead bare bulb burst in a shattering explosion, sending glass shards tinkling to the floor.

"The dog just raced out of Faith's bedroom," TJ reported.

"His hackles are up and his teeth are bared. He looks ready to attack. But Faith looks normal again. Ruth is hugging her."

A series of loud bangs echoed through the house as doors slammed shut.

"We have his attention," she told Sterling. "Let go of the planchette."

Sterling's forehead creased. "You sure?"

"Yes. He's coming. We're finished with the Ouija board." Well, *she* wasn't. But no one else needed to know that.

Sterling lifted his fingers from the plastic piece. She picked it up and clutched it tightly in her hand.

Sterling reached across the board and grabbed her arm. "What are you doing? You said handling that thing alone is dangerous."

"It's the only way."

"Kimberly, no!" Rosie shouted.

"Put that down!" Michael yelled.

A whoosh of wind blew upward through the door to the attic and whipped through the open space. The candles snuffed out. A dust devil of angry energy swirled around her, lifting tendrils of her hair.

She smelled him—the reek of alcohol seeping through pores combined with urine and the sweaty grime of a body long overdue for a bath, with a film of filth caked nearly thick enough to plant seeds in.

"Kimmy?" Michael asked. "You okay? KII is off the chart. One fifty and climbing."

"He's here," she responded. She sat perfectly still, allowing the spirit to continue invading her space, most likely trying to intimidate her. What worked on a terrified child, however, wouldn't scare her. In fact, he was behaving exactly as she'd hoped he would.

She held perfectly still, even when she felt his stinking breath on her neck, putrid with the years of rot and decay. His most pure self was evil to the core. He had cowed and threatened and bullied people to get his way. Especially women. Not this time. But she would let him believe his tactics worked, so she could spring her own surprise.

She closed her eyes and pushed all her energy to her indigo chakra, focusing on sending out her lighthouse beacon, her invitation to connect. James was furious with her. He should want to connect, if only to take control and teach her a lesson. He wouldn't be criticized and put in his place by a woman. Once connected, she would open a portal, drag him with her, push him across, and close the gap. The timing would be critical to avoid being pulled across with him.

She sunk further into herself, leaving the living world behind, allowing her psychic self to plumb for the veil, searching for the edge, so she could lift it and shove James beyond. She ran her spiritual fingers along the edge of this reality, until it rippled at her touch. She tugged. It warped, offering her the opening she needed.

Now where was James? She hadn't yet felt the click that indicated connection with another, like two puzzle pieces joining together.

"I know you're here, James. I'm the one standing between you and Faith. I'm the one you want."

She waited. Nothing happened. He didn't connect. This she didn't expect. She pulled back from the spirit realm.

Snickers' barks carried from where he stood on the second floor and ricocheted around the attic.

"Can someone quiet the dog?" Michael asked.

No one moved.

"He probably wants up here to help—"

James crashed into her with an unexpected force that left her gasping. Hands clutched her neck, squeezing tighter and tighter. She lifted useless fingers to her throat, prying at nothing. He meant to strangle her. His intent seeped into her psyche as clearly as a shouted message. He knew what she meant to do. She forgot completely about her plan and simply fought for her life.

CHAPTER THIRTY-SIX

KIMBERLY GRAPPLED with James and found fighting an incorporeal soul akin to trying to grasp fog. How he managed to maintain the intense energy level required for physical harm this long, she had no idea. She'd never seen anything like it. And had no idea how to combat it.

Sterling grabbed her arms. "What's wrong?"

She shook her head, unable to produce a sound. Cold. Cold seeped into her skin through ethereal fingers, through her body, all the way into her bones.

"Kimmy, what's wrong?" Michael asked.

Rosie dropped to her side. "What's he doing? Where is he?"

"Who?" Sterling asked. "What's who doing?"

"Something on the FLIR!" TJ shouted. "Blue all over Ms. Wantland's neck! Her temperature is dropping!"

"She can't breathe!" Sterling yelled.

"I can barely make out a humanoid shape in front of her," TJ said.

"There's no one in front of her!" Sterling answered. "She can't breathe. It could be anaphylactic shock. Does she have any food allergies?"

She shivered as she gasped futilely for oxygen, listening to her crew she knew unable to help. Gathering all her strength, she pushed against James.

Nothing. His grip held firm. He was too strong for her.

Through the sound of blood pulsing in her ears, she sensed Rosie moving beside her. And then Sterling sat behind her.

"Yes, like that," Rosie said. "Now rest your hands against her and imagine giving her strength and energy."

She felt what she knew could only be Sterling's hands against her back. Warmth flowed through her, clearing her mind and helping her focus. She pushed again. This time James' hands loosened their grip.

She pitched forward, catching herself before she faceplanted into the floor and gulping air into her burning lungs.

"I used sage," Rosie said. "I hope you didn't want to keep him here."

"No. You did the right thing. Like always. Thank you."

"What happened, Kimmy?" Michael asked.

She noticed Stan move closer, capturing her reply for the show.

"He never connected with me as I expected him too. He seemed to sense the rift I opened in the veil and figured out what I intended to do."

"What were you thinking?" Michael demanded. "Handling the planchette alone?"

"I needed to make sure he came to me and no one else."

"You saw what he's been doing to Faith."

"Exactly. I couldn't risk him doing that to Sterling. Or anyone else."

Rosie pushed her hair from her face. "Are you okay?"

She breathed deeply, trying to calm the shaking in her hands. "I'm fine now. Just need to catch my breath. But I've lost him. I don't know where he went, but he isn't here anymore."

The silence in the attic unnerved her. Her crew didn't so much as breathe, ears straining for some clue as to what was happening. In the tense quiet, the mob's shouts filled the void, a constant, angry hum in the background.

"KII reading?" she asked.

"Ambient," Michael answered. "No higher than twenty-five."

"Anything on the FLIR?"

"Nothing unusual," TJ answered. "No cold spots. Heat sources match living bodies."

"Elise, anything on the recordings?"

"Nothing. Not a word."

"He doesn't seem interested in communicating. I think he got his message across just fine."

Her plan had failed. James' spirit was too powerful for her. Now what?

"Ms. Wantland?" TJ's voice wavered. "I think something is happening in Faith's bedroom again."

She pushed herself to her feet and joined TJ at his monitor. What she saw on the screen made no sense. "What are they—"

Snickers' barking renewed, more urgent and insistent than before.

"Can someone please get that dog to be quiet?" Michael yelled. "Elise, you've been playing with him. Calm him down. Shove him out in the backyard if you have to."

The confusing images on TJ's monitor clicked. She knew what was happening. And it wasn't good. "No, wait! He wants our attention to help the family. Look!"

The rest of the crew clustered around her. On the monitor, Daniel struggled in a chair, appearing unable to stand despite gritted teeth and furrowed brow indicating he fought to get up.

"What is Ruth doing?" Stan asked.

The woman stood with her back to the wall, arms out, as if pinned to a specimen board on display. She, too, appeared immobilized. Only her eyes, wide with terror, moved.

Rebecca sat on the floor and appeared paralyzed with fear.

Faith alone demonstrated movement. On her feet, she edged backward, staring straight ahead.

All four sets of eyes gazed at something out of frame.

"What do they see?" she asked. "What's in there with them?"

"We decided to use a live feed loop with a sta-cam," TJ said, his breath coming in short rasps. "I didn't set up a motion-triggered camera."

"He's gone back to Faith. Antagonizing him only further angered him. I screwed up." She raced for the door.

"Kimmy, you are in no shape to take him on again already. At least let Rosie—"

"He's going after Faith with renewed determination. Because of me. I have to do something."

She scrambled down the ladder so quickly, she lost her footing and fell several feet. Her ankle hurt, but it held her weight and didn't scream in pain, so she turned down the hall.

The hallway appeared to stretch before her endlessly, Faith's door a tiny dot at the end of the elongating space. She heard Snickers' relentless barks calling for aid, as if miles away. Or perhaps underwater.

Limping, she willed herself on, each step taking her no closer to her goal. The throbbing in her ankle increased with each useless step.

James had seen right through her. She'd been a fool to think this would go as planned. He was too powerful—and the negative doubt and angry energy from the mob charged him further.

Out of breath, unable to drag her foot one more step on her twisted ankle, she eyed the distance remaining. No improvement.

She hunched over, hands on her thighs, breathing deeply. She had to re-center. Clutching her quartz, she focused on the door. *This isn't real.*

Her body, as if weightless, seemed to drift, like a balloon that broke free from its tether. She couldn't breathe again. She opened eyes she didn't remember closing, only to discover the world around her grainy and blurry. When she concentrated on a specific object, it swam out of focus. Was she underwater? Is this what drowning felt like?

Shadowy figures emerged around her, foggy and indistinct, only to dissipate like a puff of smoke and re-emerge again. Shapeless fingers reached for her, then drifted away like dandelion fluff on a summer breeze.

Kimberly.

Help me.

Voices called to her. Voices of the dead. Whispered murmurs, confused and scared, swirled around her.

She wasn't underwater, wasn't drowning. James had pulled her into the Nightshade—the spirit realm between the world of the living and whatever waited on the other side of the veil, where spirits who didn't cross over remained, left behind. He had maintained control of her while retreating to Faith's room to immobilize the rest of the family. What had he done to Faith? And how was he powerful enough to stretch his energy so wide? He wanted her in his plane of existence, where he held the upper hand.

But she wasn't ready to give up.

This isn't real. This isn't real.

Hands rested on her shoulders. Hands grabbed her arms. Hands pulled at her. The spirits had her. They were going to pull her—

"Kimberly!"

Rosie. Michael. Sterling. They stood with her, holding fast, anchoring her to the world of the living.

The grainy images blurred about her, morphing into shapes and colors.

She snapped back—and found herself directly in front of Faith's closed door.

Snickers' barking stopped the moment she stared down at him. He whimpered and nuzzled her hand with his nose.

"I'm back," she told him, stroking his silky fur.

From the other side of the door, she heard Ruth. "Kimberly? Help us! Faith! Faith is—"

She grabbed the doorknob and twisted hard. It turned easily in her hand, but the door didn't open.

She turned to discover her entire crew behind her. "We have to get inside this room."

CHAPTER THIRTY-SEVEN

KIMBERLY TWISTED the knob again and threw her shoulder against the door. It rattled but didn't budge.

Sterling nudged her aside. "Here. Let me." He threw all his weight against the door. And got the same result. "What in the world?"

She rested her hands on the door, opening her sixth sense to any input that might help. She couldn't detect a thing. But she was worn out. "No one is near the door, correct? Is anything blocking it?"

"No!" Daniel called. "Why won't you come help us?"

"We're trying! The door won't open."

Sterling ran his fingers along the edges of the door, examining the jamb, the floor. "What could possibly be sealing this?"

TJ appeared at her elbow, his monitor in hand. "Look at Faith."

One look renewed her efforts to get inside. James wouldn't stop at rashes and bite marks this time. "Everyone, push on the door!"

She gripped her crystal and called on every bit of psychic energy she could draw, waited for her crew to gather in close, and pushed against the blocked doorway with everything she had.

Rebecca's crying mingled with the screams of both parents. She heard Faith, screaming for help. She had to get inside.

But she couldn't open the door.

Sterling stepped back, hands on hips, brow furrowed. "What could possibly be holding this closed? The knob turns. Nothing blocking the door."

"It's James," she told him. "But how, I'm not sure." She used both fists to pound the door again and again until her hands ached with the bruises she'd surely inflicted.

"Stop. You'll hurt yourself." Sterling snapped. "A vacuum! A vacuum would cause a seal like this. Though I have no idea how one would exist in a bedroom."

Why hadn't she thought of that? "Of course! James is holding us out with his energy. Holding the door closed. He's probably surrounded the bedroom, pushing against us all with his energy, in effect sealing it shut."

"We need to break the vacuum," Sterling said.

"Yes, that would break his hold on the room! Sterling you're a genius!"

He shook his head but smiled. "Yet again, we're speaking the same language but mean entirely different things."

She pounded on the door. "Open a window!"

"I can't move!" Ruth called back.

"You have to open a window so we can get inside."

"I'll get there," Daniel said, his voice low and determined.

"He's moving!" TJ announced. "Slowly, but he's fighting against James."

She knew the moment Daniel wrenched open the window. Her ears popped and the door sucked inward, swinging open suddenly on its hinges.

She stumbled into the room, the full brunt of the noise from outside pouring in through the open window. Daniel, Ruth, and Rebecca all stared, open-mouthed, at the closet.

Following their gazes, she saw that the closet door hung open. Nothing unusual. So why did the air reek of ozone? And why did the hair on her arms stand up as if charged with static electricity? And where was—

"Where's Faith?" she asked, a terrible suspicion taking form in her mind.

"He—He—" Ruth seemed shocked beyond speech.

Rebecca pointed to the closet. "She went in there."

Sterling stepped past her. "Okay, so she went in the closet. Why's everyone being so weird?" He pushed aside hanging clothes as if playing a game of hide and seek. "Huh. Where is she?" He squatted down and rapped on the walls of the closet.

"She disappeared," Daniel whispered, his words tremulous. "The closet glowed and then . . . I can't believe what I just saw with my own eyes."

Sterling rocked back on his heels. "No hidden doors."

Daniel rolled his eyes. "I could have told you that."

Rebecca's eyes bulged and she looked like she might vomit. "She didn't *go* in the closet. Something pulled her in." The girl edged toward the door as if fearful she might be next.

"What do you mean, pulled her?" Sterling asked.

Ruth found her voice. "The closet door swung open and . . . the closet glowed. I think I saw a hand or something reach out of the light. Faith moved toward the closet, even though she wanted to stop herself. She tried to grab onto something but couldn't. She called for help. Why didn't you come?"

Daniel's faltering words indicated he didn't believe the words he spoke. "When you guys came in, the light went out and Faith was gone."

Ruth began to cry. "Why didn't you help her? Where is she? Where is my daughter?"

"I'm sorry. We couldn't open the door. We—"

Daniel's grim voice cut her off. "Do we need to call the police and report an abduction?"

Every eye in the room turned to her for guidance. This time she knew the answer. "The police can't help Faith. James has taken her hostage."

"Taken her? Taken her where?" Ruth's voice rose in pitch.

"To the Nightshade. The spirit realm. The plane of existence for those who haven't crossed over."

Ruth staggered, catching herself on the desk. The Ladies of Fashion rattled in response. "You mean she's dead?"

"No. Alive. I'm sure. But I don't know what he intends to do, and we need to bring her back to us." She watched the Ladies of Fashion, certain she'd seen them shift. "I know what to do. But I need to find her. And we need help. Michael, we're going to need the SEEPS."

"The SEEPS? Are you crazy?" Michael asked.

She gestured to the window, indicating the chanting mob below. "Crazy. Evil. Take your pick. But we need it."

Sterling rubbed the back of his neck. "I know I'm the least educated in your ghost hunting ways, but don't you use the SEEPS to feed energy to a ghost?"

"Dude, that's right!" TJ said. "You remembered."

"Yes, good recall," she agreed.

"Why would you offer more power to a ghost that apparently just choked you?" Sterling asked.

TJ beamed, and offered to fist-bump Sterling. "This is awesome! We lured him away from the dark side!"

Sterling tapped TJ's fist with his own. "Aren't I supposed to get cookies or something?"

"No, the dark side tries to tempt you with cookies. We—"

"Ahem." Michael cleared his throat. "You fan boys can geek out later. Kimmy, they're exactly right. James is far too powerful already. We can't risk him drawing from the SEEPS."

"Normally, I would agree. But James pulled me into the Nightshade, too. The ghosts of the past spoke to me while I was there. We have allies ready to help, but James overpowers them. We need to amp them up."

Ruth dabbed her eyes. "What do you mean allies?"

"Your mother, most powerfully. She's been moving the Ladies of Fashion, trying to get your attention. And I think she moved the doll that scared Sterling. Spirits are limited, normally. She didn't mean to scare you. She wants to help Faith and is trying to communicate with us."

Something clicked in Ruth's mind. "And George. He's here too, isn't he?"

"Yes. And many ancestors in between the two. They aren't as powerful as James, but they'll outnumber him. With their help, maybe I can force him across."

Daniel frowned. "James isn't limited. You say he's overpowering the others. How? How is he so much more powerful?"

"I've been thinking about that. He's of our world—he lived and breathed and died. He's not a demon. But he does demonstrate some similar abilities. I think maybe, while he was alive, he made a pact with an evil entity."

Sterling smirked. "Are you saying a deal with the Devil?"

She sighed. "More or less, yes."

"I thought you didn't believe in heaven or hell, God or the Devil."

Ruth appeared stricken by the thought. "You don't?"

"Sterling, please. This is not the time for a religious debate. Regardless of what I do or don't believe, I'm going to bring Faith back. We need to locate her first and verify that's what happened to her."

"Are you up for this?" Rosie asked.

She grasped her quartz. "I have to be."

Moving into the hallway, she searched the house for any blips, any ripples indicating unrest. She sent out a beacon, hoping to draw in someone helpful. Perhaps one of the other spirits could guide her to Faith.

She moved through each room of the house, Snickers dogging her heels, whining periodically. "I know, little guy. We will find her."

As she passed the formal living room, the vintage radio caught her attention. Would it work again? She flipped the power on and listened to the white noise of static hiss from the speakers.

Lowering herself into a nearby chair, she closed her eyes and directed all of her psychic energy to her indigo chakra. She wanted to connect with the spirit world without actually traveling to it. Until she knew for sure where the girl was, she couldn't help her. "Faith? Can you hear me?"

Snickers sat at her feet, resting one paw on her leg.

Her crew and the family had followed her and amassed in the room. Ruth dabbed at her eyes with a tissue and leaned against Daniel. Rebecca stood off to one side, arms crossed, looking guilty and out of place.

This family had suffered so much, for months and months. She had to end it. The distraction of the family motivated her, compelling her to end it tonight. Now. But they also distracted her, making it difficult to get into the right mind frame to make a psychic connection.

She tried again. "Faith?"

A frightened voice crackled from the radio. "Hello?"

Relief flooded through her. They had her.

Ruth clenched her hands together. "That's her! Faith! Where are you?"

"Mommy?"

"How is this possible?" Daniel asked.

"Yes. We're here. We're trying to find you."

Kimberly saw Sterling staring at the radio as if had suddenly grown legs and started barking. She knew his brain was probably folding in on itself as he tried to reconcile what he saw and heard with his belief system. She would worry about helping him later. Right now, Faith needed rescue. "Faith, can you tell me where you are?"

"Who are you?"

"It's Kimberly Wantland. I'm going to bring you back to your family."

"I don't like it here." The girl's voice was weak, fading.

"I know. Tell me what you can see so I can find you."

"People. There are people here."

"People?" That made no sense. Had she somehow moved outside? Did she see the crowd?

"I don't like them. I want to go home."

Ruth twisted her hands together. "She's scared! Kimberly, help her!"

"Faith, I'm so sorry!" Rebecca cried at the radio.

"Becca?"

The entire family looked to her, eyes pleading.

She stood, heart pounding. "Faith, can you come to us? Can you follow my voice?"

Barely a whisper answered. "They won't let me."

Snickers barked and raced to the stairs.

"Then tell me what you see, Faith. I'll come to you."

"It's dark. I can't see. I don't know where I am."

Sterling lifted the radio gingerly from the table. "This can't be a trick. But it can't be real. What is happening?"

Faith's trembling voice issued from the speakers again. "He's coming back. I don't want to be here. Ms. Wantland!"

She heard footsteps clomp above them. Snickers ran up several stairs, turned, and barked at her.

"Keep talking, Faith! I'm coming!" She turned and ran for the stairs. "I don't think she ever left the closet. She's still there but in the Nightshade."

She tore up the stairs two at a time. *Hold on, Faith. A little longer.*

CHAPTER THIRTY-EIGHT

IF FAITH WAS in the Nightshade, Kimberly had no choice but to go back. She shuddered. Dismal and grim, filled with miserable spirits, she dreaded returning. As frightening as the in-between realm could be for lost spirits, it was far worse for living souls.

And potentially deadly. A living soul not properly tethered could become lost and wander adrift. Forever.

She'd heard of travelers who fell into comas—comas that confounded doctors who could find no medical reason to explain the condition. But she knew what had happened. She wouldn't let it happen to Faith. Psychics could bring people back. She could do this if she could find the girl.

But Faith had been pulled into the Nightshade body and soul both—a phenomenon so rare, she'd never encountered it. A body in the spirit world couldn't last long. Faith was a fish out of water right now.

Bursting into Faith's bedroom, she went straight to the closet. She forced herself to calm her erratic heartbeat and gasping breaths. Faith needed strength and power to escape James.

Snickers crept to the yawning closet door, leaning forward, one paw up, and sniffed the space as if he knew Faith was near.

The prayer group's song mingled with the angry mob's continued chants. Both blew into the open window. Faith's blue curtains reached into the room, straining against the curtain rod as if seeking escape from the noise.

Her crew and the Johnsons crowded into the room, watching her for signs of what they should do next.

Michael held the SEEPS, the Spectral-Enhancing Energy Power Source they'd designed. The black box produced electricity at a controlled rate, offering power to nearby spirits who wanted to charge. "I still think this is the worst idea you've ever had."

"Thanks for the vote of confidence. Don't turn it on yet. Not until I've brought Faith back."

Michael set it on the floor. "Deal."

Rosie opened her medicine bag and pulled a stone from it. "I doubt you'll let me charge your chakras, since time is critical. At least hold onto this."

Kimberly looked down at the smooth silvery-gray stone Rosie pressed into her hand. "Hematite?"

"To ground you." Rosie closed her fist around the stone and pushed Sterling close. "You stay nearby too. You have a good track record of anchoring her."

"What do you mean time is critical?" Daniel asked.

Kimberly looked to Michael, who nodded. "The longer Faith is in limbo, the more confused she will become. Besides, she's a living being in the spirit plane. We need to bring her back where she belongs quickly."

Ruth's face crumbled, eyes filling with tears. Daniel put an arm around his wife. "We can't lose our daughter."

"You won't. I won't let that happen."

She sat cross-legged, clutching her rough quartz crystal in one hand and the smooth hematite in the other. One would help free her spirit; one would keep her physical body firmly rooted in place. Closing her eyes, she sunk deeply into herself, leaving behind all distractions of the living world. She breathed in light and freeness, breathing out stress and complications. Everything she loved and cared about she held close while letting go of all worry and frustration.

Her spirit rocked a bit, loose now, no longer completely attached to her body. She opened her eyes and looked around. The closet gaped open before her, sepia-toned and grainy. The scene before her shook like a poor-quality home movie, blurring in and out of focus. One more tug and her spirit loosened, nudged from her body.

Whispering voices crackled in her ears, but she couldn't grasp individual words or the meaning of the communication. Smoky fingers materialized at the ends of foggy hands. They pointed to the back of the closet, toward the wall.

She understood. They were directing her beyond the wall. To Faith? Or into a trap? Without knowing who powered these disembodied hands, she couldn't take the risk. Her spirit had to stay within sight of her body. Otherwise the risk of permanent separation was too great.

She listened for the sound of a heartbeat within the silent nothing surrounding her, the tell-tale sign of a living being in the empty void.

Faint but there, she heard a frantic *lub-dub* pulsing through the emptiness around her. "Faith? Can you hear me?"

"Ms. Wantland?" The girl's trembling voice broke her heart. The pitter-pat of her heartbeat kicked up another notch.

As if echoing through the chambers of an intricate cave system, she heard Sterling's voice. "My God. I hear her. I hear them both through the speaker. How is this possible?"

"Mr. Wakefield," she heard Ruth admonish, "please don't take the name of the Lord in vain in this home."

Despite the pressing need to find Faith, Kimberly smiled. Hearing them, knowing they were near, even if she couldn't see them, helped buoy her and strengthen her resolve.

She pushed her hand through the back wall of the closet. Separated from her body, her spirit passed easily through the flimsy reflection of the real world she wandered. "Can you see my hand, Faith?"

"No," came the quiet reply.

"No?" She was sure the girl was nearby. How did she miscalculate so badly?

"My eyes are closed. I saw . . . things."

She sighed in relief. "Yes, I see them too. I need you to be brave. Open your eyes so you can see my hand and come to me."

"I can't."

"You can. I'm right here."

No response.

She tried again. "Faith, be brave for one moment. Open your eyes, you'll see my hand. Grab it and I'll take you back to your family."

The girl whimpered. "I see lots of hands. I don't know which one is yours."

Of course. She should have anticipated that. She'd seen many hands too.

"Okay. I'm going to move closer to you. But as soon as you see me, you must come to me and grab my hand as quickly as you can. As soon as I tell you to. Do you understand?"

"Yes."

"This is very important, Faith. If we don't go back soon, we could both get lost in here."

"That would be bad."

"That would be very bad."

Michael's voice crackled nearby, floating by her as though echoing from a great distance. "Ruth, tell her to run to Kimmy, the moment she tells Faith to go."

Everyone depended on her. Trusted her. She could not fail the Johnsons. She breathed deeply, centering herself and taking note of her surroundings. She would not get lost. She could handle this. Even though her body would be out of sight and she'd never completely separated before. She would keep her feet firmly rooted in place and snap right back to her body. She took several deep breaths and pushed her head through the wall.

Faith sat huddled between wood framing some distance away. Shoot. She'd counted on the girl being just on the other side of the wall. Everything was distorted in the Nightshade, a flimsy representation of the living world, close but out of touch. Unless you knew how to cross planes.

Or were pulled into it unwillingly as Faith had been. The girl pressed her face against her knees, hiding from the bizarre landscape she'd been stolen away into.

"Faith, I'm here."

The girl flinched but didn't lift her eyes.

"Faith, it's Ms. Wantland. Remember our deal? Come over here to me."

Still hiding her face, Faith shook her head. "You might be tricking me. Some of the voices tell me they want to help."

"Please, Faith. It's really me. You have to trust me."

"There's another voice. He says he brought me here to help all the sad people. He says if I leave, they'll be so sad they'll die."

"Don't listen to that voice, Faith. That's not your job. He's tricking you. I'm here to help you and the sad ghosts."

"He says you're lying." The girl clamped her hands over her ears. "Stop it! Everyone stop talking!"

Kimberly peered around the space. Empty. No other spirits appeared to her. The gray, empty space, a shadowy facsimile of the real world stretched on and on, beyond this house, these people, this history.

A tiny blue light shimmered on the horizon. The light beckoned to her, promising warm embrace, peace, tranquility, family and friends.

Kimberly.

The scent of lavender and freesia swirled about her, drawing her forward.

"Mom?" She stepped toward the light.

She floated easily, all worries left behind with her body—

Her body. She had drifted away from her body. She tore her gaze from the welcoming light. "Faith?"

She no longer saw the girl. And she didn't recognize her surroundings. Shadows shifted alarmingly, twisting from recognizable shapes to gruesome abstraction. The floor and walls, now coated in ectoplasmic residue, tipped sideways. She grappled with the slippery surfaces, scratching her nails against nothing as she fought for a grip, feet stepping backward frantically but sliding closer to the ever-narrowing end. She struggled as the hallway narrowed until she saw where it would dump her—into a yawning chasm. The glowing mouth open before her shimmered and undulated—and seemed to have no end.

CHAPTER THIRTY-NINE

KIMBERLY HOVERED ABOVE THE ABYSS, fingers sliding along the slimy walls, feet sinking into a gooey floor. She was Alice in Wonderland, wandering through a strange reality that made no sense. If she plummeted into the depths of the mouth below her, where would she land? Could she find a way out?

Panic bubbled up her throat and choked her. *No, no, no.* She could not be lost. She would not fall into an inexplicable coma while her spirit remained trapped in this realm. She had to take Faith home.

She closed her eyes. *This isn't real. This isn't real.*

No matter how hard she willed away the oozing walls, her fingers remained covered in ectoplasm. It was real. She was in the Nightshade, and James held her completely under his control. This was his reality and he knew how to manipulate it. Her feet slid over the edge of the chasm. She dangled over a gulf of nothing.

Rather than deny the surreal surroundings, she fought them. She imagined the hallway turning on end and found herself sliding back the way she'd come. A funhouse of horrors. She could play this game too. Feet squishing, she retraced her steps.

But James wasn't done. The wall split into a hideous mouth

and wrapped around her hand like an amoeba. She pulled, but the living tissue swallowed again and again. She struggled but watched her wrist, then her forearm, then her elbow engulfed. Like quicksand, the gelatinous ooze pulled incessantly and struggling only made it worse.

Her hand drooped with sudden weight. The hematite. It would ground her in the living world and guide her back to those who waited for her there. She stopped thrashing and flailing, focusing her attention on the smooth stone Rosie had pressed into her hand.

With every ounce of strength she could gather, she clenched her fist and pulled. The wall squelched in protest as she succeeded in extracting her arm, inch by inch. A sloppy wet pop accompanied her fist as she gave one final yank. She was free of the writhing wall.

She stepped backward, thinking only of the Johnsons and her friends. The walls, floor, and ceiling shimmered, twisted, and morphed back into the house. She blinked as she tried to recognize her surroundings. The living room. How much time had lapsed? How long had she floundered in the Nightshade?

She made her way up the staircase and returned to Faith's room.

She passed through the open door. Drifting through the bedroom as if in slow motion, she saw the blurry images of all the people depending on her.

She walked past Sterling, who held the radio, ear pressed to the speaker. His mouth moved. A whispered crackle drifted past her, distorted through the frequency. "I don't hear either one of them."

Ruth and Daniel clutched one another. Images of sobbing Ruth jerked in and out of focus.

Michael stood near her body, hands pressed to his mouth.

Rosie crouched beside her, shaking her head at Michael.

Sterling set down the radio and turned abruptly. "I'm going to go look for the girl again."

He walked right through her, unaware of her presence. She smelled him, sensed his deep concern, felt every molecule of his being in a rush of intimacy that knocked her off kilter. Reaching out a hand, she longed to assure him, connect with him. But he walked away, oblivious, and the complete lack of acknowledgement left her empty—and with a better awareness of what wandering spirits experienced on a daily basis. Fresh determination rejuvenated her. She couldn't leave Faith to this dismal future, lost in the spirit world.

In all her years as a practicing psychic, she'd never had an out-of-body experience. She eyed herself as she passed by, returning to her starting point—the closet wall with a terrified little girl on the other side.

She leaned through the wall, spotted Faith, and caught her breath. Faith remained exactly as she'd left her, knees drawn close, arms hugging her legs, face pressed into her thighs. But now James bent over the girl, whose form he dwarfed in his current monstrous shape. She called out in the fiercest voice she could manage. "Faith! Run to me! Now!"

She heard her own voice crackle through the radio's speakers. Apparently, so did her crew.

"Ruth! Now!" Michael's voice commanded.

"Faith! Run, baby! Run to Ms. Wantland!"

The girl lifted her head, though her eyes remained closed. "Mommy?"

"Yes, it's Mommy. Come on, my little Faith of an Angel. Run! Run as fast as you can right now!"

Faith opened her eyes—and saw the monster crouched over her. The girl's screams tore through the Nightshade, sending feedback screeching from the radio.

"What's happening to her?" she heard Rebecca cry.

But she couldn't split her focus. Rescuing the girl had to be her only concern. "Faith! Here! I'm here!"

Time slowed to a crawl as Faith swiveled her head, locked eyes, and pushed herself to her feet. The girl turned her back on

James and never looked back as her arms pumped and feet pounded, closing the gap between them, eyes wild.

But Kimberly saw him—watched him shriek in anger as his hostage ran for freedom, watched him bear down on Faith bearing down on her.

"Keep going, Faith!" she called.

Ruth must have understood on some level that her daughter needed continued encouragement. "Run, baby, run!"

"Run, baby," Kimberly echoed, heart hammering as James closed the distance between them.

With James only a hair's breadth away, Faith launched herself forward into Kimberly's outstretched arms. She clutched the girl, closed her eyes, and leaned back into her waiting body, falling as if through a vat of molasses. The Nightshade wouldn't let her go easily. It pulled back in a tug-of-war as she struggled to escape, kicking her feet at James as he roared and grappled to regain possession of Faith.

A force hooked her, like a hand gripping her very core, and with a yank, she sailed away, back to the world of the living. Breaking through the barrier between the Nightshade and the living world, her ears popped. She landed back in her body and pitched sideways, cracking her head against the floor. Still cradling Faith, slick with ectoplasm, she gasped for breath.

The room erupted around her. Ruth and Daniel lifted Faith from her arms. Ignoring the ooze coating their daughter, they buried their faces against her, crushing her with hugs as if they'd never let her go.

Rosie and Michael each grabbed an arm and helped her sit up. She leaned forward and breathed deeply, trying to catch her breath. She caught Elise's eye, noting her usually stoic researcher teared up as she watched the Johnsons revel in the return of their daughter.

Sterling appeared in the doorway and did a double take at the scene in front of him. "What the actual hell?"

"Ms. Wantland brought her back," TJ said, his pride in the team evident in his smile.

Sterling stared at her. "I looked all over this house. I didn't see her anywhere. Where did you find her?"

"She was in the Nightshade. The spirit realm. James was strong enough to drag her there."

Sterling's forehead scrunched, his eyebrows crooked, as he shook his head. "That doesn't make any sense."

She could see him struggling to balance his innate skepticism with the inexplicable things happening around him.

Michael squatted beside her, inspecting her for visible injury. Rosie held open palms a few inches from her body, checking her chakras and energy levels.

"I'm okay," she assured them. "Just bumped my head during reentry."

"Reentry?" Sterling shook his head. He bent down and stared in her eyes, appearing to search for something, though she didn't know what. He ran one finger through the ectoplasm left behind on her arm. "What is this?"

"TJ, can you get a sample of this ectoplasm for Sterling to analyze, please? And someone get some towels for Faith."

Elise shook off the shock. "I'll grab some towels."

TJ shrugged off his backpack, extracted a plastic tube and scraped it along her arm before capping it and passing it to Sterling. "Here you go."

"Ectoplasm, huh?" Sterling shook his head but pocketed the sample. He squatted beside her. "Will you talk to me about this later? Tell me where the girl was? This would be a phenomenal stage act. Was she in the closet all along? You covered her with goop and then 'returned from the spirit—'"

A deep rumbling emanated from the bowels of the house. The hair on Kimberly's arms stood on end. She held up a hand. "Shhh. Listen."

Sterling cocked his head. "I only hear the people outside. Is that what you mean?"

"What's that smell?" An acrid burnt odor assaulted her nose.

Sterling's forehead crinkled. "I don't smell anything."

The faces of her crew and the Johnsons mirrored Sterling's. They all shook their heads in confusion. No one but her detected any of these changes.

Not good.

CHAPTER FORTY

REALIZATION HIT HARD and terror gripped Kimberly's heart. She gritted her teeth and pushed herself to her feet.

"What's wrong?" Michael asked.

She steadied herself against Sterling's arm. "Ruth, Daniel, take Faith outside."

They looked at her as if she'd sprouted a second head and started speaking Japanese.

"Go! Now! Out!" She pushed Sterling toward the confused family. "Go with them. Make sure they get her outside."

Ozone shot through the air, sulfur following like the smell of gunpowder after a shot. An electric jolt ran up her spine.

Ruth's and Daniel's mouths dropped open as they stared at something behind her.

"Not again," Faith whimpered.

"What's happening?" Rebecca asked. "What is that?"

Sterling paused to see what caught their attention. His eyes widened and he shook his head as if to clear it. "What is that?"

She locked eyes with him, and, remembering his reaction to the little girl's spirit, knew this would be more than he could handle. "Get them out of here. Please."

Sterling shifted his focus to the terrified parents. "Let's go. Come on."

Clutching Faith, Daniel tore out of the room, Sterling right behind him.

Kimberly grasped her quartz and slowly pivoted to face the looming threat.

A crack opened in the closet. A decaying hand, followed by a skeletal arm, stretched from the gap, elongated to an unnatural length, and swiped at Daniel as he disappeared from the room.

"Don't stop until you get her outside," Kimberly called after them. "I don't care what you think you see or hear!"

James' hideous form followed, bloated, rotting, no longer fully human. One foot, then another followed through the portal.

She wouldn't get close enough to touch the vile thing in front of her. But James broadcast his inner self so clearly, she knew exactly what had happened and what drove his actions.

"It's the Devil," Ruth whispered, hands clasped.

"No. This isn't the Devil, though I suspect he's seen something that could pass for him. It's James' spirit in his warped form, a fully corrupted soul, eaten up by hate and envy and desire. Evil destroys anyone who allows it in. And James welcomed it—the promises of power, wealth, status, and a whole new life. And all he wanted in return was your soul, didn't he, James?"

James' head swiveled to face her, arm retracting to roughly normal length. Black eyes bore into her, plumbing to test her mettle. "Kimberly Wantland."

"In the flesh. Which you no longer possess. Your energy in the living world won't last, James. And I won't let you steal Faith again."

"Faith will join me. The youngest of my false heirs will be my companion in the next life."

Ruth moaned and crumpled against the desk.

"That will never happen. You don't belong here, and she

doesn't belong there. You can't elude justice forever. You will pay for your crimes."

"No. My false heirs are the ones who will pay. Faith will be mine. You will join me too. Me and your mother." He gestured toward the closet, to the crack in time and space.

Her mother's image peered at her from beyond, the warm smile beckoning her to come, to find peace, to let go the fight.

All the strength drained out of her. She bent forward, collapsing like a deflated balloon, catching herself on her knees. Defeated.

James moved across the room, staring down each person in her crew and then Ruth, until they trembled in terror, homogenized with fear.

He turned back to face her again, curling his face directly in front of her like a viper threatening to strike. Her diaphragm quivered, but she couldn't draw a breath.

"Why do you linger, when your mother waits for you?"

She tried to wrench her gaze from his, hoping for a reassuring glance to the portal, but his soulless black eyes held her trapped.

He can't hurt you. He can't hurt you.

He seemed to stare directly into her very soul.

"Oh, I can hurt you. And you can't stop me." Faster than a blink, he crossed the room to the window. He opened his putrid mouth and bellowed, then stretched forward, diving outside while his feet remained on the floor, like a grotesque slinky tumbling down stairs.

A collective gasp preceded silence—the first silence she'd heard all day.

She roused herself from the stupor she'd fallen into under James' draining influence. Somehow, he'd managed to leave the confines of the house, perhaps as she had forced her way into the Nightshade. She had to keep him away from Faith and force him to cross over. Nothing else would stop him.

Screams punctured the air, arrows of confusion and horror

shot at the monster descending from the house. She dragged herself across the room on wobbly legs. The angry mob members scattered like ants prodded with a stick. While a few of them held cameras, presumably recording the bizarre scene unfolding before them, the majority ran, dove into cars, and drove away.

Zeke turned in circles, commanding his followers, arms waving. "Stand firm in the face of evil! Kimberly Wantland has wrought this demon upon us, and we must fight to the end!"

She took no pleasure in anyone's suffering, yet couldn't help but note the irony when one of his own supporters barreled into him and knocked him to the ground. Hard.

And yet Zeke remained undaunted, calling for them to storm the house and end this once and for all.

She saw Sterling leave Daniel's side and face off with Zeke. "Shut your idiotic mouth!"

Sterling's clenched fists looked ready to swing. Before the situation escalated further, James leaned lower and roared into Zeke's face.

Zeke scrambled to his feet and ran, shoving through what remained of the crowd.

The prayer group had encircled Faith. Each woman lifted high a cross and sang, harmonizing together as they protected the little girl.

James drifted closer to them.

She saw Daniel shake, clutching Faith to his chest, saw sweat soak his shirt as it dripped from his brow. And yet James moved no closer. He hesitated.

Was he confused? Did the crosses and prayers actually deflect him? She couldn't be certain. But regardless of the reason, his distraction gave her the opportunity she needed. He was correct—she couldn't stop him. Not alone. But she knew who could help.

"Michael, now. Switch it on."

He blinked. "What?"

James threw his head back and snarled. She didn't know how long the prayer group could hold him off.

"Turn on the SEEPS! Now!"

He flipped the switch. The black box buzzed to life. Crackling arcs of electricity sizzled across the wires that spanned the top of the box.

"Keep it around the midpoint," she told Michael. "We don't want to open it up full throttle."

Michael turned a dial, and the indicator stopped gyrating, settling midrange.

Shadows oozed from the walls, ink blot hands and arms stretched from the beyond. But this time the spirits drew from the SEEPS, forming into fully corporeal apparitions. Bodies appeared at the end of the arms.

Ghosts who had wandered the home for decades, either lost or keeping an eye on their descendants, manifested to protect their own. Kimberly watched as they fully materialized and nodded to her in thanks. A Native American gentleman stood before her.

"George?" she guessed.

He tipped his head at her.

"I saw what happened to you. I'm so sorry. James is still hurting people. I tried to stop him, but I need your help."

George squared his shoulders.

"Mom?" Ruth spoke in a hushed tone, as if unable to believe what she saw.

Kimberly turned and saw an older woman patting Ruth's cheek.

Tears filled Ruth's eyes. "Mom, I miss you so much."

Shouts outside caught her attention. She ran back to the window—just in time to see Faith run up the stairs and back into the house, Daniel and Sterling chasing after her.

No! While she'd been distracted by the other ghosts, James had rallied.

She whirled back to George. "Can you help? Will you fight him?"

George nodded.

Faith appeared in the doorway, glazed over, as if sleepwalking.

"Faith!" Ruth ran to embrace the girl, but Faith brushed her aside. "What's wrong, baby?"

"She's under James' influence again!"

Daniel and Sterling burst into the room as Faith plodded relentlessly toward James, who had retracted back inside and returned to a somewhat human shape.

"Please!" Kimberly called to the ghosts. "If you can help me stop him, do it now!"

She gathered every last bit of energy, reaching into a reserve she didn't realize she possessed. Grasping her quartz, she directed all her psychic energy to her indigo chakra and aimed it at James. She pushed with everything she had.

James stumbled, and she pushed again. And again—driving him toward the closet. If she could corral him and open a rift, she should still be able to force him to cross. Provided she did so quickly, before she had nothing left.

She splintered off a portion of energy and reached out, feeling psychically for the edge of the veil. When the edge of this world softened and warped, she concentrated, pressing harder until a fissure cracked open. Electric blue light poured into the room.

Utterly spent, she returned her attention to James. To her relief, she discovered George and Alta each held an arm, keeping him away from Faith. They both saw the opened crack and nodded. They seemed to understand her plan. Other spirits in the room closed in and laid hands on James as well.

James screamed as he realized the blue portal waited for him. He would no longer linger in the Nightshade. They were taking him to the Afterlife, to judgement and hopefully to justice.

Kimberly didn't know what waited after this world, but she truly hoped he would get what he deserved.

She psyched herself up and pushed James, the hardest she'd pushed yet. The spirits pulled as she pushed, dragging James kicking and screaming to his waiting fate.

She gave one last shove then collapsed, completely spent. Looking up from all fours, she silently implored the ghosts of the family's past to finish what she'd begun.

They clustered around James, overwhelming him, pushing and dragging him toward the light though he continued to thrash and twist, fighting to stay in this world.

Kimberly sighed with relief. It was over. James couldn't hurt anyone ever again.

Before she knew what was happening, James wrenched one arm free. It shot past her and grabbed Faith.

"No!" She lurched forward, grabbing the girl as James continued to be dragged closer to the portal by the other spirits. He could not take Faith with him. No living body could cross the veil. And if her soul crossed, her body would cease to live.

A whooshing filled her ears along with Faith's screams, Ruth's cries, James' indignant fury, Snickers' barks. Time seemed to stop as she watched the portal draw closer and closer. She wouldn't let go of the girl, no matter what happened. She couldn't. And yet she couldn't tell the ghosts to stop. She had to finish what she'd started.

Snickers lunged forward and grabbed her pants' leg in his teeth. The dog dug in his heels. He had the right idea. But wasn't strong enough to stop her completely.

Still she drew closer. Nothing stopped her slow approach. James seemed determined to inflict one more heart-wrenching injury before leaving this world behind.

Her muscles began to quiver. Her strength waned.

The spirits surrounding James paused and looked to her for guidance. Continue on and risk taking Faith with them? Or leave

James to continue terrorizing the family? Faith would be sick forever, tormented for something she played no part in creating.

Neither option was good.

Faith slipped from her grip. She fell to her knees, nothing left. She looked to Ruth, but the woman seemed too shocked to move.

She'd failed.

Sterling knelt in front of her. "I don't know what's happening here," he yelled over the whistling vortex cycling in the closet. "I know you're not asking me to prove my faith, so I give it to you freely. I may not fully believe in ghosts, but I completely believe in you!"

He grabbed both sides of her face and pressed his lips to hers, crushing her in a kiss so fierce it took her breath away.

Warmth flushed her skin. His energy transferred over her lips and flooded through her body. She drew his strength to her core and rose to her feet.

Clasping Sterling's hand, she faced the vortex. "Don't let go."

He squeezed her hand. "Never."

She walked toward the shining blue portal. White orbs danced across the opening, a sparkling, glittering backdrop to the horror wedged between this world and the next. James remained on this side of the portal, grappling with a still-struggling Faith.

The girl managed to grasp Kimberly's outstretched arm with both hands.

She gulped in huge lungsful of air. Drawing on her fresh influx of energy, she psyched herself up and pulled.

Faith held tight. But so did James. The girl gave a swift kick straight to his face.

James howled in fury as Faith slid closer to Kimberly. But still he held on.

She turned to Ruth, watching as if in disbelief. "Ruth! Help me! Fight for her! Fight for Faith!"

With a nod, Ruth latched on and pulled, turning the tide in their favor.

James grip slipped again. He barely held Faith by the ankles. She knew she could do this. Using Sterling's grip as an anchor, she pulled with all her might, whipping Faith into Ruth. The two crashed backward.

Ruth collapsed to the floor, sobbing, holding her daughter.

One of the orbs moved closer to the portal opening and materialized into a relatively human form.

Rebecca, she knew before the whispered name escaped from James' lips. She recognized the steely strength, the kind heart, and compassionate spirit. The spirit collected into a semblance of its former shell, and she recognized the gentle eyes passed down through generations, now alive in Ruth, Rebecca, and Faith.

"George," she said as she caught sight of her love. She reached out a hand. "I've been waiting for you. Come home."

George cast one look around then stepped through. A dazzling flash of white light burst from the portal as he left this world for the next. Kimberly hoped with every fiber of her being that the two would now enjoy eternity together, making up for the time they were denied in this life.

Alta waved to Ruth, then followed George. The ghosts continued, one after another, crossing through the portal to the Afterlife.

Rebecca's gentle eyes flashed and filled with a stormy fury. "You've hurt my family too long, James. You'll never cause another woman misery."

Rebecca's spirit reached out from beyond and grabbed him.

James screamed as she dragged him to the portal.

Kimberly relaxed and breathed deeply. Faith was safe. She turned to find Sterling watching the entire scene, mouth hanging open.

A hand closed around her wrist. She whirled to face James, now clutching her, his bony fingers digging into her skin.

He pulled her along with him. She watched him disappear as if sinking into a gelatin mold, watched the portal with its shimmering electric light glimmer before her.

She struggled, but her strength was sapped. She thought she heard shouts around her, but the noise from the vortex drowned out everything.

And yet, the closer she drew to the portal, the less fear she felt. Intense relief washed over her, along with a warmth that seemed to emanate from inside her. Her chest swelled with love and comfort. She had nothing to fear. She was going to a better place. She closed her eyes, and prepared to cross, knowing everything would be okay.

A hand took hers—soft and tender, nothing like James' harsh touch. The hand squeezed hers, then pushed her away from the light.

Not yet. It's not your time.

Lavender and freesia surrounded her, enveloped her in comforting embrace.

"Mom?"

No reply followed, but she fell backward, landing hard on her butt. She sat up, eager for a glimpse into the next life, perhaps even of her mother.

With a scream of agony, James finally crossed over. A flash of red light accompanied him, along with a momentary burst of howls of anguish. The rift snapped closed.

He was gone. For good.

CHAPTER FORTY-ONE

THE NEXT MORNING, the crew chatted as they prepared to record the final wrap segment. Kimberly had slept better than she had in a long time. The Johnsons reported sleeping well too. A morning news show played in the background as Stan and TJ readied cameras and crew members rolled up cords and packed away equipment.

Rosie watched her, a gleam in her eyes. Kimberly knew her best friend couldn't wait to get her alone and find out where she'd slept last night. She enjoyed keeping the information to herself and letting Rosie's imagination run wild.

"Hey!" TJ said. "The news is talking about us!"

Ruth turned up the volume as a photo of Kimberly transitioned to the Johnsons' house. The caption at the bottom of the screen read REAL GHOST ON WANTLAND FILES SET?

The anchor's concerned face stared gravely into the camera. "Did *The Wantland Files* have a real ghost on site? Or did a huge hoax lead to mass hysteria? That's what local Guthrie residents are asking themselves this morning after an incident at a home being investigated by paranormal celebrity Kimberly Wantland for her show *The Wantland Files*. News Six is on site to learn more."

The screen cut to a man in a T-shirt and ball cap who looked like he hadn't showered in days. He spoke into a microphone held by Cathy Rickman, who stood beside him. "I dunno how they done it, but they musta drugged us or somethin' somehow. I saw a ghost come outta that windo' right there." The camera followed where the man pointed—to Faith's bedroom window.

The camera panned to Cathy. "While some observers believe the show is behind the mass hysteria in a bid for publicity, neighbors claim followers of an obscure religious sect disrupted the neighborhood for days, then staged the hoax to gain attention and deserve nothing but contempt. Did we have a real ghost right here in Guthrie, Oklahoma? Perhaps only Kimberly Wantland knows for sure. Liz?"

"Thanks, Cathy. I guess we'll have to watch the show to see what happens. Across town—"

Ruth clicked the television off. "Well. The news just aired all our dirty laundry. Not sure I appreciate that."

Daniel put an arm around her. "Might as well get used to it. Once the show airs, everyone will know all the details."

Ruth sighed. "Perhaps our experiences will help others. I'll have to stay positive about it."

Michael looked like he'd been handed a winning lottery ticket. "We can't buy publicity like this!"

Kimberly wasn't quite as euphoric. "What about Ezekiel though? Will he be back?" They had seen only a few stragglers milling about in the street. She'd wondered all morning if the group would return, angrier than ever.

Sterling scrolled through Twitter. "Nah. They're gone. Couldn't handle the shock of something uglier than them. Zeke appears to be headed to his next location."

"That's it? He harassed me all this time and now he just leaves? And gets away with it?"

Sterling draped an arm around her shoulders. "Let's focus on the part where he's gone." He held up his camera above them. "Smile."

"Sterling!"

"Time for our morning Kimberling post."

She glanced at Rosie. "I don't think I can handle this."

Rosie grinned. "I think you're adapting."

Rebecca and Faith bounded down the stairs, giggling and brighter than she'd seen them.

"Are you okay, Faith?" she asked.

Faith held out her arm. "Look! The rash is going away. Hardly anything left of it now."

"Her hand too," Rebecca said, flipping her hand over to expose the palm. "Look. It's a little pink, but it's going away."

Sterling inspected the girl's arm. "Wow. I can't deny that looks much improved."

Kimberly held out her own palm. "Mine too. Nearly back to normal already."

Sterling ran a finger over the pink skin. "Remarkable recovery. But I'm glad to see it."

"And James is gone for good?" Daniel asked. "He can't come back?"

"He can't return," she reassured them. She shivered slightly at the memory of what awaited him on the other side. "He's no longer hiding in the Nightshade. He passed to the next life, albeit unwillingly. I've witnessed crossings before, but never like this. I think he's finally going to atone for his actions."

"I know he's gone," Faith said. "I can tell."

"This morning over coffee," Ruth said, "I noticed weeds sprouting in my garden under the oak tree. I haven't been able to get anything to grow there for months now. I may leave the weeds just to enjoy something green there."

Faith approached Sterling and shyly tugged on his sleeve.

He appeared startled by the interaction. "Yes?"

The girl held up a quarter and closed it in a hand. She waved the other hand over the closed fist. When she opened it, the quarter was gone. "Ta-dah!"

Sterling's face lit up as he clapped. "Well done! Excellent!" He passed a hand behind her ear and held a quarter between thumb and forefinger, which he offered to her. "Here's another to keep practicing with."

Rosie rested a hand on Kimberly's shoulder. "Girl, he is dreamy. How are you doing? Are you okay with this outcome?"

She took a moment to consider. "James had to go. We all agreed on that. And ultimately, though I played a part in his final crossing, I wasn't the one who forced him. Wronged souls dragged him away to face justice."

Michael shook his head. "That was truly the most incredible ending we've ever had. Wait until Randmeier hears about this." He pulled his cell phone from a pocket and left the room.

"We finally have irrefutable proof of a ghost!" TJ said. "We even made the news! All those people are—"

Sterling cut him off. "All those people are looking for any explanation other than a ghost. Have you seen Twitter?"

"But people had their phones out. They got pictures and videos."

"Won't matter. If it were me, like it used to be, I wouldn't believe it. Not a bit. I'd write it off as someone really good with Photoshop or graphics software. It wouldn't have changed my mind."

"But . . . you saw it! You have to admit you saw it."

"I don't want you to build this up and then be crushed when things don't go the way you expect."

"But it's the truth!"

Michael popped his head back into the room, cell phone stuck to his ear, and waved at them. "Sterling? Need you for a second."

He squeezed her arm. "I'll be right back."

TJ watched him walk away, then rounded on her. "We have him on record, terrified of seeing a ghost at Stone Lion. We can leak that footage and prove—"

"Please don't."

He blinked and sucked in a breath. "But we have him this

time. He was your biggest critic. He called you a fraud so many times. This proves even complete skeptics can see ghosts."

"I don't want him publicly humiliated like that. Please, do this for me."

"I don't—"

"The dynamic of the show is psychic and skeptic. Sterling may be starting to come around and realizing there really is something to these investigations, but publicly we need him to retain his role of the cynical nonbeliever. That's how the show works."

TJ threw his hands up in surrender. "Okay. If that's what you want."

"Thank you."

Sterling returned. TJ gave him some side eye and then slunk away, crestfallen.

"What was that about?" he asked.

"TJ and I had a minor disagreement about what should and shouldn't be included in the episode."

"And now he's miffed at me? What did I do?"

"Nothing. He'll get over it. What did Michael want?"

"He had me talk to Randmeier. The crew is buzzing a bit about us spending the night together. Wanted to keep things above board so we wouldn't appear to be sneaking around. He, uh, suggested we could save money by putting us both in the same room from now on."

"Oh." She wasn't sure how she felt about that. Excited, sure, but that seemed like a huge step forward for two people who were just starting to know each other.

"I told him I didn't think we were ready for that just yet."

"Thank you."

"Not that I'd mind."

"I'll remember that." She turned to discover everyone in the room listening and blushed.

Ruth hugged Kimberly. "I'm glad I got to see Mom one last

time. I wasn't here when she passed away. I never felt like I got to say goodbye. Now I know she's okay."

"I understand. I'm glad too." Kimberly so wished for the same opportunity. Perhaps someday.

Rebecca grabbed Faith in a massive hug, squeezing the breath out of the girl.

"Hey!" Faith squeaked in protest, arms waving in an attempt to escape.

"Sorry, not sorry," Rebecca said. "I'm glad you're better. I need my sister."

Kimberly looked at Rosie and then threw her arms around her best friend.

"Hey!" Rosie squirmed. "What's that for? You're not usually a hugger."

"We may not have the same parents, but you're my sister as far as I'm concerned. I want you to know that."

"Awww." Rosie teared up. "I get to be your bridesmaid, right?"

Kimberly leaned back and rolled her eyes. "For Pete's sake, Rosie."

"What? I need to know. I can start planning your bachelorette party."

"I'm not engaged! Stop planning my wedding!" She hazarded a glance at Sterling. His lips twisted into a grin. He looked entirely too amused.

Faith lifted her head from Rebecca's shoulder. "Will I be your bridesmaid?"

"Duh," Rebecca replied. "Wouldn't have anyone but you. I better get to be your maid of honor."

"Whoa," Daniel said. "Hold up. No wedding plans, please, girls. Your dad isn't ready for that just yet."

Sterling shook his head at Michael. "Girls and weddings."

"Right?" Michael agreed. "I wanted to be her bridesmaid!"

"You can be his best man," Rosie suggested.

"Stop planning my wedding!"

Michael clapped his hands together. "As much fun as antagonizing Kimmy is, let's shoot the end cap so we can wrap. Randmeier wants us to get back on the road. Next investigation will be our Halloween episode this season."

"Halloween episode?" Sterling asked her. "Ghosts aren't Halloween enough on their own?"

"We plus it a little bit," she told him. "Besides, decorations will be up everywhere. We use it to our advantage. Where do you want us, Michael?"

"How about the front porch, house behind you?"

Daniel crossed to Sterling and shook hands. "Appreciate everything. I know you're not into this stuff, but I will pray God blesses all of you. You deserve it."

"Appreciate it, man. Always glad for prayers."

The two of them followed Michael outside and allowed themselves to be posed on the front porch.

Sterling cleared his throat. "Are you going to exorcise the ghosts at Stone Lion? If there really is a little girl's spirit wandering there forever, that seems really sad."

"Sterling Wakefield, are you worried about that little ghost?" She glanced sideways at him. His concern absolutely melted her heart. "Gloria doesn't want her ghosts sent away. She likes sharing her space with them. But I gave her some ideas for interacting with the girl a bit more. Engaging her might make her less mischievous."

"Too cozy, Sterling," Michael called. "Stand a little farther apart from Kimmy. And look skeptical. Cross your arms and scowl or something."

Sterling shook his head. "My job is getting harder. I don't want to scowl at you."

"Yeah, well, that's why you get paid the big bucks."

He took a deep breath, placed his hands on his hips, and gave her a hard stare. "How's this?"

She threw her head back with laughter and clapped. "You look ridiculous. I love it!"

Michael pinched the bridge of his nose. "Are you two about finished? I'd really like to wrap this up."

"Sorry! Sorry, everyone." She shook out her limbs and fixed her features back into a concerned yet compassionate countenance.

Michael shook his head. "You two are going to make my life hell. I think I liked it better when you hated each other."

She faced Stan's camera and waited for Michael to count her in. "The Johnsons' house proved to be one of the most difficult investigations we've ever tackled. Wouldn't you agree, Sterling?"

"Pretty crazy. I'm eager to review all the footage and determine what was really happening here. Plus, I intend to stay in touch with the family. I'm curious to see if Faith's medical issues truly resolve, now that you've cleared the house of the supposed haunting."

"Learning family secrets hidden away for generations was a shock. But that enabled us to purge the home and grounds of the ghosts from the past. We leave the Johnsons to cope with some startling news they didn't expect. But I think the truth is always best."

His lips twisted into a grin. "On that we agree. The truth is always best."

Michael called to Sterling, "Want to give us your take on what's happened here this week?"

Sterling cleared his throat. "I have no idea what happened. Yet. But there is only one way I'd like to see this episode end. Kimberly, I think you know what it is."

He lifted one eyebrow. He'd been through a lot this week. She could do this for him.

She faced Stan's camera, smoothed her hair, and clasped her hands together. "This house . . . is clean."

The crew erupted in laughter. Sterling got his *Poltergeist* ending after all. Sort of.

"We will have the chance to uncover the truth again during

our next investigation. Join us next time as we venture to Hannibal, Missouri."

"And cut," Michael called. "That's it. Let's hit the road."

She descended the steps and headed for the van.

Sterling's voice stopped her. "Where do you think you're going?"

She turned and found him on the passenger side of his car, door raised. He gestured her in. "You're with me now."

SIGN UP FOR MORE

Did you enjoy *Ghosts of Guthrie*? If so, please leave a review wherever you purchase books.

Sign up for my newsletter to be the first to know of upcoming releases, chances for contests, and to receive previews and insider information http://www.larabernhardt.com/contact

I'd love to hear about YOUR supernatural encounters! Feel free to reach out and share!

PREVIEW OF HALLOWEEN IN HANNIBAL

Kayla watched her boyfriend pick the lock, shivering and sweating in the heat and humidity of a sweltering Hannibal summer. Crickets chirped in the distance. For the thousandth time she imagined footsteps, sure they were about to be discovered.

"This is a terrible idea, Cory. Let's just go home."

"I thought you wanted to see a ghost. You said you wouldn't be scared."

Typical Cory, taking her words out of context and twisting the meaning. "Not what I said, and you know it."

Cory grunted as the metal picks slipped from the lock. "Dang it!" He glowered at her and retrieved his tools. "Yes, you did. I'm doing this for you."

"I said that if your aunt was cool with it, I'd love a tour of the building. And that I didn't think I'd be scared of a ghost if we happened to see one. I never suggested you break in. Where'd you learn to pick locks anyway?" This was the sort of thing it seemed she ought to know about her boyfriend.

He squinted, angling the tiny picks back into place. "YouTube video."

"Seriously? And you had lockpicks laying around your house?"

"Nah. Ordered 'em off Amazon."

"Of course you did. Now that we've established I never requested a B and E, can we please—"

A click from the lock lit Cory's face. "Got it!" He turned the knob and opened the door.

Somewhere in the hallway, a security alarm beeped, demanding the code.

"Oh my God, Cory! They have an alarm!"

"Yep." He sauntered to the glowing panel, opened it, and tapped buttons. The beeping stopped.

Cory held his arms wide, expecting applause, praise, hugs— or maybe all of the above. "Who's awesome?"

"How did you know that code? Did you steal it?" She could not get in trouble. *Could not*. Her parents would—

"Nope. My aunt let me work here a couple summers ago and gave me the code then."

"And it's still the same?"

"You kidding? They're old. They don't change their passwords."

"We're still breaking and entering. We're here without permission."

"My aunt won't press charges. Even if we somehow get caught. Which we won't." He held out a hand. "And night is the best time to catch a glimpse of a ghost. Right? Wouldn't that be awesome? Our 'What I Did During the Summer' essays will blow everyone away."

That would be super cool. And who would ever know? "You promise I'll be home by midnight? I can't get in trouble. My parents would ground me so fast—"

He placed a hand over his heart and bowed deeply. "Your sainted curfew shall be hallowed as always."

"Hey! Just because your parents let you—"

"Come on!" He grabbed her hand and yanked. "You're wasting valuable time."

She'd crossed the threshold. They were doing this. Nerves bubbled over into giggles.

"What's funny?" Cory asked.

"I dunno. It is kind of thrilling."

He lit up, clearly delighted he'd won her over. "Hecks, yeah. What first? The stage? Props? Costumes?"

She squeezed his hand. "Show me everything."

He led her through the hallway, winding from the back entrance toward the front of the building. The flashlight from his cellphone illuminated the path, playing off old wood paneling and floors. The building smelled old, but not musty or dirty. A chill ran down her spine.

In the lobby, she could see the huge doors leading from the street entrance, plus the doors into what she knew was the actual church, where services had been held. She'd like to see that too, but Cory went straight to the stairs.

"The theatre is in the basement," he said.

"You told me before."

She picked her way carefully down the worn carpeting of the stairway. Outside the soft, limited glow of the phone flashlight, she couldn't see much of anything. The thought of being alone in complete darkness sent a shiver running down her spine. She squeezed Cory's hand.

Inside the auditorium, he led her to a row of center seats and flopped down. He patted the one beside him. "Best seats in the house."

"I thought we were going to look around," she said, though the idea of wandering through a costume shop and construction area in the dark sounded less fun and creepier the longer they remained.

"We will. Let's sit for a bit."

"I'd rather be on stage than in the audience."

"Come on. Sit."

She threw her hands up in surrender and did as he suggested. He stretched and fake-yawned and the next thing she knew his arm was around her. "What are you doing?"

"Just getting comfortable." He turned off his cellphone flashlight and pocketed the device.

She heard a noise from the stage. "What was that?"

"I didn't hear anything. Relax."

"I'm sure I heard something."

"No one else is here. Maybe it was the building creaking."

"Cory, it's really dark in here. Can you maybe turn on a light?"

"I dunno. I kinda like the dark." He leaned close and kissed her.

She forgot about the sound and kissed him back. Her parents didn't like for her to date and had only recently, and reluctantly, allowed Cory to take her out unchaperoned. Kissing was still new—and he was good at it. He wrapped both arms around her, leaning into the kiss. She opened her mouth, a fluttering excitement skipping through her stomach.

But then his hands started to roam and grope. She didn't know if she was ready for that. Kissing was one thing, but he seemed to be pushing for more tonight. She broke off the kiss and pushed him away.

"What?" he panted. "What's wrong?"

"What are you doing?"

"Enjoying being alone. How often do we manage to be completely alone? No one to interfere?"

He leaned into her again, and she once again got swept away in his delicious mouth on hers. He had a point. Maybe they could find a quiet corner in the costume shop and—

Out of the corner of her eye, she saw a figure looming over them, a dark solid mass against the grayness around them. She leapt to her feet.

Cory fell forward before he caught himself. "Okay, jeez! Just say no. You don't have to—"

"I saw someone!" She breathed heavily, trying to calm her racing heartbeat.

"What? You're so jumpy. There's no one here."

She strained her eyes, staring at the spot she'd seen the dark figure a moment ago. She thrust her hand into her purse for her phone. Whatever Cory thought about the dark being awesome, she wanted a light. A rustling sound from the stage sent her spinning around.

A face ducked behind the curtain.

"Cory! Oh my God! Someone is in here!"

"Again? After you insisted you wouldn't be scared—"

She finally got her shaking hands to operate her phone and punched the button to turn on the light. She shone it on the curtains just in time to see them shimmy back into place.

"What the hell?" Cory jumped to his feet. "Hey! You're not supposed to be in here! Come out or I'm calling the cops!"

She tugged his sleeve and crouched on the floor behind the bank of chairs in front of them and whispered, "We're not supposed to be here either! You can't call anyone. Then we'd have to explain why *we're* here!"

"I can't leave some random guy in my aunt's theatre. What if he jacks the place up? She's already having financial problems."

"Let's get out of here. In the morning you can make some excuse to your aunt to come check on the place."

"Nah. Might be a hobo or something. I'm gonna go see."

She reached to grab him, but he shook her off. "You can't leave me here alone!"

"Well, come with me then."

"No way."

"Whatevs." He trotted down the aisle and stomped up the steps to the stage.

She watched his phone flashlight bob along in the darkness, dimly illuminating his form as he thrust his head through the curtains.

She held her breath.

Cory turned. "He's not here anymore. I'll check the back-stage area. You go upstairs and see if he ran up there to hide."

"Are you crazy? We can't split up! Don't you watch horror movies?"

She could hear the eyeroll in his tone. "This is not a horror movie. Seriously. Probably just some drunk guy who wandered in and passed out."

"Wandered into a locked building?"

If Cory heard, he didn't answer. She crouched to the floor again, trying as hard as she could to be invisible and silent. Her thumping heart and rasping gasps made that impossible.

She took deep, controlled breaths and tried to reassure herself. *Everything would be fine.* They wouldn't be hacked to pieces by an ax murderer. That sort of thing didn't happen in real life.

A shadow fell over her.

She gasped and jerked her head up.

A draped figure stood directly in front of her. How? She hadn't heard any footsteps.

She crab-crawled backward, blinking and willing her brain to stop imagining things.

But the figure remained.

She turned and scrambled to her feet. "Cory! Cory, help me!"

She ran and didn't look back. She'd seen enough movies to know you don't look back. If you did, you either tripped and fell and the ax murderer got you or you ran smack into the ax murderer who somehow got in front of you when you looked away.

Okay. Okay, where were the doors? It was dark and she hadn't paid attention when they came in. And where was Cory?

She heard a noise and spun around. No dark figure. Where had it gone?

"Shit. Shit shit shit." She closed her eyes and pressed her fingers to her temples. *Don't panic. Think.* They came down the stairs into a lobby. Yes! She needed to get back to the lobby.

Feeling better, she turned, sure of the way out.

And ran right into a body.

She screamed and flailed her arms, pummeling with her fists.

"What the hell, Kayla?" Cory grabbed her arms.

Momentary relief gave way to fury. "Where have you been?"

"Looking for the hobo, duh. I can't find anyone. Did you?"

"Someone was here. Didn't you hear me yell for you?"

"You saw the hobo? In here? Why didn't you tell me?"

"I screamed for you. Where were you?"

Cory flipped on his cellphone flashlight, cutting a hazy beam through the darkness.

The curtain fluttered again.

"What the hell? I just checked back there."

"Cory, don't. Let's just go!" Tears pricked at her eyes. This wasn't fun. She wanted out.

Ignoring the stairs, Cory hopped onto the stage. Before he could right himself and investigate, the curtains parted.

A man stood there, grinning.

"What the—" Cory scrambled backwards so fast, he toppled off the edge of the stage, plunging them into darkness.

"*Where's my spotlight?*" A man's voice—not Cory's—echoed eerily through the theatre, a hollow sound that made her shudder.

The building alarm went off, angry screech piercing the dead quiet of the night.

She heard footsteps pounding from the room. "Cory? Cory!"

She sat down on the floor, tucked her knees against her chest, and rocked back and forth. Cory had left her. Left her with the ax murderer! How could he? At least she thought he had. The shriek of the alarm filled her ears, drowning out potential breathing or footsteps.

Scared to move, too terrified to breathe, she fumbled for her cellphone. Maybe Cory was still here. Maybe he'd hurt himself when he fell. But then, what footsteps had she heard pounding up the aisle toward the lobby?

She wiped her sleeve across her forehead, mopping up the sweat dripping from her temples. Taking a deep breath, she flipped on the flashlight. Careful to avoid illuminating the stage area, she shone the beam over the rest of the room—the banks of seats, the aisles. Nothing. Slowly she dragged the light to the stage edge. Nothing. She lifted it to the curtains. Nothing.

She bent forward, relieved, determined to catch her breath. Cory—that jerk! He'd ditched her and run for safety, leaving her alone. Her parents were right, he was bad news.

Scowling, she turned toward the aisle, formulating exactly what she'd say to Cory once she found him.

Her flashlight revealed the hem of a dark cloak. Her light went out.

"*Where's my spotlight?*" The question reverberated around the pitch-black room, echoing alongside her screams, drown out by the sirens. A hand clamped down on her shoulder.

ACKNOWLEDGMENTS

Born and raised in Oklahoma, I thoroughly enjoyed bringing Kimberly and her crew to my home state. I wove a little state history into the story along with some family lore passed down through the years. Additionally, the Stone Lion Inn is a real location in Guthrie, OK. Though I drew on some history and ghost tales associated with both the inn, the town, and the state, I greatly fictionalized the characters and many other elements for this story.

ABOUT THE AUTHOR

Lara Bernhardt is a Pushcart-nominated writer, editor, and audiobook narrator. She is Editor-in-Chief of Balkan Press and also publishes a literary magazine, *Conclave*. Twice a finalist for the Oklahoma Book Award for Best Fiction, she writes supernatural suspense and women's fiction. You can follow her on Amazon and on all the socials @larawells1 on Twitter and @larabern10 on Facebook, BookBub, and Instagram.

ALSO BY LARA BERNHARDT

The Wantland Files series

The Wantland Files

The Haunting of Crescent Hotel

Women's Fiction

Shadow of the Taj